Tales of Narda: Road to Andolan

TALES OF NARDA:
ROAD TO ANDOLAN

Copyright © 2020 by Donna Rae Casselman

All rights reserved. This book or any portion thereof may not be reproduced or used in any manner whatsoever without the express written permission of the publisher except for the use of brief quotations in a book review.

This is a work of fiction. Names, characters, businesses, places, events, locales, and incidents are either the products of the author's imagination or used in a fictitious manner. Any resemblance to actual persons, living or dead, or actual events is purely coincidental.

ISBN: 978-1-7353497-0-1 (hardcover)
ISBN: 978-1-7353497-1-8 (trade paperback)

www.talesofnarda.com

Printed in the USA

Tales of Narda:
Road to Andolan

D.R. Casselman

Foreword

Tales of Narda (not Narnia) is a story that has evolved over many years. I would have loved to devote my full time to the series, but alas, many other duties called, which could not be neglected. Narda was so named by the *Eldarin*, the race who colonized it. The name derives from the *Eolengwas,* their language, and means 'the crossing of the mountains from the sea to the first settlement in the high hills,' *Malta*, the name given to the region where they settled. The story evolved over time and was perhaps influenced by some of my own adventures, but the characters are all fictional. Narda is an Earth-like planet, with a diversity of races and cultures, some allied, some in conflict, and the tale is as much a coming-of-age for the protagonist as one of the conflicts and problems facing Narda. I hope you will find the adventure interesting and exciting, as my purpose in writing it is simply to tell a good story. And I hope, too that you will contribute your own imaginations in bringing the characters and creatures of Narda to life.

Donna

Acknowledgements

I want to acknowledge those who have helped to make this book series possible: Susan Stroh, my first editor; Wayne Hanson, my last editor; Joshua Shultz, for his unwavering belief in the project and help with promotion; Jaclyn Prophet for help with research; Len and Colette Williams of Design Strategies for book cover designs, website design and marketing assistance; Eric Young for website and other tech-related aid and upkeep; Scott D. Welch for publishing and marketing guidance; Nico Photos for the creature illustrations; C. James von Scholz of Gotham Artists Agency, New York, for getting me started; all of my early book draft readers, who encouraged me to continue; my children and grandchildren, who inspire me to write and my husband of 36 years, who has been the wind beneath my wings. To all of you, I offer my sincerest gratitude and heartfelt thanks.

Donna

Map of Narda

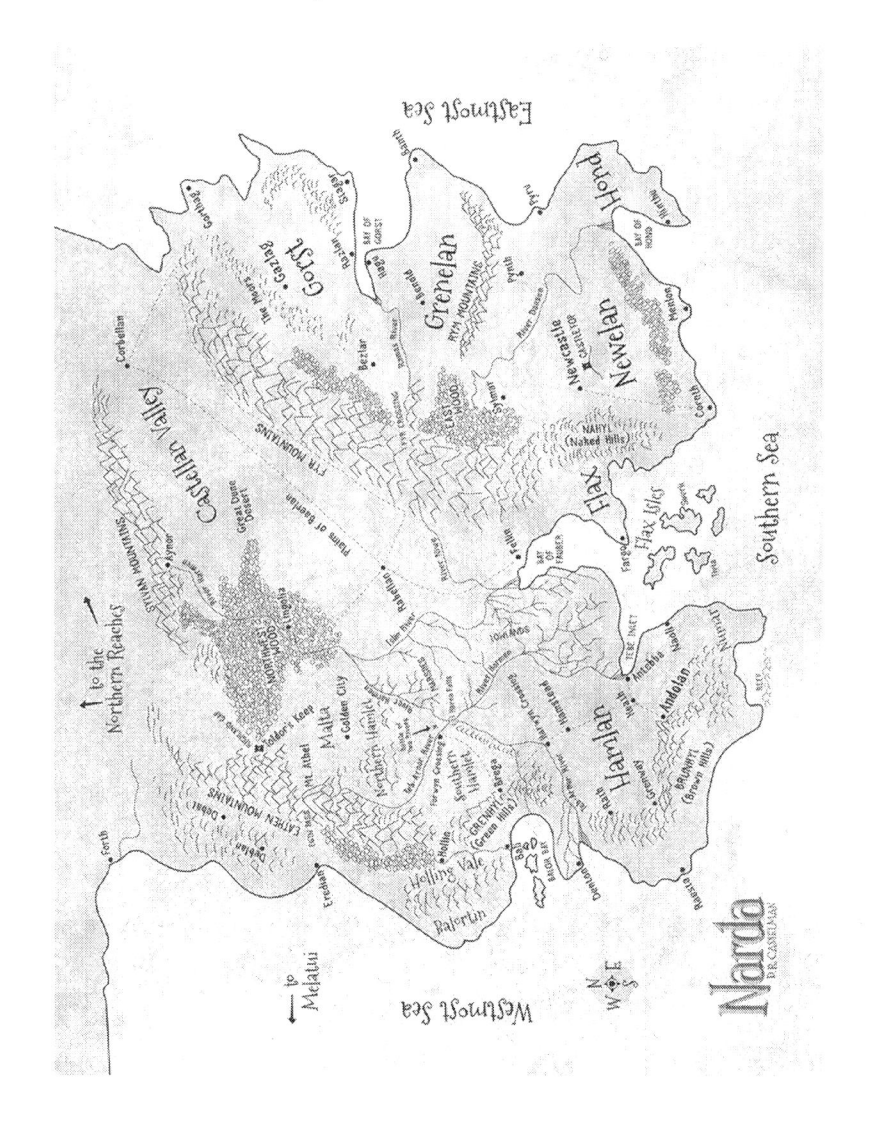

Table of Contents

Chapter 1: Voyage to Narda 1
Chapter 2: An Unexpected Turn 20
Chapter 3: The Southern Coast 28
Chapter 4: Shadow of the East 31
Chapter 5: A Premonition 37
Chapter 6: The Journey Begins 43
Chapter 7: A Restless Night 54
Chapter 8: A Friendly Surprise 61
Chapter 9: The Back Trail 81
Chapter 10: A History Lesson 94
Chapter 11: Andolan 104
Chapter 12: King of the West 117
Chapter 13: Preparations 133
Chapter 14: The Company Rides North 144
Chapter 15: Harwyn Crossing 158
Chapter 16: The Black Caat Inn 168
Chapter 17: Northern Hamlet 189
Chapter 18: A Hunting Accident 200
Chapter 19: A King in Exile 208
Chapter 20: Esol's Errand 217
Chapter 21: Parting Company 220
Chapter 22: The Golden City 233
Chapter 23: The Catacombs of Malta 248
Chapter 24: The Ghosts of the Dead 263
Chapter 25: Elvenvale 274
Chapter 26: Northwest Wood 289
Chapter 27: Lord of the Elvenkin 298
Chapter 28: Visitors in Lingolia 307
Glossary of Terms 323
Biography of Donna Casselman 343

Chapter 1:
Voyage to Narda

Dawn crept in quietly, a pale sun rising out of a black sea, its soft rays dimming night's shadow and warming its cold breath. A crisp, cold breeze stung *Eathelon's* face, as the *Sirine* cut swiftly through the dark waters of the *Westmost Sea*, but standing tall on her foredeck, lost in thought, he did not much notice. His muscular frame a shadow against the waxing dawn, he pulled his *spyglas* from its leather sheath at his side, a gift from his *Eldarin* Mother — to give him farsight, she said, an ability unique to the *Elvenkin*, a race once allied to her people. It had belonged to her Father and had helped them find *Melatui*, their adopted island home, when they'd been forced to flee Narda. They had sailed this very sea, on this very ship, and the voyage had claimed his Grandfather's life. *I wish I could have known you, Grandfather.* As the sun rose slowly over the southeastern horizon, he lifted his spyglas to look for any sign of land, but the effort proved fruitless. He turned his thoughts to his errand ahead. If they found Narda and completed their errand, would they return safely?

"Morning, Cap'n," a familiar voice said, interrupting his thoughts.

He turned to greet *Tomas,* as he stepped onto the foredeck, swinging a bucket. His crewmate squinted and brushed a tumble of curly blond hair out of his blue eyes then asked, "See any sign of land yet, Cap'n?"

"No, Tomas, not yet."

Tomas noticed the dark circles under his Captain's eyes, but said nothing. "Well, our work is never done with this small crew, so I had better get to it."

"Hold a moment — please."

"Sure, Cap'n, what is it?"

Eathelon sighed. "Tomas, why do you and *Marchal* insist on calling me Cap'n, when we have been friends all of our lives?"

"Well, because you *are* Captain of this fine vessel. We only offer you the respect you are due." Tomas grinned. "Now, what is *really* bothering you? You look … troubled."

"I am. There is much on my mind. My Father passed right before we left Melatui, as you well know, and my Mother, the Queen, assumed the throne, as is custom. But if someone was unhappy with Father's reign, then Mother may well be in danger and I am not there to protect her."

"I know this is a heavy burden on you, Eathelon, but there are others there to protect her. Trust your mother and *Celorn* to handle the situation. If they did not feel strongly about the importance of our errand, they would not have insisted we leave."

Eathelon smiled at Tomas. "I know. And you three came because I needed men I could trust," said Eathelon.

"And you have them."

The two of them stood at the rail and watched the sun rise from its watery bed, bathing the sky in soft yellow hues.

"Is there anything else?" asked Tomas.

Eathelon smiled at his perceptive friend. "A premonition. You know how I get them."

"Of what?"

"Just the feeling that things are not right."

"You have the gift of foresight, Eathelon. You have always been more prescient than the rest of us. Of course things are not right, or we wouldn't be here at all. But I know you will work things out."

"Foresight is not always a gift, Tomas, sometimes it can be a curse."

Tomas smiled. "Is it not better to know what lies ahead, even if the way seems dark? At least then we can prepare for it."

"Perhaps." He turned to Tomas. "I do not seem to have the same gift here that I had in Melatui. How can we prepare for something I cannot foresee?"

Tomas placed a hand on his Captain's shoulder. "Your worry is misplaced, Eathelon. The answer will come to you, you will see."

Eathelon smiled at his friend, whose words and faith in him gave him some comfort, though did not assuage his uncertainty altogether.

Sensing this, Tomas continued, "We are all anxious, Eathelon. We have been at sea longer than ever before, sailing to a place we have heard of, but never seen." He sighed. "But Narda will soon appear and put all of our fears to rest."

Tomas bent down, picked up his bucket, sucked in a long breath of fresh air, and grinned. "Now, I had better get to my chores."

"Indeed. Where is Marchal?"

"Below, cooking *brefas*," replied Tomas. He winked and walked off swinging his bucket and whistling a merry tune, as ever he did.

Eathelon turned into the wind and let it brush over his lightly bronzed face as it whistled through the rigging. He breathed in the smell of salty air and sea, one he'd come to love, for he'd spent much of his youth sailing and exploring the isles of Melatui's archipelago with his friends. But, as Tomas said, they were farther from home now, and he was grateful they had all come together.

He lifted his spyglas again and scanned the horizon, but when he found no sign of land, put it away and walked aft to speak with Palo, his helmsman. Marchal was just coming up from below deck, as Eathelon passed by.

"Hoy, Cap'n, see land yet?"

"No, Marchal. We are still a day or two out, I think."

"No more than that, I hope. Our stores are quite low."

"Well," grinned Eathelon, "there are plenty of fish in the sea."

Marchal grinned back, "Speaking of fish, brefas is cooked."

Eathelon appreciated his friend and crewmate with the soft green eyes and dull red hair, the ship's cook in addition to his other duties. "I am not hungry now ... perhaps later."

"Sure Cap'n, it will be there when you are ready to eat." Marchal turned and went down the galley stairs.

Cap'n, mused Eathelon, but after his talk with Tomas, he just shrugged and continued aft. He hadn't slept much of late.

Whenever he closed his eyes, his mind raced with images of the Narda his Mother *Lelar* had described to him. Narda had been her home for a time, home to her family, her people. Now he would see it himself and he wondered if it would look anything like Lelar's description. She had been a child when her family fled Narda. Perhaps her stories were more fantasy than real. She spoke of it as a far-off land of magical creatures and races. He wondered how much would prove true.

The Eldarin on Melatui taught all Eldarin children the history of their people, its language, legends and culture, including the Mallorite children, those of mixed race like Eathelon. The history and culture of the Eldarin are as important to know as the history and culture of the *Maagi*, they said.

Eathelon felt a knot tighten in his stomach as he pushed back a gnawing premonition that something did not feel quite right. But after his talk with Tomas, he reassured himself that anyone heading into the unknown would feel such uncertainty.

He stopped at the ship's rail and watched the sea foam around the hull of the Sirine, as she knifed through the deep blue waters of the Westmost Sea. He looked around and, satisfied he was alone for the moment, reached under his tunic and pulled out a small green amulet. He stared at it a moment, then put it away.

A gust of wind came up suddenly and yanked some of his dark red hair from the long, neatly tied braid at the nape of his neck. *A shift in the wind.* "Tomas! Marchal!"

"On it Cap'n," yelled Tomas.

Eathelon felt the ship turn under Palo's expert hand aft.

The crew had navigated the Sirine across the Westmost Sea thus far without incident, but Eathelon expected to reach the west coast of Narda by now. He hoped his charts, and his navigation were correct. He relied on charts made by the Eldarin when they crossed this sea to his isle, but they had found the isle by accident.

"More sail, Tomas!" yelled Marchal, as they handled the turn.

"Watch that line!" Tomas yelled back.

"Do you two need a hand?" Eathelon called out, knowing the answer, as he did.

"Shards no, Cap'n!" yelled Tomas. "If we can't handle a simple turn, you may as well throw us overboard!"

Eathelon chuckled. No reply needed.

The sails billowed out again and the ship glided along robustly. Eathelon continued aft, staring at the white crests of ocean waves that stretched to the horizon, as the last vestiges of night disappeared.

Eathelon loved the freedom of sailing the open sea, but also respected its dangers. He recalled a warning his Mother had given him on the eve of his departure: "Keep to the Westmost Sea, for it brought us safely to Melatui. Avoid the *Southern Sea* if you can. The Eldarin who entered it never reached our isle." She'd held him long in the gaze of her soft blue-grey eyes, her yellow hair framing her delicate face, and said, "Come back to me, son." Her eyes had moistened then and his moistened now, as he recalled her words and face. She had always been strong and wise, but in that moment, he'd seen an uncharacteristic vulnerability.

Lelar wished to return to Narda, to the Golden City of her youth and she shared this desire with most other Eldarin on the isle. So, the Eldarin Council had asked Eathelon to make this dangerous journey, to discover if that were possible. As the son of a King, who by Maagi custom must prove himself worthy, he could not refuse, and knew his friends, capable seaman themselves, would join him, if asked.

But on the eve of their departure, his Father, the Maagi Warrior King of Melatui, who should have had many more years of rule ahead, had been found dead. Stunned and in grief, Eathelon attempted to delay their departure, to find out what had happened and why. But *Celorn,* Head of the Eldarin Council, insisted they leave on schedule. Departures are ruled by season and tides, he'd said, and promised to investigate, as they sailed away.

Eathelon knew the Maagi custom of having the Queen assume rule upon the King's death had long ago been made for a Maagi Queen, not for an Eldarin Queen to rule over the Maagi. It could prove to be a dangerous time for Lelar, and for Melatui — and he was not there to protect her!

But he could not now dwell on something he could not change, so he turned his thoughts to his errand ahead and the need to complete it and return home as soon as possible. Perhaps the Eldarin would be able to return to Narda and the situation on Melatui would sort itself out.

A bird called out above, pulling Eathelon from his thoughts. He raised his spyglas and scanned for land again, without result. He wondered if other lands besides Narda existed out here in this vast ocean. Perhaps the Eldarin who'd entered the Southern Sea had found some other isle and settled there. But in his heart, he knew it was not likely. And what if the Sirine missed Narda altogether and simply sailed on until their stores gave out?

Just then, Marchal yelled, "Sails are trimmed!"

"She's gliding along like a bird," said Tomas, walking toward his Captain.

"Ever the poet, eh Tomas?" said Eathelon.

Tomas grinned and bowed, "It is who I am, Cap'n."

"Good, your poems and songs cheer me."

"Happy to be of service," grinned Tomas.

Marchal walked over. "I am going below. Come along, Tomas."

"I have other duties," he replied.

Eathelon continued aft, watching the rhythmic swells of the rolling sea, its white peaks foam and fall. The smallest, yet one of the finest sailing vessels in the Eldarin fleet, the Sirine had borne his Mother's family from Narda to Melatui 60 years earlier. It had been refurbished there and Eathelon considered the odd turn of events that it now carried Lelar's only son back.

When King *Maalo* died, Eathelon became acutely aware of his own mortality, something he hadn't really thought about before. The old tribal wars on Melatui stopped after the Eldarin came, long before his birth and his 'warrior' training had been one of mock battles, though he'd trained hard with some of the best veteran warriors on his isle.

If someone wanted the King dead, they must mean to harm his family. His Father had ruled well, had appeared to be well liked. Would those same people harm his Mother? He'd heard rumors that some on the isle disagreed with Maalo's marriage to Lelar, though the marriage had been sanctioned by both the Maagi and the Eldarin. Suppose their errand failed? Suppose he did not return?

In all of Melatui's known history, its Kings and Queens had been Maagi. The Maagi had no doubt not foreseen an intermarriage with another race when they'd adopted the custom of having the Queen rule in place of the King. Had he not come on this errand, he likely would have taken up rule himself, spared his Mother any danger. But the errand was too important to her and to the Eldarin. Should he succeed, the Eldarin would all be able to return safely to Narda, fulfilling their one desire. He knew it would mean the end of his family's reign on Melatui, but he didn't care.

Eathelon reviewed what he'd learned about his Eldarin ancestors: a wise and peaceful folk who'd journeyed to Narda from some far-off place in ages past. They'd created there a lasting peace and prosperity, until betrayed by one of their own, a *Tynar* Eldarin. *Tebor* wanted to rule Narda himself, but was discovered and banished from the Golden City. Angry, he set up his own house in *Gorst*, in the East, the House of Tebor. Later, his descendant, *Baele*, had recruited the giant Northmen from the *Northern Reaches* and the exiled criminals of the *Castellan Valley* into his army. They invaded the Golden City and murdered many Eldarin, forcing the rest out of Narda. The Eldarin who'd sailed into the Westmost Sea had reached Melatui. Those who'd sailed into the Southern Sea had perished.

The Eldarin found the Maagi unfriendly at first, but won them over eventually, as they had done with the races of Narda. The pact made with the Maagi King to wed Lelar to the King's son, Maalo ended any conflict. The intermarriage created a new race, the Mallorites, Eathelon its first Prince and heir to the throne. Other Eldarin intermarried with the Maagi also and the races on Melatui became three: Maagi, Eldarin and Mallorite.

Eathelon's two closest Eldarin friends, Tomas and Marchal, joined him on his errand, for, in addition to being capable seamen, they each possessed another unique ability he needed to accomplish his errand. Celorn had chosen Palo, the son of a Maagi chief who'd been a close friend to the King and, since Palo had already been a sort of big brother to Eathelon, he was pleased with the choice.

Eathelon and his crew had been given three tasks: find out if the House of Tebor still ruled in Narda and whether the Eldarin were still under death threat there; seek out the Eldarin's old allies and request their help to bring the Eldarin back; and a third, secret task, one known only to Celorn, Lelar, Eathelon and his crew.

Eathelon arrived aft to see Palo's huge hands guiding the ship well, as ever they did.

"She is running on course," said Eathelon.

"Gliding along like a fine lady," grinned Palo, his mouth spread over his brown face like a half-moon. "If I could find a lady as reliable, I'd marry her and have a whole crew of children!"

Eathelon laughed. This voyage had mellowed Palo somewhat and Eathelon liked the change. He mused that Palo, unlike the other two, never addressed him as 'Cap'n'.

"I shall feel obliged to remind you of that when you complain to me that you never have time to look for a wife. You are always busy sailing, hunting and ... well, warrioring!"

"I have other skills," Palo defended.

"Of that, my friend, I have no doubt," chuckled Eathelon.

Tomas suddenly appeared on the aft deck with a tray of food for Palo.

Seeing it, Palo complained, "Fish again?"

But his complaint rolled off of Tomas like water. "You know very well our stores are low, and besides, you like fish,"

"Yes, but for every meal?" replied Palo.

Tomas shrugged. "Save your complaints for the cook — I am just the delivery boy." He set Palo's plate down hard on the deck. "I have more important things to do than bring an ungrateful crewmate his brefas." He winked and walked off whistling.

"Cheerful as ever, that one," said Palo, reaching for his food.

Eathelon laughed, "Yes. I, for one, like it."

Palo took a bite of fish. "I have never met anyone as cheerful as those two," he said it with a mouth full of fish.

"Nor are you likely to," replied Eathelon.

True, for Tomas and Marchal often did their chores singing cheerfully. And, though Palo pretended to be annoyed at times,

Eathelon knew he secretly liked it. Eathelon appreciated the light mood his friends created on the voyage, for his mood had darkened after his Father's death.

He finished up with Palo and headed back up the port side, inspecting the ship as he went. Despite the many duties of a limited crew, they had all managed to keep the Sirine in good condition.

Eathelon felt the change in the weather before he observed it. The sky began to darken as he went below to check his charts. He sensed an oncoming storm. He had a bite of food, noted the low water stores and went back on deck.

Tomas, at work on the rigging, recited a poem:

The Sky dared the Sun to a game, painting itself in hues,
The Sun shifted yellow to gold, invading the Sky's subtle blues,
The Clouds floated into the game, playing hide-and-seek with the Sea,
The Sun dodged its puffs without shame, but the Clouds would not let it be,
They frowned at the Sun, casting gloom, as the Sea danced its playful waves high,
Then Night rolled in too soon and dropped its curtain down on the Sky.

"I like it," Eathelon called out.

"Thanks, Cap'n. I hope I can remember it."

"You will, my poet friend. Now get up the mast and tell what you see. I want your keen eyes on this weather." He handed Tomas his spyglas.

Tomas scrambled up the rigging like a *Hoona Monkey* and scanned the horizon.

"If Narda's shore is anywhere near, these clouds will soon hide it," Tomas called down.

Eathelon shrugged. *Well, maybe land will appear before this storm moves in.*

But it was not to be. The clouds thickened so fast that by the time Tomas scrambled down to the deck and handed back the spyglas, it had turned black.

Eathelon headed aft again, for Palo had 10 years more sailing experience than the rest of them.

Tomas bumped into Marchal, who was trying to catch more fish, a look of concentration on his face. "Is there something on your mind besides catching supper, Marchal? Look at the sky! I believe we are in for a storm."

"Yes, I do not much like the look of this weather, but I need something to add to our stores. To answer your question, I was thinking about how to describe this little adventure to our friends back home. I cannot put it all down in rhyme like you."

"Rhyme does seem to be my gift. What have you worked out then?"

"The two of us, sitting in front of the fireplace at the *Mali* Inn with our friends gathered around, each of us telling our adventure in his own way. Yours will be exciting and full of rhyme, of course."

Tomas laughed. "And how will you tell yours then?"

"I am still working that out."

"You, my factual friend, will probably tell it like a history lesson — boring! From the look of this sky, though, I think the journey is about to get much more adventurous!"

They laughed.

Marchal felt a tug on his line. Some hapless fish had caught his hook and struggled to get free. Marchal struggled harder and Tomas jumped in to help, for the fish was very large. Together they overpowered it and hauled it in. A single blow to its head sealed its fate. Marchal gathered up his gear, wrestled the fish over his shoulder and headed for the galley.

Eathelon passed him, as he reached the stairs. "Nice catch!"

"All in a day's work, Cap'n," grinned Marchal, and he hauled it down the stairs.

Eathelon appreciated Marchal's cooking. Palo could cook but was needed at the helm. Tomas excelled at sails and rigging. Eathelon served as Captain, crew and navigator. The four made a workable crew for the Sirine. The fact that they were lifelong friends added pleasure.

Eathelon gazed the sky with concern, as he spoke with Palo. The largest man aboard by far, Palo's hands were twice the size and his middle twice the girth of Eathelon's. He made a good helmsman. Eathelon relieved him now and then so he could go below to sleep for a few hours, but Palo preferred to spend most of his time at the helm. Tomas and Marchal brought his meals to him there as a courtesy. Eathelon liked having Palo remain at the helm. The helmsman knew every motion and strain of the Sirine and kept her securely on course.

"I do not like the look of that sky," Palo stated.

"Nor I." said Eathelon. A knot tightened his stomach, as a raindrop hit his face.

Suddenly, out of nowhere, hundreds of tiny black fish broke the surface of the water and flew into the air all around the ship. They spread transparent fins, like bird wings, thrashed about in the waves and flew into each other in mass confusion. They thumped hard against the ship's hull and emitted a high-pitched sound that pained the ears of the crew, who were forced to duck and cover their ears. They watched in astonishment, as the tiny fish fluttered and flailed about for several minutes, then dove back under the dark water and disappeared.

"That was the strangest sight I have ever seen," said Tomas.

"What kind of fish were those anyway?" asked Marchal. "They had wings!"

"I have never seen or heard of one before," replied Eathelon.

"Nor I," added Palo, "not even in tales of the old fishermen at the Mali."

"That sound pained my ears," said Tomas.

"It tied my stomach in knots," remarked Marchal.

"Well, thankfully they are gone now," said Eathelon.

Another raindrop fell, then several more as Eathelon stuck out his hand to catch them. "We had better batten her down. I think we are in for some bad weather. Marchal, see if you can rig something to catch the rainwater. We may need it."

"Aye, Cap'n," replied Marchal.

The wind picked up as the crew busied themselves preparing the ship.

"Tomas," said Eathelon, handing him the spyglas. "Get aloft again, but do not stay up long."

"Aye," Tomas replied, and he scrambled up the rigging, singing robustly:

Oh, a sailor's work is never done,
he works from dawn to setting sun,
he works his fingers to the bone,
though never does his work alone,
with crew and Captain all together,
under clouds and in fair weather,
under sail and hand in hand,
he works until he reaches land,
and then, because he's done his best,
at anchor, ship and sailor rest!

Eathelon shook his head and chuckled. *Is there nothing that dampens his spirit?*

Eathelon noticed an eerie yellow glow behind the darkening clouds and his face tightened in concern. A pang of homesickness hit him in the belly and he felt a momentary remorse. He had courage enough, but being half *Syndar* and half Maagi, he had long felt conflicted about who he was and what he might prove to be — wise, like an Eldarin, or a fierce Maagi Warrior? Probably some of both, he guessed.

"Hoy! Off the starboard bow!" Tomas called down from the rigging.

Eathelon thought maybe Tomas had sighted land, but it turned out to be something quite different.

"Greatfish! Greatfish to starboard!" Tomas yelled down, with excitement.

Marchal went over to the rail to look. Palo secured the wheel and went over to join him. Eathelon came over to see if they should alter course, but the greatfish were far enough away.

They had all heard the tales of these gigantic sea creatures and wanted to witness the rare sighting, one few had been privileged to see. They all stood at the rail and watched, as the huge undulating beasts swam gracefully several hundred yards off the starboard bow. They rose and fell in the dark water, their long sleek backs curving in and out of the churning waves. The largest of all sea creatures, the greatfish sprayed multi-colored, iridescent seawater fountains high into the air, from large holes in their dark backs. They made a show for the crew, spewing their rainbow fountains high into the darkened clouds, the eerie yellow glow alight behind them. The scene looked unreal, and almost magical. *Magical land of odd creatures ...* Eathelon recalled.

"Look, how they move in rhythm to one another," said Tomas, "and spray the rainbow fountains at timed intervals!"

"How do they do that?" asked Marchal.

"I do not know," replied Eathelon.

"An old sailor at the Mali Inn told me that greatfish have a slimy substance in their breathing holes that turns seawater into that rainbow of color," said Palo.

"How could he possibly know that?" challenged Marchal.

"He said he sailed on a ship that hunted greatfish, but much regretted doing so. The crew cut the creatures up and sold the meat and other parts. The man sailed no more with that crew after, for he could not tolerate the hunting and killing of such beautiful creatures."

"I have never seen anything like them," remarked Marchal.

"They are ... unique," added Palo.

"Magnificent," said Eathelon. He became momentarily lost in a memory, triggered by the sight of the creature's spray, of a time when he'd accompanied his Mother to Melkatu, a beach on Melatui's southern coast. He'd climbed atop a giant rock, where the sea pushed its salty brine up through a hole, spewing water forth at timed intervals, like these greatfish. He'd been 10 and the power of the sea spewing forth had frightened him. He'd scrambled back down to sit on the sand beneath the falling mist, but later, had mustered his courage and gone back to conquer his fear. He'd stood at the edge of the blowhole, arms outstretched to meet the sea and dared it to take him, a foolish and dangerous stunt. *Would the sea remember his dare?*

"They are turning!" Tomas yelled down.

The creatures had turned south.

Not that way, thought Eathelon, *but then the greatfish own the seas. They have no reason to fear the Southern Sea.*

The crew went back to their task and Palo kept the ship on course. As he worked, Eathelon thought about what they would do when they arrived in western Narda.

We will anchor at Balor Bay, stay in the best inn in Bali, take a short, well-earned rest then purchase the supplies we need to cross the Brunhyl — Hamlan's high coastal hills — to Andolan. We will continue north, across Southern Hamlan to Malta and on to the Golden City.

It was Celorn's suggested route, for his mentor wanted to ensure that they beached as far from Eastern lands as possible, until they could determine whether or not the enemy still ruled there. As they sailed closer to Narda, Eathelon grew more and more excited about seeing his Mother's childhood home. Most of her family had perished in the Golden City, but Celorn and Lelar had told him everything they could remember about it and how happy the Eldarin had been living there. Now he would see it himself, walk its streets. His heart skipped a beat.

Eathelon ordered Tomas down to the deck, then a sudden squall erupted into a wild, churning maelstrom. The crew had little time to react, as it unleashed its fury upon them and they all scrambled to meet it head-on. A gust of gale-force wind, filled with rain and seawater, hit the ship hard on the starboard side and listed it to port, sending Marchal sliding into the rail. Eathelon held onto the rigging and helped Tomas down, as Palo tightened his grip on the wheel. Lightning struck all around them as the waves and wind pounded the ship from every direction.

"Hold on!" yelled Eathelon, as Tomas landed on the deck and grabbed for the rail.

The small crew worked furiously to keep the Sirine afloat, as the tempest tossed it about like a toy. Eathelon wondered if he'd made an error in his course calculation, or if there was an error in the charts, but in truth, the growing tempest had driven them off course to a place where the Westmost Sea and Southern Sea currents collide and they found themselves in the grip of the stronger current of the Southern Sea, as the storm unleashed its full fury on them.

"Hard to port, hard to port!" Eathelon yelled to Palo over the howling wind.

Palo turned the wheel with all of his might and, though

strong, struggled to keep the ship upright.

"Tomas, Marchal, over here!" Eathelon barked. "Help me get the sail down.!"

A wave washed over the starboard side and sent them all crashing into the rail.

"Hold on!" he yelled. The last thing they needed was a man overboard!

The three men began to work frantically to get the mainsail down, as the wind threatened to rip it to shreds. Ship and crew were thrust atop mountainous waves and pushed down into watery valleys over and over again, and before they could get the sail down, the gale-force wind ripped it apart and the Sirine floundered.

The killing storm had come up out of nowhere and Eathelon knew that the Eldarin ships of old must have been sunk by a storm like it. Only by the skill of the brave crew, and perhaps a little luck, were they kept from the bottom of the sea.

But the storm did not last long. It passed after only a few hours and the exhausted crew inspected the ship and found, to their surprise, that it had sustained minimal damage. The mainsail had ripped, but they had a spare in the hold. The ship had taken on water below, which left a mess, but no critical damage. This fact cheered them and they set about making any needed repairs, after which Tomas and Marchal fell exhausted into their bunks for a few hours of sleep. Eathelon offered to relieve Palo at the helm, but Palo refused.

"Go get some rest yourself," he said.

"We are off course, Palo. I fear that we have strayed into the Southern Sea."

"You may be correct to say so, though I hope you are wrong."

"As do I." *My premonition of doom?* Eathelon could not get an accurate bearing in the low-lying clouds that now obscured sky and horizon.

Tomas and Marchal came back up on deck after two hours, so Eathelon went below to rest, but made Tomas promise to wake him in two hours more. By the time he came back on deck, the sun had almost set, and dark, low-lying clouds drifted overhead. The black night soon followed and, by morning, a thick mist had formed around the ship, the dawn a pale ghost behind it. The wind died and without wind, the Sirine drifted on the current.

Eathelon went aft to speak with Palo, whose haggard expression told much.

"How am I supposed to get us back on course in this cursed fog?" asked Eathelon.

"I do not know Eathelon. I have a bad feeling about this."

"I cannot tell where we are or which way to set our course, Palo. Even the best navigator could not navigate in this cursed fog!"

"Just do your best, Eathelon. Your instincts are good."

But without the wind, adrift on a calm, ghostly sea, encased in dense fog, the crew could see little beyond the ship's rail and do little but drift with the current.

"I must somehow reset our course," Eathelon mumbled to himself, but he had no idea how to do it. He had never before been in a situation like this. A feeling of dread washed over him and this time, he could not shake it off.

The Sirine drifted for several hours in eerie silence, punctuated by the splash of mild waves against her hull and rhythmic groans, as she rocked restlessly on the fickle sea. The crew wisely used this time to make needed repairs, and to rest.

Happily, by noon the next day the wind returned, billowing out the sails, and the Sirine began to glide along briskly over a more willing sea. The horizon remained obscured by distant fog, however, and Eathelon's instinct told him they headed south, not west. His concern deepened as he realized more fully that they had indeed strayed into the Southern Sea. There was little they could do about it now but hope they reached Narda's shores soon.

Another day and night took them closer to land but, as morning broke on the last day, the sound that came to Eathelon's ears turned his blood to ice — the sound of the sea racing to shore. The Sirine had drifted in too close during the night. By the time the crew saw the reef looming ahead, they had little time to react, as the ship was pulled portside into it.

"Hard to starboard! Hard to starboard!" Eathelon ordered,

over the chilling sound of waves breaking off the port side.

Palo turned the wheel with all his might.

"More sail!" barked Eathelon, but when he saw Marchal and Tomas already on it, he ran to help.

Too late! The ship slammed hard into the reef portside then shuddered, like a soldier who has received a mortal wound.

Eathelon looked at the immense rock sticking out of the water. *A reef? But no reef was marked on the charts!*

He had no time to think about that now. The rocks ripped a hole in the port side of the ship and the Sirine began to list steeply in that direction.

Tomas ran for the galley stairs.

"Don't go down there," cried Marchal, "it is probably flooded!"

"I must!" Tomas responded. "There is something valuable Eathelon needs!"

The ship slammed into the reef again and shook violently!

"Shards! Right!" said Marchal, realizing what it was and he followed, sliding down the stairs as fast as he could, as water poured into the ship's belly through a gaping hole in the port side.

Eathelon realized the same thing and ran for the stairs too, just as the ship slammed hard into the reef again. This knocked him down hard to the deck and, as he staggered to his feet, a piece of loose rigging struck him in the head. He fell unconscious to the deck.

No longer able to control the ship, Palo abandoned the wheel and ran to help Eathelon.

Below deck, Marchal called out to Tomas in the dim light, "Where are you?"

"Over here! My leg is stuck."

Marchal followed his crewmate's voice and found him struggling with a fallen beam that had pinned his leg.

"I will try to loosen it," said Marchal. He looked around for something to use as leverage and found a piece of wood. He dragged it through the water, which by now had risen almost to his knees, then saw why they were both not already completely submerged — the rock that made the hole in the side of the ship also partially blocked the flow of water. But he knew they did not have much time before the water rose further.

Marchal tried with all of his might but could not budge the beam.

"Leave it, Marchal! Listen! There is something you must do!"

"What? I am not leaving you, Tomas."

"I know, I know but you must listen!" Tomas held up a cloth sling with something inside.

"Get this to Eathelon! You know he must have it! Go! Then come back for me, if you will. Meanwhile, I will try to free my leg."

Marchal grabbed the sling and bolted up the stairs. When he reached the deck, he looked around for Eathelon, but did not see him, so called out, "Eathelon! Where are you?!"

"Over here!" came Palo's voice. Marchal followed it to find Eathelon sprawled face up on the deck, Palo bent over him.

"What happened?"

"It looks like a piece of rigging hit him in the head and knocked him unconscious. He is starting to come around now."

The ship slammed hard into the rocks again and this time began to break apart.

Alarmed, Marchal said, "Tomas is trapped below! Give this to Eathelon! I must go back!"

"We have to get off the ship Marchal — it is breaking up!" Palo yelled to be heard over the sound of crunching wood and crashing waves.

But Marchal had bolted and was already halfway to the galley stairs.

"Save Eathelon if you can," he called back. "I must free Tomas." Then in a voice he was not certain Palo even heard, he added, "If we don't make it out, tell Eathelon we will always have his back."

Marchal flew down the galley stairs and by the time he reached Tomas, the water had risen to his chest. The belly of the ship had filled with floating debris.

"It is no use, Marchal, my leg is pinned tight. I do not think we can free it in time." He hesitated a moment, then added, in a choked voice, "Get off the ship while you still can."

"I am not leaving you," Marchal said calmly, and he dove back under the water and felt the problem with his hands. He could barely make out the beam in the dim light that filtered in through the tear in the ship's wall and he saw that Tomas was right – his leg was pinned tight and he knew the beam was too heavy for him to handle alone. Still, he had to try. He would not abandon his friend.

Back on deck, Palo put the cloth sling over his shoulder and lifted a groggy Eathelon to his feet. He half dragged, half walked him to a small lifeboat and lifted him into it. He lowered it into the water. The Sirine hit the rocks again and nearly spilled them both into the churning sea. When they reached bottom, Palo rowed with all of his might to get them away from the sinking ship. Looking back, Palo saw the ship break apart fully and the sea rush in, unhindered.

In those last moments, luck wholly deserted ship and crew, and somewhere off the coast of southern Narda, the Sirine, pride of the Eldarin fleet, broke apart fully and sank into an underwater chasm, taking Tomas and Marchal with her. And the malevolent Southern Sea closed its hungry mouth over them.

Palo rowed desperately to keep the lifeboat from the sucking current of the sinking ship and he managed, by sheer strength and a stroke of luck, to find a hole in the reef large enough for the little boat to pass through. It landed in a calmer bay on the other side of the reef. Grunting, Palo rowed for shore.

Dazed from the blow to his head, Eathelon lay back in the boat, his eyes fixed on the sky. A window opened in the clouds above and a great white bird appeared — the largest bird Eathelon had ever seen. The beautiful creature floated effortlessly on the air currents above, watching the drama unfold below, then suddenly flew down to where the ruined ship had been, circled twice and followed the boat across the bay. Then the giant bird flew away as Eathelon watched it become a speck and disappear.

Then darkness took him.

Chapter 2:
An Unexpected Turn

Eathelon sat on the wet sand, his back against a rock, his eyes closed, and he listened to the sound of water lapping at his feet. He imagined a wolf cub lapping water from a rain pool in a Melatui forest. But the smell of the sea told him this was not a forest. *I am on the beach at Melkatu.*

He rubbed his head to ease its pain and cleared the fog from his eyes. The spiny rock he sat against dug into his back, and the sound of the sea pounded in his ears. He focused, blinked and looked around. *This beach is unfamiliar.*

He remembered, the sound of the Sirine scraping rocks, the crew crashing into the ship's rail, the vague impression of an object coming toward him.

He stood, with some effort and looked up and down the beach. He saw the lifeboat a few yards away and remembered: the Sirine had struck a reef and sunk.

No reef was marked on the charts!

Picture after picture began to flood his mind, like savage soldiers rushing an enemy — the sight and sound of water pouring into the ship, the churning waves pounding against her breaking hull, distant voices.

He stared out at the visible parts of the reef that stood guard over this bay and the gentle fingers of water that lapped at his feet, in stark contrast to the violent sea that had pushed him here. The Sirine was lost. She had survived the perils of a voyage that brought the Eldarin to Melatui, and another back across the Westmost Sea only to be struck down as she returned home.

What ill omen does this portend?

He rubbed his head and looked up and down the beach. When he saw no one, he sat back down, closed his eyes and gave in for the moment to his situation. He opened his eyes again when he heard the call of a bird. It flew across the bay and his eyes followed it. They landed on a playfish out in the bay, that dove in and out of the water, moving eastward. He watched it and only after it dove below the surface, did he notice Palo standing up the beach. He breathed a sigh of relief.

Palo appeared to be making something. Eathelon took a deep breath to ease the pain in his head some. He remembered. Palo had dragged him into the lifeboat and pushed it away from the sinking ship. He had grunted and rowed with a great anger, until he wrestled the boat beyond the reach of the churning sea and into this calmer bay.

Eathelon remembered seeing a giant white bird above but he could not be certain whether it had been real or imagined. It all seemed like a dim, unfolding dream. He leaned back against the rock; his wet clothes heavy against his cold body.

He turned and looked up the beach again to where Palo stood and saw the Warrior staring out to sea. He knew at that moment that Marchal and Tomas were gone. Tapping some reserve of inner strength, he stood and walked over to Palo. The Warrior put his hand on Eathelon's shoulder and his look told him he understood his friend's pain.

Weary with both pain and grief, Eathelon said, dully, "Tomas and Marchal are gone then."

"I am afraid so, Eathelon," Palo replied, with little emotion.

After the recent loss of his Father, the loss of his ship and two friends was almost more than Eathelon could bear. Palo helped him over to the boat and offered a sip of water from a waterskin he'd rescued from the ship.

Dazed and spent, Eathelon leaned against the boat and allowed the sweet memories of his childhood with Marchal and Tomas to flood his mind. They had laughed and played together most of their lives. Tomas and Marchal had brought that same cheer on this voyage and the memories stiffened Eathelon's jaw like the walls of a stone castle and closed his throat like its iron front gate, holding back a well of grief. But the gate could not hold for long and tears filled is eyes. His friends had come to help him with his errand and had paid with their lives. He could not be consoled.

Palo left Eathelon alone with his grief for a few minutes, then quietly laid two small wreaths on the sand near his feet. Eathelon composed himself and saw the restrained grief on Palo's face. He felt a rising compassion for his Maagi friend who had saved his life and put a hand on Palo's arm. No words needed.

"Our errand has been spared, but at great cost," said Eathelon.

"Indeed," replied Palo.

"You saved my life, Palo. Such a deed I cannot easily repay."

"It is what I came for, Eathelon."

Eathelon nodded.

They picked up the crudely fashioned wreaths, waded into the bay and laid them on the water. The current took them out, but not far.

"We offer these *alìndas* in honor of our fallen friends," said Palo.

"Yes, then perhaps the Southern Sea will be satisfied and seek no further vengeance against us," Eathelon replied, bitterly. He chanted softly in *maagahasa*, the language of the Maagi, *"Eäldor penjali diri arwa menmuki ruma,"* — "may Eäldor guide your departed spirits home."

The tradition and language of the alìndas are Maagi, usually offered to the open sea. Eathelon knew these wreaths would not reach the open sea.

"Let this quiet bay keep the spirits of our friends," said Eathelon. "May they rest in peace here."

Palo's family, like Eathelon's, had a royal background, for his father *Tualo* had been a respected Chief and trusted friend of the King. He too had passed, and only a few months before Eathelon's father, and the two sons had found comfort in each other for a time. Both knew something was amiss, but Palo had not discovered anything untoward about his father's death and Eathelon had not had time to investigate his before leaving on this errand.

Maagi custom required Lelar to take the throne and when she did, something unsaid changed between the two sons, an unspoken chasm which neither crossed. Some of the Maagi disagreed with an Eldarin ruling Melatui and Eathelon knew Palo felt conflicted by his loyalty to both. This voyage had thankfully somehow mended that breach. Perhaps Celorn had foreseen this and it was why he suggested that Palo come.

They waded back to shore and, although grief still lay heavy on his heart, Eathelon knew they must move on.

"We need to find cover," he said, as they walked back to the boat.

Palo nodded.

Eathelon knew he might one day have to rule Melatui and, in painful moment, doubted he wanted to. *What will the Maagi think of a Mallorite King ruling the isle, even if I am half Maagi, for I am half Eldarin.*

He and Palo may not always agree with each other, but Eathelon knew Palo would be a loyal protector, one who would protect their errand as well as his friends. He had already proven it.

They discussed what next to do.

"Let us find cover in that wood," said Eathelon. "I have no idea where we are, half of our crew is gone and our possessions lie at the bottom of the Southern Sea."

"I did manage to salvage a few things from the ship," said Palo.

Eathelon smiled at him. "We must get off of this beach. We are too exposed here."

Then a thought struck Eathelon like a knife in his heart and he looked at Palo in restrained panic. Reading the look, Palo took the sling from beneath his tunic and handed it to him.

Eathelon sighed with relief. "Again, I am in your debt."

"Not mine, Eathelon. Marchal brought it up from below to make certain it came to you then he went back for Tomas, who was trapped below. They did not get off the ship."

Eathelon nodded but made no reply.

Palo rearranged some of the items in the boat, and said, "Marchal said something as he ran back to help Tomas. I did not understand what he meant, but perhaps you will know."

"Tell me when we are safely off the beach," Eathelon replied, and he picked up one end of the boat.

Palo picked up the other end.

"Make for the wood ... over there," said Eathelon, pointing to a place where they might be able to get the boat up to it. "I feel eyes on us."

Palo gave him a curious look, as they hoisted it over their heads and made for the trees.

The beach was narrow between the woods and the bay and the sandy slope up to it steep. They scrambled up the embankment, set the boat down in the brush and sat down with their backs against it.

"What did Marchal say?" asked Eathelon.

"He said, 'If we don't make it out, tell Eathelon we will always have his back.' Do you have any idea what he meant?"

"Not off hand. I must think it over." Eathelon looked dejected.

"No one could have predicted that squall, Eathelon," said Palo. "I have heard tales of those from old fishermen at the Mali, tales I thought only the embellishments of bragging seaman. By the gods, that tempest must have been conjured up by some evil here. And its message to us clear enough — go home!"

"You know I do not believe in evil spells," Eathelon responded, "Such storms, while rare and unpredictable, do happen. The Eldarin who sailed into the Southern Sea must have perished in one."

"Marchal and Tomas are gone and we are sorely grieved," remarked Palo. "But the errand to which we all pledged ourselves is spared. That such misfortune has befallen us at the beginning of our journey does not diminish its importance."

Eathelon considered his words. "I know."

"We all go to our Fathers, Eathelon — some sooner, some later than their time. I believe it is *how* we go, not when or where, that measures who we are. Marchal went back to help Tomas when he could have saved himself, a true friend. But we all knew the risks when we signed on."

"Yes, but our friends trusted their Captain and now they are dead," said Eathelon, with some bitterness.

"Do you believe they would want us to grieve long and stumble after?" Palo waited for an answer.

"No," replied Eathelon. He smiled a half smile. "They would

expect us to carry out our errand, as we would expect them to do had they lived in our stead."

Palo nodded.

"But their loss has given us another problem, Palo."

"The Stones."

"Yes, and we must find a way to solve it or our errand may be in vain. But we have a more urgent problem at this moment. We are far from *Balor Bay*. Do you see that cliff over there?" He pointed to a cliff jutting up from the beach on the west side of the bay.

"What about it?"

"I must somehow get up there so I can get a bearing on our location before we go running off in the wrong direction."

"Then I will set a camp while you look for a way up."

Eathelon smiled at his Warrior friend. "Things could be worse, I suppose. We have stumbled, but not fallen, mostly thanks to you."

"Have you considered Marchal's words?"

"Yes, and I can think of only one explanation. When we were young boys, Marchal and Tomas talked me into sneaking down to the beach for a swim late one night. I foolishly got caught in a rip tide and nearly drowned before I could make my way back to the beach. One of my Father's staff had followed us and I knew Tomas and Marchal would be in trouble if my Father knew the truth, so I told them all it was my idea. I 'had their backs,' so to speak."

Dissatisfied with this explanation, Palo grunted, "There must be another meaning."

"The Maagi believe they make a journey to join their Fathers in death, so lay them in the Tombs under the mountain and leave a light for them to find their way. The Eldarin burn the bodies of the dead, to release their spirits, so they may return. Perhaps Marchal meant they would somehow return. I have no other explanation."

Palo grunted again, but he knew it was the only answer he would get.

"We will stay in the wood tonight, but let us find a more sheltered place — and build a fire. I am cold and hungry. Make for that cliff."

Palo pulled a dry cloak from the boat and handed it to Eathelon, who smiled gratefully at Palo's choice of items he'd salvaged from the ship. Then Palo attempted to add some levity to the situation, by saying, "Well, it is a good thing you have a skilled hunter and cook along. At least we will not starve to death."

"Indeed," smiled Eathelon.

Palo put the salvaged items into a makeshift pack and they started off.

The coast of Southern Hamlan is strewn with wooded hills and abundant plant life, often dense down to the shoreline. They walked now between two tall cliffs that rose high on either side of the long, narrow beach, tramping through the wood, toward the smaller, west one. As they neared it, they entered a small cove.

Palo stopped, and pointed. "Eathelon — look."

Eathelon's eyes followed Palo's finger to the long rocky reef that sank the Sirine and saw that the beach they'd just left was strewn with rocks and wood debris, more than he had first noticed.

"Ours is not the only ship to wreck here, it would seem," said Eathelon.

"Indeed."

The secluded cove had dense trees surrounding it, a suitable place for a camp. They built a fire and warmed themselves until Eathelon felt revived enough to go look for a way up the cliff.

"Hunt us up something for supper, Palo."

Palo grinned.

Eathelon walked over to the base of the cliff and began to search for a trail.

Palo cut a branch with the huge knife he always carries and began to make a spear. He glanced up now and then to watch Eathelon and a wide smile spread across his broad brown face. Eathelon was more Eldarin than Maagi, his Mother's influence, and he still wore the soft look of youth. But beneath those keen gray eyes lay a gentle heart, a Warrior, and a leader.

His spear made, Palo set off to hunt.

In the damp air of the cove, Eathelon's tunic clung to his muscular frame, and his plaited hair, once neatly tied at the nape of his neck, fell to his shoulders now and blew about his face in the light breeze coming off of the sea. He searched the bottom of the cliff and grew frustrated when he did not at once find a way up. He brought to mind the image of the last map of Narda he had studied. It showed the two large cliffs on the southern coast, an indent between, where they now camped. The larger of the two cliffs he knew was the tall cliff of *Numar*, on the east side of the beach. The storm had not pushed them that far east and he knew they camped now under the lower, western cliff.

He searched again for a trail and found the remnants of one. He followed it up and, as he climbed, recalled Celorn's words, given to him on the eve of his departure:

"I am counted wise, Eathelon, yet I cannot foresee what lies ahead for you in Narda. There may come a time when you feel hope is lost. For that time, I say, *do not lose hope!* I cannot say where your errand will take you, but your journey may be long and your path filled with many twists and turns. My heart tells me it will end well, but I can no longer trust to my heart alone. If the Eldarin are to return to Narda, our fondest hope, it will be by your hand, and those of your friends. We have no right to ask it of you, yet we do."

Celorn had put his hand on Eathelon's shoulder, and added, "There may be some in Narda who wish you harm and some you may suspect of this, who may yet prove to be your friends."

"But how will I know?" Eathelon had asked.

Celorn had smiled. "You will know, Eathelon. You must trust yourself."

The crew of the Sirine had put to sea quietly the next morning, with no one in attendance but Celorn and Lelar. None of them knew if they would return.

Eathelon looked at the position of the sun, as he followed the path up the cliff. His strength had waned from his ordeal and he expended much effort in the climb. The back of his neck began to prickle again, a sign he was watched, though it appeared the trail had not been used for a very long time.

Chapter 3: The Southern Coast

The vegetation, dense at the bottom of the cliff, diminished as Eathelon climbed the steep trail, walking or climbing over and around rocks and boulders strewn there. The trail led him over a narrow rock bridge, and in one place came so close to the edge of the cliff he nearly lost his footing in the growing shadows. The sun had fallen far down the sky now and he had little time left to reach the top for a bearing before night fell. But tired, out of breath, his head pounding, he had to stop for a brief rest. After his breath slowed, he set off again and at last came near the summit. Encouraged, he made the last, short climb to it.

The trail disappeared at the peak, onto a flat top covered in short, spongy green grass. He laid down for a few minutes to regain his strength and noticed faint dots of light starting to appear in the sky, obscured here and there by thin ragged pieces of cloud.

He stood and turned slowly in a circle and found he had an expansive view of the surrounding lands and sea. Its beauty in the waning sun took his breath away. He watched as the fading orb slowly began to sink into the Westmost Sea, sending its fiery fingers out over the watery horizon.

He turned eastward to the tall, shadowed cliff of Numar rising like a stone giant out of the Southern Sea. He felt certain now that they had run aground in Southern Hamlan, far from their intended destination of Balor Bay. His heart sank. He looked out over the bay they had crossed to the long, narrow beach and saw something that had not been visible from below — the reef, the demise of his beloved ship and friends, stretched *almost* all the way across the bay, almost. Had they sailed a little farther east they might have passed around it altogether.

But had we done so, we may have landed on Eastern shores, perhaps right into the hands of the enemy. Is it not an irony, that crashing into the reef may have kept us out of harm's way? Or, had it?

His neck had prickled for a time, after all, had it not? Had he not felt eyes on them back on the beach?

Turning northward, he could see over the tops of the trees in the broadleaf wood where they'd stashed the lifeboat and these ended abruptly at the top of the ridge. He knew, from his study of the maps of Narda, that the land fell steeply there onto a wide plain that stretched to the Brunhyl.

The Brown Hills, they are called, for it is said that they remain brown between Midsummer and Latefall and turn green only after the Earlyspring rains. It is Aldona now — Earlyfall. The hills are brown, but I cannot tell, for they lie in shadow.

The Brunhyl comprise fully a third of southern Hamlan and draw inland as they run north. In the dim light, Eathelon could only imagine the place where the coastline turned in to Balor Bay, their original destination.

He sighed. *We are far from home, our two closest friends are gone and our errand has nearly come to naught at its start.*

Still burdened by grief, he drew in a long, deep breath. He could not afford to ponder over the circumstance in which he now found himself, or how he came to it. He must decide where they should go next. A knot tightened in his stomach as he realized he and Palo now had a much longer journey ahead, and few provisions with which to make it.

As he stood there, looking north, a thought struck him. *Andolan, the fortress city of Hamlan lies that way.* He began to formulate a plan, as he recalled his Mother's words, on the eve of his departure, when he'd expressed his misgivings about the journey.

"Do not doubt yourself, Eathelon. Doubt diminishes your power and hands it to your enemy. Doubt may lie in you, but it begs death, even if only to hope. Never lose hope. Trust your instincts. Wisdom and courage lie in you and will serve you in times of need."

Recalling her words boosted his courage and offered him comfort.

Night deepened atop the cliff and he knew he must get back, but something held him. As he started toward the trail, an image of Celorn appeared ahead, one so real it looked as if his mentor were standing there. It held up a small green amulet set in gold and Eathelon smiled. He'd forgotten about the amulet. He recalled now how Celorn had used it in the Great Hall back in Melatui, when he'd addressed the Eldarin Council about sending Eathelon and his friends on this dangerous errand. He'd called the amulet to life and it had bathed all of them in a pale, green light and all, save he and Celorn had been frozen still as stone. Eathelon had stood gaping, as Celorn placed the amulet around his apprentice's neck, saying, "The Elvenkin gave this to me. When they see it, they will know I sent you." Celorn had closed Eathelon's hand over the stone and it had gone dark and dull, and all who'd been frozen in its light had returned to life, none the wiser.

"But this is magic," Eathelon had protested. "I do not know how to wield it."

"Be not troubled by its magic," Celorn had said. "Its powers are not great, but it may prove useful in times of need." The old man had smiled. "When such times come, you will know how to wield it, Eathelon. The amulet itself will show you."

He opened his shirt now and removed it and it began to glow. He stared at it for a moment and blinked. When he looked up, Celorn was gone.

Eathelon knew now where they must go and what they must do. He began his descent and, though night had dropped its black curtain down fully, set the amulet before him to light his way.

Chapter 4:
Shadow of the East

The Great Hall of Gorst, once majestic and beautiful, stood dark and gloomy now. Its gaudy, ornate decor clashed with the tall marble columns that stretched the length of its main aisle from its front entrance to the dais at the rear. Heavy woven tapestries hung over the tall, narrow windows on both sides of the hall, keeping it in perpetual twilight. The occasional ray of sun shone through small round windows above and between the tapestried ones and, along with a few strategically placed lamps provided additional light in a failed attempt to brighten up the place.

The Great Hall, a former palace that held grand parties for those fortunate enough to be on the invitation list, had been built long ago by the Eldarin and occupied by the once benevolent governor of the region. After the House of Tebor overthrew Gorst and became its new occupants, the hall took on the same distasteful personality as its new owners, who kept it a dark, dreary, lifeless place.

Behind the dais, a door squeaked open and a man entered. Once tall and muscular like his Eldarin ancestors, his body was now bent and twisted, his head cast downward like a carrion bird of the Castellan Valley. His pointed nose looked more like a sharp beak, and his long, narrow black beard and bushy brows accentuated his gaunt, almost skeletal face. He walked slowly toward the dais, his gnarled fingers grasping an ornate staff which clicked noisily on the marble floor, the sound echoing through the sad, empty hall.

Baele, self-proclaimed Lord of Gorst, robed himself in the soft silk finery of the Kings of Narda, garments given to them long ago by the Eldarin. The usurper of the Eastern throne wore it now in stark contrast to his bent, gnarled body and the colorful robes gave him an undeserved, almost regal look. The Nardan Kings had chosen robes of rich blues and greens, to represent the beauty and grandeur of Narda, they said, but Baele had commanded his robes be made of red, a symbol of his might and power, he said. It later came to be more a symbol of bloodshed from the many actions undertaken by the House of Tebor, however.

Baele's head held an ornate gold crown with several colored gems placed in tasteless, haphazard fashion, almost as if to emphasize his confused and twisted mind. As he approached the throne, the monarch smiled crookedly and chortled deep down in his throat, as he often did. He ran a gnarled hand over the smooth marbled arm of his throne and sat down on the soft pillows placed there to cushion his aging body. He mumbled something to himself, his eyes darting to and fro, then suddenly, his face frozen in terror, he stood and cried out to some unseen enemy, "Leave me alone!" then sat back down, breathing hard, his face the color of new fallen snow.

On the lower step of the dais, before his throne, stood an ornate bronze stand decorated with patterns of flames. Three larger flames stretched upward to form a bowl, which held a dark red orb. Composed now, Baele stood and looked out into the hall, his head turning back and forth, his eyes scanning every part. Convinced he was alone, he stepped down to the orb. At first glance, it looked like another hall decoration, but the hungry look in Baele's eyes as he placed his gnarled hands atop it told otherwise. He caressed the thing and spoke to it as one might speak to a pet. Then he gave it a pat, turned and struggled back up the marbled steps to his pillowed throne, and sat down.

He reached for the long, braided gold cord hanging down beside the throne and pulled on it. A bell rang in the distance and two servants came running in shortly after.

"How may we serve, My Lord?" asked one.

"Check all of the doors and windows in the Hall and make certain they are locked. I cannot be too careful, you know. Then leave ... and make certain no one enters."

"Yes, My Lord," the two servants echoed in unison.

They bowed and went off to do as they were bid, giving each

other a look, hidden from their master, that said they had done all of this before. After they had finished, they left the room, but stood nearby, in case they were summoned again.

Certain he was alone now, Baele smiled a crooked smile and chortled deep down in his throat. He stepped back down to the red Stone, placed his gnarled hands atop it, closed his eyes and chanted softly:

Firestone, come now awake,
ancient fire of Morningstar,
flame, a light of day now make,
arise and show me what you are.
Aldo, spirit-stone of old,
I bid your eyes be opened still,
come forth and let me now behold
your message, for me now reveal.

The red orb slowly came to life, its yellow flames swirling around inside like a newly lit fire. Baele stared at it for several minutes, unmoving, then the flames diminished and the Stone went dark.

He furrowed his bushy brows as a deep frown came over his face. Then, his eyes flew open wide and he cried out in a rage, "You dare to mock me? You will mock me no more!"

He pushed the stand over and it crashed down, spilling the orb, which rolled unharmed across the hard marble floor. Baele went after it, arms outstretched, calling to it the way a parent might call to a child unjustly punished. The two servants came running in, knowing as they did what had happened. One of them retrieved the runaway orb and the other picked up the stand and restored it to its place. Baele walked back slowly and sat down on his throne, head in his hands.

The two servants stood before him, waiting. They had a message to deliver that they knew Baele would want to hear, so they waited patiently for him to regain his composure. When he had, one of them mustered up the courage and said, softly, "My Lord, *Esol* has arrived."

Baele lifted his head and brightened up a little, "Well, show him in — and tell him to bring my little pets."

"Yes, My Lord." The two servants left.

Ten minutes or so later, Baele's son walked in with three creatures, each with a leather cover on its tail, one on his right arm, one on his left, one on his shoulder, secured loosely with straps. As Esol approached his Father, he loosened the straps and Baele flung his arms up in a signal for the creatures to take the air. They flew energetically around the Great Hall with speed and agility, reaching first to the rafters then darting in and around the marble columns. Baele squealed with delight as he watched them for several minutes, then he summoned them to him.

"*Raji, Muji, Fyri — acöm vit, vit!*" (Come here)

Baele stretched out his arms and the *fyrcaats* settled, one by one onto his lap and onto the arms of the throne. They nipped playfully at each other, vying for affection.

"Behave yourselves now," Baele said firmly, though not unkindly. "There, there, my little Fyri," he added, and he pulled him onto his lap and stroked his sleek, red-brown hairless, leathery-skinned body. Fyri purred in a low growl, then coughed, releasing a tiny puff of smoke from between his sharp teeth. "Careful now!" laughed Baele.

"And my shy Muji," said Baele, as he pulled his brown-yellow onto his lap and touched her nose. The creature's eyes blinked a warning and Baele scolded, "Naughty girl!"

He turned to the third fyrcaat, sitting on the arm of the throne. "My precious blue Raji," he said as he stroked the creature's back, down to the leather guard on his tail, used to protect a handler from its poisonous barbs. Raji looked at him, blinked and purred with contentment.

Esol watched the entire scene with mild contempt. "Father, you know fyrcaats are dangerous. I do not know why you keep them for pets."

"They are not dangerous to me, ungrateful sod!"

"There is no need for insults. Why have you summoned me this time? You know I have important work to do to keep things under control in Newcastle."

"I am certain you can handle that, or I would not have sent you down there. And I can summon you here whenever I wish.

Am I not the Lord of the East?"

"Yes, of course you are, Father. So, what do you need me for this time?"

In a controlled voice Baele replied, "There are intruders in the West — intruders, strangers! I saw them in the Stone, though I confess the image was rather vague. I did not see their faces, but I could tell they are outsiders, and at least one, of some race I have never seen."

"You are certain?"

"Did I not say so? If you spent more time looking for that missing Stone at Castletop, as I bid, you might better appreciate what these Stones can do for us."

"I have searched and searched Father. I tell you that Stone is not at Castletop. Perhaps *Landrin* took it when he fled to the Flax Isles."

"Imbecile! Do you think I would have allowed that? He did not have the Stone, but he fled before he could be questioned about it. We must find it before *Aneron* does."

"Meanwhile, I want you to send my fyrcaats after those intruders. I cannot have them coming here or going to *Newelan*. We need to know what they are up to, what they are doing."

"Your fyrcaats are not going to help much in that regard."

"Oh, but they will. They can stop them. Too many of our spies have been caught in the web of the West, of late. My fyrcaats are more reliable in some ways than the men I send over there. They do what comes naturally." He cackled.

"Why not just send them yourself?"

Baele flew into a rage. His face became distorted and he bellowed, "Because I am ordering you to do it, that's why! That traitorous King Aneron is up to something and we need to find out what. And after all I have done to keep his ridiculous trade agreement. He is sneaky, lulling me into a false peace when all the time he intends to overthrow us! I know he does!" Baele paused and his next words dripped out like honey, "But I will have the last word yet, son, oh yes, I will have the last word!"

Esol did not doubt his Father's words.

Baele smiled a wicked smile and motioned Esol closer. Esol bent down and Baele whispered something into his ear, as if it were some great secret that he must keep from a host of people lurking about in his empty hall.

Esol smiled as he listened and he nodded in agreement, for one of the many traits he shared with his Father, and indeed had learned well from him, was his thirst for power, at whatever cost. He would help defend the power of the House of Tebor, yes, but he also had plans of his own.

Baele stood, placed his three pets back onto Esol's arms and shoulder and fastened the straps to hold them there. He smiled up at his son, who stood a full foot taller than his Father. Then Esol left, and Baele sat back down on his throne, mumbling to himself, a crooked smile on his aged face.

Chapter 5:
A Premonition

Eathelon navigated the steep path down the cliff in less than half the time it took him to climb it. He found a low fog lay over the bay and cove as he came to the bottom, and the light from the amulet died once he was safely down.

He spotted Palo's campfire and walked toward it, gathering wood. His hope for a warm meal was rewarded when he saw Palo lift a roasted fish from the fire.

"Hoy Eathelon! Supper is cooked. Did you get to the top? You have been gone longer than I expected. I could wait no longer to cook our meal."

Eathelon set the wood down, grabbed a fish and began to eat. "Your timing is perfect Palo. This fish is good! I am hungry! And yes, I made it to the top," he said between bites.

Palo grabbed a fish, sat down next to Eathelon and began to eat. "What did you find?"

"The climb was difficult, but well worth the effort. I know now where we must go and how we will get there."

Eathelon devoured his fish as if he'd not eaten in weeks and it renewed him. His grief had diminished with food and warmth and he decided to have a little jest with Palo. "This is really good, Palo. You are indeed as good a fisherman and cook as your Father claimed."

His words had the desired effect. Palo stopped eating for a moment and looked at him. "Just when did you speak with my Father about my skills as fisherman and cook?"

"I did not say I spoke with him, only that he made such a claim." He grinned and took another bite of fish, "I quite agree."

Palo took the bait. "If you did not speak with my Father, how would you know he made such a claim?"

"Do you not have friends who frequent the Mali Inn?"

Palo scoffed, "Since when do you take gossip from the Mali?" Palo grinned back — he'd caught on. He went back to eating his fish. "Besides, if they were my friends, they wouldn't be spreading gossip about me at the Mali."

Eathelon laughed. "Do not worry, Palo they left out all the bad parts."

Palo grinned. "There are no bad parts and it is lucky for you that I *am* as good a fisherman and cook as my Father said, if he said it, or you would starve."

"This I doubt," grinned Eathelon, taking another bite. "But it is good to have such skills along on our journey ... and better yet to have a friend along."

Palo grinned.

Eathelon had accomplished his purpose, for the light banter had provided a temporary respite from the gravity of their situation.

Night deepened and the fog lifted some, but still hid the moon and stars that had so delicately dotted the sky atop the cliff. Eathelon wanted the warmth of the fire, but they decided it more prudent to put it out and wrap themselves in their cloaks for the remainder of the night, so they finished the meal and put out the fire. Although weary from stress and grief, they remained awake awhile longer to discuss their situation.

"You know which way to go then?"

"Yes. We landed on the southern coast of Hamlan, of that I am certain. Numar is east of us and *Bali* far to the north. But we no longer need to go to Bali. Celorn chose that destination to keep us as far north as possible that we might avoid any chance of meeting the enemy. But we have landed here now. Such is our circumstance. And by chance or by luck, it has actually put us closer to the fortress city of *Andolan*. We were to go there anyway, to return the Stone. So, we will go now from here and seek an audience with King Aneron. But we must first discover whether Aneron still rules the West, so we don't go walking into a trap."

"How will we do that?"

"Go with caution and trust to luck, I suppose."

"The same luck that landed us here?" Palo asked, with a bit of sarcasm.

Eathelon gave him a look of irritation and ignored his remark.

"Celorn said Aneron has always been a true friend and ally to the Eldarin. It is likely he still rules the West, for it is said Andolan has never fallen. We have seen no sign of anyone since we arrived and have made little attempt to hide our presence here. We will need Aneron's help and resources." Eathelon paused. "Fate is strange, Palo. This odd turn of events may have pushed us into a plan far better than the one Celorn set for us."

"Fate was not kind to our friends, Eathelon."

"No, and my regret for their loss is deep, and still fresh."

"I did not mean to re-open the wound, Eathelon, I am sorry."

Eathelon shook his head. "The wound will take time to mend, Palo. He smiled. We must leave our misfortune behind us now and turn instead to our errand." He stretched and yawned. "I know you are tired too, but do you think you could stand first watch?"

"Yes. I am not sleepy."

"Wake me in two hours then." Eathelon yawned again, laid down, pulled his cloak over his body and fell into a restless sleep. A dream came to him:

He stood on the deck of a ship that rocked on a vast open sea, and he breathed in the pungent air as the sun rose over the eastern horizon. Suddenly, he was lifted up and, although he did not know how, he seemed to float above the ship. He peered down at it, as it cut through the vast water, and saw a man at the helm. He reached out to him, for he seemed familiar, but his hand only met air, as the tanbark sails of the ship billowed out in the growing breeze and the ship continued on its course, the man at his work.

He rose higher and higher into the air and was afraid at first, but his fear dissolved into a feeling of calm, as the clear, deep blue sea rolled gracefully below and white, puffy clouds dotted the sky above. He hovered over the ship for what seemed hours, but he could not tell, for he moved with it and time did not seem to exist.

The sun grew hotter and a cool breeze played with the hair of the man at the helm, yet Eathelon's hair lay untouched. A voice called out to him, in a low murmur at first, then louder, and louder still until it surrounded him, and here is what it said:

Eathelon, Eathelon, sail the Westmost Sea,
onto Narda's western shores, as we have bidden thee;
Under Eathens' snow-capped peaks to fair Andolan's gate
And to far off Northwest Wood before it is too late!
Beware the Fyr Mountains, the Druid on the Moors,
and those who might betray you, who sleep on eastern shores.
Eathelon, Eldarin's hope, walk Narda's land with care,
for some may seek to hinder you and take you captive there!

He heard his name called over and over, in rhythm with the rising and falling of the sea,
"Eathelon, Eathelon ..."
Then the voice grew urgent. "Eathelon, wake up!" Palo said, in a loud whisper.
Eathelon came awake and wiped beads of sweat from his forehead. He stood and looked around to familiarize himself with his surroundings.
"Are you alright?" Palo asked. "I would have let you sleep longer, for you no doubt have need of it, but I am too tired myself to stand watch any longer, and you told me to wake you in two hours, yet it has been three."
Eathelon yawned. "I am fine, Palo. Go get some sleep."
Palo laid down under a tree and fell asleep. Eathelon, awake enough to stand watch now, considered his odd dream, then shrugged it off.
The rest of the night passed without incident and the morning light crept through the branches of the tree above Palo. Eathelon had not awakened him. The sun climbed up the sky and still Palo slept. When it burned away the fog and nearly reached its zenith. Palo awoke and looked around. Eathelon was nowhere in sight. He made a brief search and found him several yards off, fast asleep, his back propped against a rock.
Reluctant to wake Palo, Eathelon had stayed at the watch all night. When he'd sat down to rest for a few minutes, he'd fallen

asleep, one sorely needed. Seeing this, Palo could not pass up an opportunity to tease Eathelon back for his Mali story.

He shook Eathelon awake and said, "Some watch you turned out to be."

Eathelon realized what he had done. "Shards Palo! I fell asleep at my watch. I must have been more tired than I thought."

"Indeed," agreed Palo, a mock frown on his face, then he added, "and I slept well past mine. It is fortunate for us this area is deserted. We needed sleep, but we must be more careful next time."

"There will not be a next time," Eathelon proclaimed.

Palo nodded.

The sun had risen almost to its zenith and hunger gnawed at them. They wanted to get started, but not without food. Moisture from the sea kept the air in the cove damp and cool and the sunlight had melted away most of the fog. Eathelon could see patches of blue sky through the ragged, drifting clouds. He drew in a long breath of air, brushed himself off and set about gathering more wood.

Palo picked up his makeshift spear. "I will go get us something to eat. I would not want to disappoint my Father!" he said, a wide grin spread across his broad brown face. He took off at a run, down to the water before Eathelon could make any reply.

Eathelon built a smokeless fire, despite the risk. He knew they needed a decent meal before starting off on the next leg of their journey. True to Palo's reputation, he returned with two large fish, gutted and ready to roast.

They talked together as they cooked and ate the fish and, when they'd finished, Eathelon put the fire out. They returned the camp as much as possible to its original condition, left the cove and made their way back to the boat.

Trailing behind Palo, Eathelon stumbled onto a familiar plant and, smiling at his unexpected good fortune, picked a few leaves and placed them in his pack. They came to the boat, retrieved the rest of the items Palo had salvaged and, satisfied they'd hidden the boat as well as they could, searched for a trail north, over the top of the ridge.

The Stone that Tomas and Marchal had given their lives to

save sat securely now in the sling tied to Eathelon's belt, hidden beneath his tunic. As it brushed against his body, his grief momentarily resurfaced.

Had I not left the Stone below, Tomas and Marchal might be here. He sighed and wiped the moisture from his eyes. *But what is done cannot now be undone.* He vowed to not let the Stone out of his sight until it had been safely returned to Andolan.

Their search for a trail north over the ridge proved fruitless, so in the end they simply set off in a northward direction through the broadleaf forest. Earlyfall was not far off now and the leaves of many of the trees had begun to turn. The sun turned the forest into a colorful landscape on its slow descent to the horizon. They had gotten off to a late start and traipsing through the forest without a visible trail did not help their pace, but they plodded on, keeping watch for a trail.

As they walked, a pair of eyes followed them a few hundred yards back.

Chapter 6:
The Journey Begins

After trudging through trees and brush for another hour, Eathelon and Palo stumbled onto a trail leading north, and followed it.

"We have gotten off to a late start Palo, but I want to reach the top of the ridge by nightfall, if we can."

"Well, now that we have a trail to follow, perhaps we can. But we need to find a water source before we go down onto the plain. There is little left in the waterskins and we have no idea if there will be water fit to drink there."

"Perhaps there is a water source between the here and top of the ridge. Such springs are common on Melatui."

"This is not Melatui."

"Trails often pass near a water source. Listen, and watch for a side trail."

Eathelon liked this broadleaf forest and recognized many of its trees — oak, cedar, hackberry, rosewood. It had quite a lot of mixed scrub too, and the trail appeared well-traveled, at least at one time. Few had evidently walked it of late.

They saw the last blooms of a variety of wildflowers and heard the chatter of jays, the tap, tap, tap of a woodpekir and the rustle of creatures in the bushes, likely *rabets*, usually plentiful in such wooded areas.

The trees thinned out and grew farther apart as they climbed toward the ridge, leaving them more exposed than they liked, but they had little choice than to follow the trail.

"Perhaps you can catch us a rabet for supper," grinned Eathelon. "You know how I like them."

"Indeed, I do," grinned Palo. "Or, perhaps I can find a chikka for us. You like fowl too."

"Chikkas are more likely to be found on the plain."

"Then rabet it is."

The light conversation kept them focused on the errand and off of recent losses, and helped pass the time as they hiked. They found the trail easy to follow now and fell into a steady rhythm for a time. By the time the sun had fallen halfway down the sky, they came to a flat area below the ridge and stopped there to rest, though not for long. Eathelon was still determined to reach the top before nightfall.

They started off again, but before they'd gone far, a large flock of giant black birds sitting in the trees ahead suddenly launched themselves into the sky and dipped and dove together, as a group, making a loud, raucous noise.

"Eathelon, do you recognize those birds? I have never seen one before."

"No, I do not."

The hikers stopped and watched the black mass move about the sky, then continued up the trail past the trees the birds had occupied. Once the hikers had passed, the birds dropped with a *whoosh* and settled back into the trees behind them, twittering and chattering away, as if to discuss the rude intruders.

"It seems we interrupted a social gathering," Palo remarked.

"Perhaps, but for some odd reason I feel those birds' eyes on us. They chitter away to each other as if they are talking about us."

"They are as ugly as the bottom end of a *Hoona Monkey*, do you not think?"

"Better not to insult them."

"They are *birds*."

"I know, but my intuition says they may be something more and I have felt eyes on us off and on since we left the cove. The birds unsettle me."

Palo shrugged. "We cannot think every odd creature we find is some plot against us."

"Perhaps, but we must be cautious. We have no idea how far the enemy's fingers reach." Eathelon had learned to follow his intuition. But he said nothing more about the birds.

They continued up the trail as the day waned. They still had far to go to reach the top of the ridge, so Eathelon quickened the pace. When the trail narrowed, they walked single file, in silence but when it widened again, they resumed their conversation.

"The top is in sight now Palo. Perhaps we can make it down to the plain tonight."

"That seems unlikely," replied Palo. "Look at the position of the sun. Night is not that far off."

Eathelon's neck prickled. "We must try. We are too exposed up here. We will be less exposed in the tall grass of that plain."

"The wood seems deserted enough," said Palo.

"I have felt eyes on us, as I said. Perhaps it is not as deserted as we believe."

But they could find no evidence of recent hikers on the trail. They plodded on and came to the top, as the sun fell to just above the horizon, leaving much of the wood in shadow.

Eathelon stopped abruptly.

"What is it?" Palo whispered.

A rabet scurried across the trail and ran under a bush.

"Supper," replied Eathelon, grinning.

As they crossed the ridge, Eathelon's mood darkened, for no apparent reason. Palo attempted to lighten it with conversation, but Eathelon just motioned him to silence. Palo became a surly companion, as Eathelon's anxiety grew. He had learned to trust Eathelon's intuition and he kept a closer watch on the surrounding area.

Patches of colorful wildflowers bloomed at the top among the sparse trees and the sight seemed to lift Eathelon from his somber mood, to Palo's relief. They stopped for a brief rest.

Palo sneezed. "It is late in the year for blooms," he said.

"Do these flowers disagree with you?" Eathelon smiled.

Palo sneezed again.

"I see they do."

Palo frowned.

"I like this wood. I could hike it for a month and not tire of it," said Eathelon.

"I prefer the sea." Palo sneezed again.

"I too, love the sea, but there is something special about a broadleaf wood that attracts me."

"That is the Eldarin in you, Eathelon."

"Yes, I know."

"Tell me something of the forests in Narda," said Palo, "from your teachings."

"Well, the forests of the *Eathen Mountains* are ancient, it is said. The Eldarin crossed those mountains in the First Age and settled in the high hills of Malta, where they built the Golden City. *Northwest Wood,* the forest of the *Sylvan Mountains* farther north, is home to the Elvenkin. *Forsil,* a visible star in the northern sky, beckons me there. I do not know why."

"Are there other forests in Narda?"

"The forest of the *Fyr Mountains* in the East is old and twisted, it is said – dead. The mountains spewed foul gases in ages past that killed all living things around them. But I do not expect us to go there. That is enemy territory, as far as I know."

"Good, I have no desire to traipse through a dead wood. There are no other forests then?"

"Another ... *East Wood.* The Elvenkin once lived there, but I doubt they still do. That wood lies in enemy territory and the Elvenkin have always been allies of the West."

"Let us hope they are still."

Eathelon nodded.

They walked in silence awhile, then Palo sneezed again.

Eathelon chuckled. "These Earlyfall blooms smell sweet, but your nose protests their perfume."

"The blooms of Melatui do not tickle my nose so."

"No doubt because you are used to them. Do not worry, Palo — your secret is safe with me." Eathelon grinned.

The mention of Melatui brought a pang of nostalgia, as Eathelon breathed in the sweet smell of wildflowers. He thought about how the wild *Tocuni River* rushes off the snow-capped peaks of *Mt. Malucan,* free-falling from the high cliffs and bouncing down over boulders to the flatlands, spreading its fingers out at the end of its journey to the sea, how the sun's rays fall on *Saluna Meadow,* the beauty of the misty morning as the sleepy sun rises over the top of the mountains. Then he thought about the tiny biting insects that come with the Earlyspring rains and shuddered.

Eathelon suddenly became aware of the sound of water in

the distance and stopped to listen.

Palo heard it too.

"West," said Eathelon.

Palo nodded. They went off in that direction and made their way through the sparse trees and undergrowth toward the sound. Eathelon thought about how Lelar and Maalo had taken him into the forest, taught him to walk with stealth, to look for signs that another had passed, showed him signs he had unwittingly left himself. The Eldarin taught him everything he knew about Narda and its geography. He'd brought those teachings, and their maps, on this journey. But he must rely on his teachings alone now. His charts and maps lay at the bottom of the sea, with the rest of his possessions.

After a time, they came to a brook, fed by a small spring and drank their fill. They filled the waterskins with the cool clear water and, Eathelon's intuition validated, his confidence rose. They returned to the trail and, shortly after, began the descent from atop the ridge. The trees thinned, the undergrowth grew sparse and the flowers dwindled away as they hiked. The color and shape of the land changed, but the cool water refreshed them and melted away some of the unease Eathelon felt.

The sun had fallen almost all the way down to the horizon and only a thin veil of light remained. The wood lay in shadow. The trail brought them close to the edge of the cliff, so they walked over to watch the sun slowly sink into the Westmost Sea.

"It is as lovely a sunset as any on Melatui," said Palo. "Perhaps there will be other such sights on this journey."

"I would not be surprised to find it so," replied Eathelon.

They stared out over the grassy plain to the shadowy outline of the Brunhyl far in the distance and Eathelon followed its silhouette north. As the sun's giant orb fell into the sea's watery bed, a gentle breeze ruffled Eathelon's hair and blew through the branches of the trees, which murmured in rhythm. They took in the beauty of the scene until night's curtain fell, then they walked back to the trail and continued down the north side of the ridge.

As they did, a pair of eyes watched them from several yards

back and Eathelon's neck began to prickle again.

"Narda seems hospitable enough," said Palo.

"Let us hope so."

"You do not expect us to continue down to the plain on the meager brefas we had this morning, do you, Eathelon?"

"You thought your meal inadequate?" Eathelon teased.

"You know very well it is my way of saying it is time to eat."

"Yes, Palo, I know you well," grinned Eathelon. "It may be unwise for us to build a fire and take a meal here. We should continue down to the plain and stay the night there."

"We cannot make a fire down there in the grass. When would we next have a meal? We still have far to go once we get down there."

"You have a point, but we should not take time to hunt," Eathelon said firmly.

"If I do not remind you when it is time for a meal, we will both grow too weak for warrioring, should that prove necessary."

Eathelon thought about the eyes he felt on them. What if they encountered the enemy and were too weak to fight, as Palo said?

"I still think it unwise for us to make a fire, but I admit I am hungry, too."

Palo argued his point until Eathelon agreed, his decision influenced by his own hunger. At least they would continue on the plain rested and fed, he justified.

"Alright, see if you can hunt up a couple of rabets then," said Eathelon.

"Rabet, it is!" Palo ran off with naught but his knife.

True to his reputation, he returned a little while later with two rabets in hand and a wide grin plastered across his broad brown face.

"Those will do nicely," Eathelon remarked, stoking a smokeless fire, his mouth watering at the sight of the rabets, already cleaned and ready for roasting. But guilt nagged at him. He felt his decision had been foolish. "I cannot shake off the feeling that we are watched, Palo, though I have no real evidence of it."

"I, too, have felt it," Palo confessed, turning the rabets over.

"Then why did you not say so? Perhaps my decision would

have been different."

"Yes, and then we would be hiking down to the plain on an empty stomach."

Eathelon gave him a look of irritation.

"Well, what is done is done. Let us finish up and get going. We will have to hike in the dark now, but the grass below should provide us good cover. If someone is following us, perhaps we can lose them there and I saw some large boulders from up here that would make a good shelter for the night."

Eathelon took a rabet from the fire and began to eat it. As he did, he caught a movement out of the corner of his eye and started to say something. But before he could investigate, a winged creature came streaking toward them at lightning speed.

"Watch out!" he yelled, as it bore down on them. He dropped his rabet.

Palo jumped in front of Eathelon on instinct, as the creature whizzed by.

Eathelon looked for it.

It came whizzing back and Eathelon looked more closely, as it did.

"Watch out, Palo! It's a ..."

The creature headed straight for Palo, who stood holding his half-eaten rabet and Eathelon guessed it wanted the rabet. It came at Palo with its front claws extended.

"Palo, drop the rabet!"

Too late! Palo dodged the creature at the last minute but instinctively put his arm up to shield himself and the wretched thing swung its tail around and fired off a barb, hitting Palo square in the forearm. It grabbed the rabet and sped off.

The Warrior reacted at once to the searing pain, swiping in vain at the creature, as it sped off and disappeared into the night. He grabbed his forearm and writhed in pain, as it quickly swelled to half-again its normal size. His face went pale and his eyes glazed over.

"What is happening?" choked Palo.

He leaned against a tree; his breathing labored.

"I think you have been hit with a fyrcaat barb, Palo. Those

creatures are poisonous. Lie down so the poison cannot spread too fast."

Eathelon recalled what he'd learned about fyrcaats. The barbs are poisonous and can even sometimes cause death. He said nothing of this to Palo.

Eathelon helped his Warrior friend lay down. His heart raced in his chest. What if he lost Palo? What could he do against a fyrcaat barb, here in the middle of nowhere?

Palo began to slip into unconsciousness.

Eathelon felt his forehead — hot. He ribbed a shirt and wet a strip of cloth in the cold water from a waterskin and placed it on Palo's forehead. He placed another on his swollen arm. Then he remembered the leaves he'd picked in the wood by the cove. *Lothingel!* He had nearly tripped on it but had forgotten about it after placing it in his pack. He grabbed his pack, found a leaf and crushed it into a cup Palo had salvaged from the ship.

Palo's eyes opened. "What is it?" he groaned, "what are you doing?"

"Lothingel, Palo, an Eldarin healing herb. I found it growing wild near the cove and thought it would help if we encountered those biting insects I so dislike. Its healing properties do not last long once picked, but these leaves are still fresh."

Lothingel had been a staple of Eldarin healing for ages and Lelar had taught Eathelon what she knew of it. "A ruling hand is a healing hand," she'd said, and he should know the basics of the healing arts. He had not looked for the plant, nor even thought about it, until he'd spotted it, but it turned out to be fortunate for Palo that he had.

He poured the warm liquid onto Palo's wounded arm and it appeared to give the Warrior some relief, though his head still felt hot with fever.

Palo moaned.

"It is a strong herb Palo and should help counteract the poison from the barb, but you may feel discomfort for a time."

"Discomfort? My arm is on fire!" Palo exclaimed.

"Which is no doubt how the fyrcaat earned its name."

Eathelon had thought fyrcaats a legend. Would other such legends come to life here?

He placed a hand on Palo's forehead and said softly, *"Lothingel, ratintha lamnatha loh lohwren,"* then dribbled a small amount of the liquid onto Palo's lips. "Rest, my Warrior friend."

Palo fell into a labored sleep and Eathelon examined his wound and found a fragment of the barb imbedded there, so removed it. He poured the liquid onto the wound and wrapped it in a clean strip of cloth. He sat at Palo's side until his breathing quieted, then made more liquid from the remaining leaves.

He thought about warming his uneaten rabet, but it had fallen to the ground and he no longer felt hungry. He sat and stared at the fire, fighting back the grief that tried to assail him from his earlier losses. It seemed that just when things improved, they worsened. He hoped it would not prove so on the rest of their journey.

Once Eathelon composed himself, he realized how out of place the fyrcaat was here. *The creatures inhabit the caves of the Fyr Mountains, in the east, it is said. Why would one be found so far west?* He recalled what he could about the one that had attacked Palo. It had ripped through the air faster than any creature he'd ever seen, but he'd gotten a glimpse of it's red-brown color and fierce yellow eyes.

Weary from the long day's hike and from tending Palo, Eathelon closed his eyes and fell into a sort of waking-sleep. When Palo stirred, Eathelon came fully awake and checked on the Warrior's condition. The lothingel appeared to be working. He gave Palo another draught and the Warrior fell into a more restful sleep.

Eathelon considered his limited training in the healing arts. He knew something of herbology and knew lothingel had been used effectively against other poisons. It is why he'd picked it to use when those biting insects injected a tiny bit of poison under the skin that made it itch and burn. He'd never expected to have to use it on something more poisonous, but he'd seen his Mother use it once on a child who'd stepped on a poisonous stonfish and survived. This reassured him and his fear of losing Palo diminished.

Palo slept all the next day and Eathelon did not wake him or leave his side. He continued to nurse the Warrior's wound with the last bit of lothingel. Palo's arm slowly returned to normal and his fever abated. The Warrior woke up the second morning after the attack, much improved, but weak. The incident had cost them a day and a half but, thankfully, the fyrcaat had not returned.

Palo insisted on continuing down to the plain, but Eathelon felt it was too soon and he managed to persuade Palo to wait. As the hours passed, the Warrior grew more and more anxious to leave however, so Eathelon relented when Palo said he felt up to it.

They packed up, cleared the camp and began to follow the trail down the cliff. It fell gradually at first, then more steeply until they reached a flat shelf just above the plain. They stopped there to rest.

"How are you feeling?" asked Eathelon.

"I am still a little weak, but I do not wish to delay us further."

"Rest here as long as you need, Palo. We are near the bottom now and have seen no more sign of fyrcaats. It appears to have strayed here and must have been the eyes I felt on us. It only wanted your rabet, I think."

"That seems likely." Palo laid back and closed his eyes.

Eathelon mused about his friend, as he lay resting, for while Eathelon could find his way out of a dark cave at night in a new moon, Palo sometimes became lost on his own island. The Warrior had evidently not been endowed with the usual Maagi Warrior sense of direction. Few knew this but Palo's Mother *Ulu* and his close friends. Eathelon would get them where they needed to go, and Palo would make certain they arrived safely. The two made a good team. Now that they knew what to look for, the fyrcaat would not get the best of them again.

The moon rose high in the sky and gave off sufficient light for them to see the dim trail, so although Palo had not fully recovered, he announced he felt ready to continue. Eathelon knew they should eat something, for neither of them had finished their rabets, but he knew they could not now risk another incident.

As if he had somehow read Eathelon's thoughts, Palo patted his stomach and announced, "I am shrinking."

Uncanny, thought Eathelon, the accuracy of his intuition sometimes. His own stomach protested too, but they simply could not risk a fire so close to the plain.

"We will have to content ourselves with whatever we can find to eat along the way now, Palo. A fire is too risky."

Palo nodded. He was too weak to hunt or even argue and he knew Eathelon was right. They pressed on, looking for anything suitable to eat — berries, nuts, mush-rooms, tubers, eggs, grubs – well maybe not grubs.

Their descent from the shelf proved treacherous in places, more so in the dark and they picked their way down carefully.

"This land must hold little value to the West," said Palo. "It is rocky and deserted."

"Perhaps we will reach the Brunhyl without any further hindrance then."

"Odd to find it so empty, though, do you not think?"

"No. It probably lies too far south to be of value, perhaps too close to the East for safety."

"There seems little evidence anyone ever lived here."

"The trail from the cove was man-made."

Palo grunted.

They found no more traces of water after leaving the spring. Eathelon guessed water would be scarce on the plain, perhaps even undrinkable. They drank sparingly from their waterskins.

The trail narrowed as it dropped to the valley floor, forcing them to walk single file. When they reached the bottom, the tall grass swallowed them. They fell into a steady rhythm on the flatter plain, but the moon and stars disappeared behind a torn curtain of clouds and soon it became too dark to see. They found it almost impossible to continue.

Eathelon heard a rustling in the grass behind and the hair stood up on the back of his neck. "Hurry Palo. We need to find those boulders!"

Chapter 7:
A Restless Night

They followed the trail across the plain as best they could in the dark, peering out over the top of the grass to see if they could spot the boulders Eathelon had seen from atop the ridge, or perhaps find some other suitable shelter. But they saw little beyond the tips of their fingers at this point. *Now would be a good time for farsight*, thought Eathelon, but his spyglas lay at the bottom of the Southern Sea.

The prickling sensation on the back of his neck had subsided and, with it, his anxiety. He expected the trail to lead northwest, perhaps to the front gates of Andolan, but his navigator instinct told him they headed in the opposite direction. The clouds obscured any light from moon or stars and the trail had taken several twists and turns. Eathelon felt challenged to keep his sense of direction, something rare for him.

Still recovering from the poisoned fyrcaat barb, Palo stopped. "I must rest, Eathelon." He sat down.

"I did not mean to push you so hard, Palo. We will rest here until you feel strength enough to continue. We both need food and rest."

They drank from the waterskins and laid back in the grass, which felt warmer in the cold night, and Eathelon considered what next to do. When the moon crept out from behind the ragged clouds and provided enough light for them to see ahead on the trail, Palo stood and announced he was ready to go on. But, after they'd walked several more yards, the trail took a sharp turn eastward.

"Shards!" said Eathelon, "this trail is not taking us where we wish to go!"

"We must have missed a turn back there in the dark," said

Palo. "Surely there is a trail from Numar to Andolan."

"So, I thought, but this is clearly not it."

They searched ahead, turned back and made a search behind, but could find no other trail. The moon disappeared back behind the clouds and they lost what little light they had to see.

"We cannot continue forward in the wrong direction," said Eathelon. "We must turn back."

"We could stay the night here and look for another trail in the morning," Palo offered. "I am tired, and hungry. And something about this grass seems to sap what little strength I have left."

"I have noticed that about the grass also. I feel more spent than I should, though the day has been long and the food little. I am not certain remaining here is our best option."

"Have you a better one?"

"I am working on it."

"Well, work faster! I am tired, cold and hungry!"

"Indeed, or you would not be so cross with me!"

"You would be cross too, were you poisoned, half-starved and the air in your lungs feeling like a hot, stuffy cave!"

"Well, fortunately for both of us the fyrcaat barb missed me, but as to the rest, I share your condition, yet I am not cross."

"That is no doubt because you are a Mallorite Prince and I a Maagi Warrior! Warriors are easily irritated. We depend on it for warrioring!"

"Is that a warning?"

"Take it as such, if you will!" Palo sulked.

"Duly noted. Now please mind your manners. I am in no mood for an argument."

Eathelon knew their annoyance with each other had more to do with circumstance than their friendship. But he knew they must solve their predicament as quickly as possible and get some food and rest.

The light breeze they'd felt atop the ridge disappeared when they entered the grass, and although it felt warmer here, the air felt close and stifling, which did not help their mood any. Beads of sweat formed on their brows from the effort expended walking in this odd, tall grass that indeed seemed to sap their strength. The valley floor, while more or less flat, was yet strewn with tiny sharp rocks that penetrated their shoes and pained their feet as they walked.

Palo, feeling a little remorseful for his outburst, apologized. "I was not myself back there, Eathelon."

"Do not worry, Palo, you cannot unmake our friendship so easily. We are both tired and hungry and have become irritable with every step in this grass. I felt no such burden until we entered it. There is something peculiar about it affecting our mood."

"What do you think we should do?"

"We have four choices, I think. One, continue on this trail and hope it turns north, but I doubt it will. I believe we missed any turn in the dark, as you said. Two, leave the trail and continue north over open ground, which is risky. We may lose our way and have yet to confirm if the enemy is about here. Three, remain here, as you suggest, but we are little protected and the grass affects us."

"And four?"

"The best choice, I think ... turn back and look for the boulders I saw from the ridge. If we can find them, we will have shelter for the night and can resume our search for the northwest trail in the morning. "It is not the easy choice, perhaps, but the best one, under the circumstances."

Palo knew better than to argue with Eathelon once he made up his mind, but he trusted Eathelon's judgment, and sense of direction.

"Agreed."

They started back the way they'd come, peering into the night to look for the outline of the ridge, the one reference point they could use to estimate the location of the boulders. It proved almost impossible in the dark night, but they continued down the trail and hoped for the best.

As luck would have it, the wind picked up and parted the clouds, allowing more light for Eathelon to see the shadowy outline of the ridge. And, going more on his navigator instinct than anything else, he veered off the trail at a place he thought would take them over to the boulders. He found the cluster about a quarter mile south of the trail and smiled with satisfaction as they approached. Palo sighed with relief. The boulders sat atop a small rise of land.

"Your Eldarin instincts are worth a hundred navigators, Eathelon!"

"We each have our skills, my friend and yours are no less valuable than mine." He paused. "This will give us a better vantage point than expected."

The grass diminished some as they walked to the boulders and thick underbrush surrounded the base. They walked around behind them and found a way up the back side. They climbed to the top and found a space large enough for both of them to lay down. Palo rummaged around in his pack and pulled out a few things he had found while hunting earlier.

"I know you want meat, Palo, but we dare not hunt or risk a fire."

"I am too tired anyway, but I have a few things I picked up along the way. Here." He handed Eathelon some sort of berries he found and a few mush-rooms.

They ate these in silence then Eathelon said, "I will take first watch."

Palo did not argue, for he had not yet gained back his full strength. But after an hour, unable to get comfortable on the hard rock, he rose and relieved Eathelon at the watch. The cold night air seemed to handle his lethargy, so he stayed the watch for a few hours until Eathelon woke up and relieved him.

Palo fell into a restful sleep and Eathelon did not wake him again. He knew the black night hid them well enough, so he slept too. The warmth of the sun woke them early the next morning and they made their way back down to the trail After following it for about half an hour, they found what they had missed in the dark — a meeting of trails.

"It is as I guessed," said Eathelon. "See, this trail leads west. Perhaps it will turn north ahead. At least it does not turn back east, to Numar."

"It is not surprising that we missed it in the dark," said Palo. "See how overgrown it is? It must not have been used for a long time."

"This is Numar territory so it seems logical that the east trail would the one most used. These lands have probably been deserted since the Great War. There may be little use now for a west trail."

"Well, let us hope we cross to the hills without further hindrance," said Palo.

"And do our best to remain hidden in the event the enemy is about in these lands."

"That seems unlikely now," Palo remarked.

"Nevertheless, it is good to remain cautious."

Relieved to be on the westward trail, they hiked along more energetically now, despite the peculiar effects of the grass and the increasing heat from the waxing sun. But the effects of the grass diminished as they walked, a fact for which they both felt grateful.

They hiked all morning and, as the sun reached its zenith, a breeze sprang up and sent fingers of cool air through their dampened hair. The hard, stony trail softened as they walked westward, but took them up and down little hillocks and into and out of the tall grass, exposing them more than they liked.

"This land is thirsty," said Palo.

"And neglected, it would seem," replied Eathelon.

Indeed, cracks and fissures in the ground forced them to walk around and through the flanking underbrush, some of which was weed-choked, twisted and thorny.

"The sooner we are off this plain the better I will like it," added Palo.

Eathelon nodded. He knew the Brunhyl would offer better protection, but the hills were on the far west side of the plain.

Their second night on the plain, they made camp near a large black oak. A thick blanket of clouds obscured the moon and threatened rain. Thankfully, none fell, though the land clearly cried out for it.

The third night, they camped in a small cluster of rocks that offered little space to stretch out, but whose position permitted them a good view of the trail in both directions. Eathelon took encouragement from their progress, but reluctant still to make a fire, they did without a proper meal again and Palo's noisy stomach let them both know about it.

"Your belly talks much," grinned Eathelon.

"It becomes more irritable each day," Palo smiled and patted his stomach.

"Perhaps the trail turns north ahead and can take us to the front gates of Andolan. We will have a proper meal then."

"Perhaps, but in the end, we must go where the trail leads — or get off of it altogether. And our means to purchase a proper meal in Andolan lies at the bottom of the Southern Sea — or have you forgotten?"

"No, I have not. Perhaps there is some small service we can offer in exchange for a meal."

They continued to follow the trail west for four more days. They heard creatures scurry about in the underbrush and heard chikkas chirp and twitter in the grass. This only served to make their mouths water and their stomachs complain all the more. *We must find something more substantial to eat,* thought Eathelon, *before we reach the other side of the plain.* He noticed a *sinter hawk* circling above and recalled he'd learned about them, as he watched with interest. It must be hunting a meal, he guessed, as it hovered above, riding the air currents, its red-tipped wings and tail visible from below. *A messenger bird of Narda,* he knew, though this one did not seem to be on an errand.

They dined on berries and odd bits of edible vegetation they found to keep up their strength, but after a week of this, their bodies had weakened and Eathelon knew they needed something more substantial to eat. Palo hunted and Eathelon made smokeless fires to cook whatever Palo brought back and the food renewed them.

The eighth day brought respite from the hot sun as large grey clouds covered it, and they hiked along in a cooler climate, a welcome change. They had long since become immune to the effects of the grass, which had diminished, and Eathelon perceived a gradual rise in the land. To their disappointment, the west trail did not turn north and they stared at the Brunhyl in frustration.

"This trail evidently does not lead to the front gates of Andolan. I do not understand. There must have been travel between Numar and Andolan."

"Who can say why?" said Palo.

They would have to follow the trail west to the foot of the Brunhyl, then turn north from there to the front gates of the city, a longer route than Eathelon hoped for. He estimated it would take two days more to reach the hills and two weeks after to reach the city. Discouraged, they trudged along with less enthusiasm.

Rock formations had all but disappeared now and they found themselves in rolling hills of short grass, which left them uncomfortably exposed. Late on the ninth day, they veered off toward a copse of black oak a hundred yards off to camp for the night. On the way, they heard a loud screech above and looked up, but saw nothing. Eathelon's senses sharpened on instinct.

"Keep watch on the sky," he said to Palo.

"It is probably another hawk hunting up supper," said Palo.

A covey of chikkas suddenly erupted from the grass and exploded noisily into the air.

"Perhaps you are right, Palo ... a hawk hunting up supper."

Then, three fyrcaats sprang out of the grass, burst into the air and began a wild display of antics. The chikkas scattered. But the creatures did not attack the hikers. They dipped and dove in and out of the grass and whizzed around each other, as if in play. Eathelon watched with some suspicion until the creatures flew off eastward and disappeared.

The hikers puzzled over the incident for a few minutes, then continued to their chosen camp site. As they neared it, they noticed a thin wisp of smoke rising out of the grass where the fyrcaats had been and Eathelon realized the creatures had set fire to the grass. The dry grass would burn quickly and trap them!

"Run Palo! Follow me!"

Chapter 8:
A Friendly Surprise

Eathelon and Palo ran back toward the trail as fast as they could, then crossed it and continued south, away from the fire. They looked for any cover that might shield them from the growing flames, to no avail. Their only chance now was to make a run for it. Eathelon feared they would not be able to outrun the blaze. He looked back to see the fire gaining speed. The dry grass provided good fuel for the growing inferno; whose flames created a hot wind that served to further fan the fire. The grass and brush, so long without water, burned like kindling.

The hikers ran as fast as their feet would allow, over the rocky land, as the fire crept closer. Eathelon knew it would soon overtake them and he felt a pang of regret for their circumstance, for his loyal companion, for those who'd sent them on this failing errand. But he refused to give in to his circumstance. He quickened the pace. Palo kept up.

They heard a rumbling in the Earth, and it grew louder with every step. Eathelon did not look back. He thought the fire rushed to consume them, so he ran faster. He shuddered at the thought of being consumed in this manner. A warrior, he expected to die in battle, perhaps, but not like this.

Their faces red from heat and effort, and every drawn breath painful, they did not slow their pace, not as long as they had even the slightest chance of escaping the fast-moving inferno. The smoke had become thick and they could see little ahead, as they continued south.

Suddenly, out of the thick smoke a man rode up on Eathelon's flank, slowed his horse and pulled up alongside. He extended a hand and yelled, *"Hlep — jump!"*

Almost without breaking pace, Eathelon reached up, grabbed the man's hand and leaped with all of his might. The man pulled him onto the back of his horse and, as he did, Eathelon saw several other horsemen around them. Over the roar of horses' hooves and fire, Eathelon yelled, "*Mel-la!* My friend!" The man pointed and Eathelon saw Palo had jumped on the back of another horse.

The fire gained on them, as the horsemen slowed to pick up the endangered hikers, but they rode off at a full gallop now and managed to stay just ahead of the flames. After several minutes of heavy riding, they veered eastward, uphill into rocky terrain, leaving the burning inferno behind.

The man in front of Eathelon slowed the company after a time, then led them to a large outcropping of rock and around it into the mouth of a cave large enough for them to ride into. Once inside, the huge cavern dwarfed them and Eathelon gratefully breathed in the dank cool air. He'd no idea who these men were, or why he and Palo had been spared from an unthinkable death. He looked around and noticed a small opening in the top of the cave. It let in just enough light to see. The man in front of him dismounted and motioned Eathelon to do the same.

"Stay here," the man said, not unkindly, yet with authority and he walked over to speak with a yellow-haired man.

Eathelon watched as the two men spoke in animated voice and gesture, though he could not hear what was said. Palo stood across the cave, guarded by two men. Eathelon had no idea what these men planned, but guessed that, had they intended harm, they would not have made such a daring rescue.

The fire slowly burned toward the cave and, as it crept closer smoke began to filter into the opening. The man who'd saved Eathelon walked back leading a *flaxling* horse and motioned for Eathelon to mount. The tall, slender mare danced with restless unwillingness at first, but Eathelon spoke softly to her and she let him mount. He saw Palo climb onto another flaxling, one wider in girth, and smiled at the match. He'd heard of them and knew they belonged to the men who ride the southern plains. He surmised these men to be one and the same.

The leader mounted and motioned the company forward to

the back and single file into a dark, narrow tunnel. The light soon vanished, but the horses appeared to know their way in the dark. After a quarter of a mile, the company emerged one by one onto a rocky shelf and Eathelon had to shield his eyes from the bright light at first. They made their way down a stony path toward the plain below and, as they descended, Eathelon saw a clear blue lake. He stared at it in awe.

The man riding ahead had turned around to check on his captive and, catching his look, said, "There are a few such lakes in these lands. A man may find one, if he knows where to look."

He speaks the common tongue!

Eathelon started to reply, but the man motioned him quiet. He looked back to find a sullen Palo riding a couple of horse lengths behind and gave him an encouraging smile, which Palo weakly returned.

The company had ridden southeast to outrun the fire, but as they descended to the plain, Eathelon knew they now rode west, confirmed when the Brunhyl came into view. Two hours more brought them north, back to the main trail. They followed it until dusk, when the leader veered the company off the trail to another small copse of black oak. The tall, yellow-haired man ordered the company to dismount and set a camp.

Eathelon could clearly see the shields of the men now — polished bronze with an *N* emblazoned in the center, confirming what he guessed, that these men are the Rangers of Numar, those who patrol Narda's southern plains. But, why would they be so far west then?

Most of the Rangers, save their leader and the yellow-haired man, had long dark brown hair and brown eyes. Eathelon noticed something familiar about the leader. He reminded him of an Eldarin friend back home. *Could it be?* The man stood taller than the rest and his hair was nearly the same color as his bronze helm, his features fine. Most of his men were shorter and thicker in girth, though all shared a weathered look, no doubt from years of riding under a hot sun.

The leader noticed Eathelon's observations and his golden-brown eyes danced as they locked with Eathelon's a moment. He wore a dark green cloak over a brown tunic, and leather trousers, as did most of his men, but Eathelon noticed an uncommon dark green jewel set in gold that fastened the man's cloak. When the leader saw this, he brushed back the side of his cloak to reveal a beautiful sword with a silver hilt, peeking out from its leather scabbard. Eathelon recognized the symbol on the hilt, one no other man in the company possessed, and a look of wonder came over him. *This man is an Eldarin!*

Seeing Eathelon's look of recognition, the man smiled, confirming the guess, and an unspoken understanding passed between them.

The gesture went unnoticed by the rest, all but the yellow-haired man, who said curtly, "What do you intend us to do with these men, Captain? If we are to uphold our code, they must be taken prisoner. They have entered our lands without permission."

The young Captain turned to his lieutenant and said, not unkindly, "Patience, *Farli*. I know well the code. Did my Father not make it? Its intent is to protect us from the enemy. Unless I miss my guess, these men are not the enemy."

Eathelon nodded. "You speak truly, friend."

Farli looked unconvinced as he stared at Palo. He made it clear by his look that he did not trust the Warrior. "We tracked you many leagues after you left the cove. You walk with stealth, but your fires revealed you."

Some of the men snickered at the comment and Eathelon knew it had been foolish for them to give in to hunger, but he knew also they could not have hiked this far on empty stomachs so, he did not regret his decision.

"We remained well behind you," Farli continued, "to watch where you would go. When you took the east trail, we thought you may be spies returning East, but then you backtracked and took the west trail, so we thought perhaps you intended to infiltrate Andolan. Catching spies is part of our job, but luckily for you our Captain sent us ahead with orders only to track you until he could join us. Had he not given that order, we may have slain you. Spies entering our lands do not leave it."

Palo overreacted to this and reached for his knife, which until now had been concealed. Two Rangers quickly drew swords and held them at Palo's neck.

"We are not spies," said Palo, staring daggers at Farli. "You believe yourselves brave, slaying two with 20? I would not boast such odds, were I you. Let us show you how we can slay 20 with two!"

"Enough, Palo!" said Eathelon. Such aggression was not only unnecessary, but dangerous.

The Captain signaled the two Rangers to drop their swords.

"It would be very wise for you to listen to your Captain," Farli remarked.

"And wiser still for all of us to keep our weapons, and our tongues sheathed," added the Captain, stepping in front of Palo. "Farli only meant to do his duty." He gave Farli a look.

"Indeed," said Farli, with little sincerity, "I meant no harm."

The young Captain turned to Eathelon, "Come, it must be clear to you by now that we do not intend you harm. It is not confrontation I seek, but conversation. In spite of what Farli said, I had you tracked for that one purpose."

"What do you wish to know then?" asked Eathelon.

The young Captain smiled. "More about the two of you, for one. I searched the wood near the cove to learn something of you and found there something I did not expect, evidence that you are indeed friends. But Farli was correct to say the Rangers likely would have slain you had I not intervened."

"Then we are grateful for your wisdom," said Eathelon. *Are these the eyes I felt on us? An Eldarin — so unexpected!*

Eathelon recalled Celorn's earlier words that they might find some in Narda who would claim friendship, yet betray him, and some who he might think an enemy who may yet prove a friend.

Is this man pretending to be a friend, or is he one? He saved us. He is an Eldarin, but so is the enemy Baele, of the House of Tebor, even if he is no longer acknowledged as such.

The Captain read his look and smiled. "We serve Aneron, King of the West. He rules these lands ... and all of *Hamlan*."

The men raised their swords and declared, in unison, "to King Aneron!"

"You serve Aneron," Eathelon repeated, with relief.

"Yes, we are not his soldiers, but we are in his service."

Eathelon gave him a puzzled look.

"I see a better explanation is in order. I have questions for

Tales of Narda: Road to Andolan

you also. We have more to say to one another than may be said here, I think. It is well that we found you before Aneron's soldiers. He has grown over suspicious of late and his soldiers may care little whether you are friend or foe before taking you prisoner, or worse."

"Aneron's penalties are swift and harsh," said Farli, "but none of us act out of hatred, only survival. The West has long been under scrutiny by the House of Tebor in the East. The earlier wars wiped out entire populations."

Yes, including my Mother's family. Eathelon nodded.

"Come, we are good judges of character," said the young Captain. "Are we not right about you two? Come and give me whatever information you are willing to offer, and I will do the same."

Farli stared at Palo and asked, "Of what race are you? I have never seen any man like you in Narda. There is some similarity between you two, yet you are quite different."

Eathelon answered before Palo could speak, "You have a good eye, friend. We are not from Narda." He let that sink in as the Rangers murmured and stared.

"I am Palo, a Maagi Warrior, a native of our island home, Melatui, which lies far out in the Westmost Sea."

"Palo and I crossed the sea together," added Eathelon, "a long voyage in which we lost our ship and two companions."

"I am sorry," responded the young Captain. "It is difficult to lose a command and more difficult still to lose one's friends."

"I thank you," replied Eathelon. He guessed the man spoke from his own experience.

"Palo and I are different, yet similar, as you observe," said Eathelon. His parents are Maagi. I am Eathelon, a Mallorite ... Warrior. My Father was Maagi, but my Mother is ... of a different race. I am a mixture of the two."

"I am *Darian*," said the young Captain, "a mercenary of sorts, I suppose, and as you have seen, leader of these men, the Rangers of Numar. We patrol Hamlan's southern lands."

Eathelon nodded, "So, I guessed."

Eathelon and Darian each held something back and each being intuitive, knew it, so Darian took Eathelon aside and said,

"Let us go talk together in private, to loosen our tongues."

Eathelon nodded. He took Palo aside and spoke with him briefly, then walked off with Darian. Harlen, a Ranger, engaged Palo in conversation, but Palo kept one eye on Eathelon and noticed where he went.

Darian spoke briefly with Farli and led Eathelon to a small private campfire built in a little hollow, set for him by some of his men. He motioned for the man tending the fire to leave, then he and Eathelon sat down to talk.

Eathelon spoke first. "You said you found something that told you we are not your enemy. You risked your life and the lives of your men to save us. Why?"

"That we followed you is our duty. That we spared you certain death, only decent, were you spies or not. I am interested in all things Eldarin, as you may have already guessed. I saw your look of recognition when I revealed my sword, and you noticed the jewel at my neck."

"Yes."

"I will say more about that, but first I will tell you where you are."

"I know where we are ... west of Numar on Hamlan's southern plains. Andolan lies north."

"I see you know something of Nardan geography. Numar lies at the southernmost tip of Hamlan and my home is there, though those lands are empty now and I am rarely home."

"Did the Eldarin live there? I found lothingel growing near the cove and finding it proved fortunate for my companion. He ... fell ill to an unexpected poison." Eathelon did not mention fyrcaats — not yet.

"Some Eldarin lived there, yes, and a few Elvenkin also."

"Elvenkin? I thought they only lived in the north."

"Some also live in the East," replied Darian. "Those few Eldarin who lived in Numar left during the Great War. Some returned to the Golden City and perished there. But I suspect you already know that. The few Elvenkin in Numar returned to East Wood. The citizens of Numar fled to the cities ... most to Andolan, some to *Antebba*, a few as far west as *Hollin* — anywhere far from eastern shores. My home lies near the wood where you beached, but it has long since fallen into disrepair. I spend all of my days with the Rangers, riding the southern plains."

"The wood near the cove is fair," said Eathelon, "but the beach is strewn with much rock and debris."

"Yes, the reef is treacherous and hides a deep trench on the seaside. Yours is not the first ship to wreck there."

"So, we discovered."

"You are not from Narda, you say, yet you seem to know much about it."

"I have made a study."

"You can tell me more about that, but to continue my tale, when the citizens of Numar fled, I stayed behind, as did many of my men. The southern lands are part of Hamlan, but are too vast and too far south for adequate protection from Andolan. Numar once produced many goods for trade. *Naoli*, on Numar's east coast, was a thriving seaport until plundered by the House of Tebor. It fell into ruin and Antebba is the only working southern seaport now."

"Numar is under Aneron's rule, then?"

"Yes, and no. Aneron rules all of Hamlan, as was said, but Numar has always governed itself. My Father, a good friend of the King, gathered a force to watch over the southern lands at the King's request. He created the Rangers. After the Great War, my Father passed and the Rangers disbanded for a time, believing Aneron would send soldiers to protect Numar. But the King did not want to send soldiers so far south. He needed them more in the north. Hamlan is a vast territory. So Aneron asked the Rangers to reassemble and I picked up where my Father left off. I rounded up those I knew and we recruited others. Numar is our home and we would have protected it whether asked by the King or not. Long have we suspected Baele of trying to infiltrate the West and plot to take it over. This has been confirmed only recently by the spies we have caught in Numar."

"If Baele intends to take over Narda, why does he not simply attack?"

"He will when he is ready. But the man is mad now, we are told, though he is still clever. The House of Tebor has always lost its bid to take over the West and with it, domination over Narda. They have never been able to take Andolan, Hamlan's stronghold. Andolan is impregnable and Baele had little choice than to sign the extant trade agreement with Aneron. He has more or less honored it, but Aneron is not stupid. He would sooner trust a path snake than his enemy. He made the agreement with the usurper to avoid another costly war. The Great War laid waste to much of Hamlan and divided its allies. Aneron has little stomach left for war and believes he lacks the resources to win. He chose the trade agreement as an alternative and although I do not share his view, I find no fault in his decision."

"The Rangers continue to protect the southern lands then."

"Yes, mostly lands south of here, in Numar. We are duty bound to do so. We must keep the House of Tebor out of Numar, for it is a gateway to the rest of the West." He paused. "Now, it is your turn. Tell me, why you have come to Narda. You must have a good reason for making such a perilous journey."

"I will tell you, but first tell me more about your men. Their look differs from yours. Are they mercenaries?"

Darian laughed. "No, although we are all mercenaries of a sort, I suppose. The real mercenaries live in *Rabellan*, in the Castellan Valley. They are an unsavory lot, mostly exiled criminals, allied to the East. These men remained in Numar, so I united them to a common purpose, is all. We patrol the southern lands from Antebba to Naoli, scouting day and night, resting little. It is fortunate for you that we came so far west. We do not often do so, but I had an errand for the King.

"Is this all of the Rangers?" asked Eathelon. "There are so few of you."

"No, there are other companies, each with a lieutenant like Farli. They report to me whenever they can. We are like a spider's web, reaching out our net. This company is the eyes of the spider. A stranger seldom enters our lands who does not turn out to be allied to the East. You two are an exception. Our justice with intruders is swift, but merciful. Baele's men suffer a much crueler fate should they return East having failed. Baele and his son Esol are cruel, evil men. From what we know of the self-proclaimed Lord of Gorst, he is little more than a coward sitting on a throne he stole from *Landrin*, the rightful King of the East."

"Landrin is dead?"

"He lives in exile on Suvrii, largest of the *Flax Isles*. Aneron arranged for his safe passage as part of the trade agreement."

"If Baele agreed to Landrin's safe passage, that seems to me a reasonable thing, not the act of an evil madman."

"Baele was a different man then and Aneron gave up much to buy Landrin's life, probably much more than we know. The men in Baele's service are mere slaves to him, willing to carry out his dirty deeds without conscience. They murder, pillage ... and worse. I ask you, are those the deeds of a sane man?"

"I see your point."

"From what we have learned, Baele's men fear him while yet hoping for some small reward to carry out his work. This led them to pillage Numar, take our women, our homes, our food and possessions. It is why Numar lies empty now. Its citizens all fled to the cities." Darian sighed. "It falls to the Rangers to ensure that any eastern enemy who enters our southern lands does not leave it."

"But surely you cannot catch them all."

"Few escape, if any. We are good at our task, though the job is distasteful. We have eyes and ears of our own in the East, those who travel freely back and forth and are rarely detected. They are capable actors, who slip in and out, bringing us valuable information. But it is a dangerous game that few play well. Still, we have managed to obtain useful information about Baele's activities and feed him false information about our own." He laughed. "It is a fool's game, Eathelon, one meant only to delay the inevitable."

"Darian, how can you trust a spy?" asked Eathelon.

"We do not, for our part, though some men of the East are in our pay, for having seen Baele's true nature, they wish to serve the West and cannot safely leave. So, we buy them, for a price. But you are right, of course. Those bought cannot be wholly trusted. Still, they report to Baele and Esol what we ask of them, it seems, which makes them of some value. It is a dangerous game and the outcome unpredictable. But it has worked to our advantage thus far. Baele is a vain, self-absorbed man who evidently pays little heed to who comes and goes in the spy business now. It is his son, Esol who most concerns us, for he is a cunning, hateful man, and more intelligent and calculating than his Father. At least those are the reports we have received. Baele is half mad now anyway. We take whatever advantage we that we can."

"This is information you have gleaned from those who come from and go to the East?"

"Yes."

"I do not see how they can possibly cover all of the Eastern lands, which are as vast as Hamlan's, if I am not mistaken."

"You are not, and we cannot cover all of it, at least now well. But the East has a natural divide. Esol occupies *Newcastle* and rules over Newelan, the southernmost portion. Baele is in *Gazlag* and rules over Gorst, the northern territory, though he has proclaimed himself ruler of all eastern lands. His influence does not appear to extend to Hond, or Flax. *Grenelan* divides the two primary regions he rules, north and south. But like Numar, it is mostly empty, occupied only by the nomads who roam there, and they have no loyalty to East or West. But they have occasionally given refuge to our men in times of need and permitted some to travel in their caravans. Some men of the west have also taken refuge in East Wood, when needed. The Elvenkin there despise the House of Tebor. The men of the East dare not enter East Wood."

"This is a remarkable story, Darian, and you are a remarkable man. It is my great honor to be your friend."

Darian smiled. "I simply carry out the task of my Father before me and serve my King. I was told only recently that Esol may be onto our little spy game. Some say it is only a matter of time before I am caught and killed." He let out a hearty laugh and Eathelon could not help but smile at his confidence.

"They are empty threats," Darian continued. "But our informants have said that Baele is planning a move against the West. It is something we have long predicted, but I was on my way to Andolan to bring this news to the King when we discovered you. Personally, I prefer the peace of the trade agreement too, but war will come to us whether we seek it or not. The sooner we all face up to that the sooner we can prepare. Baele and his pea-brained son will not be content to share Narda much longer. I am surprised they have done so this long."

"Then perhaps my coming here is better timed than I thought."

"What do you mean?"

"I will tell you, but first answer my original question. What made you follow us without intent to do us harm?"

"We thought you spies, at first, as Farli said. Palo is large and of an unfamiliar race, so I thought perhaps Baele had recruited some new race from the North. The opening on the east side of the bay where you beached faces east so, I thought you had come to spy on us. But all of the other spies we caught had landed on Numar's eastern shores, no doubt to avoid the reef and treacherous currents. I watched you on the beach. It is fortunate for both of us that I decided to return home for a few days, or my men may would probably have captured or slain you. I watched you make some sort of tribute in the bay, for your fallen friends, I now know."

"Yes."

"When you left the cove and headed north over the ridge, I instructed Farli to follow you, from a distance. I searched the wood to see if I could learn something of you before deciding what to do and I found your boat." He smiled. "You did not hide it well."

Eathelon smiled back. "No, we thought the area deserted and we did not expect to return."

"Again, it is fortunate that you left it there for me to find, for I found something else I did not expect. I recognized the symbol on your boat, knowing that few in Narda would know it."

"*Sirine,* the Eldarin word for guide," said Eathelon.

"Yes. For that reason alone I followed you to speak with you. And I have confirmed what before I only guessed — that you and I are ... kin."

A chill went through Eathelon's body as Darian's words sank in. The hilt of his sword and the jewel at his neck had confirmed it. Eathelon owned a similar clasp, one Celorn had given him and it sat in a treasure box in Melatui. He mused that, had he not left it there, it would lie at the bottom of the sea with the rest of the possessions he'd brought.

"I recognized the symbol on your sword and the jewel that fastened your cloak," said Eathelon. "But in truth, I doubted you at first, for such treasures could be the trophies of the enemy. Baele is of Eldarin ancestry. But my intuition told me otherwise."

"An Eldarin trait," chuckled Darian. "Well, it seems my Eldarin ancestry is known to the enemy now and Esol has threatened to hunt me down and kill me. When I elude capture it only serves to further ignite his hatred for the Eldarin, and for the Rangers. But I confess, I derive a certain pleasure from his discomfort — a trait not so Eldarin, I am afraid."

Eathelon laughed. "Perhaps we are more alike than you think. How long did you hide your ancestry before being discovered?"

"Most of my life. When the Eldarin fled Narda, my Grandmother and my Mother remained behind, and my Father's family. My Mother and Father later married and, when I was old enough, they taught me the Eldarin language and history I now know. My Mother was a *Nydar*. Her family fled the Golden City and came south to Numar. When they took to the ships, my Mother refused to go, so my Father's family, who had also refused to go, took her in. No word ever came back of her family or the other Eldarin who sailed from the shores of Numar. My Mother said the southern coast was later strewn with debris, so she guessed their fate. But I ask you now, though without hope — did any of the Eldarin who sailed from Numar reach your isle? If so, would you know if my Mother's family was among them?"

"I am sorry, Darian. The Eldarin on our isle said that those who sailed into the Southern Sea must have perished, for none reached Melatui. Palo and I survived our own voyage here by the grace of Ealdor. Once the Southern Sea currents grabbed our ship, we were doomed."

Darian nodded. "Well, as I said, it was a question without hope. My first Father, also a Nydar, kept watch over Numar, formed the Rangers and trained most of the men for this duty. His work claimed him. I serve Aneron largely for that reason.

The King treats me like his own son — in honor of my first Father. My second Father was a Nardan and kept my ancestry a secret. He loved my Mother and me well. Both of my parents have passed." He hesitated, then added, "I am without kin."

Eathelon smiled at him. "Until now," he said, on impulse.

Darian smiled back. "Yes, until now — with a bit of Nardan rebel thrown in for good measure!"

Eathelon laughed, then paused. "My only brother died shortly after birth and as you no doubt now know, I am half Eldarin. My Father was the Maagi Warrior King of Melatui. He passed on the eve of my departure. My Mother is a Syndar and rules the isle in his stead. In Maagi culture, a Queen is duty-bound to rule if the King passes before his time. I am the first Prince of the Mallorites, the new race born of the union of Eldarin and Maagi, and heir to the throne of Melatui. The Eldarin call our isle *Mayurna*, 'Morning Star' after the ship that brought them to Narda in the First Age, or so it is said. One day, should I prove worthy, I am to rule Melatui."

"Those names are familiar," Darian remarked. He looked at Eathelon with newfound respect. "You. You are the one in the legend, the one for whom we have long waited, Eathelon."

"What are you talking about? What legend?"

Some of Darian's men nearby heard Darian speak and came over to find out what had happened. Darian bowed slightly to Eathelon and said to his men, "There is a Prince among us — show him your respect."

Somewhat puzzled by his words, they nevertheless did as he asked and bowed.

Uncomfortable with the gesture, Eathelon said, "Please, such tribute is unnecessary." *And unearned.*

Seeing Eathelon's discomfort, Darian motioned his men away, but they stared back curiously as they left.

"What you have just revealed here is a confirmation of something for which we have all long awaited — a sign of hope. An Eldarin has returned!"

"Half, half Eldarin. And I came on an errand, not as a sign of hope."

"Oh, but you are. You are a sign that the Eldarin survived, that they still exist! That is a sign of hope, not just to the Rangers, but to the West. We did not expect a Mallorite Prince, perhaps, but we have long awaited the return of the Eldarin."

"It is true that we came ahead to see if it was possible for the Eldarin to return, but that has not yet been determined."

"See? I am right about you!"

Darian began to recite:

Island in the Heavens, Mayurna.
Thou art no more, fair Ealdor.
Mayurna is the Morningstar,
Eldarin, once from Narda gone,
Return. North, Mayurna,
Morningstar, Mayurna.

"They are words from an ancient Eldarin prayer that tells of the arrival and departure of the Eldarin, but also predicts their return, or so it is said. I do not know the rest of it, but your isle is mentioned."

"I do not think so. Mayurna is the name given the ship that brought the Eldarin to Narda, as was said. That it is also the name given our isle by the Eldarin is merely a coincidence. And I see no connection to the north."

"The Golden City of the Eldarin lies north."

"True, but their history books are missing much from the First Age, only tales and legends handed down and such are often altered over time."

"Point taken. Tell me, how did you and Palo manage to cross the sea safely, while the Eldarin perished?"

"Not all Eldarin perished, as you know. We crossed the Westmost Sea, like the Eldarin before us who landed on our isle. Trouble found us only after we reached the place where the Southern Sea and Westmost Sea currents collide. We were warned against that place, but a tempest blew us off our course. The Westmost Sea is not subject to the same storms that occur in the Southern Sea, apparently, though the voyage is still long and the outcome unknown. We planned to lay anchor at Bali, but the storm pushed us into that reef and only by the grace of Ealdor did Palo and I reach the shores of Numar. We are most grateful that you found us before the enemy, or the King's soldiers."

"Is Bali where you wish to go then?"

"No. Our plans have changed. We were going to Andolan anyway so were merely heading there now, when you found us. We seek an audience with the King. I have something to return to him — a gift from the Eldarin, one taken from Andolan long ago, when the Eldarin fled. That is why we took the westward trail. I hoped it would turn north ahead, but it did not."

"No, the west trail does not turn north until it reaches the foot of the Brunhyl. From there it is another two weeks to the front gates of the city."

"I guessed correctly then."

"But I know a shorter way."

Eathelon's eyes grew wide. "There is a shorter way?"

"Yes, and I will take you! I may also be able to help you get an audience with the King, for as I said, I am in his favor. This shorter way will enable us to travel unhindered to the back gates of the city."

"The city has back gates?"

"Yes, a fact not highly promoted."

Eathelon smiled and the two men clasped arms.

"I have no words to say how grateful I am to you, Darian."

"Well, it seems you have a guide — and I, a ... brother." Darian smiled.

Eathelon smiled back. "Yes, I see that we are brothers of a sort."

"You are no doubt hungry by now," said Darian. "I will send for food. My men should have supper ready."

"We had little to eat on our journey from the cove, which is why we gave in to hunger and made the fires Farli said revealed us."

"I do not fault you for your hunger and it turned out alright in the end. You shall eat your fill tonight. My men are good hunters and the hunting has been good!"

Palo arrived, looking for Eathelon, in time to hear "hungry" and "eat," hope for his complaining stomach. Eathelon said, "Palo is a good cook. Perhaps he would be willing to help with supper."

Palo smiled, "I am, and I would."

Harlen, a Ranger who had befriended Palo and accompanied him said, "The men will welcome a good cook. I confess, I am a much better hunter than cook."

Some of the men, having overheard him, added,

"He speaks truly!"

"We would welcome a good meal!"

Harlen ignored the men's remarks and led Palo to the main fire where the Warrior showed him a few culinary tricks. Palo looked more cheerful than he had in days, no doubt at the prospect of new friendship and a good meal. Harlen had already set out the fare from the hunt ... rabet, chikka, tubers, herbs, apples — enough for a feast.

A cheer went up for Palo that night, for the meal was better than any the men had tasted in months. They asked Palo to be their new cook for now and Harlen agreed with much enthusiasm.

Eathelon and Darian continued their conversation at their private fire, grateful for its warmth, as the night grew cold. Darian's men brought food and wine over and Darian complimented the meal. After supper, Eathelon and Darian talked into the night, until weariness overtook them and they were forced to retire. Darian's men stood watch.

Before he fell asleep, Eathelon saw Palo engaged in animated conversation with his new Ranger friends and guessed they asked the Warrior about life on Melatui and some of his fighting techniques, which Palo later confirmed. The Rangers had never met anyone like Palo, a large, unusual man, nor heard of the Maagi, or of Melatui, a far-off isle in the Westmost Sea, where none but the Eldarin had ever gone.

The Rangers in turn told Palo about life on the southern plains, how Numar had flourished before the Great War and later been abandoned. They told of their adventures hunting spies, described Antebba's famous Bazaar, how anything made in Narda could be purchased there, for a price, how it had diminished after the war. The Rangers and the Warrior talked until their tongues tired and their eyelids faltered, then all, save those who stood watch, retired for some needed sleep.

Eathelon slept well in the company of his new friends and Palo remarked later that he'd had his best night's sleep since leaving the cove.

Eathelon rose at sunup and saw that the morning meal had already been cooked and eaten and the men were busy breaking camp. Palo was not in sight, so Eathelon walked over and joined Darian at his private fire. Palo followed soon after.

"I trust you both slept well," said Darian. "We have far to go today and must leave soon."

Eathelon sat down to eat and Palo, having been appointed cook only the night before, gave Darian a puzzled look as he ate.

Seeing the look, Darian added, "We thought it only fair to give you respite from the morning meal, Palo, after the feast you made last night. There is little Harlen can do to ruin brefas."

Eathelon laughed and Palo, having been relieved of his morning obligation, smiled gratefully. They ate in haste, and finished up, for the company was almost ready to ride.

Darian's men brought the horses over and they mounted. The company set off with Eathelon, Darian and Palo riding abreast, at the head.

"I thought we would have crossed the plain in better time," said Eathelon, "but several things hindered us." He did not tell Darian about the fyrcaat on the ridge and he wondered if Darian knew about fyrcaats.

"If you reached the place where we found you in less than a fortnight, you made good time," said Darian, "especially on foot. The plain is deceptive. It appears flat, but is rocky, as I am sure you discovered."

"Yes, and there is something about that grass that stifled our breath and brought on some kind of irritability and lethargy."

Darian chuckled. "*Caleopsi grass* — its seeds make you drowsy until you become immune. Fortunately, that does not take long. My men and I have long since been immune to its effects, so we give it little thought."

They talked together most of the day and on the evening of the second day after breaking camp, they arrived at the foot of the Brunhyl. Eathelon saw that the trail here turned north and followed the hills, as Darian had told them.

"This trail leads to the front gates of Andolan," said Darian, "two weeks more of travel. But as I said, we will take a shorter way."

Darian explained that, in his service to Aneron, the men he sent east to spy for the West reported to a handful of trusted men, including Farli, who brought the information to Darian. He then took it to the King. He told Aneron he could deliver the information faster if the distance to the city's gates could somehow be shortened. The King knew of a little-known back trail that had been blocked off, no more than a cut in the hills that would cut a week off of the journey to the city. He had his soldiers restore it and placed sentinels there. This path they would now take.

"You and Palo must swear on whatever you hold dear to keep this back trail a secret," said Darian. "You must do this in service to King Aneron if I am to show you the way. I could be imprisoned just for revealing it to you, though the King trusts my judgement."

"We will keep your secret," Eathelon agreed. Palo nodded.

"Then I will swear you into the King's service."

Eathelon and Palo swore allegiance to King Aneron in the presence of the Rangers and were drafted into the King's service.

By now, the sun had fallen far down the sky and the hills lay mostly in shadow Darian ordered his men to make camp.

"We will enter the back trail in the morning," he said. "The entrance is narrow and hidden, too difficult to find in the dark. We leave at dawn."

The men made fires and Palo, the new cook, made supper and joined the Rangers again at the campfire. Darian and Eathelon sat with them this time and Eathelon answered questions about life on Melatui, his family and the Eldarin living there.

Then Farli set a watch and they all retired.

They woke at dawn to a pale sun rising behind the shadowed hills. After the morning meal, the men broke camp and Darian called Farli over.

"Take the Rangers and return to Numar, Farli. Keep watch on the southern lands and have the other Ranger groups report to you. I will return as soon as I can or get word to you."

The two clasped arms and said goodbye.

Farli rounded up the Rangers and they turned to leave.

"We will miss your cooking!" Harlen called out to Palo.

"More than you know!" one of the men shouted and they all laughed, including Harlen.

"We will miss the stories at campfire," added another.

"As will I," said Palo, a wide grin on his face. "Safe journey, my friends."

"Safe journey," the men called back.

"Safe journey," Farli said to Darian. "Do not forget to send word!"

"Safe journey, Farli." Darian waved them off.

Then he, Eathelon and Palo entered the back trail.

Chapter 9:
The Back Trail

The entrance to the back trail was little more than a cut in the hills, as Darian said. Eathelon and Palo followed him in, single file. The narrow trail twisted and turned deeper and deeper into the hills, winding its way into a canyon, which eventually widened out enough for the three of them to ride abreast. The walls of the canyon, low at the start, soon dwarfed them, but later shrank, as they wound their way up through rocky soil into the Brunhyl. When the sun reached its zenith, they stopped under a rocky outcropping to rest in the shade.

They ate leftovers and drank from the waterskins, as they talked together quietly. Eathelon surveyed the canyon walls, which told him much. Many ages had formed the canyon, visible in the colorful striations and he knew they sat where a river once flowed.

"Drink your fill, my friends," said Darian. "Andolan is not far now and there is plenty of cool, clean water in the city — and many other pleasant things to drink." He grinned.

"Like what?" asked Palo, chewing on a piece of dried chikka meat.

"Local brew, for one, and *Holling Vale* wines. Also, the juices of local fruits from Andolan's orchards, and milk from their bovines and goats."

Eathelon laughed, Darian joined in and Palo added his low voice to the mirth, but they quickly fell silent when they heard the echoes bounce off of the canyon walls.

"We have wild goats on Melatui," said Eathelon, chewing an apple.

"And *conteberis* (pigs) ..." interjected Palo, "but ..."

"What is a bo-vine?" the two asked, in unison.

"An animal smaller than a horse, different, but tasty, and its milk is smooth and refreshing," said Darian.

"Then I must try this bo-vine meat and milk," said Eathelon.

"And I," said Palo.

Darian chuckled. There were evidently many things in Narda new to his companions. But they had lived their lives on an island far out in the middle of the sea, after all. "Andolan has much to offer weary and hungry travelers," he said.

"When do we reach the back gates?" asked Eathelon

"If all goes well, by nightfall tomorrow."

"I am eager to see the fortress city," said Palo, still chewing. "Andolan is legend on Melatui."

Eathelon, finishing his apple, started to say, "I ..."

When Darian suddenly motioned them quiet. Palo drew his knife, but Darian shook his head and whispered, "No, Palo ... put it away."

Palo did.

They listened for a few minutes and, when they heard nothing more, they relaxed and resumed their conversation.

"We are near the fortress city now," said Darian. "The trail is patrolled. We have revealed ourselves, so should we encounter the King's soldiers, let me speak. No harm will come to you as long as you remain in my company. You must keep your weapons sheathed."

Eathelon and Palo nodded.

The trail climbed more and more steeply as they rode higher into the Brunhyl, and the walls of the canyon shrank until they barely rose above their heads. The sun had fallen far down the sky now, leaving much of the trail in shadow.

"I know a place ahead where the path widens," said Darian. "We can stop there for the night and make a fire."

"A fire would be most welcome," said Eathelon, pulling his cloak around his body. "It is colder up here."

"Is a fire a good idea?" asked Palo. "I could hunt something up for supper, though I do not know what I would find in this canyon."

"There is no need to hunt," said Darian. "We have plenty of

food left. I am not concerned about a fire. The King's soldiers are bound to find us on this trail sooner or later. Darian halted them and wrinkled his brow in concentration, then relaxed. "But you ..." he started to say, as they came around a bend in the trail and a company of King's soldiers confronted them. The leader barked, "Halt, or you are dead men!"

They halted and Darian gave his companions a look to remind them to leave their weapons sheathed. The small company of soldiers quickly surrounded them, their shields up and swords drawn.

Eathelon noticed each soldier wore a leather tunic and dark blue cloak, fastened at the shoulder with a gold clasp. Each wore a gold helm also, with a short white plume and each shield bore an emblazoned white *T* in the center.

The House of Toldor. Eathelon stared unafraid at the King's soldiers of Andolan, whose regal garb and manner contrasted much with the weathered Rangers of Numar.

"Who are you and how did you find this trail? Speak while you have a tongue!"

The gruff words came from a tall, handsome soldier, evidently the Captain of this company. His black hair fell to his shoulders and his bright blue eyes and tight jaw conveyed his stern warning.

"Come, *Arestor*," said Darian, casually, "do you not recognize me?"

Palo had pulled slightly ahead of Eathelon (ever his protector) and the young Captain, staring at Palo the entire time, had failed to at once notice Darian.

"Well, lose me in the *Lowlands*, if it isn't my spy-chasing friend!" Arestor signaled his men to lower their weapons.

Darian raised his eyebrows and gave him a half-smile.

"I was taken back by your companions. You have been gone many months, Darian. I thought perhaps Baele snared you in one of his little traps."

"You know me better than that, Arestor."

"Indeed, I do," laughed the Captain. The two men dismounted and clasped arms. "Well met! It is good to see you safely back." Arestor paused. "The circumstances here have changed much since you left, Darian. We captured two spies on this trail only two weeks ago. Do you believe it? Soldiers patrol night and day now, under orders from the Captain of the Guard, though I do not always accompany them."

"Your Father is wise to order it," replied Darian. "And it is fortunate for us you came along this time or we may have been skewered by one of your men. Speaking of spies, we have captured several in our southern lands. I did not realize they had infiltrated so far west."

"The King ordered Father to have us capture any man on this back trail. He is to be taken at once to Andolan for interrogation. Aneron is deadly serious about keeping spies out of Andolan. We could be imprisoned if we let any pass."

"And so, you should be!" said Darian, a look of concern on his face. He paused. "Though I doubt Aneron would imprison the next Captain of the Guard."

"I am not so certain," said Arestor. "As I said, circumstances have lately changed."

"Indeed, I see they have. Are things so bad in the city then?"

"Less so than in Numar, I expect. Who are these two?"

"I will tell you, but first know they have been sworn into the King's service."

Arestor gave him a puzzled look. "So you say?"

"Take us prisoner if you are duly sworn to it. I would not wish to harm your reputation with the King ... or your Father."

Arestor replied, with some irritation, "This is hardly about my reputation, Darian. It is a deadly serious matter."

"Indeed, I see things have grown much more serious in my absence."

"More than you know," said Arestor grimly.

"Well, you will no doubt tell me about it. Meanwhile, these two seek an audience with King Aneron. I was bringing information to the King when I found them and now I am also bringing them to the city for that purpose. Escort all of us in if you wish. The message they bring is urgent and they bring a gift for the King."

Arestor looked at Eathelon, then Palo, then back to Darian. "What message? What gift?" He pointed at Palo. "Your look differs from any man I have seen in Narda." He paused. "Of what race are you?"

"All will be said in due time, Arestor."

"Alright. If the Rangers have sworn you both into the King's service, then I will accept Darian's word for you."

"Indeed, I have hunted spies far longer than you, my friend," said Darian. "These two are not only not spies, their message is urgent and hopeful."

Arestor relaxed a little and turned to Eathelon, "Perhaps you can tell me your message so I may determine its value to the King. One does not so easily gain audience with him of late."

Eathelon replied, politely, "Thank you, but my message is for the King's ears alone and he alone may determine its value."

Darian gave Arestor a look of exasperation. "I can only imagine the trouble you must give your enemies."

"It is my job to trouble my enemies."

"Well, there is no need for you to trouble us."

"I suppose I sometimes err on the side of caution, Darian, but had you been in Andolan these past few months you would understand why."

Darian sighed. "Well I am still waiting for you to tell me. Look, I know you are doing what the King and your Father have ordered and I have no quarrel with that."

"Indeed, many lives are at stake should spies enter the city, and no less the King's life," said Arestor.

"Well, many more lives may be at stake if you do not help us," said Eathelon.

Darian took a deep breath, "We will tell all, Arestor, just give us escort to the back gates of the city."

Arestor smiled. "Of course we will. Come, there is a place ahead where we can camp for the night and discuss ... recent events."

Arestor motioned for his men to form up and move out. He rode next to Darian. Eathelon and Palo rode behind. Four soldiers led and four brought up the rear.

"What kept you for so many months?" Arestor asked Darian. "You used to come more often."

"Andolan is not the only target for Eastern spies," Darian replied. "The Rangers have caught several in Hamlan's southern lands, as was said. We have extracted information that Aneron must hear. You and I are both flushing out Eastern snakes, it would seem."

"You know me, Darian. I have little taste for the spy business, but my Father has ordered us to keep this trail secure and apprehend anyone entering it. Otherwise, we will have to close down the back trail. The King is worried that spies have already infiltrated Andolan."

"He is right to be concerned," said Darian. "I believe the real threat to the city is from within. It has already proven it can withstand an assault from without."

"The city is not Aneron's only concern," said Arestor. "He is restless about the Northern Reaches. He is sending reinforcements to Toldor's Keep. The men are to complete the restoration at once. The garrison there keeps watch on both the Highland Gap and Hamlan's northern lands." He paused. "Do you bring news of Baele then?"

"Yes, we have reason to believe he is planning a move on the West, though it has not been confirmed."

"It comes as no surprise. Baele is a cunning man. He feigns friendship, like a snake that waits to strike until your back is turned. But Aneron is no fool. He knows the man. What makes you suspect this?"

"Information gleaned from captives, though some may feed us false intelligence, as we do them." He paused. "Enough spy talk. It is genuinely good to see you, my friend! I am eager for news of the city. You said circumstances have changed. What do you mean?"

"I will tell you, but first I want to know more about your companions. The larger one is clearly of a race I do not know."

"No, nor could you. My companions are not from Narda."

Arestor looked puzzled. "How is this possible?"

"What I tell you next may stretch your beliefs, Arestor. Eathelon is a Mallorite Prince, from Melatui, an isle far off in the Westmost Sea and Palo a Maagi Warrior native of that isle." Darian said this next thing with restrained excitement. "They have come to let us know the Eldarin settled there, on Melatui. Arestor, the Eldarin survived!"

Arestor looked at Darian almost in disbelief. "You are certain of this?"

"I have verified its truth myself. The Eldarin live on their isle under the rule of Queen Lelar, a Syndar Eldarin, Eathelon's Mother. Eathelon is half Eldarin and half Maagi. His Father was the King of Melatui, only recently passed."

"I have never heard of the Maagi, or the Mallorites." He paused. "I thought the Eldarin did not marry outside of their own races. How did Eathelon's Mother come to marry a Maagi Warrior?"

"Eathelon will no doubt tell us the tale." He paused. "Many things may change in times of conflict, as you well know. I ask that you trust my judgement. Eathelon's message is important, not just for the King, but for us all. These two have braved the open sea to bring it to us. The bearer of the message alone should be evidence enough of its importance. Eathelon is not only half Eldarin, but a *Prince*."

"I trust you, Darian, though I must admit this news indeed stretches my beliefs. I will see what I can do to help persuade the King to see them, but I cannot promise he will do so. For now, comes the change of which I spoke, and it is ill news." He paused. "Aneron mourns the recent passing of the Queen of Hamlan, and of his baby son, second heir to his throne."

Darian gasped. "The King had another heir?"

"Yes. The Queen was with child, a son."

"But how? The healers of Andolan are much skilled at birthing."

"We have all asked the same question. Something is clearly amiss. The Queen seemed to be in good health, all of these past months of her condition."

"Andolan must grieve," said Darian, still in shock.

"Yes. The citizens of Hamlan love the King, and no less his family. Some say the Queen counseled with him often and that her influence on the people was great. Father said Aneron is in deep despair."

"As any man would be at such a loss. But Arestor, it must be clear to you by this fact alone that not all in Andolan loved the King's family."

Arestor grimaced. "I know."

Eathelon and Palo overheard the conversation and gave each other a telling look. Another unexplained death. Eathelon felt empathy for the King.

"Aneron has been sequestered since he laid the Queen and babe to rest in the Tombs," said Arestor. "The people of the city turned out for the funeral procession. Rumor says the birth went wrong."

"Well, something went wrong, for certain, but the skill of the healers is well known, so there must be more to it, something undiscovered," Darian stated, with cold certainty.

"Are you are saying you think the Queen ... was murdered?" asked Arestor.

"That is for you to discover," Darian remarked.

"The whole affair stinks like rotten eggs and should be investigated," replied Arestor.

"Then do so," Darian responded.

"That is up to Father and *Stefen* now. My duties do not permit me that luxury."

They rode in silence awhile after that, until Darian broke it. "I understand Aneron is in mourning, but you must try to convince him to give Eathelon an audience, nevertheless. I am certain he will be glad you arranged it. He will validate you for having courage enough to bring him Eathelon's message and gift, even in his time of mourning."

"I will see what I can do, but you must understand Aneron is not wholly himself right now — and some say not just from his recent loss."

"Do not listen to such cabal, Arestor!"

"I do not, for my part, but some others do. I have seen a change in him myself. Stefen tends the affairs of the city and *Scirra*, jewel of his heart, often waits long hours to offer him comfort. A great cloud of sorrow hangs over Andolan, Darian. You have not picked a very good time to return."

"Circumstance has picked the time, not I."

They arrived at the place where they were to make camp and Arestor ordered his men to set camp, prepare a meal and set a watch. That done, he motioned Eathelon, Palo and Darian to a private fire.

"A Syndar, you say?" he asked Eathelon. "I know little of the Eldarin except what history and legend have taught, and an occasional tale from my Father and the King. I know Aneron misses the Eldarin, and the advice they once offered. Tell me what you will of your reasons for coming. We cannot travel the back trail tonight anyway."

Darian looked at him with curiosity and made a mental note to ask him about that remark. He had often traveled the back trail at night.

Arestor continued, "I have brought ill news today — perhaps yours will be more hopeful."

Before Eathelon could reply, Darian interjected, "Long have we discussed our desire to help Landrin regain his throne in the East, Arestor. But that goal has been little more than a far-off glimmer in a dark sky that hangs over the House of Tebor. Hamlan maintains an uneasy alliance with the East, but Aneron suspects Baele only feigns peace. It falls to Hamlan, to Andolan's soldiers, to prevent the House of Tebor from taking over Narda. And we seem to have few allies these days."

"Baele is as poisonous as a path snake," agreed Arestor. "I, for one, look forward to cutting off the head of the snake." He paused and changed the subject. He looked at Darian then back to Eathelon then back to Darian. "There is something familiar about the two of you. What is it?"

"Darian's Father and Mother are ... or were Eldarin ...Nydar," said Eathelon, before Darian could speak.

Arestor looked at Darian and laughed. "I knew there was something different about you, my spy chasing friend, but I could never put my finger on it."

Darian raised his eyebrows and gave Arestor a half-smile.

"I thought you had a Nardan Father," Arestor added.

"That is a long story, my friend," replied Darian, "one to which you are welcome, but one better left to another time."

"Why did you not tell me of your ancestry? You know you can trust me."

"I trust you as I would a brother, Arestor. I told no one. It is better to keep certain information close in the spy business. It is a survival point. Do not take it as an insult. Only two outside of my immediate family have ever known my ancestry — Aneron and Stefen. And Stefen knows only because Aneron keeps nothing from him." But Darian lied. There was another who knew, but that too, was a closely guarded secret.

Arestor nodded. "No harm done," he said.

Eathelon continued, "My Mother is a Syndar Eldarin and, as was said, my Father was a Maagi Warrior, the last King in a long line of Maagi Kings that to rule Melatui. I am expected to take up rule when I return. I am the first Prince of the Mallorites, the new race born of the union of Eldarin and Maagi."

Arestor's brows went up.

Eathelon continued, "Palo and I have traveled far under great hardship to bring this news and gift to King Aneron. We lost our ship and two of our companions on the voyage. It is urgent that we speak with the King. He has long been an ally of the Eldarin."

Arestor looked at Eathelon with new-found respect. "Many Nardans have talked of the return of the Eldarin, including my Father," he said, "but few have kept any hope of that alive. It has been 60 years since the Eldarin were exiled. We assumed they had all perished. News came of the debris strewn across the southern shores. The King will welcome the news that they survived."

"There are some who do not wish the return of the Eldarin," said Darian."

"Yes," said Arestor, "but we know who they are."

"Perhaps, perhaps not all," said Darian.

Arestor turned back to Eathelon. "Why have the Eldarin not sent someone sooner?"

"As you know, many Eldarin perished, both here and when they fled Narda. It appears that the Eldarin are still under death threat here, even today. Why would they wish return under such conditions? Palo and I came to discover if it is safe for them to return. From what I see, the House of Tebor still rules the East and now you say may be planning a move on the West. Clearly it is not safe for the Eldarin to return. We have just arrived, but I see there is much to do here to make it safe for the Eldarin to return. We hope to seek the help of their old allies. Conditions must change." He said nothing more about the true nature of his errand.

"It is true that the House of Tebor still holds power in the

East," replied Arestor. "But largely due to Aneron's skill, their power has thus far been contained there. Still, I believe they will not remain content to keep it so much longer."

"Many Nardans bury their heads in the desert sand," said Darian, "and go about their daily lives unaware of the growing Eastern threat. If we do not teach our children, they will grow up knowing little or nothing about the Eldarin, or their contributions. They have no idea what life was like here before the Eldarin were unjustly cast out. And the children are our future."

"People can become blind given enough time and circumstance," said Eathelon.

"And history lost or rewritten," added Darian.

"Perhaps Baele knows this and expects to take advantage of it."

They fell silent awhile then Arestor addressed Eathelon with a different topic. "Where will you and Palo go after your audience with the King, should it be granted?"

"To Malta. I wish to visit the Golden City. It has long been deserted, but I have an errand there. Where we go after will depend upon what I find."

"You are a man of mystery," said Arestor. "You go north then."

"Yes." Eathelon paused. "I hope to find anyone there, in Northwest Wood, who might give me information about a matter important to my errand. I wish to visit the Elvenkin. I heard tale of an Eldarin couple living with them in Northwest Wood. Do you know anything of this?"

"I believe they perished in the Great War, but there is a tale of a child, a daughter," said Arestor. "She may still be there, for she would be in great danger if she left the wood. But the Elvenkin have little tolerance of strangers, Eathelon. Few Nardans dare enter that wood." He paused. "I visited the Golden City once, though long ago. I fear it is no longer golden."

Darian listened, but his mind had wandered back to Arestor's comment about not being able to travel the back trail at night. He brought it up. "Arestor, why can we not travel the back trail at night? I have done so often."

"Oh — that," replied Arestor. "It slipped my mind. I meant to tell you that, by order of the King, we must set traps on the back trail. We cannot keep watch on every step of it to our back door."

"What kind of traps? When had you planned to warn me—after I was caught in one?"

"In my defense, you have been away a long time and I told the soldiers to watch for you. The traps are set closer to the back gates, not in places you have already passed, obviously."

"You failed to recognize me," Darian reminded, "and many of your men do not yet know me."

"That is not altogether true. I did recognize you, just not right away because my attention was on Palo. And I expected you to be traveling alone."

"Do not worry, Arestor, I hold you blameless for following your orders, but you might have told me earlier about the traps."

"You were not here. You only just arrived."

"Alright, a fair point. How did spies find their way into the back trail? Did I somehow betray the entrance?"

"No, I hold you blameless. I believe they found it by accident. My Father believes that one of the soldiers loosened his tongue in a tavern. Soldiers are not permitted to drink in public taverns now for that reason. We keep a private one for them for when they are on furlough. Any who disobeyed have been disciplined, but we cannot know for certain whose or how many ears may have been reached. And Aneron has grown concerned that we have traitors in the city."

"I see there is more work to do in Andolan than I thought," said Darian. "I have sent Farli back to Numar with the Rangers. They will have to patrol the southern lands in my stead. It looks as if I may be here awhile."

"Farli is capable enough to act in your stead," said Arestor. "I am glad you are back." He paused. "Come, you can tell me what you will of your errand and adventures over supper. We must leave at dawn if we are to reach the back gates of the city by tomorrow night and I am due back then."

Palo perked up at the prospect of a meal. They followed Arestor to the main campfire, where several rabets roasted and carried three back to Arestor's campsite. They ate and talked into the night and Darian told Arestor of his latest adventures in the southern lands. Arestor asked Eathelon and Palo many questions about Melatui and their travels in Narda thus far and the two recounted their sea voyage, the blackfish, greatfish, sudden storm, and their loss of ship and crew. They told Arestor about Darian's rescue, but revealed nothing of the specific nature of their errand with the King.

Arestor answered many questions about Andolan, the greatest city in Narda, he said. Such tales are long in the telling but the listeners absorbed every word. When their tongues grew tired and their eyelids heavy, they bid each other goodnight and laid down to sleep. Eathelon slept as well as possible on the cold hard ground, grateful for another new friendship, and for once again being spared the watch.

Chapter 10: A History Lesson

Eathelon woke at dawn and found Arestor and his men eating at the campfires. Hungry, he walked over to join Arestor and Darian at theirs and Palo arrived shortly after.

"Hoy!" said Arestor, as Eathelon approached, "Take a meal while you can — we must leave soon. I am anxious to return to the city. I left soon after they laid the Queen and babe in the Tombs." He tore off a piece of chikka meat and popped it into his mouth. "Some of my men have gone ahead to unset the traps. They will reset them after we pass."

Darian's face twitched at the mention of the traps.

Eathelon noticed. *He still feel irritation about those traps.*

One of Arestor's men signaled from up the trail that it was now safe for them to pass and Arestor acknowledged with a wave.

They finished up their meal and put out the fire. Arestor gave an order for the company to mount and they all rode off in the same formation as before. After riding for a couple of hours, they reached the top of the canyon, where the trail widened enough for the four of them to ride abreast, and they resumed conversation.

"Tell us about Andolan," Eathelon said to Arestor. "You have lived there all of your life?"

"Yes. It has changed much due to the increase in population. Many more people moved to the city from the outlying lands."

"Darian mentioned this," said Eathelon.

"Andolan is built on hills, is it not?" asked Palo.

"Yes, 10 levels, in the Brunhyl. The King's home is at the top level."

"I understand its architecture was much influenced by the Eldarin," said Eathelon.

"Indeed," replied Arestor, "it was and is. The Eldarin architects created our system for bringing water in from the hills and built us a House of Healing."

"It sounds much like what I learned about the Golden City," remarked Eathelon.

"The two have much in common," Arestor concurred, "but Andolan is the oldest and fairest city in Narda. The Golden City is, or was, nearly its equal, but for the 10 levels. Andolan is the most ancient city in Narda, built long before the Eldarin arrived. But they did much to improve it for us."

"It is said that any assault made on Andolan brings a heavy price," Palo added, ever the warrior.

"Indeed," said Arestor. "For the enemy. Andolan has never fallen, despite many attempts to break down its walls. It is for that reason that many Nardans have chosen to live there. It is probably the most secure city in Narda."

Arestor told them more about Andolan from his personal experience, and Darian felt obliged to add an occasional fact or two of his own. The four companions rode and talked together from morning until sunset, and here is some of what they said:

"After the Eldarin arrived in Narda in the First Age, until well into the Fourth, things became more and more peaceful and prosperous," Arestor said. "They built the Golden City and set out from there to explore other parts of Narda. Both West and East eventually came under Eldarin influence. The Kings employed Eldarin advisors to help them with their affairs."

Darian added, "The Eldarin made friends easily and taught anyone willing to learn their techniques in many things, including architecture, engineering, shipbuilding and the arts. The Eldarin built beautiful ships, ones more seaworthy than ours, so in time their designs became the standard for all trade ships."

"We are familiar with Eldarin ships," said Eathelon. He felt a pang of remorse for losing the *Sirine.*

"Some areas of Narda have always been difficult to reach by foot or horse," continued Darian, "and some of them are more easily accessed by ship."

Arestor jumped in. "Our ships were well-constructed, but flawed. They faltered in the storms off of the eastern coast. The

Eldarin shipbuilders corrected these flaws and provided better navigation tools, so trade became more profitable as the ships gained access to areas of Narda not previously reached. The demand for goods increased."

"What kinds of goods?" asked Palo.

"The fine wines of Holling Vale, for one," said Darian, grinning.

"Like *Dark Horse Red*, a favorite of the King," noted Arestor. "Come to think of it, I haven't seen many bottles of that arrive to Andolan of late."

"That is no doubt because Baele is fond of *Dark Horse Red*," interjected Darian, "or so it is said. There are probably plenty of bottles in his storeroom."

"Wine is not the only thing he has plundered from the West," Arestor commented. "But getting back to your question, citizens in the eastern regions could now purchase the fine wines of Holling Vale, and those of us in the West get the better grains from *Hond*."

"Any many other goods too, including all types of clothing, leather goods, fine furniture, jewelry and just about anything else anyone might need or want," added Darian.

"Various regions of Narda are abundant in natural resources," Arestor pointed out. "Nardans grew in wealth and some became quite prosperous. Peace grew between East and West, where once there had been friction. The House of *Began* and the House of Toldor became close allies."

"The ship trade has continued," said Darian, "but it is only a fraction of what it was before the war. And Baele and his greedy son extort what they can from everyone."

"Extort?" asked Eathelon. "Would not the trade agreement even out trade both ways? Does Aneron not oversee this?"

"It is difficult for Aneron to keep watch on all of the trade for Hamlan. The soldiers keep security in the north and the Rangers in the south as best they can, but trade is overseen primarily by the merchants of East and West under the trade agreement and they are depended upon to keep it. The King has received reports that Baele demands the best goods for the lowest prices and his men sometimes intimidate the merchants into compliance. Some merchants are also dishonest, it seems."

"What is to be done to handle this?" asked Eathelon.

"Aneron is more interested in keeping the peace than in gaining wealth," said Arestor. "There is little to be done. Not all criminals can easily be brought to justice. We do the best we can."

Arestor continued. "Anyway, under Eldarin influence, the Kings, their families and some of their friends helped finance the shipbuilding, to expand the trade. This increased their wealth and they chose to invest it in Narda, so built roads, bridges, cities, schools and Houses of Healing. They upgraded Andolan, created the bazaars and open markets and improved the quality of life. The Eldarin assisted the Kings' visions to benefit all."

"Baele does not share this vision," said Darian. "He is greedy. He wants it all."

Arestor continued, "Yes. Anyway, the Kings had the Eldarin architects design and build *Castletop*, in Newcastle and improve Andolan. Castletop, once King Landrin's home, is built atop the highest peak in Newcastle, *Mt. Castle*. Andolan, already built into the Brunhyl long ago, was remade on the 10 levels it now has. These can be sealed off from one another in the event the city is breached. The city was in need of repair but is fully restored now."

"Interesting Arestor." Eathelon changed the subject. "I am curious about something else. In my study of Narda, I learned that Landrin is a descendant of the House of Began and Aneron a descendant of the House of Toldor, but I learned nothing of the lineage of the Captain of the Guard."

"We are descendants of the House of Toldor also."

"You are related to Aneron then?"

"In lineage, yes. Began was the first recorded King of the East in Narda, thus the name, House of Began. The Eastern Kings descend through his eldest son, Betan. Landrin, the rightful King of the East lives in exile in the Flax Isles now. Baele overthrew him in the Great War."

"So, I was told," replied Eathelon.

"Landrin owes his life to Aneron, who negotiated his friend's exile as part of the trade agreement. That is why the East was allowed to plunder western goods. Aneron would have traded all the goods in Hamlan to save his friend. It is but one example of the lengths Aneron has gone to in order to keep the House of Tebor on its own side of Narda."

"It will be my great honor to meet him," stated Eathelon.

"And mine," added Palo.

"Aneron is a good King," Arestor remarked, "but he has suffered much."

"As most Kings do," said Eathelon, remembering his Father.

"He needs time to recover from his loss," noted Darian.

"Tell me about your lineage, Arestor," Eathelon reminded.

"*Toldor* was the first King of the West and all such Kings down to Aneron descend from his eldest son, Teold. But there existed another line, one through his daughter Teolin and that is the line from which the Captains of the Guard descend. Teolin wed Thyrstan, a soldier of some renown, who had gained the favor of the King. Thyrstan formed the Guard to protect the King and his family and became the first Captain of the Guard, and a worthy one. The King decreed that, upon Thyrstan's death, his male heir should inherit the post, should he prove worthy. A high and trusted post, one that commands all of the personal guards of the King and his family, the post and title pass to any worthy heir upon retirement or death of the Captain. Every heir of every Captain of the Guard from Thyrstan down to me has proven worthy. The line has remained unbroken."

"Most impressive," said Palo. He gained a new-found respect for this young Captain.

Arestor continued. "The Captain of the Guard changes when the crown passes to the King's heir. When Stefen takes the crown, I will become the new Captain of the Guard."

"You have your own place of honor then," said Eathelon.

"Yet to be earned," said Arestor.

As is mine, thought Eathelon.

Having ridden all day, the company stopped to rest and take a meal. As they did, the conversation resumed. Arestor and Darian gave a more detailed description of their own knowledge of the Eldarin, and of Andolan.

"The Eldarin brought advanced skills to Narda," said Arestor. "They taught us to grow the healing plants from seeds they'd brought, and how to use them. Our own healing methods were much cruder."

Darian added, "They gave us the common tongue. The languages of Narda were diverse. Sometimes this led to war over even petty matters. The common tongue, taken from the Eldarin language, eventually became the primary language of Narda. Other languages exist, of course, but these are little used today. The common tongue served to unite us and put an end to most conflicts."

"It seems an irony that the Eldarin stopped war in Narda, only to have one of their own create a war that nearly wiped them out," said Palo.

An awkward silence ensued.

"Perhaps the Eldarin can help prevent another Great War," Darian commented, looking at Eathelon.

Such is my hope, thought Eathelon.

"I meant no disrespect to the Eldarin," Palo offered.

"I know," Darian responded.

"Eathelon," said Arestor, "there is a legend which references a magic device the Eldarin brought here in the First Age. I do not believe in magic, of course, but I am curious about this. Have you heard of it?"

"Yes, the *Seontir*," replied Eathelon, "a Seeing Stone."

"How can a stone possibly see?" Arestor queried, with some sarcasm.

Eathelon's eyes met Palo's briefly, then looked away.

"Sometimes things may be difficult to believe and yet be true," Eathelon responded.

"You are a man of mystery, as was said," Arestor noted, but to everyone's relief, he did not press the matter about the Stones. "Not everything introduced by the Eldarin was new to Nardans. We have always possessed our own talents, some used for many ages. We are skilled smithies, for example, a craft long used to make instruments of war. The Eldarin helped us put such talents to better use. We make decorations and utensils for trade, in addition to weapons for war. Unfortunately, such weapons will always have a use, so long as evil exists in these lands."

"So, it seems," said Eathelon.

Darian continued, "Nardans are fond of music. We are excellent musicians. The Eldarin brought new instruments and taught us to play them." He paused a moment. "Narda has lost much with the exile of the Eldarin."

"Indeed, we are no longer as prosperous a people as we once were," Arestor added, "despite the trade agreement."

The conversation waned here and they finished up the meal in silence, then mounted and rode off again toward the back gates of the city.

"What else can you tell us about the fortress city?" asked Palo. "I would like to know how it has withstood its enemies for so long."

"You are persistent," laughed Arestor. "The rebuilding of Andolan was the largest undertaking of its time, yet even before that, it was a fair city."

"Well, if it was so fair, why did you rebuild it?" asked Palo.

Arestor laughed, "You ask a fair question, my Warrior friend. Hamlan had become peaceful but the King knew little about some of Hamlan's more remote regions — like the lands north of *Eredian*, for example, near the Northern Reaches. The King thought it good foresight to build a city large enough to protect, not only his family and Hamlan's government, but any citizen of Hamlan who wished to live and work there, whether by choice or because they were forced to flee from an enemy or natural calamity."

"Natural calamity?" asked Palo.

"Like flood, or fire. Heavy rains sometimes flood the lower plains and the grasses can catch fire from lightning or a careless campfire, sending ranchers and farmers fleeing for their lives."

There was nothing natural about the fire that chased us, thought Eathelon. He and Palo exchanged a knowing glance.

"The King did his utmost to make decisions that best served all Nardans," continued Arestor, "but some of his decisions were not popular."

"I understand," said Eathelon. "My Father had to make many such decisions, as any good leader must do."

"Toldor knew the task of rebuilding Andolan would not be

completed in his lifetime," said Arestor. "He wanted the King's house built high in the hills, where his family would best be protected, but he also wanted fast access to those who governed with him. He called on his most skilled architects and builders who, aided by the Eldarin, designed and built Andolan on the 10 levels it now has. Prior to its expansion, the levels were four, which is why the back trail leads to what used to be the front gates of the city. The rebuilding of Andolan was completed under Aneron's Father, Feorn. No city in Narda today is its equal, not Castletop, not even the Golden City."

"One enters Andolan the first level now. The top of the city lies right below the highest peak in the Brunhyl, *Vinte*. From the Watchtower, you can look out over the Brunhyl in every direction."

"That sounds strategic," said Palo.

Eathelon smiled, for Palo always seemed to consider things from his Warrior point of view.

"The Watchtower rises from the middle of a large courtyard, between the 10th level gate and the King's house," continued Arestor. "The buildings that house the King's staff lie at the perimeter of the courtyard, whose outer walls are of thick, grey stone, high and wide."

"A large iron gate sits in the 10th level wall," Darian noted. "Only those known to the King or the Guard may pass."

"The Guard is posted outside and inside the gate at all times," added Arestor. "Were you not with us, you would not pass."

"We are fortunate to be in the right company at the right time," claimed Eathelon.

"From the tall front gates at the base of the Brunhyl, a wide paved road twists and turns up to the 10th level," said Darian, "and strong metal gates seal off one level from the next to the top."

"Again strategic," Palo offered, clearly impressed.

"Many citizens also live outside the city walls," Arestor continued, "and enter to sell their goods at the Open Market, on level one. The front gates remain open by day. A bell tolls their closure at dusk. Soldiers are posted outside the main gates at all times, not the King's Guard, but soldiers of Andolan. Anyone who lets an enemy pass risks his own life."

"Is this true for the back gates also?" asked Darian.

"Yes," said Arestor, "for as I said earlier, things have changed. Darian is known here, however, and because Eathelon and Palo are in our company, all shall pass."

Eathelon and Palo continued to ask Arestor for more details of the city, and because no one had ever asked him this before, he eagerly answered.

"Along the streets of the city, in its courtyards and on its roofs, pipes collect rainwater and divert it into aqueducts. Our waste system lies far beneath the city, in stone tunnels that take it over rock and stone to underground pools, where plants turn it into usable water to grow our crops."

"Seeds from those plants came from the Eldarin, no doubt," said Eathelon, with a smile.

"Of course," grinned Arestor.

"Could a spy not simply enter the city through the underground tunnels?" asked Palo.

"Another thoughtful question Palo, but no. Large metal grates buried deep into the rock below prevent entry by anything larger than a raat."

"Impressive," replied Palo.

An Eastern spy would certainly qualify as one, thought Eathelon, but he said only, "It appears to be a well-planned city."

"The Eldarin had foresight," said Darian. "They knew the population would increase over the years."

"It is unfortunate their foresight did not predict their treachery," said Eathelon.

That brought about another brief silence.

Darian broke it. "Fruit and nut orchards grow outside the city walls, fed by streams in the Brunhyl. Some of these dry up in summer so the reclaimed water is used on the orchards until the rains return to fill the streams."

Arestor continued, "Andolan now houses more than half of the citizens of Hamlan. Those who live outside its walls grow many of our crops, graze our herds and bring their goods to the

Open Market." Arestor paused. "But no more questions, please! My tongue is tired."

By now the sun had fallen to a point just above the horizon.

"We will arrive to the fortress city soon," Darian stated.

Eathelon shifted uneasily on his horse, weary from talk and sitting a horse.

"The back gates are just around that bend," said Arestor. "*City in the Clouds* Andolan is sometimes called, for from the Watchtower you can see above the clouds to the multitude of stars shining in the night sky. This I have witnessed myself."

They rode on only a short distance then rounded the bend and beheld the back gates of Andolan.

Chapter 11: Andolan

Eathelon sat atop his horse, in the dusk of the waxing evening and stared in awe at the enormous back gates of Andolan, which towered far above his head.

"The front gates are even higher and wider than these," said Darian.

"It is a sight, for certain," agreed Palo.

Wrought of thick gray metal, the massive gates bore a *T* emblazoned in the centers and lothingel leaves on an unbroken vine around their outer edges, an obvious tribute to the Eldarin. The high walls were of smooth gray stone, cut and set with such precision that Eathelon almost could not see any flaws in the face. Above the gates, these words of warning had been carved into the stone. Eathelon read them aloud:

Enter all who bear good will and safely dwell herein whate'er thy path.
Beware those who bear us ill, for nothing will protect from Toldor's wrath.

"Toldor's warning to enemies, which stands today," said Arestor. "The fortress city will never fall." He said it with great conviction. He dismounted and walked over to a small stone building on one side of the gate. A soldier stood before it and he spoke briefly with him, then returned and mounted his horse. The huge gates swung open and the company rode through, but the guard gazed long at Palo as he passed and continued to stare at him until the gates closed behind them.

"He has never seen a Maagi Warrior before, Palo," explained Arestor, "and is no doubt uncertain about his decision to let you pass. But I command these soldiers." Arestor grinned, "He had no choice."

It would not be the last stare Palo would get on his journey in Narda.

"The soldiers know Darian by name and reputation, though not all know his face," continued Arestor. "It is dusk. The guards have orders to bar entry to anyone after sundown now."

"How far is it to level 10?" asked Eathelon.

"This trail brings us into the city at level four," said Arestor, "which cuts off half or more of our journey to the top. The levels shorten as we climb. But we are not yet to the main road."

Stars began to dot the sky above and lights flickered on in the city. After riding a short distance, they came to the main road, and another, small gate. The guard, seeing Arestor waved them through, as he too stared with curiosity at Palo when they passed.

"Am I to be the object of stares throughout our journey?" asked Palo.

"So, it would seem," said Eathelon, grinning. "You cannot hide your impressive size and color."

"Nor do I wish to," huffed Palo.

They turned onto the main road and found it bustling with activity. Eathelon expected people to be eating supper, preparing to retire for the night, but it was not so.

"Is the city always so active so late?" he asked.

"The hour is not late," said Arestor, "and anyway, Andolan sleeps little." He paused. "I must ride ahead now, to make arrangements for your lodging, but I will return again soon. I will leave you in Darian's care, for now." He rode off.

"Arestor is right about the city," said Darian, "Some ale houses are open all night and serve brefas the next morning. One need never go to bed!"

They all laughed.

"You have come to the ideal place, Palo! You can drink all night and take brefas as the sun rises," Eathelon teased. "But some of us still require sleep."

"Sleep was also on my mind," replied Palo. "I am weary of sitting a horse all day and sleeping on hard ground. A bed would be most welcome."

People acknowledged the riders as they passed, and the companions returned the greetings.

"The people here seem friendly enough," Eathelon stated. "They are no doubt curious about us."

"No doubt, but the folk of Andolan are usually friendly, and generous," added Darian. "Many of them share willingly with those new to the city."

"Even someone who looks as different as I do?" asked Palo.

Darian laughed, "Yes Palo, even then, though they are probably curious to learn something more about you."

"Well, some people trusted may yet have bad intentions. If everyone had good intentions, there would be no need for Warriors — or for hunting spies."

"A valid point, my Warrior friend," said Darian. "But the good folk of this city depend on Andolan's soldiers to keep out undesirables. They may be curious about you, but I doubt they believe you to be anything than what you are — a large, brown, friendly guest!"

Palo grinned.

But Eathelon knew from Arestor's report that someone with bad intentions lived in the city, for the Queen and babe had died.

Arestor returned a while later and joined them again. "There is a small inn ahead where you and Palo can take supper and stay the night. It holds few patrons and should be ideal. It is arranged. I will take you there, then I must go find my Father to see if I can help arrange your audience with the King."

"We are grateful for your help and friendship, Arestor," said Eathelon.

The four of them rode on and came at last to a stone-faced cottage set back from the main road. A narrow cobblestone path led to its front porch and above its yellow door a sign said:

Cärmindôl
Lamplighter Inn

They tied the horses to beautiful black wrought-iron horse-head posts set in the ground for that purpose and before they had finished unpacking their belongings, a man appeared and stood ready to take their horses to the stable. They walked the short path to the front door and entered. The inn, as Arestor said, was small — only six sleeping rooms off of a main corridor with a small dining room to the right of the lobby. Arestor went to the front desk, retrieved the key to their room and handed it to Eathelon. He led them down the hall to the last room on the right and Eathelon opened the door.

"Two beds?" he asked, a puzzled look on his face.

"I do not stay," replied Darian, "I have business in the city. But I will take supper with you and return for you in the morning. I will go find a table, while you two unpack."

"The room is modest but the beds and pillows soft and the blankets warm," said Arestor. "Return the key to the desk when you leave. I must go now but I, too will return in the morning. Your horses are stabled behind the inn and the groomsman will bring them up for you when you are ready to leave. Sleep well and enjoy your supper! I understand the food here is excellent." He turned and left.

Eathelon and Palo put their belongings in the room and walked back to the dining room to join Darian, who had taken a table in the back corner. As they walked over to it, Palo ignored stares from the few patrons and Eathelon, on impulse, felt for the Stone secured beneath his tunic.

Palo grumbled as they sat down and Eathelon realized his clothing differed much from the other patrons, which made him stand out all the more. They would need to find more suitable clothing.

They'd been seated only a few minutes when a lovely young waitress brought supper over and laid it on the table. She gave Eathelon a shy, warm smile and he smiled back. His eyes followed her as she walked with a youthful bounce across the room, her skirts swaying back and forth. Palo and Darian looked at him and grinned.

"What?" he asked, grinning back.

"Nothing," said Darian, with raised eyebrows and a suppressed smile.

They helped themselves to the food and began to eat.

True to Arestor's words, the food tasted excellent. They talked quietly together as they ate, and when they had finished Darian excused himself.

"I must go," he said, "but I will return in the morning, as I said." He left some coins on the table to pay for supper, then turned and left.

"Perhaps he has a lover here," mused Palo.

Eathelon scoffed. "I doubt his duties leave time for such pleasures." Eathelon's attention strayed back to the young Nardan girl who kept refilling his mug and flirting. This time, as his eyes followed her across the room they landed on a swarthy, sinister-looking man at a table on the far side. Eathelon would have given him no notice, but the man called attention to himself, for when he saw Eathelon looking at him he quickly hid his face.

"Palo, did you notice that man across the room — the one in the corner?" Eathelon discretely tipped his head in that direction.

"What about him?" asked Palo, as he munched on a piece of warm bread.

"He hid his face when he saw me look at him. He is hiding something more."

"This I doubt, Eathelon. He stares because we are strangers and I, strangest of all." Palo took a drink from his tankard of ale.

"Why should he hide his face then?"

"He is probably just some drunkard who cannot hold his brew."

"My instinct says otherwise," responded Eathelon.

Palo shrugged.

But the young waitress kept distracting Eathelon by coming over again and again, and he soon forgot about the man in the corner. Then, their bellies full and the long day's ride behind, they finished up the meal and retired to their room. The beds and pillows proved a luxury they had not felt in months and they fell at once into a restful sleep.

Eathelon awoke at sunup and found Palo up.

"Well slept," said Palo.

"Indeed," yawned Eathelon, "and well rested."

Palo grunted. "I am hungry."

"Well then," grinned Eathelon, "I guess we had better go get some brefas."

They walked to the dining room, but Darian was not yet there. Eathelon saw that the same corner table from the night before sat unoccupied, so claimed it. The same young waitress who'd served them supper now served brefas and, when she saw Eathelon, she hurried over with a basket of fresh cakes and smiled at him. He took one and smiled back. She giggled and hurried off to wait on another patron.

"Does the girl never sleep?" asked Palo.

The question needed no answer.

Palo ate enough for three men because the girl kept bringing food over and each time made some little contact with Eathelon, whether a look or an "accidental" touch.

"She is after you like a foxx after a chikka" Palo said, a wide grin on his face. He stuffed down another brefas cake.

Eathelon said, in restrained amusement, "I, like Darian, have no time for such distractions."

"Last night you looked as if you would welcome it."

"I played along."

"But do you not think about taking a wife one day, Eathelon? I do." Palo stated with a wide smile.

"My mind is occupied with other thoughts," he said, grinning. He ate his last bite of sweet cake.

Darian and Arestor walked in as Eathelon and Palo finished up.

"Well met, and well timed," greeted Eathelon.

"Well met," Darian responded.

Arestor walked to the desk and settled the account, while Darian accompanied Eathelon and Palo to their room to collect their belongings.

"How was your night, Darian?" asked Palo, with strong interest. "Where did you stay? Do you have family here?" Eathelon scowled at Palo for prying. He thought it bad manners.

Darian laughed. "The King's family is my only family here, Palo." He glanced at Eathelon. "But to answer your question, I have friends here. I have no need to stay at an inn."

Palo shrugged.

Eathelon knew Palo hoped for something more from their spy-chasing friend but Darian said nothing of the nature of his errand and Palo did not press him. Packed and ready, they passed by the dining room and joined Arestor in the lobby. The young Nardan girl brushed by Eathelon one last time, smiled and giggled. Darian grinned and Eathelon rolled his eyes then politely returned the girl's smile.

They left the inn and followed the main road up to level five. Eathelon watched the activity in the city with interest. People walked and milled about on the wide paved road as shop after shop opened its doors.

He noticed as they rode along that several narrow roads branched off from the main one, and asked Darian, "Where do those lead?"

"To more shops, and homes, mostly."

They saw children walking to school and Eathelon said, "Andolan is fortunate to have so many children."

"Yes, and many schools to accommodate them," said Arestor.

"We have many Maagi children on Melatui but few Eldarin children, and even fewer Mallorite children."

Darian smiled. "Many citizens of Hamlan live here, as was said, which is why our population here continues to grow."

Eathelon read some of the signs on the shops they passed:

Shalia Jewelry, Babia Clocks, Dara Clothiers, Nori Music Palace.

They rode past street vendors too, and artists sketching or painting, musicians playing and singing and those who stopped to watch and listen, and drop coins into waiting baskets.

They passed other inns, most small like the Lamplighter, passed by gardens, outdoor cafes with people in them, eating and talking together.

Eathelon saw a shop whose large front window displayed malea leaves and ratintha, herbs of the healing arts. They passed a shop that displayed Holling Vale wines and local brew, and a leaf called *Tip*, that Darian told them came from *Rath*, a small village in the Brunhyl on the west coast.

Despite the activity, Eathelon perceived a sadness, heard in the music, noticed in the way some people walked and interacted with each other.

"Sorrow still lingers here," he stated bluntly.

"Yes," Darian replied. "It will take time for the city to recover its loss."

"The King has not been seen down here since the Queen passed," Arestor said. "He used to visit, at least once a season."

"He must make his own recovery," said Eathelon. "He is no doubt still in mourning." Eathelon empathized with the King. The loss of his Father and friends still lay heavy on him.

"A King may mourn, but he cannot neglect his people," remarked Arestor.

"Take care your words Arestor," warned Darian.

They rode in silence awhile after that, until Eathelon broke it.

"Andolan is indeed a fair city, Arestor. No doubt it has the provisions we will need to continue our journey, but our means to procure them lie at the bottom of the Southern Sea. Perhaps there is some small service we can offer in exchange for what we will need."

"Do not worry, Eathelon, the people here are generous, and no more so than the King himself. I spoke with my Father last night. Aneron is sending Stefen and me north with a company of a hundred men, to *Toldor's Keep*, our northern fortress far up in the Eathen Mountains. You said you will ride north, so you may as well ride with us. There is safety in a company of soldiers and you will have no need for provisions. Even so, if you did, the King would provide them. My Father speaks with the King this morning. By the time we reach the top of the city, you should have your answer. I believe the King will grant your audience."

"You have proven a good friend in a short time," said Eathelon. "We will ride north with you and be glad of your company." He grinned and added, "Besides, you no doubt have more tales to share."

Arestor laughed. "Indeed, many, but your ears have already outlasted my tongue, so I may regret saying so. I confess I do love to tell them, but I give you fair warning — you may beg for sleep before I am finished!"

Eathelon laughed. "Sleep is a necessity, my friend, but your tales are like bread at my table. You will find me an eager listener, I am afraid."

"And me," Palo chimed in.

They laughed.

"Well, the campfire will be lively, at the least," Darian noted.

"Surely you must have heard all of Arestor's tales by now," remarked Eathelon.

"Sadly, I have not," proclaimed Darian. "Our duties keep us apart, and if you recall, he did not even recognize me on the back trail."

"Ouch!" Arestor interjected. "Do you plan to bring that up over and over?"

"Indeed, until I am satisfied you have been properly chastised!"

They laughed again.

The main road twisted and turned up to the level-five gate, which stood open, but had a posted guard.

The guard grew curious when he saw Palo, but seeing his Captain with these strangers, said nothing.

"The gates between the levels remain open unless the city is under threat, or the King orders them shut, usually for a drill."

They passed into and through a short tunnel, that ran under the wall between the levels, a gate and guard at each end.

"Are all of the gates so constructed?" asked Palo.

"Yes," replied Arestor. "A gate on each side of the wall, a short tunnel between them. The levels can then be closed off from one another, if necessary, trapping the enemy. Holes in the ceiling allow archers to assail anyone trapped from above."

"A most interesting idea," said Palo, "If the city has never fallen, it is untested though, yes?"

"An event anticipated may be one prevented," Eathelon offered. "So, I was taught."

"A fair point," conceded Palo.

As they passed through the tunnel, they saw it matched the thickness of the wall, one wide enough for soldiers to walk upon and high enough to assail an enemy from above.

"Untested or not, it is a thoughtful defense," declared Palo, as he rode through.

"If an enemy penetrated this far, the city surely would fall," Eathelon commented.

"The city will never fall," countered Arestor, in a tone that ended further discussion.

They rode on through level five, residential, and came to a set of clean, well-built stables.

"Who owns those?" asked Eathelon.

"The top breeders of Hamlan," replied Arestor. "The best horses in Hamlan are stabled here — the *pizos,* steeds of the King's Guard."

"Like yours," noted Eathelon, for he had noticed Arestor rode a different horse today than the one he'd ridden on the back trail.

"Yes," Arestor responded. "I see you noticed my horse."

"Flaxlings are the chosen breed of the Rangers," said Darian, "for they are swift and hearty, good for long days of riding on the southern plains."

"The pizos are a regal, muscular breed," added Arestor, "wide in girth, slower in gait, bred for battle. My other steed is stabled here, the one I rode on the back trail. I will ride him north, for it is a long, hard journey. He is neither a pizo, nor a flaxling, but a breed used for endurance."

"You are fortunate to own two such beautiful horses," exclaimed Eathelon.

They rode on through level five and Eathelon noticed a few large homes that stood out from the rest. Some had an upper level, which intrigued him. "Who lives in those?" he asked.

"Many of them belong to Andolan's merchants," said Arestor, "some to artists of renown or other citizens of wealth."

"Why do those houses have steep roofs?" asked Palo.

"Between the houses or other buildings by the wall lies a narrow trench, one wide enough for only a single man," replied Arestor. "The roofs are meant to be too steep to stand on and the alley too deep and narrow for anyone to breach the wall."

"An archer on the wall could easily assail anyone who attempted it," Palo stated. "Another impressive defense."

"Exactly the point, my Warrior friend," said Arestor.

"We have no such walls on Melatui," Palo noted. "Maagi Warriors fight each other on open land. Such is our code and we would never harm a woman or a child."

"It is a good code," Arestor confirmed.

"After the Eldarin arrived on Melatui, the Maagi stopped fighting, for the most part," Palo stated. "Oh, there is the occasional quarrel, of course, but Warriors are a dying breed, I fear."

"There will always be a need for Warriors, Palo to protect our isle and its people," claimed Eathelon, "just as Andolan's soldiers protect its people. And Warriors will always hold a place of honor, so long as I am King."

Palo's broad face beamed in appreciation.

"The soldiers of Andolan would not harm a woman or child, if such could be prevented, but the men of the East have no such code. They will kill anyone who gets in their way, man, woman or child."

"You are talking about Baele," surmised Eathelon.

"Yes, and his son Esol, and those who serve them," replied Darian.

"Who could possibly serve such evil men?" asked Palo.

"The Northmen, tribal men of the Northern Reaches, and the mercenaries of Rabellan. The Northmen are not very bright, and the mercenaries are criminals. They both lack honor and serve the East willingly." He paused. "Andolan may have been overbuilt, as some say, but considering the fate of the Eldarin, I do not think so. Had the Golden City been better protected, the Eldarin may still be here. If Andolan were to fall, no one in Narda would be safe."

"Surely not all in the East serve Baele and his son," remarked Eathelon.

"Unfortunately, many do," Arestor responded, "but there are no doubt some in the East who have remained loyal to Landrin and the House of Began. They could not say so, of course, for fear of reprisal."

The companions rode in silence, until they came to a place where the road widened and split. A narrow channel of swift-running water appeared down its middle and Eathelon scratched his head and looked puzzled, for no such water had been visible on the previous level.

"Where does that water come from?" he asked, "and where

does it go? It just appeared."

Arestor smiled. "Its source is in the Brunhyl. It dives beneath the ground at this level and surfaces at level two."

"An underground river," Eathelon said with admiration. "Andolan is a city of many interesting qualities."

They rode on one side of the channel and passed by several little bridges that spanned it at intervals, permitting people to cross from side to side.

"This is the main water supply to the city," Arestor pointed out. "Underground channels take it to the buildings and homes and another set far beneath the city carry off waste. Andolan is the cleanest city in Narda."

"Indeed, I see the truth of it with my own eyes," Eathelon asserted.

"Architects have studied Andolan's structures to build other cities like it," added Darian. "But its placement in the Brunhyl makes it unique, impossible to duplicate. Newcastle has a similar water and waste system, for it was built also to house a King and a large population, but their system is not as extensive as ours."

"Andolan has no equal," said Arestor, "though expansion here is limited now. Many of Hamlan's citizens have moved in since the Great War. Many others live outside the city walls, in the hills. The King has limited building in the city now and directly outside of its walls. He does not want to undo what the Eldarin worked hard to do to keep the city and surrounding lands clean and free of disease. There is little room left here for new construction now."

"People may take refuge here in times of calamity — or war, however," he continued. "There is a large cave system in the Brunhyl used for this purpose. That is how the Eldarin escaped to the ships. Most of its tunnels are natural, but some are manmade. The tunnel system has been under construction for more than 100 years, yet remains unfinished."

"Andolan must have architects capable of completing the project," Eathelon stated.

"Yes, though much of the earlier Eldarin technology and skills have been lost."

"In only 60 years? The Eldarin left nothing behind?" asked

Eathelon.

"It has been lost over a much longer period of time," said Darian.

They rode through levels six and seven and each level grew colder as they climbed farther into the hills. They passed by a House of Healing on level seven, its tall smooth columns rising from porch to roof. Empty chairs and benches sat on its porch and in the surrounding gardens, for it was too cold for anyone to occupy them now. Eathelon read the familiar message carved in stone above the columns, as they passed:

Enter here and be made well. In health and healing may you dwell.

A House of Healing is meant to be a place of comfort and trust, but it had not been so for the Queen and her babe. Anger welled up in Eathelon for the King's betrayal, fueled by the betrayal of his own Father.

Palo noticed the change in Eathelon and asked, "What is it Eathelon?"

Eathelon just shook his head.

Palo did not press him.

They rode through level eight as the sun fell farther down the sky and there passed through the seat of Hamlan's government and the residences of those who governed.

They came to level nine and passed through its gate.

"This level houses the royal servants, the King's Guard, their families and their steeds," said Arestor. "We are near level 10 now."

The road had become steeper through level nine but flattened out as they reached the level 10 gate ... the top of the Brunhyl. The gate bore a *T* in its center and lothingel leaves around its edges. The only entrance to the house of the King and his family, the gate was shut tight and members of the King's Guard posted before it. Eathelon noticed that the walls here stood higher than those on the previous levels.

As they rode up to the gate, two Guards stepped forward and crossed swords in front of the gate. Then six more came out of nowhere and surrounded them.

Chapter 12:
King of the West

Arestor dismounted and walked up to one of the Guards, his jaw tightened and a controlled urgency in his voice. "At ease, Thyrl, *a somë ando passarë* — let us pass. We bring an urgent message for the King."

He spoke briefly with Thyrl, as the other Guards stared uneasily at Palo. Then he and Thyrl clasped arms, Thyrl motioned the Guards to open the gate and the companions rode through, into the realm of the King of the West.

When they entered the courtyard, a tall handsome man approached, wearing the bright blue cape of the House of Toldor. His yellow hair shone in the waning sun and his blue eyes sparkled, as he walked up to greet them. Eathelon stared at the ornate silver headband with the small blue sapphire on the man's brow, and noticed the carved silver handle of his knife, which sat just above its leather scabbard, at his side.

"Well met, Stefen!" said Arestor, dismounting.

"Well met, Arestor," replied Stefen.

The companions had dismounted and stood by, as Arestor and Stefen clasped arms in greeting.

Stefen turned to Darian, "Well met, old foxx!" The two clasped arms. "You have returned at last. How fares our southern lands? Caught any Eastern spies of late?"

"Indeed, a few. We thought these two spies at first but, as it turns out, one is ... well, sort of kin."

Looking more curious than surprised, Stefen replied, "I see there is a story here. I trust you will tell me."

"I will, but that must wait. We bring an urgent message for the King, as you must know."

Eathelon and Palo were introduced to the Prince of Hamlan.

"Well met," said Stefen.

"Well met, sire," they replied.

"I spoke with the Captain of the Guard last night," said Arestor, "and asked him to request an audience with the King for these two. I have not spoken with him again since. Do you know if he was able to arrange this?"

"I spoke with your Father this morning," replied Stefen. "He passed the request on to me."

He turned to Eathelon and Palo. "The King has agreed to see you, albeit reluctantly. He awaits us in the Hall. I hope you understand that he is not at his best. He mourns the death of my stepmother and baby brother. I do not know what will come of your audience."

"I have no expectations, My Lord," Eathelon stated. "We have come to return a gift I believe will be of value to the King, and to deliver a message to him ... from an old friend."

Eathelon perceived a restrained grief in Stefen and he wanted to offer him some words of comfort, but decided he would wait for a more appropriate time.

"Come, leave your horses," said Stefen. "My men will see to them."

They followed Stefen up a winding path, through a wide expanse of lawn and well-tended gardens between the gate and the King's house. They passed by the Watchtower and Eathelon saw that it indeed rose high above the other buildings, as Arestor said, and the flag of the House of Toldor flew at its pinnacle. The wind stung their faces, as they crossed the courtyard, for they were not only at the top of the city, but the top of the Brunhyl.

"The wind can be fierce up here at times," Stefen pointed out. "Unlike the lower levels of the city, there is little up here to shield us from it."

"I have climbed the Watchtower," added Arestor. "It sometimes rises above the clouds ... an odd sight to see clouds below and stars above."

"It is a concern," Stefen continued, "that our enemy might approach from up here in the hills. We post Guards in the Watchtower at all times and soldiers in the smaller towers scattered in the hills. Should they see anyone approach, they toll bells in the towers and the Watchtower tolls a warning to the city. The gates shut tight and the soldiers go to battle posts. The King has sometimes tolled the bell without warning, as a drill to remind everyone that an uneasy state exists with the East. He has not done so for some months now. His attention has been on other matters."

"Perhaps he trusts the trade agreement more than he should," Arestor commented.

Stefen gave him a look of irritation for the remark, but Arestor just shrugged it off — he had evidently not been one to hold his tongue.

They arrived at the King's house, a large, two-level building with many windows. A porch spanned its width beneath several large columns, and behind them, two high, wide ornate doors stood with a *T* in the center and lothingel on a winding vine around the outer edges, as before. The King's Guard, posted at either side, opened the doors for Stefen and his guests to pas through. They stared at Palo as he passed by and he just grinned at them.

They entered the foyer, then walked through another set of doors into a large, rectangular hall, furnished with hand-carved tables, chairs, couches, woven rugs, wall hangings and sculptures. Huge stone columns lined the sides of the wide center aisle and both side aisles and furnishings sat in groups between them. Many of the columns bore images and tall, color-glass windows lined the outer walls on both sides of the hall.

"What images do those columns hold?" asked Eathelon.

"The history of Western Narda is depicted on them," replied Stefen.

One of the nearby columns caught Eathelon's attention. He walked to it and saw their faces, and the image of a full-scale battle. "The Great War," he commented.

"Yes," Stefen confirmed, coming alongside.

"It is one thing to learn about it, another to see its images," Eathelon admitted.

"All of the Kings of the West down to my Father are depicted on these columns. The story of each King's reign, important events — all the way back to the founding of this hall."

"I have never seen anything like it," said Palo.

"Who makes these images?" asked Eathelon.

"Various artists from the city — we have many such talents here."

The images and carvings encircled the columns bottom to top, but some columns stood empty.

"What about the empty ones?" asked Palo.

Stefen pointed first to one, then to another. "That one is for my Father's reign and that one is for mine. Those over there are for my sons and grandsons."

I wonder what happens when they run out of columns? Eathelon mused, but he did not ask.

They arrived at the marble steps leading to the dais. A high-backed, beautifully carved chair sat upon it — empty. Then a door opened behind it and a tall man emerged, dressed in the fine clothes befitting a King, including a dark-blue cloak fastened with a gold clasp. A simple gold crown with a large, deep-blue sapphire sat on the King's head, the bottom nearly lost in a tangle of dark brown curly hair that spilled down onto his shoulders and mingled with a long flowing beard. Both hair and beard were speckled with gray. Though not old by Eldarin standards, Aneron walked like an old man, his head and shoulders bent almost as if he'd not noticed his guests standing there.

"Father," Stefen spoke softly, "our guests have arrived."

The King nodded, gave a wave of his hand then straightened up his frame and walked over to stand before them. He gave them a weak smile of welcome. "Well met," he said. "Stefen has said you bring some urgent news."

Eathelon saw the grief in the King's hazel eyes, the same grief he'd seen in his Mother's eyes when his Father had passed. His own grief began to well up, but he managed to stay it. He felt empathy for this noble King so, fell to one knee and placed his arm across his chest. Palo did the same. But before either could speak, the King motioned them both up, saying, "We may dispense with any formalities today. If my only son brings strangers into my house, they are no longer strangers. Your message must be urgent indeed for you to request an audience in my time of sorrow. And while as a man, I may wish to refuse you, as your King I may not."

Seeing his opportunity, Eathelon addressed his next words to both the King and his son. "We learned only recently of your loss, My Lords, and we are deeply saddened. We are grateful that you have granted us this audience."

"Yes, Eathelon, is it?" the King said, with a vacant voice. "Well, life goes on whether we will it or not. Sometimes an ill wind blows, as it has for us — an ill wind that has come to our land and people, and any attempt I have made to forestall it has been in vain." He paused. "But you have not made your long journey to hear the rantings of a tired old King. Tell me, what message is so urgent that you interrupt my mourning?"

"Its importance is for you alone to decide, My Lord, and I bring you a gift from an old friend."

"Indeed, My Lord, I believe you will find his message hopeful," said Darian.

"What message could possibly be hopeful now? I doubt hope will find audience here."

"My Lord," Darian offered, "Eathelon is Prince of the Mallorites of Melatui, an island far off in the Westmost Sea. He does indeed bear a message of hope. Hear his message and you will see."

"A prince, you say? What about your companion?" He sighed. "We will have to retire to the couches for this. My tired old body does not so easily tolerate this hard throne for long, and I see there is a story here."

Stefen placed his hand on his Father's shoulder, as they walked to the couches, remarking, "Your body may be tired Father, but you are not yet old, and your strength will soon return."

They sat in the section nearest the dais and Aneron motioned Eathelon to begin his story, then stopped him before he could do so.

"Wait. Before you begin, tell me, what is a Mallorite? I have never heard of this race, nor of your isle." He turned to Palo. "Are you a Mallorite?"

"Hear my story, sire, and all of your questions will no doubt be answered," Eathelon stated.

Eathelon began his tale, handed down to him by the Eldarin, of how they arrived on Melatui after they fled Narda. "You no doubt heard that many Eldarin perished in the Southern Sea when they fled, including Darian's kin."

The King looked at Darian.

"I had heard this about the Eldarin," said the King. "The Southern Sea is treacherous in certain seasons of the year and word reached Andolan of the debris scattered across our southern beaches. I surmised the rest. We feared that all Eldarin who'd sailed in ships had perished, but of course hoped it was not true."

"Many did perish, but not all," Eathelon went on. "Of those who sailed into the Westmost Sea, most survived, including my Mother Lelar, a Syndar Eldarin. A child when her family fled Narda, they survived the genocide of the Golden City and made a new home on our isle. They called it *Mellærna*, or 'Morning Star', after the name of the ship that bore their ancestors to Narda in the First Age." He took a breath before continuing.

"My Father, the Maagi Warrior King of Melatui, wed my Syndar Mother, so I am half-Eldarin and half-Maagi, the firstborn Prince of the Mallorites, the new race created from the union of those two races. The name Eathelon means 'wise Warrior' in the Eldarin tongue. My Mother said I am so named for the wisdom of the Eldarin and the Warrior blood of the Maagi. My companion, Palo is a Maagi Warrior of Melatui, my protector, and friend."

Palo sat up a bit straighter in his chair.

The King leaned forward and listened with more interest now.

"I am surprised the Eldarin permitted your Mother to wed a Maagi, when such unions have long been against their custom, even unions between the Eldarin races themselves."

"Indeed, My Lord, though I confess it was a custom I did not fully understand, created long ago out of a need long since forgotten and carried forward out of its time and place, perhaps. But the Eldarin no longer keep this custom."

"What changed it?"

"Survival forced a change. Other Eldarin took Maagi husbands or wives, after my Mother's marriage, though some have remained true to the custom.

"What do you mean by survival?" asked Stefen. "You said yourself the Eldarin survived the voyage to your isle."

"Yes," replied Eathelon, "but the Eldarin races were much diminished in the Great War. They decided their intermarriage with the Maagi would help ensure their continued survival."

"Not as Eldarin." said the King.

"Well, the Eldarin still do exist, as was said, the three races in Melatui have continued to grow, albeit slowly. The races are three now: Maagi, Eldarin and Mallorite."

"This is a strange tale, Eathelon," the King commented, "but continue please."

"My Father passed just before I left to come here. My Mother rules in his stead now. Maagi custom holds that a Queen should rule should a King pass before his time and has no heir to sit the throne. Had I remained behind, I most likely would have taken up rule in my Mother's stead, but she sent me here."

"Then your errand must be important indeed," said the King.

"The passing of rule to a son is common here," said Stefen. "I have never seen rule pass to a Queen."

"You have undertaken your journey here in your own time of sorrow, it seems," said the King. "For this reason alone I am justified in granting this audience." The King smiled. "A Syndar Queen rules Melatui. I would never have expected to hear such a thing. Here only men rule. Perhaps our custom, too, will one day be outdated."

"This, I doubt," remarked Stefen.

"What do the Maagi think of this arrangement?"

"Most agree with it because it is custom, but clearly some disagree, for my Father lies in his tomb, yet he was a good King and in good health."

"And the Queen of Hamlan, although in good health and with child, lies with our son in the Tombs. Our tales are not so dissimilar, Eathelon."

"Sadly, they are not, My Lord. But this errand was too important to the Eldarin for me to remain on Melatui. Tides and seasons do not wait, my Eldarin mentor said. He agreed to investigate my Father's death. He has remained true to Eldarin custom, despite the fact that he arranged my Mother's marriage to my Father. He has long been the Head of the Eldarin Council both here and on Melatui. You no doubt know him — Celorn?"

Aneron sat up straight and his eyes went wide. "Celorn? Celorn lives?"

"Indeed, My Lord, it is Celorn who sent us."

The King sat back, a look of wonder on his face. "Your tale is indeed strange, Eathelon and, as you said, one of hope." He smiled. "Celorn! I have not heard that name for more than 50 years, yet often in my private thoughts have I wondered what became of my dear friend, whose company I most assuredly miss." He chuckled. "Celorn must be old now, like me."

"He is not old for an Eldarin," said Eathelon, "and his mind and spirit are yet young. It is Celorn's fondest hope that the Eldarin can return to Narda — to their Golden City. They, too, wish to see old friends again, friends they sorely miss. And Celorn said he wishes to right the wrong perpetrated on the West."

"Wrong? No, any wrong done to the West by our enemy was done first to the Eldarin. We failed to protect them."

The King became lost in his thoughts for a few moments, as his guests waited patiently. Eathelon perceived a change in the King. His grief had diminished and a light came into his eyes. Hope had indeed found him.

Twice after, the King called for food and drink, for Eathelon's tale was long in the telling. The sun's glow faded in the windows and Eathelon worried that he had kept the King overlong, but the monarch hung on his every word. Near the end of the tale, the King asked, "But why have the Eldarin not sent someone before now?"

"It has taken many years for them to recover their injury and sorrow, My Lord," Eathelon responded. "Most of them lost family and friends at the hands of the House of Tebor, betrayers of their people."

"We know well the story of that House and its ancestry," said Stefen, "and of the traitor Tebor, the Tynar Eldarin who set up his own ruling house in the East and paved the way for his descendant Baele to later plot the murder and exile of the Eldarin."

"But, for 60 years we have not known the fate of our Eldarin friends who fled Narda in their ships, so long ago," said the King.

"Nor could you, sire. The Eldarin did not expect to return. Only after their intermarriage with the Maagi did they consider the possibility. They believed it unwise to attempt it. They are still under threat of death here even now, so they had foresight in this. And their ships reached Melatui only by the grace of Ealdor. Palo and I, skilled seaman, barely made it here safely, and lost our ship and friends in the end."

"Grief has stricken everywhere, it seems," the King stated, looking sad again. "It comes as a thief in the night, when least expected, and slinks out again with the dawn, leaving a trail of sorrow in its wake."

"Then let us put our sorrow behind us, My Lord," offered Eathelon, "and turn our eyes forward. Palo and I need your help to bring your friends back. We did not know what we would find when we arrived, whether friend or enemy. By good fortune, Darian found us first and lifted us to safety, and Arestor befriended us and brought us here to you and Stefen. You are Celorn's most trusted friend and ally and he would be much relieved to know you still rule the West, that it has not fallen to the House of Tebor."

"By my Father's skill alone was the delicate trade agreement made possible with Baele," Stefen asserted.

"And Celorn's earlier influence on me," added the King.

"And Baele's incessant greed for Holling Vale *Dark Horse Red*," interjected Darian.

The King laughed for the first time in many weeks. "The man does seem to have a weakness for our best Holling Vale wines," he confirmed.

"I am not certain if that is good, or bad," said Stefen.

"Good, if it keeps him on his own side of Narda," replied the King. He turned to Eathelon. "You shall all remain here, as my guests. We have many rooms and I would like the honor of your company."

"The honor is ours, My Lord," Eathelon declared. "Of course, we will stay."

In truth, Eathelon felt relief at the King's invitation, for he wanted more time with the monarch, preferably alone. He'd been trying to decide how best to request this without offending his companions and, in the end, having come up with no other solution, he simply asked.

"I mean no disrespect to my companions, My Lord, but there is an urgent matter I must discuss with you ... in private."

Darian, Palo and Arestor all gave him a curious look, as he awaited the King's reply.

"I keep nothing from Stefen," Aneron pointed out. "He is my heir and needs to know my affairs. Was it not unexpected that my wife would die before her time?"

"You shall outlive us all Father," Stefen commented. "I will be an old man before I take the throne."

The King smiled at his son.

"Very well," Eathelon agreed, "then I would like to request a private meeting with you and Stefen."

Darian, astute in such matters, rose and spoke to the others, "Come, Arestor! Show Palo and me to our rooms." He slapped Palo on the back, "I have some important matters to discuss with you, my Warrior friend!" He winked at Eathelon and the three men left the room.

"What is so important that it is for the King's ears alone?" asked Aneron.

Eathelon reached under his cloak and pulled out the sling. Stefen and Aneron watched with interest as he held it in his hands and told them another story.

"Celorn told me that long ago your Father, King Feorn, had an Eldarin advisor Faras, a Nydar Eldarin, who kept a Seontir, a Seeing Stone, in this house, used for functions of great importance to King Feorn and the West. Faras brought the Stone to Andolan from the Golden City and it remained with him throughout all of his time here, for these Stones can be wielded only by an Eldarin."

Eathelon paused, as the King thought for a moment.

"I remember this Stone," he declared, chuckling. "I explored this house often as a boy and, one day I discovered an entrance to the Watchtower, previously hidden to me. My Father had left the door unlocked and, curious, I entered. It led to a long hall, which I followed to the end, where I found many stairs and began to climb. I was young and tired before I could reach the top. When I sat down to rest, I heard Father's voice and walked toward it. I tried the few doors on that level but all were locked, save the last, which stood ajar. I peered into the room and saw Father and Faras standing across from one another, a green Stone sat atop an ornate stand between them. They had their eyes fixed on it and they spoke together in a language I did not understand. Distracted, I slipped and the door creaked open, revealing my presence. My Father hurried over and sent me away, not unkindly, then closed and locked the door. It was the last time I saw that Stone, but my memory of it is quite clear. Father kept the door to the Watchtower locked after that and he possessed the only key. When asked him about the Stone, he said only that one day he would tell me about it, but he passed without doing so. When I became King, I found his keys among his possessions and unlocked the doors leading to the Watchtower. I found the room, hoping it still contained the Stone, but I found there only the stand, not the Stone. I searched the entire house and never found it. After I became involved with my duties as King, I forgot about it. I kept that room locked, as my Father had done before me, but never entered it again."

"You did not find the Stone because Faras took it when he fled Narda. He followed the tunnels out of the city and into the Brunhyl with many other Eldarin who had taken refuge there. They boarded their ships in Bali and sailed into the Westmost Sea, without any idea of a destination. Celorn said that Faras, old even by Eldarin standards, perished on the voyage, but the Stone came safely to Melatui, where Celorn has kept it safe for the past 60 years."

Aneron grew visibly excited, as he gazed at the cloth, no doubt making a guess about what it held.

"There existed five Stones in all," continued Eathelon. "Three went to the extant Kings of Narda — one to Feorn, two to *Laenig* in the East — Landrin's Father."

"Why two to the East?" asked Stefen.

"Each Stone was accompanied by an Eldarin advisor to wield it. Laenig sent one of his, Aldo, the Fire Stone, to *Madrin*, Governor of Gorst at the time. He kept *Ule* — the Wind Stone and its advisor at Castletop, home to the House of Began. Parma, a teaching Stone, and *Yala*, the Power Stone remained with the Eldarin, in the Golden City. So, you see two Stones went East and three remained in the West."

"I see," said Stefen.

"What are these Stones used for?" asked Aneron.

"Celorn said only that the Stones are, or were used for functions of great importance to Narda. He did not say *how* they were used, only that they somehow linked Andolan, the Golden City, Castletop and *Gazlag,* in Gorst, and that instructions for their use would be contained in the Book of Stones."

"Where is this Book of Stones?" asked Aneron.

"He said it did not come to Melatui, that it is hidden in the Golden City."

"Do you believe these Stones are some kind of magic?" Stefen queried.

Eathelon smiled, remembering the amulet. "I do believe some kinds of magic, but if what Celorn stated is true, these Stones are not magic exactly, but some kind of ancient system of communication. I suppose they may seem much like magic to us now. Celorn said the wielder can see images in the Stone, of places and things near or far, but, without the knowledge and instruction contained in the Book of Stones, he cannot be certain of the message revealed in the Stone." Eathelon paused for a breath.

"Did Celorn tell you where to find this Book of Stones?" asked Stefen.

"Not exactly, but he did give me some idea where to look for the book."

"I am beginning to understand more about your errand," the King stated,

Eathelon had unwound the cloth as he spoke, and he came to a point just short of revealing its contents, as he continued his tale.

"Of the three missing Stones, the Power Stone seems the most vital, but Celorn did not say why. It was one of the Stones kept by the Eldarin in the Golden City. They evidently do not work well individually — they must be linked."

"Then they are of no use, unless all five are located," said the

King.

"Correct," replied Eathelon. "Celorn believes the Fire Stone may still be in Gorst. He fears Baele has it, but doubts he knows how to use it."

"That is ill news," said Stefen.

"Did Celorn say why he believes Baele has the Stone?" asked the King.

"It went missing before Baele invaded Gorst. He said it is only a guess, but a good one, I believe. My presence in Narda may be known to Baele, whether by use of the Fire Stone or some other intelligence."

"What do you mean?" asked Stefen.

"Palo and I have been dogged by fyrcaats since we arrived and we found a collar on one killed by a sinter hawk. In fact, I believe the hawk may have saved my life. I understand fyrcaats live in the East. The collar suggests it is someone's pet."

"I have heard Baele keeps fyrcaats for pets," offered the King. "Darian's informants have suggested it. If you have been dogged by fyrcaats bearing a collar, Baele is the likely owner."

"It is also said Baele has grown mad, whether by improper use of the Stone, or another reason. I do not know," mentioned Eathelon.

"Baele *is* mad," Stefen exclaimed, "though I doubt this is due to the Stone. Still, this is troublesome news."

The King frowned. "What of the other Stone, the one held by the House of Began at Castletop? That House is occupied by the enemy now."

"That Stone was last at Castletop, but Celorn has no idea if it is still there or if perhaps Landrin took it into exile."

"Landrin did not take the Stone to the Flax Isles," said the King. "He would have told me. We have long been friends and allies and we remain in touch even today."

"Perhaps he kept this information from you to ensure it did not fall into the wrong hands, Father," volunteered Stefen.

"A valid point, Stefen, but I doubt Landrin has this Stone."

"I have not shared all of this information with my companions," admitted Eathelon

"Why not?" asked Stefen.

"Only my Mother Lelar, Celorn and our three friends knew anything of our errand concerning the Stones. I will tell the others when the time is right." He sighed. "Baele is plotting war against the West, it is said. Until this threat is removed, it is not safe for the Eldarin to return. I am tasked with finding the missing Stones and the Book of Stones, for only then can I have some idea of how to restore the Stones to their full power, to help the West."

"How can we help?" asked the King.

"This errand of yours will lead us to war," Stefen proclaimed, bitterly.

"My intent is to prevent another genocide, Stefen, not start a war," Eathelon clarified.

"War will come to us Stefen, whether Eathelon finds the Stones or not," the King commented. "It has been brewing for some time, as well you know."

"The Stones are of such value that should Baele find them before we do, he would no doubt use them to wipe out the West."

"And is it not our intention to wipe out the East with them?" asked Stefen.

"Wipe them out? No," replied the King, "but put down the House of Tebor, yes. It is only a matter of time before Baele makes his move. I believe he intended this all along."

Eathelon unwrapped the last bit of cloth and held up its contents. "Behold — I give you the Eorth Stone! I return it now, to its rightful place in Andolan."

Aneron and Stefen gazed at the dark green orb, which sat dull and lifeless in Eathelon's hands.

"Of what use is the Stone to us here, without the rest?" asked Stefen.

Eathelon replied, patiently, "It is of little use, as was said. But with this Stone tucked safely away in the fortress city, it cannot fall into enemy hands and there is little they can do without all five of them. Our shipmates who perished came with us to wield two of the Stones, should they be found, so their loss is grievous. But, by luck we have found another who can wield this Stone, someone I did not expect to find. You know the Eldarin of whom I speak."

The King sat back and smiled, but said nothing.

Eathelon saw a light come on in Stefen's eyes. "Darian. But even if he knew about the Stone, he does not know how to wield it."

"No. I must first find the Book of Stones, and I will tell him when the time is right. Until he knows how to wield the thing, why burden him with the problem?"

"Did Celorn tell you where to find the Power Stone, Eathelon?" asked the King.

"He said they last had it in Malta, but does not know what became of it when the enemy laid waste to the Golden City."

"Let us hope they did not find it," Stefen remarked.

"Such is my hope," replied Eathelon. He paused. "Here then, is how you can help us. My companions and I would like to ride north with your company, Stefen. Arestor has offered it. We will need provisions, once we leave the company, but our means to procure them lie now at the bottom of the Southern Sea."

"You shall ride with our company, Eathelon," said Stefen.

"And I will provide whatever provisions and funding you need for the rest of your journey," added the King.

"Thank you, My Lords. I ask now that the Eorth Stone be placed in its stand and the room locked, as before. Keep the key with you at all times, My Lord, until we can activate the Stones, assuming we find them. Celorn said the Stones only work in their designated stands. And there is one more thing."

"Yes?" asked the King, his eyebrows raised, for no one, save his wife and children, had ever spoken to him in this way.

"You understand now, the importance of the connection between the Eldarin and the Stones. I seek an Eldarin maiden, said to inhabit Northwest Wood, with the Elvenkin. Celorn mentioned the couple and I wish to go there after I leave the Golden City. Celorn gave me something to return." Eathelon offered nothing further and Stefen did not press him.

"I have heard tale of this maiden," replied Aneron, "though little enough, for the Elvenkin have long been sundered with Andolan."

"Eathelon," Stefen suddenly changed the subject, "you are half Eldarin. "Why can you not simply wield a Stone yourself?"

"I would try, should it come to that. But I am only *half* Eldarin, remember, so my ability to wield a Stone is in doubt. Darian can do it."

"Should he return," Stefen stated, thoughtfully.

"The future is uncertain regarding for any of us at this time," Eathelon admitted, "but we intend to return to Andolan."

He turned back to the King. "Can you tell nothing more about this maiden then?"

"No. I traveled once to Northwest Wood ... long ago. *Mengalan*, Lord of the Wood, is an old ally of mine, but as was said, our relationship has long since been sundered. The Elvenkin keep mostly themselves. I do not know if they will welcome you."

Eathelon thought about the amulet. "I believe they will."

"Well, Arestor and I must leave with the company in the morning," Stefen remarked. "Our journey north will take us to the Southern Crossroads. We are escorting a large company of soldiers to Toldor's Keep, our northern fortress in the *Highland Gap*. You can ride with us as far as the Crossroads. The trail splits there. The east trail will take you to Malta and on up into the Golden City. The ride to the Southern Crossroads is long, so we shall be glad of your company for a time. There is still much to learn about you, my Mallorite friend."

"We shall delay your departure for a day or two, Stefen," the King declared. "I want to complete my counsel with Eathelon. Purchase any extra provisions he and his companions will need after they leave your company."

The King addressed Eathelon again. "I regret that I cannot tell you more about the maiden, Eathelon, but you will no doubt find out what the Elvenkin know once you reach their wood. Let us adjourn. The hour is late and we are all in need of rest."

Stefen walked Eathelon to his room, one that sat between those of his companions. A fire had been set to warm it and he climbed gratefully onto the soft bed and fell into a restful sleep.

Chapter 13: Preparations

Stefen and Arestor left to complete preparations for the journey north, and Darian offered to give Palo a tour of the city. Eathelon met with the King again and, during their last meeting, a young woman entered.

"There you are Father," she said.

"Scirra," replied the King, "come and meet our guest."

"Where have you been, Father? Is everything alright?" she asked, as she approached.

Eathelon stared at Stefen's sister, whose earlier description matched what Darian had told him — fair of skin, cheeks the color of *petiperls*, eyes the color of *blubels* and long yellow curls that poured down in waves over her slender shoulders.

"I am much improved, daughter."

Indeed, for he stood straighter and color had returned to his pale cheeks.

Ignoring his guest for the moment, Scirra asked her Father, "To what do we owe this good fortune?"

"Not to what, but to whom," replied the King. He turned to Eathelon, "My daughter, Scirra."

Eathelon bowed slightly and smiled warmly. "Well met, My Lady."

She acknowledged him with a smile and slight curtsy.

"Our guest is Eathelon, Prince of the Mallorites of Melatui," the King explained.

"Well met ... My Lord."

Like a yellow songbird on the branch of a cherry tree in spring, Scirra cocked her head and surveyed him from head to toe. "Meaning no offense, but what exactly is a Mallorite? I have not heard of one."

Eathelon smiled. "I will leave the explanation to your Father, My Lady. He knows well my tale."

"He is kin to Darian," added the King.

Scirra gave her Father a look of skepticism. "But I thought Darian had no kin." She looked at Eathelon. "How are you two related?"

"As ever, daughter, you are astute, but impertinent," the King said proudly.

Eathelon smiled, "It is alright, My Lord." He turned to Scirra. "Darian and I discovered this fact only days ago, My Lady."

"I see," she replied. She paused as if the fate of the world depended on her next words, while Eathelon waited patiently. At last, she smiled and said, politely, "Well then, I would love to hear your tale, perhaps at a more appropriate time."

"Did I not say what a treasure she is?" the King asked Eathelon, grinning.

"Indeed, My Lord." It was evident that Scirra had captured her Father's heart.

"We are all fond of Darian," Scirra offered. "He is family to us." She blushed a little then changed the subject. Her reaction did not escape Eathelon's notice.

"Father, there is a matter I wish to discuss with you, in private. I am afraid it cannot wait."

He turned to Eathelon. "If you will excuse us, Eathelon."

"Of course, My Lord." He walked to the other side of the hall. He could not hear their words but he noticed intangible similarities between the King and his daughter. Her poise impressed him and the fine drape of her dress on the lovely curves of her body did not escape his notice. He watched them with interest, but remained respectfully aloof.

After the conversation ended, the King motioned Eathelon back. Scirra curtsied and smiled, then walked away, as Eathelon's eyes followed her long lake-blue skirts swaying to and fro. His eyes lingered in her direction a moment, and the King chuckled.

"Her Mother had the same effect on me." He sighed. "Scirra is my sun and moon, as her Mother was, but she is a challenge for me at times. She is somewhat unique, is she not?"

"Indeed, My Lord, and beautiful."

The King smiled. "She is the loveliest woman in Andolan, at least to my eyes, but not just in her physical beauty. Her little outburst of disbelief is unusual but, as she has grown older, she has become more outspoken. In wisdom and manners, she is much like her Mother, I think."

"But she appears to command herself much like you, My Lord."

Aneron gave him a half-smile. "Perhaps," he said. He paused. "I have had — and lost — two wives, Eathelon. I did not expect to outlive either of them. Fate is strange."

"Indeed, My Lord. My own journey here has already turned out far different than I expected. But I believe a man may bend fate to his own purposes."

The King smiled. "I think you will make a good King one day, Eathelon."

His comment signaled the end of their meeting.

The next morning, one day before their scheduled departure, the three companions sat for brefas at the King's table, but dined alone. Darian offered to show Eathelon the city.

"It is a most interesting place," said Palo, putting away a large helping of eggs and sweet cakes. "Darian showed me parts of it yesterday." He washed his food down with the juice of oranges, brought in from a nearby orchard. He looked at Darian. "Perhaps we can visit some of those shops we passed." He wiped his face with his sleeve, and grinned.

Eathelon grimaced at Palo's bad table manners.

"A Warrior wants to visit our shops," Darian commented. "I see Andolan is growing on you, Palo."

"Well, we may as well look while we are here," Palo defended. "I can use a few things for our coming journey."

"Take us where you will," Eathelon said to Darian. "It may be our last opportunity for a long time."

"Alright then meet me outside the level 10 gate in an hour," Darian remarked. "I will fetch our horses."

Eathelon spent the hour in his room, pouring over a map of the city with Palo, one Stefen had provided. They met Darian outside the gate at the appointed time and mounted to leave, as Stefen rode up with Scirra. Eathelon smiled at her and she returned the gesture.

"I had hoped to complete my preparations and accompany you," said Stefen, "but too many tasks remain yet. Scirra has offered to show you the city. She has lived here all of her life and knows Andolan well."

Darian laughed, "Of course she does! She roams the city, while I am off riding the southern plains." He winked at her.

Stefen turned to Eathelon, "Father said the two of you have met."

"Last evening," said Eathelon. He addressed Scirra. "This is Palo, my Maagi companion, My Lady."

"You may call me by my name, Eathelon."

He nodded.

"Well met," Scirra addressed Palo with a reserved smile, "What is a Maagi?"

"Would you like the long version, or short, My Lady?" Palo replied politely.

"The short one, if you please."

"Maagi is short for *Maagigasci*, the name of my race and the isle from which it originated. That isle was destroyed in an eruption of *Mt. Minatoa* long ago and my people migrated to Melatui, the isle on which we now live. The name Maagigasci was later shortened to Maagi. We are a Warrior race."

"Most interesting," replied Scirra.

Palo acknowledged her with a nod.

Stefen listened politely then turned to leave. "Enjoy the sights of the city while you may, friends. Our journey north will be long and without such pleasures." He winked at his sister and rode off.

Eathelon wondered at the meaning of these unspoken messages that passed between Father and daughter, brother and sister. Some sort of family code, he decided.

Darian said to Scirra, playfully, "Come Scirra, take us to whatever parts of the city you believe may have remained hidden to me."

Scirra gave Darian a half-smile and maneuvered her horse next to Eathelon, then paused as if to see if Darian reacted. But Darian just laughed and put his horse behind hers, next to Palo and they set off, two and two down the wide paved road toward the lower levels of the city.

Eathelon found it difficult to keep his mind off of his coming journey and his anxiety rose as he posed questions with few answers. Would he find the missing Stones? The Book of Stones? If he found the Eldarin maiden in Northwest Wood, would she be able to tell him anything about the Stones? Would the Elvenkin welcome him, as Celorn said? Was Darian a family friend, or was something more going on between Darian and Scirra?

They rode down through the levels, passed by the government buildings, the House of Healing, the merchant's homes, a school, a park and arrived at the fourth level, where they had first entered the city.

"Scirra, our tour of the city thus far has mainly been to pass by these shops," said Darian.

"Well, perhaps that *is* the tour. I understand Palo requested it."

Darian smirked, "I see our tour is to the city shops. I suppose I could have better spent my time on preparations."

"Let us not underestimate how much our guests may like the shops," Scirra replied. She looked at Eathelon and smiled.

Her capricious attitude captivated him.

"How much *you* like the shops, you mean," Darian challenged.

Scirra ignored the remark.

They rode on and a moment or so later, Palo said, "Stop!" They halted before a clothier shop. Palo had evidently seen something he liked in the window. He dismounted and entered, and others followed. He went to the window, removed a leather vest from the display and held it up to his large body. Too small. He put it back. He walked over to a nearby table, rifled through some others, but found nothing large enough.

"Andolan appears to carry few vests for a tall, wide-girthed Warrior," Eathelon exclaimed with a smile.

Palo frowned.

"Wait here," said Scirra and she walked to the back of the shop. She returned a few minutes later with a large vest. "Try this one, Palo. It looks suitable for a Warrior of your stature."

Darian smiled, "Scirra is a master at shopping, Palo. You would do well to take her advice."

Palo grinned and put the vest on, then removed it and handed it back. "Thank you, My Lady, but it is not quite what I looked for."

Scirra put the vest on the table with the others.

Eathelon pulled Palo aside. "What is it Palo?" he whispered. "I thought the vest perfect."

Palo gave him a look and a gesture, hidden from Darian and Eathelon understood. They had not brought any funds with which to make a purchase.

"Perhaps another shop will have what you want," Scirra commented.

Coming to Palo's rescue, Eathelon urged, "There are some other parts of the city I would like to see, if you are willing, perhaps the House of Healing we passed by earlier."

They left the shop and mounted their horses to continue the tour.

"You may ride with Darian, My Lady," Eathelon said to Scirra. "I have some things to discuss with Palo."

Darian grinned. "Certainly ... My Lady."

Scirra, pulled Eathelon's horse alongside of her own. "I would not think of it. This is the first, and perhaps only time I will have an opportunity to tour a Mallorite Prince around the city." She smiled.

Darian laughed and took his place next to Palo.

Eathelon smiled at her, as they started off again. They toured for most of the day, and this took Eathelon's mind off of his unanswered questions, as he took in the sights and sounds of the city. He felt happy in the company of his new friends. He again mentioned his desire to see the House of Healing.

A shadow passed over Scirra's face, as she replied, "Perhaps another time, Eathelon."

Realizing his error, for he had unintentionally reminded her of her recent loss, he offered an apology. "I am sorry, Scirra. I am curious, is all. I am a student of the healing arts."

Scirra nodded and smiled but made no comment.

Truthfully, Eathelon hoped to look around the House of Healing for ... what? Some clue to help unravel the mystery surrounding the Queen's death? Birthing was a basic skill all healers learned well, even for complicated births. But it was really none of his business and he would not help resolve it any more than he would help resolve his Father's death back on Melatui. Both only served to remind him of the urgency of his errand — and his own uncertain future.

The day waned, as they rode back up the levels toward the King's house. Soon the sun fell into the cradle of the Brunhyl, leaving the city in shadow.

"The Eldarin influence in the city is very visible," Eathelon commented as they neared the top level.

"Yes, the Eldarin influence in Narda has been great," Darian confirmed.

They arrived back at the King's house at dusk and were urged by the staff to clean up and go at once to the Banquet Hall, where a feast had been set to honor the soldiers leaving to Toldor's Keep.

"The soldiers are gone for many months," Darian remarked. "The King always holds a banquet in their honor that includes their families, who live without them for half a year or more. It has become a tradition."

"I am hungry enough, after the long day of riding," said Palo. "I am eager for a feast."

"You will not be disappointed, my friend," Darian assured him.

The companions cleaned up and walked to the banquet hall, where the festivities had just begun. The tables were set with every kind of food Hamlan offered, purchased from the Open Market: meat from the ranches of Southern Hamlet, fish from nearby lakes and streams, fruits and vegetables from orchards and farms, local brews from Grenway and Rath and fine wines from Holling Vale, including a rare bottle of *Dark Horse Red* visible at the King's table.

The King, Stefen and Scirra already seated, gestured for the companions to join them at the King's table. It sat perpendicular to a long table, forming a "T." The King sat in the center at the head, with Stefen to his right and Scirra to his left. Darian took a seat next to Scirra and Eathelon next to Darian. Arestor sat next to Stefen and Palo took the empty seat next to Arestor. They were seven in all, at the King's table.

Some departing soldiers of renown and some government officials sat at the long table and smaller tables, scattered about the hall, accommodated soldiers and their families. The staff served food to all and the King stood and made a toast to the soldiers and their families. After the meal, much lively conversation and merriment ensued, including dancers, musicians and a magician.

An honored guest at the King's table, Eathelon remained reservedly polite and drank sparingly. He did not want the effects of wine to cloud his judgement or loosen his tongue. Such could not be said of his companions, however and of Palo in particular, whose large frame and girth gave him a near bottomless stomach. Palo ate and drank great quantities of everything with little effect.

During the meal, a soldier approached Arestor, spoke with him briefly, then left. Arestor whispered something to Darian and the two left on some errand. Stefen motioned for Palo to take Arestor's vacant seat and Scirra had Eathelon take Darian's. She explained to Eathelon that they considered it bad manners to leave a guest next to an empty chair. Soon all had engaged in lively conversation again, Palo with Stefen, Scirra with Eathelon.

Scirra called a server over to pour them each another glass *Dark Horse Red*. Eathelon accepted only to be polite and although he sipped it slowly, the wine soon began to loosen his tongue. He began to talk without inhibition. So did Scirra.

"Ours is a life of privilege," said Scirra, taking a sip of wine. "But it is also one of burdens, do you not think?"

"I do," agreed Eathelon. "Most people do not understand. They believe ours only a life of privilege, yet we sometimes carry heavy responsibilities and burdens they will never see."

"Indeed, we are taught to put our people's needs ahead of our own, whether we wish to or not, even if it is not best for us … personally."

"I suppose so, yes."

"Were you not chosen for this errand because you are the Prince of Melatui?"

"I do not understand the question, My Lady."

"Well, there must have been others equally qualified to

make the journey. It seems a dangerous journey for the only son and heir to the throne to make himself. Suppose something happens? Who would take the throne in your absence? Did you not say you have already lost two companions? Palo is a Warrior, so his choice seems suitable enough, but why would your people want to risk sending the King's only heir?"

Eathelon smiled with tolerance. Her questions and comments bordered on impertinence, but he knew she meant well. "I, too, am a Warrior, Scirra," he said, "though perhaps I do not look the part as much as Palo. And he accompanied me not only because he is a Warrior and protector, but also because he is my good friend."

Seeing her error, she offered, "I meant no offense, Eathelon. I made the point only to say because you are the son of a King. I should think the King would want to protect his only son." She took another sip of wine.

"The King agreed to my errand, though he passed before I left. And being the son of a King, much is expected of me, as I suppose is also the case with your brother."

She confused and charmed him in equal measure but he felt off balance around her. Or, perhaps it was the wine.

Scirra sighed. "True, I suppose. Responsibility is our lot, in any case."

He realized at that moment that something had to be troubling her. "What is it Scirra, what troubles you?"

She turned her body toward him, away from the King's eyes and lowered her voice. "I must wed a man I do not love ... or even know. Father arranged it when we were infants, if you can imagine. It is a silly, outdated custom." She pouted.

"The King seems reasonable enough. He even told me you are his moon and stars." *Or was it sun and moon?* He definitely was feeling the effects of the wine. "Surely, he will let you out of this arrangement, if he knows how strongly you feel about it

"He will not. I have asked more than once but he stands fast on his decision. The arrangement would create an alliance important to Narda, he said. My feelings are hardly of primary concern."

"What alliance?"

"One between East and West, of course," she replied. "Father and Landrin, the rightful King of the East living in exile, believe that East and West should unite under a single rule, for the good of Narda. Father said he cares little who becomes King, whether Stefen or Landon, Landrin's son, who I am to wed. But I know he would prefer Stefen to be King of Narda."

"If your Father wants Stefen to be King, then Stefen should marry Landrin's daughter. Would that not solve the problem?"

"Well, yes, but of course Landrin would like his own son to rule. The two Kings made a pact ... for both children — Stefen is to wed Liana and I am to wed Landon. The two Kings are assured of a united Narda either way."

"But if Landrin lives in exile and Baele now has the Eastern throne, how could such a marriage pact unite Narda?"

"Father is willing to wait. He believes Landrin will be restored to his throne."

Eathelon knew there was little comfort he could give Scirra in her dilemma, so he simply took her hand and smiled, "Well then, it is my fondest hope for you that you may marry whomever you truly love."

She smiled warmly at him and gently withdrew her hand. "My marriage to Landon is to be my fate, I am afraid, even if I must live a life I do not rush to embrace."

"I understand," replied Eathelon, and he did, to some degree, for he'd not volunteered for this errand yet could not refuse it. He did not seek to be King, yet one day he would be. He took another sip of wine, sighed and wondered what it would be like to simply remain here, in Andolan, perhaps with Scirra, or another woman worthy of his affections. Had he not already pledged himself to the King? But before he could answer his own question, Darian returned and Eathelon moved back to his own seat.

Scirra quickly engaged in conversation with her Father and Eathelon watched with interest. Darian watched Eathelon watching Scirra, who was bold, but respectful with her Father. Then Scirra turned and began a conversation with Darian and Eathelon perceived the two of them held something back from each other. Whatever it was, he knew it would remain a secret.

The banquet lasted far into the night but the companions

excused themselves well before it ended and left to their rooms to sleep. They were to begin their long journey north at dawn and wanted to be well rested.

The next morning, the King bid them farewell at the level 10 gate and wished them all a safe journey. "Send word to me of your progress, as often as possible, Stefen," he instructed.

To Eathelon's disappointment, Scirra did not come to say goodbye.

The King offered an excuse, saying, "Scirra asked me to bid you all 'safe journey'. Her scheduled duties kept her away this morning."

Or, was it something else?

Several young women had caught Eathelon's eye on Melatui, but none had captured his heart, or even his interest, beyond a fleeting amusement. He felt drawn to Scirra's energy, beauty and intellect, and after talking with her at the banquet, he found that he also admired her courage and loyalty. But he decided he had misjudged her interest in him. He turned his thoughts to the journey ahead.

Stefen and Arestor met them outside the level 10 gate. They mounted their horses and joined them, and the five men made their way down the winding paved road to the front gates of the city. They exited and joined the company, which was already assembled on the grassy fields of the lower Brunhyl.

Stefen called the company to order and Arestor gathered the soldiers into five groups of 20. He appointed a leader for each group and brought them together for a briefing, then gave an order for the company to move out. They rode off, with Eathelon, Darian and Palo behind Stefen and Arestor, at the head of the company.

As they rode away, Eathelon turned back to look at the majestic gates of Andolan, the expansive fortress city in the hills. *City in the Clouds*, he recalled, and he considered his time with Aneron, a King who inspired him very much, and with Scirra, the coy princess with cheeks the color of petiperls and eyes the color of blubels.

Chapter 14:
The Company Rides North

"Where do we go first?" Eathelon asked Darian.
"To *Heath* — about 20 leagues north, much of it downhill. We should arrive there the day after tomorrow, if all goes well."

Eathelon told Darian how much he liked Aneron's family, and he gently approached the subject of Scirra.

"She is rather unique," said Darian. "Everyone is taken with her when they first meet her ... but she is promised to another."

"So she said."

Eathelon quickly changed the subject. "Narda's geography differs much from our isle. Melatui has flat lands, high mountains and a long coastline, but Narda's lands and coastline are far more vast by comparison, even if we count our archipelago, which includes other small islands."

"Narda's geography is indeed diverse, more so than what you have seen thus far," Darian agreed. "Hamlan has several interesting regions, but the Lowlands, the natural divide between Western and Eastern Narda are mostly inhospitable."

"Which region of Hamlan do you like best, Darian? Which areas do you find the most beautiful here?"

"Well, the Eathen Mountains and Sylvan Mountains, both ancient, are tall and majestic, and their forests lush and green, though they differ somewhat in quality. Hamlan's northern plains are green and lush with grass. The southern plains dry, as you discovered, yet many rivers, lakes and streams abound in Hamlan and our flowers are varied and beautiful. Our bridges and structures, designed by the Eldarin, are unequaled in Narda."

"I am eager to see more of Hamlan. Have you ever been to

the East?"

"No, for it is not safe, but I have heard tales of it. The Fyr Mountains are barren, and foul creatures still dwell in some parts of the East, though none are fouler than the House of Tebor itself and that has little or nothing to do with geography." He grinned.

Eathelon smiled.

"Newcastle was once a beautiful city, but after being occupied by the House of Tebor these past 60 years, I doubt it has remained so."

They rode and talked thus and, on their first night out of Andolan, camped on the open plains below the Brunhyl, the five groups of 20 men each at their own campfire and the five companions at theirs. After the meal, Stefen and Arestor went to brief the group leaders and set a watch. Eathelon wrapped himself up in his woolen cloak and laid down near Palo and Darian, grateful that the air had warmed as they'd descended from the hills. It was Earlyfall and Eathelon knew winter would soon follow and spread its frosty fingers over the northern lands, where he and his companions now headed.

"I am not much accustomed to cold weather," Eathelon stated, "though it does get cold at the tops of Melatui's peaks."

"Our trek north should give you time to acclimate yourself," said Darian. "It will be cold in Malta and Northwest Wood." He yawned. "The Northern Crossroads lie at the foot of the Eathen Mountains and we will take that road to reach the Wood."

The air is damp here," exclaimed Palo, "almost like down by the sea. I did not expect it to be so."

"The wind sometimes blows down off of the Brunhyl, bringing moisture from the sea," Darian pointed out. He yawned again. "Get some sleep now. We leave again at dawn."

But Eathelon did not fall sleep. He laid back and stared up at the multitude of stars in the clear night sky, punctuated by ragged clouds drifting by that partially hid the moon. But sufficient light remained for him to see the outline of the Brunhyl they had left behind and he suddenly thought about Scirra. *One day I will take a wife. I hope the woman I choose will awaken the same feelings in me Scirra did.* He paused. *Aneron said I will make a good King, but he knows little about me. Father was a good King* ... but that thought got him thinking again about his Father's untimely death and the mystery surrounding it. He decided he would probably never solve it and he drifted off to sleep. When he awoke, his thoughts had vanished and he felt ready to resume his journey and meet head on whatever circumstance it may bring.

After a light meal, they mounted and started off and, after a time, came to a wide dirt road that looked well-traveled. Riding at the head of the company as before, the companions talked together, as the company continued at an unhurried, comfortable pace.

"These lands looked flat from atop the Brunhyl," said Eathelon, "but this road rises and falls through the lands."

"Like the southern plain we crossed," added Palo.

"Yes," replied Darian, "the southern plains do rise and fall, but they steadily rise toward the Brunhyl. That land is rocky and hard. This one is smooth, by comparison."

"And this road is well-traveled, it seems," noted Eathelon.

"Yes, for it is traveled often by Andolan's soldiers."

"At least the grass here does not make one drowsy," Palo interjected.

Darian laughed. "No, caleopsi grass is an oddity of Numar, planted long ago to provide protection for caravans traveling between Numar and Andolan. It turned out to be both a good, and not so good idea."

"What do you mean?" asked Palo.

"Caleopsi grass is taller than a tall man, as you no doubt discovered, so it provided excellent cover for the Nomad caravans. But it also hid the thieves who sometimes ambushed the caravans. The grass originates in *Grenelan*, where it grows wild between the *River Dansen* and the *Rym Mountains*. The Nomad caravans once carried goods to *Sylmar* and *Pynth*. They were sometimes robbed, so the Nomads seeded the routes with caleopsi grass. They had long since been immune to its effects, of course, and intended it to slow down the thieves, which it did. When the Nomads expanded their routes to include Numar and Heath, and later Andolan, they seeded the southern plains with the grass. But once the House of Tebor took over the East, the caravans stopped. Esol's spies try to hide their tracks in the grass, but the Rangers know Numar too well and are immune to the grass, so spies do not stay hidden for long." Darian laughed. "Caleopsi grass turned out to be more useful to the Rangers than to the Nomads, or the East."

They talked thus the rest of the way to Heath and by evening, arrived at the edge of the city. The soldiers pitched tents against a threatening sky and made campfires in their groups, as before.

"I need a word with Stefen," said Darian. "My friend *Dar Bartil* owns an inn in Heath — *Bartil's Bed and Supper.* I stay there when I travel this way, for it gives me an opportunity to catch up on local gossip, which can be useful to the Rangers, and the King. I have been away long this time and I need to see Dar. I will ask Stefen if he has any objection to having you two accompany me."

"I would welcome a bed," Eathelon confessed.

"So, would I," added Palo.

Darian went to speak with Stefen and the two returned a few minutes later.

"Eathelon, Palo, you know I would not keep you from Darian's hospitality," Stefen stated, "or the hospitality of his friends. You two are not under my command so are free to go where you wish, as long as it does not endanger the company or our errand. But I must caution you of the risk you take, should you decide to go into Heath, and trust you will make the right decision whether or not to go."

Stefen turned and addressed Palo directly. "Your race is wholly unknown here, Palo, which makes you stand out. Given the nature of Eathelon's errand, it may be unwise for you to call attention to yourself. People here are unpredictable in such times as these. When they see one whose appearance differs so much from their own, they can make trouble. It is human nature, I suppose. Many Nardans live in fear now, after the purging of Eldarin from our lands, fear that it may happen to them. It is useful for Darian to go into Heath to learn what gossip he can, but he is known there. Eathelon's appearance is not so unusual as yours and to say he is Darian's kin would not be a lie."

Stefen paused to give them a few minutes to think it over.

Eathelon and Palo discussed the matter quietly. Eathelon knew Palo should stay in camp but he felt Darian should have thought that through before offering for Palo to go.

After giving them time to talk it over, Stefen asked, "What is your decision?"

"Darian should go, as you said. Palo and I will remain in camp."

Then, unexpectedly, Palo exclaimed, "No, Eathelon. You go with Darian. I will remain here. I want to look around and speak with some of the soldiers here anyway. Perhaps they may even ask me to cook." He grinned.

"I am certain they will welcome your help," smiled Stefen. "I am given to understand you are a good cook."

Somewhat surprised at Palo's concession, Eathelon nodded and smiled at his companion. He knew Palo would be in good company, for a Warrior had much in common with a soldier.

"Good, it is settled," Stefen confirmed. "I suggest you choose another name. Eathelon. is ... well, too Eldarin, I should think."

"Darian is an Eldarin name," claimed Darian.

"Yes, but it is also common. Many Nardans are called by this name. I have never before heard the name Eathelon used here."

Darian thought for a moment. "Ethan. It is a common enough name, one taken from the Eathen Mountains and it will not draw attention."

"Ethan," repeated Eathelon. "I like it."

Stefen smiled. "I will see you two in the morning. Come Palo!"

Darian and 'Ethan' mounted their horses and rode off to Dar Bartil's, as Palo and Stefen walked over to join Arestor.

"I must caution you," Darian declared, grinning. "Dar loves to talk."

"Duly noted," Eathelon grinned back.

The ride to Bartil's Bed and Supper was short. The well-kept inn of wood and stone had plants growing along its stone walk and many flowers that had begun to prepare for a winter's sleep. They arrived and dismounted, and a groom came to take the horses to the stable. They entered and a moment later, Dar came forward to greet them. Well past his middle years, the short, rotund proprietor had a cheery disposition and greeted them effusively. His gray hair fell onto his shoulders and mingled with a short gray beard which covered much of his round face. His large, bulbous nose held a pair of wire-rimmed glasses over pale blue eyes. Dar was clearly eager to see Darian.

"Well met, I say!" said Dar. "I thought Baele must have caught you in one of his little spy traps, you have been away so long, though in truth, I doubted it. How fare things in our southern lands, Darian ... and who is this?"

"Things change little there, Dar," replied Darian. "This is Ethan, a ... kin of mine."

"Kin? I thought you said you had no kin."

"He is only late arrived here and we had no prior knowledge of one another, but we are like brothers now." Darian slapped Eathelon on the back, while giving him a big smile.

Eathelon grimaced a little from the slap then grinned. "Like brothers," he agreed.

Darian quickly changed the subject to avoid any further explanation. "And how are things here in Heath, my proprietor friend? I am eager for any news."

"Well, to be honest, things have been difficult of late, and there is little to report, I am afraid, except that I have not been able to get my favorite wines from the East for many months, not since Esol convinced his Father to cut off the wine trade with Antebba. My stores of Eastern wines is nearly gone and some of those wines are favorites with my customers. And they bring a handsome price too, being imported from the East. I have the Holling Vale wines, which are excellent, of course, but as you know, last winter some of the Holling Vale vines were damaged in that early freeze, so now I am short on wine altogether. And leaf is short too because that freeze affected some of the leaf crop. Fortunately, most of my regular customers are content with local brew and there is always plenty of that, so I manage." He sighed. "But I miss having the Eastern wines."

"You miss the *profits* from the Eastern wines, you mean," said Darian, with a smile.

"Of course ... I am a businessman, after all."

Eathelon saw that what Darian said was true — Dar liked to ramble on. But Darian stood by patiently, nodding here and there as Dar's oration continued, so Eathelon did too. Dar stopped momentarily to offer them brew.

"How rude of me, you are both probably thirsty. Would you like some Grenway brew?"

"No, thank you Dar."

"Well, alright, then if you will excuse me a moment, I have something I want to show you." He walked away.

"He does like to talk, as you said," 'Ethan' said to Darian.

"Yes, but though he said he has nothing to report, I can assure you, he will have something of value to tell me."

Dar returned a few minutes later, holding a rare bottle of Holling Vale *Dark Horse Red*. Eathelon and Darian looked at each other with curiosity, as Dar motioned them over to the main counter, opened the bottle and offered each a cup. Guessing by his generous offer that Dar had something important to tell him, Darian did not refuse, and out of courtesy, Eathelon took a cup also.

"To what do we owe this generous gift, Dar?" asked Darian. "This must be one of very few bottles left in the West outside of the King's stores."

Dar took a sip and replied, "Indeed it is. In fact, it is my precious last bottle. Do you remember what you promised me, if I could get you some really good information?"

Darian paused, trying to recall what he had promised. "Oh, now I remember, you wanted gems from *Aynor*. I thought you said you did not have any information to offer."

"I have little information, but what I do have is really good. And gems from Aynor are more valuable here now than Nardan coins. It is why I offered you some of my last bottle of Dark Horse Red. I am hoping you will make good on your promise." He said it with restrained excitement.

"I am listening, but I warn you that I reserve the right to decide whether or not your information qualifies as really good."

"Fair enough," replied Dar, a little deflated. "For years, strangers have stopped at my inn on their way West, or East, and more of them lately, it seems. They rarely stay more than a night or two, and most are simply passing through to the surrounding villages or are on their way to Andolan." He chuckled. "For a while, I thought perhaps Baele had stopped sending his wormy little spies over here and had gone back to minding his own business, but that turned out to be wishful thinking. He is still up to his old tricks. The number of strangers passing through has steadily increased and I began to take more of an interest."

"Go on," said Darian.

"I doubted you would return anytime soon because you are always patrolling with the Rangers and are gone for long periods of time. Your visits have become fewer and further between it seems."

"A necessity these days, I fear."

"I understand. Well, anyway, I worried that I would not be able to remember everything I wanted to tell you when you did come. I am not very good at writing things down ... I have staff to do that and I am getting old. My memory no longer serves me as well as it once did. I wanted to be certain I could tell you the important things you would want to know, so you would make good on that promise. I had to figure out a way to keep track of the strangers coming and going at the inn because I knew you would want to know about them. I wanted to know if they'd been here more than once because I guessed such information could be valuable to you, but I knew I would never remember it all."

Eathelon could not quite see where Dar was going with this, but Darian stood by patiently and listened with interest, so Eathelon did too.

"Most of the strangers coming through are obvious to me," chuckled Dar, "but more and more they started to blend in with the regular crowd. I cannot remember everyone who walks through my door. We are on the main road here and I have the only inn of any decent size for miles around, you know, so I am bound to get most of the travelers passing through Heath."

"Your point, Dar?" Darian finally asked.

Eathelon smiled.

"I am coming to it. There is a regular customer in here almost every day, name of Cob. The man practically lives here because he has no family of his own and ..."

Darian coughed and looked at Dar who began to talk faster.

"It turns out that Cob began sketching the patrons. He is discreet about it, of course, and the customers are usually too busy talking and drinking to pay much attention. After he finishes a sketch, Cob takes it over and offers it to the patron in trade for brew. Most are amused by it and are usually so full of brew themselves that they make the trade. I have not intervened because the patrons pay for Cob's brew and I sell more brew. Of course, now and then, someone makes a scene."

Darian gave Dar a look of impatience, which Dar ignored.

"I had planned to put a stop to it, until I realized it might be useful to both of us. Most of the patrons seemed to like Cob's sketches, Cob got brew, I sold more brew, so it worked for everyone. I grew curious about the patrons who objected to his sketches and it gave me an idea."

Darian glared at him.

"I *am* coming to my point, Darian, and I promise you will like where this is going. When I took the trouble to look at the sketches, I found them to be excellent — Cob has a real talent for it. He even did one of me." Dar grinned.

"Dar," urged Darian.

Dar talked faster. "Cob got a few coins because some of the patrons invited him to sketch the family, so sometimes Cob even bought his own brew, but that is not my point. My point is, when I got to thinking about our last meeting and your promise and, since my memory isn't so good anymore, I came up with an idea to help both of us."

Eathelon was practically out of breath listening to Dar and waiting for him to get to the point.

"Which is?" asked Darian.

"I offered Cob free brew to sketch anyone I asked him to, and I made him promise to do it with such discretion that the person sketched would not know he was being sketched. Once he completed the sketch, he would simply turn it over to me."

Perhaps Dar Bartil is not as stupid as I thought, Eathelon said to himself.

"Come," Dar whispered, "and I will show you."

They followed Dar to a tiny room behind the main counter, one barely large enough for the three of them. It contained a chair and a small desk, piled high with papers, disorganized. Dar walked around behind the desk and unlocked the door to a closet, the contents of which were equally disorganized — except for one neat stack of papers tied with string. He brought that out, cleared a space on the desk, and laid it down.

"Here are Cob's sketches of all of the strangers who entered the *Bed and Supper* over the past few months. I had him sketch anyone I didn't recognize and if the person came in more than once, there will be more than one sketch of him. If you go through the stack, you will get a good idea of who has been here, and how often. I thought perhaps you might recognize one or more of them."

Eathelon chuckled to himself, *not stupid indeed.*

Darian smiled. "I admit Dar, you have surprised me. If this turns out to be as useful an idea as I believe it may be, you can rest assured that I will fulfill my promise."

Dar grinned from ear to ear and Eathelon heard him mumble under his breath, "You, fat old buzzard, in your mostly wasted life you have come up with two great ideas — buying this inn and hiring Cob's sketches."

Darian took the sketches and put them under his cloak. "I will need to borrow these tonight so I can look them over. I will return them to you in the morning."

"Yes, yes, keep them as long as you need," replied Dar.

They returned to Darian's room, at the back of the inn, which held two beds. Darian reviewed the sketches but did not recognize anyone. He committed them to memory and asked 'Ethan' to do the same, which took some time. When they had finished, they went for some supper then went to bed. They arose at sunup and Dar had brefas waiting for them in the dining room. They ate, then returned the sketches to Dar.

"Keep them locked in your closet, Dar," Darian remarked.

Dar nodded and walked them to the front door. Dar had their horses brought up from the stable and they mounted and turned to leave.

"Safe journey, Ethan, safe journey Darian," said Dar. "Don't forget your promise!"

"I will not forget, Dar," replied Darian.

"Thank you for the bed and meals," said Eathelon. "Both were excellent."

The two companions rode back to camp.

It had grown cold in the night and the morning air felt chilly and crisp under the clear, blue sky. The wind stung Eathelon's nose as they rode back to camp and, when they arrived, they found it already cleared and the company ready to ride. Palo approached, leading his horse and said, with some envy, "I trust you both slept well and that your visit proved fruitful."

"Yes, to both," replied Darian.

Eathelon nodded.

Arestor rode up behind Palo and announced, "The company is ready to ride."

"There is a brief matter I would like to discuss with you first," said Darian.

Arestor dismounted and the two walked away to speak in private. Eathelon saw Arestor nod in agreement with whatever Darian had said to him, then the two returned and Arestor gave the command for the company to mount up. They all rode off northward.

"Where do we go next?" Eathelon asked Darian.

"To *Hamstead*," replied Darian. "We should arrive in four days — providing there are no incidents."

"What do you mean by incidents?" asked Eathelon.

"When Stefen escorts the soldiers between Andolan and Toldor's Keep, the citizens along the way sometimes stop them and ask them to take their letters and packages to loved ones north. There is no regular mail service, so the people of the towns and villages along the way count on Andolan's soldiers to carry the mail. Before the Great War, mail carriers traveled regularly, but after the war, it became too dangerous and unreliable. People became poor, and messengers were sometimes robbed, or even murdered. Eventually, no one would do it. The people in the lands north of here are poor and cannot afford to lose what few possessions they have. Mail is important to them and they know it will be safe with the soldiers."

"That Stefen permits his soldiers to carry mail to and from these villages shows how much he cares for his people," said

Eathelon.

"Yes, both he and Aneron care a great deal for the people of Hamlan. Nevertheless, Stefen cannot let the mail slow him down too much, so he devised a system whereby one person from each town or village brings and receives mail at designated stops along our route. Scouts go ahead and news travels fast when they are spotted. Stefen appoints a few soldiers to make the mail exchanges and occasionally, a dispute arises. Someone does not receive something expected or brings a piece of mail too late to be taken or falsely accuses a soldier of theft or damage — that sort of thing. Then Stefen must step in to sort it out, which creates a delay. That is what is meant by an 'incident'."

"Well, let us hope no such incidents slow our progress. *Wintereve* is approaching and we still have far to go," said Eathelon.

The ride to Hamstead proved to be without incident and the mail exchanges were handled efficiently by those appointed to the task. The mail consisted primarily of letters that fitted easily into the pouches on pack horses brought for the purpose.

The mornings and evenings were cold, but the days remained warm and dry, under a clear sky. Earlyfall bathed the lands north of Andolan in color, as the leaves of the deciduous trees turned from green to yellow, orange, red and gold and fell to the ground.

They arrived at Hamstead on schedule.

"Hamstead appears to be only a large village," Eathelon observed. "I thought perhaps it would be like Heath."

"We have left the cities behind now, though Hamstead is one of the larger villages outside of Andolan," Darian replied.

"Is there an inn here too?" asked Palo, no doubt hopeful of a soft bed.

"I am afraid not for us, Palo. I have a friend here, but he is away. We shall all remain in camp tonight. I keep two Rangers in Heath and they visit Hamstead now and then to collect local gossip, but they reported to me in Andolan before we left. It will take all day tomorrow for us to reach *Harwyn Crossing* and we will likely set camp near there once we cross the river."

Palo looked disappointed.

"Do not worry, my Warrior friend," Darian stated assuredly.

"The best inn of all — *The Black Caat* awaits us in Brega, our next stop after Harwyn Crossing. That inn surpasses Dar Bartil's. The beds are equally soft, there is plenty of brew and Holling Vale wine, for Brega is close to wine country, but a surprise awaits us there."

Palo cheered up some. "How long does Stefen plan to stay in Brega, do you know?"

"I doubt he will wish to stay more than a day or two to take on any additional provisions the company may need for Toldor's Keep. Once we leave Brega, there will be no more towns or villages of any size all the way to the Keep, just a few outlying farms and ranches. The Hamlets are mostly deserted now, except for those with courage enough to remain. But do not worry, we shall all stay a night or two at the Black Caat Inn and I will show you around Brega myself."

"Excellent," Eathelon exclaimed, cheerfully.

Palo smiled, but looked doubtful. He must have guessed he would again be denied the opportunity to stay at an inn.

But Darian declared, "I will speak to Stefen, Palo, and convince him to let you join us at the Black Caat."

"Thank you, Darian," grunted Palo, his response an indication that he held out little hope for it. "I would like the opportunity to sleep in a soft bed this one last time. I expect we will be sleeping on hard ground after Brega, all the way to the Golden City."

"Any smart Warrior prefers a bed to hard ground," Darian grinned, "particularly when he must be well rested for a fight."

But none had a soft bed that night. They once again spread their blankets out on the cold ground.

After a restless sleep, Eathelon rose at dawn with his companions, ate a light brefas, packed and mounted to leave. It was a short ride to Harwyn Crossing now, but one over a rocky, twisting road that wound steadily down toward the river. Eathelon took in the surrounding scenery as they rode north, and about mid-day, noticed clouds gathering above. Expecting rain, he pulled his woolen cloak over his body, as his thoughts strayed back to Cob's sketches. One of the faces had seemed familiar to him, but he could not quite place it and he puzzled over why his attention stuck on it. His intuition told him it might be important but, unable to sort it out, he made no mention of it to Darian.

Chapter 15: Harwyn Crossing

True to Eathelon's guess, a light began to fall when the company had gone about halfway to Harwyn Crossing. Black clouds covered the sky and hid the sun, and Eathelon pulled a thick woolen cloak around his body for warmth, one supplied to all of the soldiers of Andolan. Darian and Palo did the same.

"These are good in rain," Darian noted. "They will keep you warm when wet, and from the look of that sky, we are about to get soaked. The wool comes from the finest sheep of Southern Hamlet and is woven into cloaks by skilled weavers. They are sold at the Open Market, but the King has adopted them as standard issue for every soldier and purchases them directly from the weavers."

"It is thick, yet light," Eathelon commented." He and Palo would not have been able to afford this luxury without the King's generosity.

The wind picked up and sent the rain hard against them, as they rode. They bent their heads against it and talk proved nearly impossible, so they rode in silence. Eathelon's spirits dampened with every hoof beat as, left to his own thoughts, he worried about whether their errand would succeed. *I wish I had the same gift of foresight Celorn has.* But he took comfort in Lelar's words and brushed off his nagging doubt.

The rain slowed to a drizzle and the sun popped out, as they approached the bridge at Harwyn Crossing.

"The bridge is not far now," said Darian. "The road ahead winds down to the river from here."

"We camp on the other side?" asked Palo.

"Yes, in the *Grenhyl*, just below Brega. Some of the soldiers will probably have a short leave to visit the city for a few hours. There are no more cities between Brega and Toldor's Keep and their tour will last six months or more. Stefen will want them back in camo by dusk. But we will have no such restriction," grinned Darian. "We shall all sleep in comfort tonight, at the Black Caat Inn."

Eathelon smiled but Palo did not, no doubt still uncertain about whether or not he would go.

They rounded a bend in the road and, as they descended to the river, Harwyn Bridge came into full view. Its beauty and architecture took Eathelon by surprise. Stefen halted the company before they reached the bridge and Arestor joined the three companions.

"Behold, Harwyn Crossing," he boasted, "the southern crossing of the *Teb-Arnor River*, the longest and swiftest river in Narda." Arestor paused. "Well, what do you think of it?"

"It is magnificent, Arestor," exclaimed Eathelon. "I have not seen its equal."

"Indeed," echoed Palo. "Some of the bridges of Melatui are ... unique, but we have none like this."

"Its architecture matches that of Andolan," added Eathelon.

"Yes, its architects were one and the same," replied Arestor. "Harwyn and its sister bridge at *Forwyn Crossing* both had Eldarin designers."

"Of course," grinned Eathelon, his pride in his Eldarin ancestry increasing.

The wide bridge, constructed of the same grey and white stone as the walls of Andolan, held beautiful, hand-crafted lamp posts at its two entrances and along both sides. The posts sat at evenly spaced intervals atop the walls, two lamps in each post, the stone walls curved down between them. The posts bore the familiar *T* for the House of Toldor, and the walls bore lothingel leaves, signature of the Eldarin, in a scrolling pattern along their length.

The road dipped down to the entrance, where the riverbank fell steeply to the rushing water below.

Eathelon could not fathom how the anyone could build a bridge over such deep, swift water, and he said so. "However did they manage to build such a magnificent bridge in such a difficult place?"

"Many Nardan architects have asked that same question," Arestor replied. "Harwyn and Forwyn, like Andolan, are wonders left to us by your Eldarin ancestors. They left other such marks in Narda, I have heard, though I have not seen them all."

"Had the Eldarin not built this bridge," added Darian, "we would have had to ride many leagues north to reach the next crossing of the Teb-Arnor."

"Yes, and it would have added two weeks more to our journey," remarked Arestor.

"And that crossing is not always passable," said Darian. "Sometimes the water rises too high at *Rena* (Earlyspring) and covers the bridge altogether."

"I am surprised that any bridge built by the Eldarin would suffer such a condition," commented Eathelon.

"That bridge was not built by the Eldarin," Arestor pointed out. "Perhaps they saw no need of it, once Harwyn and Forwyn were built."

"How far is it from here to Forwyn?" asked Palo.

"A five-day journey from Harwyn to Forwyn, or six days from Brega. Forwyn lies at the north end of Southern Hamlet. The Teb-Arnor flows fast in a narrow channel between the two bridges, too dangerous to navigate. The sister bridges offer a passable overland route between Southern and Northern Hamlan, one suitable for Andolan's soldiers."

"This side of Narda seems to offer many geographical challenges," commented Eathelon.

"Indeed," agreed Arestor. "No river offers a greater challenge than the Teb-Arnor. Its source is near Mt. Athel, up in the Eathen Mountains. Yet, Toldor's Keep is farther north still."

"Your journey to the Keep is a long one then," said Eathelon.

"Yes, and we take 100 men or more up and back twice a year," Arestor stated. "Stefen and I sometimes make other journeys to the Keep, with fewer men. We are restoring and fortifying it. The soldiers change at *Rena* (Earlyspring) and *Aldona* (Earlyfall). It is very isolated up there and most men remain six months or more. The restoration of the Keep is a priority, but is nearly completed now, and none too soon, it would seem."

"You anticipate trouble?" asked Palo.

"It would be foolish for us to do otherwise," replied Arestor. We must not be caught unprepared again. The Keep fell once, long ago. It will not fall again. Aneron wants Hamlan ready for any confrontation with the Northmen. Toldor's Keep is an important northern defense."

"Aneron is wise in that regard," said Eathelon.

They rode down to the bridge.

Arestor raised his voice, to be heard over the rushing water.

"The Teb-Arnor is swift and dangerous here, but it calms as it flows south, where it is more easily navigated. The land flattens out there and the current slows, so the boats can manage it. Many tributaries feed the farmers' fields, and aqueducts carry water to local villages along the way. The river meets the Westmost Sea on the southern side of the peninsula, below Balor Bay."

Balor Bay, Eathelon mused, their original destination.

They reached the entrance to the bridge and Stefen halted the company again. He brought the group leaders together for a brief conference. The rain had stopped altogether by now and the sun, though low in the sky, peeked out from behind the dark clouds, though the late afternoon sun provided little warmth. It did provide a break from the gloomy drizzle that had kept them all soaked, however, much to their relief.

Arestor ordered a small group of soldiers onto the bridge and Eathelon watched as they filled and lit the lamp posts, at the entrance and along the walls.

"We replace the oil in those lamps each time we cross," Arestor remarked, "but the poor villagers come and take it for their own lamps."

"Life is difficult out here now," added Darian.

"These lands produce little," continued Arestor, "so the inhabitants have little. But they are a proud people. They do not care much for charity. Sometimes people are driven to do things to survive they would not normally do."

Arestor joined Stefen and they crossed the bridge, passing

the soldiers filling the lamps. Eathelon and Palo followed. The rest of the company remained back.

When they reached the bottom of the embankment on the other side, a band of surly, unkempt men jumped out of the surrounding bushes and stopped them in the middle of the road. They stood staring at them, but said nothing.

"Let us pass!" Arestor insisted, with authority.

The interlopers stood their ground, though with somewhat less certainty now. The men evidently did not see the soldiers on the other side of the bridge, but must have noticed those filling the lamps. Those soldiers stopped what they were doing started forward, to join their Captain, but Stefen motioned them to stay back. He motioned Darian forward and the three of them, Stefen, Arestor and Darian dismounted and walked up to face the men who blocked their path, as Eathelon and Palo watched.

"Who are you and why do you block our way?" asked Stefen.

The man in front stared at them but said nothing at first. The men behind him took a step backward, leaving him alone.

"Speak, while you have a tongue!" Arestor commanded. "Do you not see who we are?"

The man in front came out of whatever fog had clouded his eyes and realized who stood before him. "My Lord, I ... that is we ..." he stammered. "I did not at once recognize you."

"That is evident," Stefen stated bluntly, "but I see that now you have. Answer my question. Why did you block the road?"

"We are from *Hamil*, sire, a nearby village," the man blurted out, as another man stepped forward. "Just over there, My Lord." He pointed east.

"We were out ... hunting," said the first, "and saw what we thought to be strangers passing through. We live in fear for the safety of our families and we only wished to see who passed."

"See who they might rob, more likely," Palo whispered to Eathelon.

"I thought the same," Eathelon responded softly.

"Well, now that you know who we are, go about your business and leave us to ours," Stefen said, not unkindly.

Darian whispered something to Stefen.

Stefen nodded. "My companion here wishes a word with

you. I suggest you listen to him."

The man in front swallowed hard as his group left him to deal with Darian by himself.

Darian spoke briefly with him and afterward, the group dispersed.

Stefen, Arestor and Darian mounted their horses and Eathelon and Palo rode up behind them, as the soldiers on the bridge completed their task. Arestor signaled for the rest of the company to cross the bridge.

"What did you say to that man?" Eathelon asked Darian.

"I asked about these strangers he claimed to see more than once in this area. These are ignorant men, Eathelon. They offered little information of value and I doubt what information they might give would be truthful anyway. I believe they meant to rob us, until they saw who we were, though some of what that man said is no doubt true — they do live in fear for the safety of their families here. They probably rob for their own survival, but that is of little consolation to those robbed. I told him we travel this way often and if we find any of them blocking the road again, or hear of anyone being robbed, we will hunt them down and throw them in the dungeons of Andolan."

"Andolan has dungeons?" Palo queried.

"No," grinned Darian, "but I doubt they know that. I doubt they have ever been out of their village. If they believe Andolan has dungeons, it serves our purpose and if they do not, I think they got the point. They are fearful, despite their false look of bravery. I told them if they even think about doing anything illegal, we will find out about it. That seemed to be warning enough to deter them for now, though I doubt it will hold up their activities for long."

"Do other such bands roam these lands?" asked Palo. "I could try my hand at warrioring. I feel a little out of shape."

Eathelon suppressed a smile. The only thing out shape on Palo was his growing mid-section, the result of much improved rations from the King's table.

"You may have other opportunities to test your warrior skills in the coming months Palo, though I hope I am wrong," replied Stefen.

"Let us not be too eager to look for trouble," said Eathelon.

"Trouble has already found us in recent months," stated Stefen, "though we have not looked for it."

"It is why we are fortifying the Keep," added Arestor, "even if only out of an abundance of caution."

Eathelon knew he and Palo would be on their own soon enough, without the protection of Andolan's soldiers. He was glad Palo wanted to be at his best.

"Stefen is more familiar with this region of Hamlan than I," said Darian. "He travels here while I scout the southern lands. But I remember these lands well enough from previous visits to see that they have changed. The people here were once well mannered and well off. Now they scratch out a living and rob unsuspecting travelers. Narda has regressed much since the exile of the Eldarin. I hope they return to help us set it right again. Baele's poison is not confined to the East, it would seem — it has already spread far into the West."

Eathelon thought about the fyrcaats. Baele indeed had spread his poison into Hamlan. *There is so much to accomplish before the Eldarin can return and the outcome lies with us.* He hoped they would prove up to the task.

They rode along in silence, as the trail climbed into the Grenhyl — the Green Hills, so named because, unlike the Brunhyl, these hills remained green throughout all of the seasons. The climate grew colder as they climbed and when they stopped to make camp, the soldiers set several campfires, as before, and this time set tents against the growing threat of rain, for swollen clouds loomed above and ahead and it looked as if they might burst and pour a torrent of water down on the company. Eathelon helped gather firewood and Palo offered to help cook.

Stefen declined, saying, "Your offer is both generous and appreciated, Palo, for Darian informed me that you are an excellent cook. But you are my guests on this journey, so I hope you will be content to eat what my men prepare, even if the meal is somewhat less fair than yours would be."

"Whatever your men prepare will no doubt be fair enough," replied Palo.

Stefen and Darian are having an influence on Palo, thought

Eathelon. *His tongue grows fair.*

Their tents up and belongings stowed, the companions sat together at the fire and warmed themselves until two soldiers brought food over. Eathelon waited to see if Palo would make a comment on the meal and he did not have to wait long.

"The meal is indeed fair, surpassed only by the King's table," Palo said, as he chewed on a piece of chikka meat.

Eathelon rolled his eyes and gave Palo a look of disapproval for his patronizing manner, but he caught Stefen's smile, which said he had not been fooled. Being a man of good manners, Stefen acknowledged the comment. "Thank you, Palo. I will pass your compliments on to the cooks."

His meal finished, Stefen stood and said, "I must go meet with my men now, but I will return," and he left.

Eathelon turned to Palo, "You know very well the cooks don't care a raat's hair what you say about their cooking. They cook what they catch and do their best to make it tasty, but it is certainly no King's fare."

Palo took another bite of chikka meat and replied, with a grin, "I may have exaggerated a little."

Darian laughed, then Eathelon laughed and Palo joined in and almost choked on his chikka meat. Then Eathelon had an epiphany, a sudden realization, "Oh, you are a clever Warrior, Palo. You want to go to the Black Caat Inn and you need Stefen's approval. Is that why you flattered him so?"

Palo said nothing, he just smiled.

"How far is it to Brega?" Eathelon asked Darian, as he broke off a piece of chikka meat and popped it into his mouth.

"Five days from here, if the weather holds," replied Darian.

"If it doesn't rain, you mean," Palo noted.

"Yes."

The rain had slowed them and, if they had to set up and take down tents, it would delay them even more. The land here was hilly and rocky, making tents a challenge. All of this added time and Eathelon began to feel pressured for time to complete his errand.

But thankfully, the sky did little more than drizzle and they reached the outskirts of Brega on schedule. Palo received permission to go with Darian and Eathelon to the Black Caat, but

Stefen cautioned him and gave him an idea for a cover story, should he need one:

"It is obvious that you are not Nardan, Palo. I have an idea how you would answer, should you be questioned about your origins."

"Why not simply tell the truth?" asked Palo.

"That is too risky. You travel with two Eldarin companions, who are under threat of death. Better that you all keep your ancestry a secret," replied Stefen. "But you could say you hail from *Forth*, Hamlan's northernmost coastal village. It lies just below the Northern Reaches and few Nardans go up there. The Northmen have invaded that region several times in the past and took our women. Few Nardans outside of Forth have ever even seen a Northman. All that is generally known about them is that they are large of build and fierce."

Eathelon smiled. "I believe Palo can match that description."

Palo made an appropriate face and they all laughed, deflating him a little.

"I have no doubt that you can act the part Palo," remarked Stefen, coming to Palo's rescue. "You are a Warrior, and you fit the general description."

"A Northman would never venture so far south," countered Arestor, challenging the cover story.

"Brega is not so far from Forth that it would seem implausible," Stefen defended.

"It is Earlyfall," Arestor continued. "A Northman could not cross *Egin Pass* this time of year. It would be snowed in."

Stefen considered his point. "Perhaps, but he could have come down the Highland Gap and made the short overland trek to Brega."

"The soldiers at the Keep would not have permitted a Northman to pass," said Arestor.

"The Gap is wide enough in places that one could slip by," Stefen noted. "Is this not why we are headed up there, to handle that situation?"

"Alright," conceded Arestor, "but what reason would a Northman have to come all the way down to Brega?"

Stefen thought a moment, clearly making this up as he went. "He came in search of his Mother's family. His Mother's family moved to Brega for safety after she was taken by the Northmen.

Palo left the Reaches in search of her family."

"The story is thin, but I suppose it could work," admitted Arestor.

"Alright, it is settled then," said Stefen.

"I have never seen a Northman in Brega," challenged Darian.

"Well, now you have," Stefen responded. "Not only have you seen him, you have befriended him." And that ended the discussion. Stefen turned to Palo. "Keep to your cover and enjoy your stay at the Black Caat Inn." He turned to Arestor. "Come, Arestor, we have business to discuss." As they turned to leave, Stefen added, "We will join you at the Black Caat for supper and stay the night there. Make the arrangements Darian."

Darian acknowledged him and turned to Palo. "See, did I not say you would have a bed tonight?"

Palo grinned, showing his large white teeth. He pushed his chest out and banged on it. "Northman," he said.

They all laughed.

The three of them rode off to Brega, in anticipation of a memorable night at the Black Caat Inn, the inn Darian claimed to be one of the best in all of Hamlan.

Chapter 16:
The Black Caat Inn

Brega, like Andolan, was built into hills, but without levels. Its unpaved main road wound around and over the gentle slopes of the Grenhyl, its narrow streets intersecting it in a disorganized, haphazard way. The population of Brega was only a tenth the size of the population of Andolan, and most of the inhabitants had either been born there or had migrated in from the surrounding area.

"Is there much to see in Brega?" inquired Eathelon.

"Not that I have seen, but I do not come often and, when I do it is usually on some errand that keeps me no more than a day or two," replied Darian. "Still, I know the town well enough."

He led them up the main road toward town, then suddenly veered off onto a narrow trail.

"Why did we leave the main road?" asked Eathelon.

"This is a shortcut that will take us to the inn without our having to ride through town." Darian grinned.

"Of course," laughed Eathelon.

"I care little which trail takes us to the inn, so long as we arrive," said Palo, with a wide smile.

They followed the trail up, over the slopes of the Grenhyl, until they reached a bend and came to another road, where Darian halted them and pointed to a large building visible at the top of a high hill.

"There it is," he pointed out, "the Black Caat Inn. This road will take us the rest of the way up."

They followed him single file to the top and there came to a long, single-level, stone-faced building. A sign above the porch bore the image of a black caat and a flag on the roof, with the same image, flapped in the wind.

"Well, there is no mistaking the name," grinned Eathelon.

"Why a black caat?" asked Palo.

"You will see," Darian responded.

They dismounted and tied the horses to carved black wrought-iron posts in the image of a cat, set for this purpose. As they unpacked their belongings, a man with a balding head and tufts of white hair on the sides walked toward them with a lilting gait.

"Evenin' gents," he greeted, then he added, "Oh, Darian is it?"

"It is indeed!" replied Darian. "Well met, *Jom*. I trust you have been well since my last visit."

"Indeed, I have," said Jom, his smile showing his crooked teeth.

Darian handed him a coin.

"Why, thank you, Mister Darian. I will see to your horses and ensure they are well cared for, rest assured."

"Thank you, Jom."

They left Jom with the horses and started walking up the long, winding path toward the front door.

"Do all guests at the Black Caat receive such service?" asked Eathelon.

"Most do, I suppose, though I may be a favored patron."

"Why?" from Palo.

"I reward good service and am polite with the staff. Some patrons are ill-mannered. A smile and good manners can go a long way ... and a coin or two also helps." Darian grinned.

"And no doubt helps you gather information," smiled Eathelon.

"Perhaps," beamed Darian.

The path wound through the pine and fir, past stone benches set at intervals, and past a small brook that meandered its way down the hill.

"It is a lot of work to reach the front door," Palo grunted.

"From this trail, yes but the view at the top will be worth it," replied Darian.

When they reached the summit, they stopped to take a look out over the wide, green plain below, and saw, in the distance, the mighty Teb-Arnor River flowing south to the sea.

"It is a spectacular view," said Palo. "We climbed higher than I thought."

"Yes, the inn sits on one of the highest peaks in the Grenhyl. Come! Let us go check out the inn!"

They took the stone path to the front porch. Many rocks, of various sizes, shapes and colors had been set into the front wall, in no particular pattern and it gave the inn a unique look, but not a particularly aesthetic one, compared to those in Andolan.

"This inn's architecture is most unusual," said Eathelon. "I do not think this design is one created by the Eldarin."

"Indeed, it is not," replied Darian. "This inn, built long ago, had fallen into a state of ruin. It was restored to its present condition by its proprietor."

"Well, I care little how it looks so long as the beds are soft and the food tastes good," grinned Palo.

"I see you have your priorities in order," smiled Eathelon.

"Jak, the proprietor, is both friendly and accommodating," said Darian.

Eathelon chuckled. "Darian, is there any inn in Hamlan where the proprietor is *not* accommodating and friendly to you?"

"None, that I have yet visited," grinned Darian. "But one cannot have too many friends and acquaintances, in my line of work."

"Indeed not," replied Eathelon.

Darian opened the large wooden doors and they stepped through into the foyer. It held a variety of Nardan mementos: a large *baer* rug, a stuffed foxx, a sculpture of a sinter hawk in flight and another huge, stuffed creature that Eathelon did not recognize.

"What is that one?" he asked, pointing to it.

"A *baerwolff*," said Darian. "Come to think of it, I do not recall seeing that here before today."

"What is a baerwolff?" asked Palo. "It is neither a wolff, nor a baer. I have encountered both before."

"Correct, Palo. A baerwolff is an ancient creature of Elvenvale, the valley adjacent to Northwest Wood, home of the Elvenkin. Jak must have purchased this from some mercenary hunter. If so, he would have paid a great price for it. Baerwolffs are under the protection of the Elvenkin. They would be most unhappy to see it here. Fortunately, Elvenkin rarely venture from their wood these days. I must ask Jak about it. It seems unlike him to purchase such a creature and put it on display here."

"Are baerwolffs dangerous?" asked Palo. "It is about the size of a full grown baer."

"Yes, they can sometimes be dangerous," replied Darian, "though the Elvenkin would not harm one, without due cause. It is best that we not mention this when we see the Elvenkin."

"Indeed, we have no desire to offend the Elvenkin," said Eathelon. "Should we encounter a baerwolff, it will not suffer any harm by our hands."

"Baerwolffs are wary of strangers and keep to themselves, it is said, but it is nevertheless wise to be cautious."

"Are there other such beasts in Narda?" asked Palo, "besides fyrcaats, I mean."

"None I have yet encountered, but who can say for certain?" replied Darian. "Some parts of Narda are inhospitable and men do not venture there."

Eathelon stood admiring a painting of the Eathen Mountains in Midsummer, then moved to a large wrought-iron sculpture of a black caat.

Then almost as if on cue, there came a soft "meow" and Eathelon looked down to find a short-haired, sleek black caat rubbing Darian's boot.

"Hello," Darian said, as he reached down and stroked the caat's head. "This is *Midnight*, the proprietor's caat ... and the inn's mascot."

"Of course," grinned Eathelon.

Midnight purred and rubbed against Darian's leg.

"Another of your friends in Hamlan, I see," said Palo.

"Indeed, the best kind," replied Darian. "He offers affection and does not talk back."

They all laughed.

Palo reached down to pet Midnight and the caat instantly arched his back and stood his fur straight up. He bared his sharp white teeth and hissed, then doubled his size and flashed two large yellow eyes at Palo.

"Midnight is not at all certain about you, Palo," said Darian.

"He ... just got ... he, he grew!" Palo spluttered.

"What kind of caat is he, Darian?" Eathelon inquired.

Darian laughed. "I suppose I should have warned you, but I derive a certain pleasure from the surprise Midnight gives new patrons. He is a *ché caat*."

"A what?" asked Palo.

"A ché caat — a shape-shifter, of sorts. He cannot change *what* he is, only his size. Ché caats are possessive. He belongs to Jak and must somehow feel threatened by you, Palo."

"Palo is supposed to be intimidating," noted Eathelon. "He is a Warrior, after all."

"Midnight probably senses I have little love of caats," Palo responded, "though I would not harm one ... unless it threatened my survival, or Eathelon's."

"A ché caat can do beyond scratch or bite," Darian stated. "They cannot grow large enough to threaten a man."

"Midnight seems comfortable enough with you, Darian," Eathelon declared.

"I have visited several times." Darian reached down, stroked Midnight's head and spoke softly to him. "We are old friends." The caat returned to his normal size and purred softly, but kept an eye on Palo. Then, as suddenly as he had appeared, Midnight walked away, shrinking as he went, until he was the size of a mouse. Then he disappeared through a small hole in the foyer wall.

"Well, this is something to add to the strange things I have seen since coming to Narda," admitted Palo.

"I doubt ché caats exist outside of Narda, or perhaps even outside of Hamlan."

"Narda is unique," declared Eathelon, "with its ché caats, fyrcaats, baerwolffs and who knows what other creatures we may yet encounter."

"I must admit Midnight is one of our more unique creatures," said Darian.

"Are there other ché caats in Brega?" asked Eathelon. "Midnight must have a mother and a father."

"Yes, he no doubt once did, but he is the only ché caat I have ever seen here," replied Darian.

They knocked on the main door to the inn, one with a small window in its center.

"Curious," Palo pointed out, "that a patron must pass through two doors to get inside the inn."

"This door has been added since I was last here," remarked Darian. "Jak must have wanted another measure of security. I see things have grown as serious here as in Andolan. The reach of the House of Tebor must be greater than I thought."

"This is a clever security measure," Palo agreed.

"Yes, Jak can lock this door at *latenight* and leave the door to the foyer unlocked. That way he can see anyone who enters before deciding whether or not to let him into the inn."

Not yet evening, the door to the inn was unlocked, so they stepped through into the main lobby.

"I will go find Jak," said Darian.

Eathelon and Palo continued to browse and Eathelon found the inside of the inn warm and inviting. It smelled of forest, a favorite odor, second only to the smell of the open sea.

Darian returned momentarily with a squat, middle-aged, olive-skinned man, and made introductions. "Jak has promised to take good care of us."

"Well met," he greeted his new guests, and offered a tour of the inn.

"That will not be necessary," said Darian. "I know your inn well enough. Please show us to our room."

Jak nodded and toddled down the long main hallway in front of them. They followed him past the check-in counter to their left, where two men tended guests, past a large dining room to their right, then a smaller one on the left. They walked past several sleeping rooms to the end of the hall, then through it, into another hall. They passed by more sleeping rooms on their right and came to the end of that hall. Jak opened the door to the last room on the left and they entered.

"A bit out of the way, is it not?" asked Palo.

"That is precisely the point," declared Darian, "privacy."

They entered the spacious, well-furnished room. Several lamps burned on the walls and colorful rugs covered the floor.

Like the foyer, various paintings and other decor hung on the walls and a fire had been set in the large fireplace to warm the room.

"It appears we are expected," suggested Eathelon.

"I received word of your coming from one of the King's soldiers," Jak responded. He continued. "Those doors," he pointed to one on the right and one on the left, "are to sleeping rooms. Each has three beds. That one …" he motioned to another on the left, "leads to that small dining room we passed in the main hall. This door to it is usually kept locked, but I will unlock it and lock the door to from the main hall so you can take your meals in private, if you like. This is our best room — the best in all of Brega, in fact. I keep it for special guests — which you are, of course. Let me know anything you may need during your stay and I will do my best to provide it."

"Thank you Jak, we shall be quite comfortable here," Darian confirmed.

"Your horses are stabled behind the inn, so should you need them, just ask at the front counter and Jom will bring them up to you. My own room is behind that counter and I keep someone on duty at the counter all night. Supper will be served in half an hour."

"We will take our supper in the private dining room, as you suggested," said Darian. "Please ask Prince Stefen and Captain Arestor to join us when they arrive."

"As you wish," Jak responded, and he left.

Eathelon and Palo walked around the large common room, viewing its wall art and furnishings, then Eathelon headed for the sleeping room on the left, but before he could open the door, Darian said, with a grin, "Let us take this other room, Eathelon. Come and see why."

So, he and Palo followed Darian into the large room on the right, which held three large beds, piled high with quilts and pillows. Next to each bed sat a small table, with clean towels and a large bowl, with a capped pipe above it. On the far wall sat another fireplace, dark but with a stack of wood piled beside it. Another door, to the right of the fireplace, sat partially open.

"An excellent room," declared Palo, bouncing up and down

on one of the beds.

"It gets better," grinned Darian. "Follow me."

They followed him through the door by the fireplace into a small room.

"A bath!" exclaimed Palo.

"Well, what a welcome surprise," confirmed Eathelon.

"Indeed," grinned Darian. "Now you understand my choice."

They stared at a tiled bath large enough to hold all three of them, as water steamed from its surface.

Eathelon dipped a hand into the water. "Perfect," he said.

Darian smiled, "I believe this is the only room with a bath, indeed the only inn with one outside of Andolan."

"Shards," Palo stated. "You were right to say it is the best inn in Brega, though it is the only one we have seen."

Darian laughed. "And why would I lie to you about such a thing, my Warrior friend, knowing as I do your desire for one last luxury before departing on your long journey?"

"Darian, we should offer this room to Stefen," Eathelon stated. "After all, he is royalty."

"Are you not a Prince, and Stefen's guest?" asked Darian. "First come is first served, I say." Darian grinned.

"You are a scoundrel, Darian!" Eathelon laughed.

"Well, unlike me, Stefen has impeccable manners and would offer it to you anyway. He has stayed here many times."

"How does this work?" queried Palo. "How does heated water get into the bath and how does it leave?"

"Both questions I had myself," replied Darian. "Jak said the system is rather ingenious, for its time, considering it is old and crude. The bath was here when Jak bought the place and he said there are huge pots of water atop fires on the other side of that wall. The fires warm the water in the pots and pipes take it from them to the bath. Simple, but effective."

"Well, I assume someone must tend the fires then," said Palo.

"Indeed, but they are lit only while we are guests here," Darian responded. "This room is otherwise little used."

Eathelon looked at the capped pipes, just above the water line.

"See that lever? When the caps are removed and that lever pulled down, the water flows in. After the bath fills, the lever is pushed back up and the caps replaced to stop the flow," said Darian. "A hole beneath those plugs in the bottom of the bath drains the water into Brega's waste-water system."

"Well, I am ready for a bath," said Eathelon. "It is the only such luxury we shall have on our journey, until we are back in Andolan."

Darian located the soap as they shed their clothes and stepped into the warm water. They bathed and changed into clean clothes then headed to the private dining room. Stefen and Arestor had already arrived and sipped on wine, awaiting their guests. Supper had been placed on the table.

Stefen raised his glass, as they walked in, "Well met! I have taken the liberty of pouring you a glass of one of our best Holling Vale wines, *Hollindale Rosé*, a sweet, light red." He gestured to the glasses on the table.

"I see we are late for supper," said Eathelon, sitting down and raising his glass. Darian and Palo did the same.

"Not at all," replied Stefen. "It just arrived."

"You all smell ... clean," Arestor noted, grinning. "I see you found the bath."

"Indeed, we did," Eathelon responded. "It is good for a man to have a bath after long days of riding on muddy roads."

"Especially when sharing a room with his traveling friends," added Darian.

They all laughed.

The five of them ate supper and talked together. As usual, Eathelon drank his wine slowly. As they finished up, a key turned in the locked door to the main hall and Jak entered.

"Well timed, Jak," said Darian. "We have just finished."

"I apologize for the interruption, sires, but a stranger in the main dining hall has been asking about your Warrior friend here and I thought you would want to know about it."

"Indeed, thank you, Jak," said Stefen.

"I will leave the door to the main hall unlocked and have someone clear your table after you retire to your rooms." Jak left.

"I have done as you asked, Stefen," Palo stated, "and kept to my cover."

"I do not doubt you Palo," replied Stefen. "It is difficult for you not to draw attention to yourself, though most people here tend to mind their own business. I am curious about anyone asking about you, especially considering the company you keep."

Stefen turned to Darian, "Go and look, Darian. Have Jak point the man out to you and see if you recognize him. Be discreet."

"Discretion is my business," smiled Darian. He stood to leave.

"I will go with you," said Arestor.

The two left and returned several minutes later.

"I did not immediately recognize him," Darian stated. "He could be the same man I saw in the dining room at Dar's *Bed and Supper* in Heath, but I cannot be certain."

"Do you think it a coincidence that this man was at Bartil's when you and Eathelon stayed there, then turns up in Brega after you arrive here?" asked Stefen.

"I do not believe in coincidences," replied Darian.

"Nor I," Stefen agreed. "Perhaps you are followed."

"Or perhaps he has business here, like the rest of us," Palo offered.

"It is his business that interests us," said Stefen. "There is little reason he should take an interest in you, beyond one of curiosity."

"Perhaps curiosity is sufficient reason for him to follow us," Eathelon suggested.

"After all, Palo is posing as a Northman, Stefen," stated Darian. "A Northman would not only be a curiosity, but perhaps also be feared."

"Well, I am getting tired of this curiosity thing," said Palo. "I will go ask this man to his face what business he has with me. It is the Maagi way. I do not like all of this sneaking around."

"Think it through, Palo," said Eathelon. "Of course, you are a curiosity, but let us not start something. We need more information."

"Eathelon is right Palo," Stefan concurred.

"Well you at least look like you belong," Palo pointed out to Eathelon, grumpily. "And I doubt we will find out what this stranger wants without a direct confrontation."

"Nevertheless, it is wise for us to wait," cautioned Stefen.

"I have been thinking about it," said Darian. "Palo did not go to Heath with us, he remained in camp, so that man could not have seen Palo in Heath."

"Darian makes an excellent point," Eathelon remarked.

"He could be one of the men from the mail-stop outside of Hamil," added Arestor.

"I do not think so," said Stefen. "Palo did not accompany you to the mail stop."

Arestor rubbed his chin in thought. "You are correct, he did not. An old woman came by camp and begged us to take a piece of late-arrived mail. Perhaps she saw Palo and told a husband or son."

"Was Palo with you when the woman came?" asked Stefen.

"Yes, but she did not enter our camp, of course, for it is not allowed," replied Arestor. "But Palo accompanied me much of the time Eathelon and Darian were in Heath."

"I saw the woman," said Palo. "It is possible that she saw me."

Stefen probed, "She was a woman, not a man, unless a man disguised as a woman."

"No," chuckled Arestor, "she was a woman."

"Definitely," agreed Palo. He grinned and made a hand gesture for a woman's shape.

They all laughed.

"Isn't Hamil the village that group of ruffians at Harwyn Crossing claimed to be from?" asked Darian.

"Yes," replied Stefen.

"I don't recall seeing that man in the group," said Arestor. "I remember their faces because I believe they meant to rob us."

"We thought the same," Eathelon agreed.

"Perhaps the men at Harwyn delayed us intentionally," offered Stefen, "though to what purpose I cannot say."

"If true, their purpose would have been to give this stranger and his companions time to reach Brega before us," said Darian.

"And when they saw Stefen and our company, they changed

their plans in a hurry," said Arestor.

"Darian chased them off before they could make further mischief," noted Stefen. He thought a moment, then added, "It is wise for you three to remain with the company as long as possible."

"This is all only speculation, Stefen," remarked Eathelon.

"Perhaps, but when you leave us, I advise you to watch your backs."

"We can send an escort with you to Malta," Arestor offered.

"Thank you Arestor, I think not," said Eathelon. "Let us not alter your plans for the Keep. Perhaps it is better that we go alone."

Arestor nodded.

The companions turned to lighter, more jovial talk after that. Eathelon noticed the waning half-moon through the small, high window in the dining room, and smiled. They finished up, locked the door to the private dining room and adjourned to their rooms, where fires now blazed in the hearths.

Palo fell immediately to sleep, as evidenced by his heavy breathing, while Darian slept peacefully. Eathelon remained awake half the night, thinking about the stranger, the men at Harwyn, the fyrcaat incidents, and if they were all connected somehow. He thought about the Golden City, Northwest Wood, the maiden and countless questions swirled about in his head, but sleep did come to him eventually.

Palo woke him in the morning. They dressed and went to the private dining room, where Darian awaited them.

"We overslept," said Eathelon.

"No, Stefen and Arestor ate early and left," said Darian. "Stefen is making the final arrangements for the provisions we need, but he and Arestor will join us for supper. The company leaves tomorrow morning." He grinned. "We have the day off, however, so let us go explore Brega!"

The largest township in Southern Hamlet, Brega is still but a tenth the size of Andolan and there is little to see outside of an old part of town preserved for historical purposes, businesses, shops and ale houses. They visited a few hand-picked shops where Eathelon purchased a pair of boots and Palo the vest he had wanted, with money Aneron had provided them. That done they decided to look around for the stranger. They looked in a few of the alehouses, to no avail, then Darian took them to *The Silver Foxx*, his favorite place. They selected a corner table that enabled them to see anyone who came or went through the front door, ordered a light meal and a local brew, Grenway *Golden Ale,* which Darian recommended. Palo drew the customary stares from patrons, which he ignored. As they drank and waited for their meal, they noticed three men enter and stare menacingly at Palo. The three took a table across the room and sat down.

"It looks like we no longer have need to look for our stranger," said Darian. "He has found us."

"I want to know what he is up to," said Palo.

"So, do I," said Eathelon, and he started to get up.

"Hold," said Darian.

Eathelon sat back down.

"Let us observe awhile," said Darian. "We can learn much from simple observation."

"It appears they are doing the same with us," said Palo.

When the food arrived, they talked as they ate, glancing up only now and then to observe the strangers.

"I would still like to question those men before we leave," said Eathelon.

"They have done nothing yet to warrant it," said Darian.

"I believe they have," said Eathelon, "but you know the spy business better than I, so I will defer to your wishes. But know this Darian, I do not care to be followed without knowing the intentions of those who follow."

"I suspect their intentions may become clear soon enough," replied Darian.

They finished up the meal and exited the Silver Foxx, leaving the strangers at their table, but when they arrived outside, they discovered their horses missing.

"We left them tied right here," said Palo.

"Yes," said Darian, "Someone has either taken our horses, or they have miraculously freed themselves."

They searched the immediate area for the horses, to no avail. The strangers exited the Silver Foxx and one smiled malevolently at them as they did.

"Now would be a good time to confront these men," said Palo.

"We still do not know if they are following us," said Darian. "I have an idea. Follow me." They walked, casually, around to the side of the *Silver Foxx* and into an alley between it and the shop next door. They went halfway back and stood behind a stack of crates piled against the alehouse wall. The back of the alley was dark, but a light at the entrance enabled them to see anyone who entered the alley from the street.

"Watch and listen," said Darian.

Only moments later, they heard voices.

"They went in there," said a man.

"I saw 'em go in," said another.

"What if they are armed?" asked a third.

"Shut it, coward!" said the first.

The companions drew knives and waited.

Darian peeked around the crates. "Those are the men from the dining room, as we guessed."

"I told you they followed us," said Eathelon. Fed up with this caat and mouse game, Eathelon stepped out of the shadows to confront the strangers, against Darian's advice. Darian and Palo had no choice but to follow him out.

"Why do you follow?" demanded Eathelon.

The leader, talking like a hissing snake, replied, "You misstake us. We are ssimply out for a walk."

"You lie," said Darian. "Answer his question."

"Alright then, just say we are curiouss about that one." He pointed at Palo. "He iss not from around here, iss he?" He addressed Palo, "Where are you from? The north? And what race are you?"

"My race and home are my business," replied Palo. "Why make it yours?"

The man did not answer his question, but instead asked, "What brings you to Brega?"

"Are you Shirif here, or just looking for trouble?" asked Darian.

The man smiled, revealing crooked yellow teeth. "We are merely concerned citizens."

"I have heard those words before," said Darian, "at Harwyn Crossing."

The man reacted, but quickly recovered himself. It was all Darian needed to confirm his suspicions.

"That man is not from around here," said one of the strangers. "We want to know who he is and what he is doing here."

Palo's face practically glowed red in the dark.

"Why?" asked Eathelon. "Prejudice is ignorance begging trouble."

"Go on about your business," said Darian, "and leave us to ours."

The three strangers did not move.

"Leave us, I said!" Darian repeated.

The men stood fast.

For a moment, no one moved or said anything. Then Darian spoke.

"I remember you now," he said. "You were at Dar Bartil's — in Heath." It was just a guess, but Darian hoped it would bring another reaction.

The leader's mouth twitched under the light and he smiled a crooked smile. "You are misstaken, friend," he said.

"I think not," Darian replied.

Another momentary silence.

The man looked at his companions then yelled, "Now!" and the three of them bolted into the alley, drawing knives as they came.

The companions stood their ground, their own knives drawn.

The largest of the three strangers went for Palo, faltered a little when he realized the Warrior stood more than 4 inches taller, then continued forward.

Another man went for Darian and the man who'd done most of the talking went for Eathelon.

Palo dodged his attacker's first lunge. He had already sized up his opponent and anticipated his move, so when the man lunged again, the Warrior side-stepped his knife, throwing the man off balance. This infuriated his attacker, who struck out in anger. Palo knew an angry man could make a mistake in a fight and it proved little more than a caat and mouse game with the trained Warrior. The man lunged three more times and Palo dodged all three then, on the last, caught the man around his neck and held him fast, knife to his throat. "Who are you and what do you want with us? Answer me or I will slit your throat!" The man struggled to get free from Palo's grip, to no avail.

Meanwhile, Darian faced his attacker and also managed to dodge the first lunge. He came back at the man with his knife and wounded him in the arm. The man jumped back, ignored the wound and lunged again. Darian side-stepped the attack and his blade cut his opponent's side this time. The man howled in pain, reeled a little, then came back hard at Darian. This time, Darian disarmed him and hit him hard in the face, knocking him to the ground. The man lay still, bleeding from his wounds.

Eathelon confronted his attacker, and like Palo, anticipated his first move. He countered without wounding the man and positioned himself for the next attack. *Clearly these men are not trained warriors.* He did not want to kill the man, he just wanted to know who they were and why they attacked. His opponent lunged again and Eathelon side-stepped him causing the man to lose his balance. Seizing on this opportunity, Eathelon hit him over the head with the butt of his knife and the man fell, face down in the dirt, stunned. Eathelon put his foot on the man's neck and held him down.

"Who are you and what do you want with us?" he demanded.

The man could not reply, so Eathelon loosened his foot a little. "Answer, if you value your life."

The companions appeared to have everything under control, with two attackers down and the third in a headlock, when suddenly two more men appeared at the top of the alley, stood a moment, assessing the scene, then drew swords and came in. They both went for Eathelon.

Despite their prowess, the companions knew knives were no match for swords. Darian left his opponent in the dirt and rushed to defend Eathelon. Palo, Eathelon's sworn protector, went to defend his Captain, dragging his captive by the neck.

Eathelon, his foot on his opponent's neck, was forced to take it off and back up, as the two swordsmen approached. His captive rose, brushed himself off and joined the two attackers.

Darian's opponent rose and made a fourth.

Seeing this, Palo thrust his knife into his attacker's back and the man crumbled into the dirt and lay still. One down, four to go.

The four attackers pressed the three companions to the back of the alley, to trap them. The companions stood their ground and, as the men advanced, he recognized one from Harwyn Crossing. Seeing Darian's look of recognition, the man smiled as he advanced.

Darian quickly broke off two pieces of wood from a crate and threw one to Eathelon, to use as a shield. Palo grabbed another for himself.

The two attackers with only knives engaged Palo and Darian. The two with swords pressed Eathelon the rest of the way back in the alley.

Palo's knife struck flesh and his attacker went sprawling face down in the dirt. The man looked up and, seeing he was no match for the huge Warrior, rose and feigned to fight, then turned and fled the alley. Two down, three to go.

Palo saw that the two swordsmen had Eathelon pinned at the back of the alley, swords at his throat and ran to help.

The back door of the Silver Foxx suddenly slammed open and the noise caught them all by surprise and momentarily halted the fight.

Two men stepped into the back of the alley; swords drawn.

"What do you say, Arestor, shall we even the odds?"

"Indeed!" said Arestor, "I prefer a fair fight."

They approached Eathelon's attackers, who had no choice now but to defend themselves.

Stefen's sword clanged against one of the attacker's sword, again and again, as the two men danced back and forth in the alley. Stefen forced his attacker back up the alley, away from Eathelon, and his sword pierced his opponent's sword arm. The man dropped his sword and Stefen halted and encouraged him to pick it up. When he did, he turned and fled. Three down, two to go.

Arestor kept himself between Eathelon and his opponent, thrust, parry, thrust, parry, thrust and finally pierced the man's arm. He turned and fled. Four down, one to go.

Darian still fought his attacker up the alley. The man circled and thrust his knife at Darian's mid-section, but Darian successfully dodged the blow. He attacked back. The man dodged and circled again, but this time before he could attack, Darian's knife went into the attacker's arm and hit bone. The man screamed and dropped his knife and, seeing he was alone and unarmed, turned and fled.

The companions came together.

"Why did we let them go?" asked Palo. "We thought we wanted information."

"Those two with swords had plenty of time to skewer me, yet they did not," said Eathelon.

"Indeed," said Stefen. "Had they wanted Eathelon dead, he would be, though I am certain not without injury to themselves." He grinned at Eathelon.

"We will never find out now why they came after us," said Palo.

"Those men, except for the two with swords, perhaps, were not trained fighters," said Darian.

"And the two with swords not highly trained," smiled Arestor.

"Those men fought well enough," said Palo. "I was about to get information out of one of them, when the other two showed up."

"How did you know where we were, Stefen?"

"We did not, at first," Stefen replied. "We evidently arrived to the Silver Foxx right after you left. When we did not see your horses, we thought you had already returned to camp. Then Arestor spotted them wandering back from up the street and we knew you would not have set them loose. We searched inside the Silver Foxx and, when we came back out, we saw those men skulking at the top of the alley and surmised the rest. We ran back into the Foxx, through the kitchen and out the back door into the alley."

"You were more observant than we, it seems," said Eathelon. "I did not see the back door in the dark."

"It was locked from the inside," said Stefen. "You would not have been able to open it."

"I would have liked to take at least one of those men captive," said Darian, "but Eathelon's safety was our first priority. They will not attempt to follow or attack us again, now that we know who they are."

"Others may come," said Arestor.

"Yes," said Stefen. "Those men must have followed you from Heath, though to what purpose, I do not know."

"Spies for the East, most likely," said Darian.

"We cannot know that for certain," said Eathelon.

"What would eastern spies be doing this far west?" asked Palo.

"What they do best," said Darian. "Spy for the East and take whatever information they find back to Baele."

"Perhaps they only wanted to rob us. You said yourself, you thought the men at Harwyn intended to do that," said Palo.

Darian looked at Eathelon. "I think not, my friend. Baele or Esol, or one of their minions likely sent those men to follow us."

They exited the alley and went to find their horses, who had not wandered far and were quickly rounded up.

"Those two men with swords must have turned your horses loose," said Arestor.

"Well, I still want to know why they came after me," said Eathelon.

"Clearly, they only meant to capture you, Eathelon," said Darian. "They did not kill you when they had the opportunity. If they are in league with the East, it is reason enough."

"They cannot possibly know anything of my errand," said Eathelon.

"No, they cannot," replied Darian. "And they erred when they revealed themselves to us, a fact for which those men will no doubt pay." He paused. "I have friends in Brega. I will give them a description of the men and have them look for them. If they find them they will lock them up, so they cannot make any further mischief. Those men are of no further use to the East now that they have revealed themselves. Perhaps my friends will get some useful information out of them. I will meet you back at the Black Caat." He left.

"Arestor and I still have a few things to attend to. We will meet you back at the Black Caat for supper." They left.

Eathelon and Palo mounted their horses and returned to the inn. They bathed again, to remove the dirt and tension from the incident. They all gathered in the private dining room for supper, discussed the day's events as they ate, then turned the conversation to the journey ahead as they sipped the last of the wine.

"Where do we go after Brega?" Eathelon asked.

"We will take the north road over the hills," replied Stefen. "They shorten and flatten out as the road winds down to the plains of Southern Hamlet. Forwyn Crossing is on the north end of the plain, its bridge a smaller version of Harwyn bridge. The river narrows there and runs swift and deep."

"The Teb-Arnor joins the *Harmen River* just above *Harna Falls*, south of Forwyn Crossing," continued Arestor. "The two rivers split again below the falls. The Harmen reaches its fingers into the Lowlands, as it winds its way down to *Tebe Inlet*. The Teb-Arnor continues its 800-mile journey south and enters the Westmost Sea near Balor Bay."

"Our original destination," Eathelon chuckled, thought-fully.

"Well, I am glad your path led you to us instead," said Darian.

"As am I, Darian," smiled Eathelon. "Our journey has taken many unexpected twists and turns already, as Celorn foresaw."

"After Forwyn Crossing," Stefen continued, "we make a gradual climb into the hills of Northern Hamlet, to the Southern Crossroads. There, we will part company. You three will continue northeast to Malta, then north up into the Golden City. The company will take the northwest road, which turns north ahead and follows the Teb-Arnor into the Eathen Mountains, and on up into the Highland Gap, to Toldor's Keep."

Stefen stood and Arestor joined him.

"We must return to camp now," said Stefen. "The company will leave soon after dawn. Be back on time so we are not delayed. Meanwhile, enjoy your comforts here. There will be no more such comforts after we leave."

Stefen and Arestor left for camp and the companions retired to their sleeping room.

Chapter 17: Northern Hamlet

Eathelon rose before dawn and joined Palo and Darian for a quick meal in the private dining room. They packed their belongings, thanked Jak for his hospitality. They rode to camp and reached it, as dawn broke and, soon after the company mounted and started off on its northward journey.

"How far is it to Northern Hamlet?" Eathelon asked Stefen.

"Two days to reach the plains, two more to Forwyn Crossing."

The five companions rode and talked together throughout the first day, under a gray sky then camped in the Grenhyl for the next two nights. As Stefen had said, the hills grew shorter and the grass grew a little taller as they crossed Southern Hamlet. Soon they began to see burned-out abandoned homes, one after the other. These had overgrown, weed-choked yards and fields, broken fences and front doors that gaped open to reveal dark, empty rooms that suggested the fate of the owners.

"A gloom lies over this land," commented Eathelon.

"It is thick with despair," Palo noted.

"Like Numar, these lands were ravaged by the East, mostly mercenaries out of Rabellan," said Arestor. "Yes, Aneron told us the citizens who arrived to Andolan, Hamstead, Heath, Brega, or other smaller towns once lived here. Those who remained here perished."

"Few live on this Hamlet now — only those brave, or foolish enough to have returned home after the Great War," said Stefen.

"They must no longer live under threat here," said Eathelon, "yet we have not seen anyone."

"Those who remain live closer to Forwyn Crossing," Stefen

replied.

"Well," Palo stated, "should we encounter any of these mercenaries, I will have reason to test my Warrior skills again."

"That is unlikely," remarked Stefen.

"Mercenaries, were they about at all, would not dare to attack a large group of Andolan's soldiers," Arestor added. "They only prey on defenseless people."

"Let us not look for trouble," said Eathelon. "but focus on our errand."

"Trouble has already found us, though we did not look for it," Darian offered.

That ended that conversation for the time being and they rode in silence awhile after that, as they continued north the rest of the day. Drawing closer to Forwyn Crossing, they passed more occupied homes, as evidenced by sheep, goats and horses roaming in the fields and chikkas running freely in some of the yards. People tended their orchards and fields and, when they saw the company approach, they stopped and came out to greet them, waving and bowing to the Prince of Hamlan, who nodded and waved in reply. Some of the boys saluted the passing soldiers, who rewarded them with a salute in return.

"Narda's future soldiers," said Eathelon. "I confess, I did not expect to find so many people out here."

"They remain for the same reason I and my men remained in Numar," responded Darian. "This is their land and home and they believe they can defend it."

"They cannot defend it against mercenaries," Arestor claimed. "Those men are lawless, ruthless. If mercenaries penetrate Hamlan this far west, these people will no doubt perish. They would be mowed down without conscience, and none left alive, not even the woman and children."

"Do not underestimate these people," Stefen insisted. "They are brave, courageous and resourceful."

"They will perish all the same," Arestor replied.

"Then we must do whatever we can to protect them," said Stefen.

"Can you not warn them, if you believe them threatened?" asked Palo.

"We will, of course, but they are proud and believe in their right to remain here, to own their land and defend it," replied Stefen.

"And why not?" added Darian. "People do have rights here, only men like Baele, and those in his employ, driven by greed and power, care nothing for people. They seek to rule all of Narda and everything and everyone in it."

"We are no doubt a welcome sight, when we pass," said Stefen. "Our presence here offers some small hope of safety for them. But these people are mostly eager for news of loved ones, from Andolan or towns and villages south of here. They wait for the letters and packages we bring. We are their link to loved ones and, when we come, it gives them cause for celebration."

Some of the soldiers dismounted and distributed mail. Stefen and Arestor dismounted to speak with some of the men, to encourage them to move their families to the city for protection, telling them there has been rumor of a possible conflict with the East. But they respectfully declined the offer, saying the East is far from them and they doubted any conflict would reach so far west. So, when the mail had been distributed, the company continued on and the people waved as the soldiers rode out of sight.

Late on the fourth day out of Brega, as they approached Harna Falls, Eathelon saw hundreds of sinter hawks circling overhead. "Darian, why do so many hawks gather up here?"

"We are near Harna Falls now," replied Darian. "The hawks build their nests high on the cliffs here. It is mating season and a sinter hawk mates for life, so must choose a mate with great care — like us." He grinned.

Eathelon grinned back and watched the hawks until the company had passed beyond their view.

They came to the bridge at Forwyn Crossing and Eathelon saw that what Stefen had said about it was true — a smaller version of its sister bridge at Harwyn Crossing. He watched the Teb-Arnor rushing down to meet the Harmen to later spill over the falls.

"Have you been to the falls, Darian?" asked Eathelon.

"No, and the sight is worth the climb, it is said," replied Darian. "Our path lies a different way today, but perhaps we shall return and visit them, once your errand is finished."

"Perhaps," said Eathelon, thoughtfully.

The soldiers filled the lamps with oil, as they crossed, while the company waited patiently on the other side. Shortly after, they came to an expansive grassy field and stopped at a large stone monument, one of a tall, handsome soldier sitting atop a pizo. Eathelon saw that the soldier bore the helm and shield of the House of Toldor. Stefen and Arestor saluted it, as they passed and Eathelon looked back to see the men of the company do the same.

"Who is that man?" asked Palo.

"The greatest hero in Hamlan," replied Darian, and he explained. "After Tebor, the Eldarin traitor, was banished to the East, he made a feeble attempt to take over the West and as part of that, made a pact with the Northmen. The brutes are not very bright and Tebor promised them the spoils of Hamlan if they would join his army to help defeat the West. I doubt Tebor had any intention of delivering on his promise, but the Northmen agreed to join with him and they invaded Hamlan through the Highland Gap. They did not succeed in overpowering the West, largely due to the fortress city of Andolan, but the Northmen did overtake Toldor's Keep, for it is close to their own region, the Northern Reaches."

"That is why you are restoring the Keep," Palo remarked.

"It is one reason, yes," replied Arestor. "We cannot permit Northmen to take our northern fortress ever again. Anyway, the Keep fell and seeing they had been defeated, Captain Teold, King Toldor's only son, led the survivors in a retreat to Forwyn, but found the bridge taken and the route cut off, so, they stood battle on this field. The Elvenkin of Northwest Wood, allies of the King, after successfully defending their wood and Elvenvale against the mercenaries, cut the eastern army's numbers in half, but too many remained they eventually overtook Teold and his men. The stand is known in our history today as *The Battle of Two Rivers,* for this field is near the meeting of the Teb-Arnor and Harmen rivers. Many Northmen fell here, but so too did Teold's men and the last to fall was Teold himself, it is said — Hamlan's greatest Warrior and beloved Prince."

"It is a brave, but sad tale," Palo commented.

"Yes," Stefen said. "So aggrieved were the citizens of Hamlan that they mourned all the seasons after, from Earlyfall to Earlyfall, and King Toldor never fully recovered from the loss of his only son. When Toldor passed, Teold's son and heir, Eatnin took the throne. He commissioned this monument in honor of his Father and the men who fell on this field defending Hamlan."

"You and Arestor salute your lineage then," said Eathelon.

"Yes," replied Stefen. "We pay homage to a common ancestor."

"The fortification of the Keep has been a long, arduous task" added Arestor, "but the Keep will not fall again."

"The Northmen are still a threat then?" asked Palo.

"They will always be a threat, so long as the Highland Gap remains open," replied Arestor. "The Northmen are huge, stupid brutes, willing to follow orders from a despot like Tebor, or his successors, Baele, or Esol. They may well have already recruited the Northmen into their armies, for all we know. We would be wise to expect this."

"If the Northmen are enemies, why did you have Palo pretend to be one, Stefen?" Eathelon asked. "Perhaps that is why we were followed."

"I do not think so, Eathelon," replied Stefen, "If anything, Palo, as a Northman, should have proved a welcome sight to those men, if Northmen have again been allied to the East. I, for one, doubt his cover story fooled them, for clearly he was not the object of their attention — you were."

"I still do not understand what reason those men would have to come after me," said Eathelon.

"That, my Mallorite friend, is something you will need to discover," replied Stefen.

"Darian said his ancestry is known to the East," said Arestor. "You are half Eldarin, a stranger in Darian's company, sufficient reason for the East to have you followed."

"Those men could not possibly know my ancestry," claimed Eathelon.

"You said yourself Baele probably has one of the Seeing Stones," Stefen pointed out. "Perhaps he used it to learn of your presence."

"Stones?" asked Darian, giving Eathelon a curious look.

Palo gave Eathelon a sideways glance.

"I will explain it to you later, Darian," replied Eathelon.

"The Northmen dared not enter Hamlan before their alliance with the East," said Darian, "except on occasion to take some of the women of Forth, as was said. But the Northern Reaches are harsh and cold, and the Northmen tribal. They war amongst themselves, 'tis said. It is not unreasonable to believe some of them might wish to live in a warmer climate."

"I do not believe the brutes capable of such a thought," said Arestor.

"Perhaps not all of them are brutes," Eathelon suggested. "Any man can be turned into one, given sufficient time and means of duress."

"Perhaps, but ignorant people are easily led by someone like Baele," Stefen noted.

"Those brutes are hostile by nature," said Arestor. "They have aided our enemy and are likely to do so again, so let us not let philosophy get in the way of good judgement."

"It does seem that Northmen are bred for war," said Palo. "Of course, the Eldarin have always tried to recognize the good in people, an admirable trait, but we must not forget that some men are simply evil."

"I, like my Father, prefer peace," declared Stefen, "but war will come to us, whether we want it to or not, and the Northmen will likely to be on the side of the enemy."

They rode on in silence after, until Stefen ordered the men to make camp at the north end of the grassy field.

"I want to go back for a closer look at the monument," Eathelon stated. "Would anyone care to join me?"

"Not me," replied Darian. "I have some things to discuss with Stefen."

"I will come," from Palo, whose job required it, of course. "I want a closer look at this Warrior-hero."

The two rode back to the monument in the fading light, as a low mist began to form over the grassy field.

"What is it you expect to find?" asked Palo. "It grows dark.

Perhaps we should look for whatever it is in the morning."

"You know very well the company leaves at dawn. No, whatever is there to find must be found tonight."

"Well, what do you expect to find then?"

"I do not know. I am drawn to it, for some strange reason."

"That is not the answer I expected. Must we search in this cursed fog for something unknown while supper waits?"

Eathelon gave him a look of annoyance, which Palo failed to see in the dark, and ignored his question. He walked around the base of the monument, examining it, but in truth, did not know what he expected to find and simply trusted his instinct.

Clouds took over the sky and even Eathelon's keen eyes discerned little as the fog, and night set in. He felt a vibration on his chest. *The amulet!* He pulled it out and it began to glow, bathing them, and the monument in its pale green light. Palo watched, intrigued. He had never before seen Eathelon use it.

Palo walked along behind Eathelon, as they circled the monument again. "Eathelon, if you do not know what you look for, how will you know when you find it?"

"Instinct. I need just a few minutes more, Palo. Please be patient."

Palo shrugged.

"Go keep the horses company, if you must," said Eathelon.

Palo grumbled and went over to join the horses, his stomach reminding him it was time to for supper, but he kept an eye on Eathelon.

Eathelon made a third pass around the monument but noticed nothing unusual. He was about to give up his search, when a sudden screech from above pierced the night. He looked up to see the shadowy outline of a sinter hawk perched atop the shrine. *What is a hawk doing here, and at night? It must be from the falls, and has lost its way.* But he had no time to puzzle over it, as something came streaking toward him from out of the dark. The hawk launched itself from its perch at the same time, talons outstretched and Eathelon ducked as both creatures raced past his head with a *whoosh*. The hawk screeched as it plucked the creature out of mid-air, wrestled it then tossed it to the ground, landing it with a *thud* at Eathelon's feet.

Palo heard the commotion and ran over to see what happened. He found Eathelon on his knees, examining the creature in the light of the amulet.

"What is it?" Palo asked.

"A dead fyrcaat, Palo — thanks to that sinter hawk." Eathelon looked around for the hawk, but it had vanished.

Palo pulled out his knife, kneeled down and slit the fyrcaat's throat, spilling its blood onto the grass. Eathelon grimaced, but could not blame him, for the Warrior had suffered much from the earlier fyrcaat wound in Numar.

"That hawk probably saved my life, Palo. I believe the fyrcaat meant to harm me, though I have no idea why, or why the hawk intervened, grateful as I am that it did. I have no more lothingel to counter a fyrcaat barb."

Palo bent over the creature. "Eathelon, look. The creature has a collar. It must belong to someone. Now who would keep a fyrcaat for a pet?"

Who indeed? thought Eathelon.

"The *Fyrls* keep them, or so it is said. But they supposedly tame them. They live near the creatures in the caves beneath the Fyr Mountains, in the East. I doubt a Fyrl would collar a fyrcaat. It must be a pet of the East, perhaps one of Baele's, or Esol's creatures. If true, it would certainly explain some of the things I have puzzled over since we arrived."

"Should we bury it?" asked Palo.

"No. We should get back to camp. Say nothing of the incident to the others."

"Darian, at least should be told."

"These fyrcaats are pursuing us for a reason we have yet to discover, Palo, though I believe you only got in the way on the ridge. They have missed their mark three times now and this time one paid with its life. If this creature belongs to Baele, he will not be pleased. He may want revenge for its death."

"If the creature belongs to Baele, I care little for its loss, or his. You could have paid with your life, Eathelon."

"Yes, and yet, Baele cannot possibly know anything of our errand, Palo. This is still a puzzle."

"His House is of Eldarin ancestry, or have you forgotten

Eathelon? Perhaps he has one of those Seeing Stones, as you said, and perhaps he knows how to use it."

"I have thought of that Palo, but even if he has the Stone, I doubt he knows how to use it. He would need the Book of Stones for that and Celorn said it is hidden somewhere in the Golden City."

"Perhaps someone from the East found it when they invaded the Golden City."

Eathelon did not reply to Palo's comment, but said, "When whoever sent this fyrcaat learns of its death, I doubt he will send another against us, at least not while we remain in the company of soldiers. But we shall not take any more side trips alone for now. And I will tell Darian about this later. For now, let us keep it to ourselves."

"I do not agree, Eathelon, but I will do as you ask."

"I ask that you trust me."

"You know I do."

They rode back to camp and found supper waiting.

"What did you think of the monument?" Stefen asked, as Eathelon and Palo helped themselves to supper. "I trust you found it as inspiring as we do."

"I found the craftsmanship excellent."

"And so you would," said Stefen, "for it was sculpted by one of the finest Eldarin artists in Andolan." He took a sip of wine and looked at Eathelon.

Eathelon simply said, "Of course," smiled and changed the subject. "How far are we now from the Southern Crossroads?"

"Seven days, providing we have no delays."

"More mail stops?" asked Palo.

"No," replied Stefen, "only weather. It grows late in the seasons now. Few people live in the Hamlet between here and the Southern Crossroads, thanks to the mercenaries who emptied it long ago. These lands are too far north and too difficult to protect, so its inhabitants did not return. I expect we will arrive at the Southern Crossroads in seven days, as planned."

Eathelon nodded, still a little distracted by the fyrcaat incident. Three now.

The journey to the Southern Crossroads did prove uneventful and they did reach it in seven days, as Stefen predicted. The soldiers set camp and a watch and the five companions sat at their own campfire, as before. They ate supper and talked about their upcoming journeys.

"What will you do when you reach the Keep?" asked Palo, taking a bite of roasted deremeat.

"Drop the men off, inspect the work completed since our last visit, and return some of the men to Andolan, ones who have been at the Keep six months or more, who wish to return," replied Arestor.

"The restoration of the Keep should be nearly complete now," said Stefen.

"How long will you stay then?" asked Eathelon.

"Until *Dèrnon* — Latefall," replied Stefen, "perhaps as late as *Énan* — Wintereve. But we will have to start back before the heavy snowfalls."

"How do you get any work done in winter?" asked Eathelon. "Does the snow not prevent it?"

"Some work, yes," replied Stefen, "but weather little affects areas inside the Keep. We have plenty of warm clothing, tools and provisions, so the work continues. The restoration has taken several years, but when completed, the Keep will withstand any enemy."

"I see it is a key defense for Hamlan," said Palo.

"Indeed," replied Stefen. "It is meant to cut off access to Hamlan from the Northern Reaches, to keep the Northmen out of Hamlan."

"There is no such fortress in the southern lands," Darian pointed out. "Numar is unprotected, but for the Rangers. But the greater threat lies in the north. Still, Numar lies closer to eastern shores and is a vast area to cover."

"We are fortunate to have the Rangers to keep our southern lands safe," said Stefen.

His comment reminded Eathelon of something he meant to ask Darian. "Darian, will you return to your southern lands and rejoin Farli and the Rangers, or come to the Golden City with Palo and me?"

"I have often considered this question during our journey, but I left Farli in charge of the Rangers because he is capable to act in my stead. My purpose in coming with you has been to assist your errand. I want to see that through. I will accompany you to the Golden City, though I fear it is no longer golden."

Eathelon gave a nod and smiled. "We shall be glad of your company, Darian."

"Eathelon," said Stefen. "The Golden City holds the ghosts of the dead now, I have heard. You should prepare yourself for what you may find there."

"Nothing in my past experience has prepared me for what I have already encountered in Narda," replied Eathelon. "I can only expect the unexpected and be as prepared as possible to meet it. I have no fear of these ghosts of the dead."

"Nor I," said Palo.

"That is well," said Stefen. "I find fear an unwelcome companion in my own travels."

Eathelon turned to Darian. "Your knowledge of Nardan geography is not only helpful to us, Darian, but vital to our journey. It is one thing to see something on a map, another to follow someone who has walked ... or ridden its paths."

The five of them continued their conversation into the night, until sleep begged and they were forced to take to hard beds on the ground. Excited and anxious about the next leg of his journey, Eathelon fell asleep dreaming of fyrcaats, strangers following and wondering what other unexpected things he might encounter in this sometimes wondrous, sometimes frightening land of Narda.

Chapter 18:
A Hunting Accident

The sun's rays filtered down through the evergreen trees onto plentiful undergrowth in the Sylvan Forest, its abundance the result of Midwinter snowfalls and Earlyspring rains. Such conditions made for good hunting. The grass, high and green, smelled sweet and the streams, filled to the brim, teemed with fish. Those whose livelihoods depended upon it hunted rabet, squirl, dere, foxx and any other forest creature whose flesh or pelt they knew would bring a good price at market.

Oni and *Hagi*, two of the best *Lit'l* hunters in all of Aynor — the city of Lit'ls far up in the Sylvan Mountains — had hunted here for two weeks. Lit'ls are smaller than normal for Nardans — being three to three and a half feet tall, but are otherwise like anyone else. By now, these two Lit'ls had accumulated enough pelts to return home to the Autumn Market.

"The end of the hunt makes me think of the stew my Lili will cook when we get home and how the young'ns will hang all over me and beg for stories of the hunt."

"I think about what I can buy when we give over our pelts at the Autumn Market — jewels for Bibi and hunting knives for my son."

"And what about that large baer rug you've wanted? You can get it without having to kill the roaring beast yourself!"

"Ha! That's the best way! Those baers are more than thrice our size and turrible hard to kill — if they don't kill us first!"

"Yes! And we can tell our adventures of the hunt over Grenway brew at the tavern. I can taste the salty liquid now, just thinking about it."

"We should earn enough from selling our pelts to buy all of the brew we want for the whole winter!"

They laughed. It had been a fruitful hunt and today they started for home.

Now Oni and Hagi always kept to the main trail because they knew it to be the safest way home. But, a long, twisting and turning trail, it did not prove fast. They had started their trip later than usual and had already pushed their luck to be back in time to compete at the Autumn Market. They knew if they did not get the pelts back in time, they may not earn enough to pay for all of the things they had just discussed so, after a short debate, they decided to cut through the forest and pick up the main trail farther east, cutting off some time.

But traipsing through the forest turned out to be more difficult than they anticipated. They wound their way through the trees, did their best to avoid the thorny underbrush and soon found themselves in a deep thicket of tall blue *rinna fern*. At first glance, they saw no way through it, so stopped to discuss their situation.

"We need to go back to the main trail," said Oni. "It's over *this* way." He pointed in the direction he thought led back.

"No, it's over *that* way," countered Hagi, pointing in a different direction.

They debated for a few minutes then decided Hagi would take the lead and started off in that direction.

Oni stopped. "Wait," he said, "I need to tie my bootlace."

But Hagi had gone on ahead and, before Oni could finish the task, he heard Hagi cry out, "What the ...?"

His view obscured by high rinna fern, Hagi had stumbled onto a group of Northmen. The brutes sat in a circle, resting. Hagi tried at once to backtrack but one of the Northmen stuck out his arm and nabbed him. The Lit'l struggled to get free to no avail, so he yelled at the top of his lungs, "Run, Oni! Northmen! Run!"

When Oni heard his friend yell for him to run, he felt torn with indecision. He hesitated. He wanted to help Hagi, but instinct told him to do what Hagi insisted and run.

"Run Oni, run!" Hagi yelled again. "Run for your life!"

Oni took off running back the way they'd come, doing his best not to lose his pelts.

One of the Northmen jumped up and ran after him, hot on

his heels.

Oni heard the huge Northman tramping through the trees behind him and he zigzagged through as fast as he could, but the heavy pelts slowed him down. With great reluctance, he cut the pelts from his belt and let them fall, knowing as he did there would be no brew, no jewels for his wife and no hunting knife for his son. His heart sank as he picked up his pace.

Northmen are large and clumsy, and Lit'ls run very fast. They dodge, ditch and dive in and out of the trees and underbrush almost as fast as a rabet. Oni ran as fast as his short legs would carry him and, as he did, he remembered a cave he had once seen in the general direction he was headed. He made for it. The Northman had gained a little on Oni as he'd slowed to free his pelts and Oni could hear the brute's hard breathing close behind him now and the sound of twigs and brush breaking under the Northman's massive feet. Oni knew he could be caught at any minute. He ran faster and faster and he reached the cave entrance just ahead of the trailing brute.

He dove headfirst into the hole, and squeezed through it, one in which his body barely fit, and tumbled down to the bottom of the cave. The Northman halted at the entrance and tried to stick his head in, the only body part that could possibly fit, but it didn't.

"Come out, you ruddy rodent, or I will come in after you!"

Oni smiled in the dark. The Northman's threat didn't frighten him — he knew the brute could never fit through the entrance. He sat down to think and it occurred to him that there might be another entrance the Northman *could* fit into. Out of breath and exhausted from running, he forced himself to rest calmly and reason out his situation.

The Northman stuck his huge arm down the hole, hoping to grab the Lit'l, but Oni was too far down.

The brute stood up and cursed, "Come out of there you ruddy rodent!"

But the Northman's words fell on deaf ears.

Once his eyes had adjusted to the dark, Oni surveyed the cave and saw two adjacent tunnels. He did not know which one to take, so he tried the left one. It came to a dead end after a short distance, so at least he knew there was no other entrance in that direction. He backtracked and took the right tunnel, which led deeper into the cave. He felt along the cave wall in the dark for several minutes then glimpsed a dim light ahead, which he guessed could be an exit. He worried that the Northman would find it too. But he knew he could not stay in the cave too long — he had to get back to Aynor and sound the alarm! Northmen afoot in the Sylvan Forest? It had never happened, not in his lifetime!

The tiny opening sat many feet above his head and, grasping any nub and crack in the cave wall that could hold him, he started to climb. At one point his foot slipped, but he held his grip. He reached the opening at last and wriggled out through the hole, one only slightly larger than the cave entrance. He blinked and looked around as his eyes adjusted to the light.

He crawled out onto a wide flat rock that jutted up against a rock wall to his left. He surveyed the immediate area then crawled with stealth over the flat surface toward the cave entrance. He peered down carefully over the edge and found the Northman down on all fours, cursing, his arm still in the hole.

Oni smiled. Not a very bright fellow, he.

He did not want to wait around and risk discovery, so he crawled back to look for another way down. But the rock wall blocked his exit on that side and the stubborn Northman waited at the entrance. His only way out was back down the hole into the cave and out the way he'd come. He was trapped! Tears filled his eyes, tears for Hagi, who probably lay dead, tears that he could not get out to sound the alarm and warn his people. He crept back to the area over the cave entrance and peered down again. The stubborn Northman was still there, cursing and grumbling.

Suddenly, the brute stood up and Oni flattened himself on the rock and lay still! He slowly crept back to the rock wall, wriggled down into a large crevice, curled up and lay as still as stone, tears staining his face.

He heard the Northman cursing and stomping and throwing things down the cave entrance for some time. Finally, the Northman stopped cursing and Oni heard the sound of twigs breaking and snapping, loudly at first, then fading away. The Northman had left. Oni stuck his head up and listened intently. When he heard only the sounds of the forest, he climbed out of his hiding place. He guessed the fate of his friend and long-time hunting partner, for he'd heard tales of rare attacks by Northman on Lit'ls and no Lit'l had ever survived one.

He mustered his courage and climbed back down into the cave. He knew the Northman could be lurking in the forest, just waiting for him to come out but he couldn't stay in the cave. He had to get back to Aynor. He made his way in the dark back to the cave entrance, climbed up and wriggled his body out. He stood at the entrance for a moment, letting his eyes adjust to the light and listening, ready to dive back down if he had to. When he heard only the sounds of the forest, he took off in the direction he thought led back to the main trail then, relieved to find it, ran as fast as he could back to Aynor.

Oni felt terrible leaving Hagi behind, but he knew he could not go back for him. Even if Hagi were still alive, which he doubted, the two of them were no match for even one Northman. Oni knew Hagi would do the same if the situation were reversed. He hated leaving his pelts, but what choice did he have? He was lucky just to be alive. Hot tears fell down his face as he ran and he did not brush them away.

* * *

Back in the Northmen's camp, Hagi was *not* dead, though he may have wished it so. He laid there, limp, eyes closed, while five Northmen debated about what to do with him. One of them picked him up and dropped him hard to the ground. With all of his will and might, Hagi did not move a muscle or make a sound, despite his pain. He knew his life depended upon it. Attacks by Northmen on Lit'ls, though rare, had occurred during the Great War and a Lit'l, being so much smaller than a Northman, had never survived. Hagi could not help wondering what Northmen were doing on this side of the Sylvan Mountains. They lived on the *other* side. It never occurred to him that the brutes might cross over. He'd heard tales of Northmen, but until now had never seen one. He knew of nothing the Lit'ls had done to provoke their wrath but then, Northmen are not known for their brain power and Lit'ls are pretty intelligent. Did these Northmen even know about the city of Lit'ls? Hagi thought about all of this as he lay injured. He knew the Northmen were not considered Nardans — they lived up in the cold Northern Reaches. They were said to be mean-tempered, even toward each other and Hagi could certainly confirm that.

Almost as if a Northman had read his thoughts, one gave Hagi a swift kick. It took all of Hagi's will not to react. The Northmen laughed, but he stopped when the one chasing Oni came crashing back into camp.

"Where is that other little rodent?" asked Grel, their leader.

"Aw, he got away," the Northman replied. "That rodent crawled into a hole this big (as indicated with his hands) and I couldn't get to him. I yelled and waited for him to come out, but he never did, so I left."

Hagi recalled one of the first things he had heard about Northmen — *huge, aggressive, mean-spirited and a brain the size of a petiperl seed.*

"You weed under a tree!" cried Grel. "You let that little rodent get away? He will run back to Aynor and sound the alarm! You'll be roasted at the stake, you worthless piece of baerwolff dung and so will the rest of us!"

"Well what was I supposed to do?" the Northman whined, "go in after him? He is tiny and fast as a sparrow. I am large and well ... not so fast."

"*Brik*, you ..." Grel didn't finish his sentence. He hit Brik on the head with his club and the Northman fell to the ground, dazed.

"What do ya want us to do with 'im, boss?" asked a Northman, pointing to Brìk.

"Bury him alive, for all I care! He's gonna get us all killed."

Taking Grel literally, the three Northmen grabbed Brìk under the armpits and dragged him off. They began digging a hole with their huge hands.

"What the ...?" Brik came to his senses and saw what they intended. He struggled to his feet and took off running.

Grel arrived just in time to see Brik disappear into the forest. The other Northmen stopped digging.

"Good riddance!" Grel called after Brik, then to the rest of his crew, commanded, "If he comes back, throw him in that hole!"

"Yes, boss," they all replied.

They walked back to camp where Hagi still lay on the ground, unmoving. One of the Northmen put a foot against his captive's side and pushed hard. Hagi suppressed a cry of pain.

"What are we gonna do with this one?" one of the Northmen asked.

"Can't ya see he's already dead?" another added.

"Too bad," said a third, "we coulda had some fun with 'im."

"Naw," responded the first, "these rodents are no fun. There's more sport in a squirl."

"Well, what *are* we gonna do with 'im — eat 'im?" The Northman who'd said that guffawed and the others joined in, as if he'd just made a brilliant joke.

Everyone but Grel, that is, who scowled at them. "Leave 'im for the carrion birds. Let's get out of here. We have more important work to do."

The men just stood there.

"Now, dogs!" barked Grel.

They all stomped off into the forest, but not before one of them gave Hagi one last kick. Tears flooded the Lit'l's eyes from the pain, but he didn't move, and the Northman didn't see.

When Hagi felt certain the brutes had been gone long enough, he dragged his injured body into the rinna fern with a great effort. He knew his legs must be broken because he couldn't stand. He dragged his body deeper into the dense fern and lay there, breathing hard. He had worked so hard to get those pelts and now they were gone. The Northmen had taken them. But he was still alive — perhaps the only Lit'l to ever survive a Northman attack!

As he lay there, he realized there would be no way to get home. He was simply too injured. Well, perhaps Oni made it back. That thought comforted him.

The sun had fallen far down the sky now and the forest lay in deep shadow. It grew cold. But before the sun disappeared altogether, it thrust a ray down into the fern and it fell on a *blu-tailed sarow* that sat on a branch above Hagi. The bird looked at the injured Lit'l, cocked its head, chirped and flew away. Then all went dark.

Chapter 19:
A King in Exile

A soft breeze rocked the fronds of the *paalam* trees on and above the beach, another balmy evening on *Suvrii*, largest of the Flax Isles. As the sun sank slowly into the Southern Sea, it marked the end of another lovely day, one that nearly made Landrin forget why and what he was doing here. He looked down on the beach from a window of his home on *Mt. Fava* and watched the gentle waves lick the white sands that stretched across the island. But he knew well the treachery of the Southern Sea, how it could turn with a fickle wind into a raging tempest, unleashing its fury upon those who sailed into it, for such had been the fate of his Eldarin friends. They had sailed into it knowing full well its dangers, but having no other choice, and the sea had swallowed them like hapless chikkas plucked from the plains of Newelan by hungry fyrcaats.

Newelan. Castletop. His home, so close he could almost reach out and touch it! Yet here he sat still, a prisoner in this beautiful island chain. He stared out at the blue-green waves, their unruly crests and rhythmic flows lapping at Suvrii's white sandy shore as if to rush in, wear down her defenses and penetrate her long, peaceful valleys, like the House of Tebor had done to his lands, people and home. Castletop had fallen and its King had fled in exile, when he should have remained and fought for what was his! He sighed. But he could never risk his Aliana's life, yet her exile had claimed it anyway. But they had made a good life here, at least for a time.

He had been a persistent, unrelenting King, in whom desire and determination had once burned. He felt old now, spent, but the ember had not gone out altogether. It still burned, one of a desire long buried beneath broken dreams and illusions. And what would it take to bring it back to flame? His Aliana could have done that, had done it before. How he missed her! She had made his exile so much more bearable, had kept his hopes alive, that one day they might return to Castletop and the House of Began might rule again there.

His mind, imprisoned with regret from past failures, had created in him a deadening apathy, but he somehow knew his lethargy was only one of a resignation to his fate of growing old here, weighed down by a surfeit of loss.

And there were still two who could raise him out of that lethargy — his son, Landon and his daughter Liana. Their efforts to rekindle his hope irritated his apathy, like the discomfort of a leg long asleep, that wakes to a prickling pain.

Landon shall rule Newelan one day, and whether I am alive to see it or not is of little consequence, so long as Newelan is restored to the House of Began. But in his heart, Landrin knew he wanted to see that day.

Landon entered the room and pulled his Father from his reverie. The old King looked at his handsome young son, who'd inherited his Father's dark brown hair and hazel eyes, a look so different from that of his sister, her Mother's namesake.

"Landon, good, you have returned. What kept you?"

"Delays, Father, delays. I awaited information I only just received. When are we going to go after that raat Baele and his flea of a son, Esol? You are 10 times the man Baele is. Why do we not act to take back your throne?"

"Patience, Landon, patience. To act in haste is to waste the act. We do not yet have the resources together to make such a move. We must plan our moves, as we do in King's Chess. Have you not learned this?"

"A man may lose King's Chess if he hesitates too long — or becomes otherwise distracted." Landon drew in a long breath and sighed. "You are right, of course Father. You know I am not a patient man. That is not a trait I inherited from you, I fear. Sometimes I want to strike out the eyes of that Eastern snake!"

The old man sighed. "We are both right, Landon, me with too much patience, perhaps and you with too much impatience.

But save your aggression for the conflict that is sure to come, for there will it best serve us. Now, tell me what you have discovered."

Landon walked over to join his Father at the window. He stared down at the beach and brought his emotions under control, as he watched the sun fall into the Southern Sea.

"It is lovely here, Father, I will give you that. I see how easy it might be to become complacent."

"Perhaps I do sometimes forget why we are here, Landon, for I have come to love these isles. Exile could have been much worse."

"I love these isles too, Father, did I not grow up here? But we must not forget what you and Mother left behind, what is rightfully yours."

"Nor have I, son, though I am afraid the fire that burned hot in me then, has long since cooled." He turned and smiled at his son. "Come, that fire has not gone out altogether! Give me what information you have."

"Something is brewing in the East."

"Well, that is little hidden to us, even on Suvrii. Things have been quiet there overlong, and a puffin fish can only puff so long before it must exhale or explode. But what information prompted you to say this?"

"The trade ships arrived from Antebba yesterday morning. *Lesil* was aboard the entire voyage and sent a messenger yesterday to bring us news that some of the ships bound for *Cornth* had disembarked special cargoes and sent it overland to Newcastle, to satisfy the demands of that selfish son of a traitor, Esol. How I despise that weakling living in your house, Father, sitting on *your* throne! He takes what he wants from Newelan and Hond and it still does not satisfy his obsessive appetite, so he robs Hamlan's best, too. And that fool of a King Aneron lets him do it!"

"Take care with your words, Landon," the King stated sharply. His voice softened. "Aneron is no fool. His trade agreement with Baele bought my life and your Mother's and keeps our family safely here. Be grateful that Aneron's negotiations with Baele have kept The House of Tebor out of Hamlan — and out of these isles. We could just as easily have suffered the fate of the Eldarin."

"I know, Father. I did not mean to disrespect Aneron. I learned only recently that he mourns his wife and baby son, and I am sorry for that. But rumor says he neglects his people."

The old man, instead of getting angry, smiled at his son's critical remark, and said, "When you have sat a throne and suffered a loss like his, or mine, you will better understand his pain. Do not judge Aneron until you have lived as he has. Things are not always black or white, Landon, but often shades of grey."

"But there is so much to accomplish, if you are to have your throne back before you pass, Father, and shards in my side, I want it to happen soon!"

The old King sighed, remembering his own impetuous youth. "The House of Began will rule Newelan again, Landon. Whether or not it happens before I die, I cannot foresee."

A shadow crossed the old man's face.

"I am sorry, Father, are you alright?"

"I am fine. I just thought about your Mother for a moment and how much I still miss her. She would probably feel as you do."

"No Father, she would chastise me for my impatience, and impertinence. She always was your greatest ally."

The old man smiled at his son. "Finish your report please, Landon."

"Well, Lesil set eyes and ears in Antebba before he sailed, as requested. His man there reported that Esol is up to something, a fact he verified from an origination by a drunken merchant seaman, in one of the taverns. He said Esol has traveled north to Gorst again. He usually returns in a few weeks, but this time, he has been away six weeks or longer. Esol dislikes Gorst and its dreary hall, so it seems odd that he has remained in Gorst so long. The man also said there has been much unusual activity in Gorst, of late."

"What kind of activity?"

"Ships entering the *Bay of Gorst* at night, unloading soldiers, and fires burning in the lower regions of Castletop. Have fires burned beneath Castletop before, Father?"

"No. That area was only used to store supplies."

"Lesil's messenger said many of Newelan's citizens are imprisoned there."

"We never had prison's beneath Castletop. That is Esol's doing, or Baele's."

"Lesil's man said he did not learn much about Baele's plans but implied there has been an expedition north. The man was found dead in Antebba this morning."

"This is ill news, Landon. There can be only one purpose for Baele to dispatch an expedition north — to recruit the Northmen. The House of Tebor has done so before."

"We cannot know that for certain, Father."

"I know Baele. He has stewed long in the juice of his past defeat and it has poisoned him. He will not rest until the House of Tebor rules Narda, not just the East." The old man sighed. "The peace of these isles has distracted me, Landon, and lulled me into thinking that the trade agreement between East and West would keep the peace. It is all too easy to remain here, far from the troubles of Hamlan, but Aneron is our friend and ally, and I can no longer deny what my heart desires. Baele may be a madman, but he is clever. Though his initial intention with the trade agreement may have been to keep the peace, I believe he uses it now to convince Aneron that he desires peace, while he schemes in secret to conquer the West."

"Then we must act, Father."

A flicker of the old flame of determination returned to Landrin's eyes — one his son had inherited in abundance.

"The spy business is risky, Landon, and treacherous. That man found dead in Antebba — find his family and make certain they are cared for, though I fear there is little comfort we can offer them in their loss."

"I have already done so, Father, and with such discretion as I knew you would want."

The King nodded his approval. "There is nothing north of Gorst but the Great Dune Desert of the Castellan Valley. The ruffians who eke out a living in Rabellan dislike each other almost as much as they dislike us." He laughed. "They would probably kill each other over a loaf of bread, if provoked. If those men are allied to Gorst again, trouble will find the West sooner than we may think. And these isles will not be overlooked. We will be pulled into the thick of it."

"I thought the mercenaries have always fought on the side of the House of Tebor."

"That is true, so we have no reason to expect that would change." Landrin paused. "How reliable is the information Lesil gives you?"

"He has never given us bad information."

"We must get a message to Aneron. He must have this news."

"I will see to it, Father."

The King smiled, "You will make a good King one day, Landon."

Landon frowned. "I doubt I will make one as wise as you, Father."

They clasped arms and, as Landon turned to leave, he added, "Oh, I forgot. There is one other thing ..." But before he could finish, Liana entered the room, a wide smile on her face and the King turned to greet her. Landon did not finish his sentence.

Tall and lithe, Liana's long auburn hair fell below her shoulders and covered her breasts. A circlet of gold that held a bright green jewel in the center sat on her brow and nearly matched the color of her bright green eyes. She walked to her Father and planted a kiss on his cheek.

"Hello Father," she said, then turning to her brother, added "hello, Landon."

"Liana," Landon nodded.

"You were saying, Landon?" his Father asked.

"It will keep until we next meet."

"Come then Liana, tell me about your visit to *Tívia*." Landrin grabbed her by the hand and pulled her over to a chair.

Landon smiled at his sister. She had always commanded her Father's attention and he sometimes envied her in that regard. "I must leave you to Liana's adventures, Father, I have business elsewhere. You can tell me all about Tívia over supper, Liana. We will speak again later, Father." He turned and left.

"Well daughter, tell me, where did you go, and what did you do on Tivia? Did you bring me a gift, as promised?"

Liana laughed.

"A King you are, Father, yet sometimes you are like a boy asking gifts from Ealdor's bag."

Landrin laughed. "Well, even a King has something of a boy left inside, though few people but his children ever see it. And how disappointed you would be if I did not ask about my gift — is that not true?" He smiled at her with affection. She was much like her Mother in appearance, but very unlike her in manner. Aliana had been a responsible Queen who'd offered hope and encouragement to him. Liana liked to socialize and she appeared to have few ambitions. *I have indulged her too often and her Mother has not been here to prevent it,* thought Landrin.

Misreading his thoughts, Liana said, "You miss Mother, don't you Father?"

"What? Why yes, of course, I shall always miss her." He paused, then said, thoughtfully, "We must take her back to Castletop ... when the time comes."

It seemed off the subject, but Liana acknowledged it. "Landon and I will see to it, Father."

"So, you will daughter, and you will see to me too, if I join her in sleep before we take back my throne."

"Do not talk of such things, Father! We will all return to Newelan together, you will see."

The King smiled. "Alright, Liana, now tell me of your adventures."

"Tivia is much smaller than Suvrii, as you know, but it is very beautiful and there are many amusing things to do there." She paused, thoughtfully. "It is lush with vegetation and waterfalls and many different kinds of trees, not just the paalam trees that are so plentiful here. The water is clear all the way to the bottom, and many colorful fish visible there. Why have you not taken us there before now, Father?" She giggled. "The place is simply magical!"

The King laughed.

"I am pleased you like it so, Liana. Your Mother loved it as you do. As to why I haven't taken you, for one, I am getting too old to traipse about Tívia, and two, the isle is full of memories of your Mother, and the time we spent together there. She loved the marketplace." He sighed.

"So *Sinda* said, though despite her age, she is as much a child as I."

"Of that I have no doubt. She accompanied your Mother to *Tivia* often and the two of them ran from booth to booth buying up whatever struck their fancy, as if we'd a fortune hidden away for the purpose." He stared at the picture of his wife in his mind and his smile lingered, then faded. "It was good of Sinda to take you. I know she misses your Mother too, and I do not worry about you when you are with her. Now, what did you bring back?"

"Something befitting a King, Father."

She pulled out a small box, opened it and held up a wide-banded gold ring with a large green jewel in the center and smaller white ones on either side.

"It is magnificent, but, however did you pay for it?" He frowned. "Sinda better not have indulged you in this and I gave you only a few coins to make a purchase. This must have been priced well above what I gave you."

"Do not worry, Father, Sinda did not pay for it. You are right, of course, it was priced well above what we could afford, but are you not a King, and I the daughter of a King?"

The old man questioned her with his eyes.

"Do you believe a jeweler could charge for such a gift when he knows it is bound for the King's finger?"

"I am not King here, Liana."

"Perhaps not, but you are loved and respected as one here all the same. Everyone here knows you are the rightful King of the East and many still believe you will return to Castletop one day, including the jeweler who made this ring for your finger. He said it is his gift to you, for that day. He asks only that you remember who gave it to you — *Somi*. He said you know of him."

The old King's eyes moistened, "Indeed, I do. He made that beautiful jeweled necklace your Mother always wore."

"Where is the necklace now, Father? I have not seen it since

Mother ..."

He cut her off. "It is in safekeeping, Liana and it will be yours one day, should you sit beside Stefen as the Queen of Hamlan."

Seeing her Father did not wish to pursue the matter, Liana changed the subject back to the ring. Holding it up, she said, "I believe it is a good advertisement for the jeweler too, which is no doubt why he offered it free of charge."

Perhaps there was more of Aliana in her than he thought.

"I may have to consider putting you in charge of public relations, Liana."

She pouted. "You know very well that even if I aspired to such a post, which I do not, it would never be allowed. Our outdated custom is clear in that respect."

"Well, such customs do not exist here and besides, a King has the discretion to change an outdated custom, if it no longer serves a purpose."

"Perhaps so, Father, but you know I would not place any shadow on my brother's hopes for the crown, though I expect I will wed Stefen one day."

He smiled at her. "So you shall, Liana."

She placed the ring on Landrin's finger and he admired it. "Thank you for the lovely gift, Liana. I shall always treasure it."

He took her hand and listened to her talk for the rest of the day, as she told of her adventures with great enthusiasm. They dined together that night and continued their conversation, but Landon did not join them. When they said goodnight, Landrin passed by his son's room on his way to his own and saw the light on. And it was still on when he passed by it again the next morning, on his way to brefas.

Chapter 20:
Esol's Errand

Esol paced back and forth in the foyer of the Great Hall of Gorst. He hated to be kept waiting. *Father treats me like a common servant, but I will rule here one day and we shall see then who waits.* A crooked smile crossed his face like a zig-zagging path snake, but it faded when he realized that, in order for him to inherit the throne, his Father would be have to be dead, and that fact alone would rob him of any satisfaction he might have in reversing his circumstance. Esol could not gain a victory at anything, when it came to his Father, it seemed.

Esol had always found the Great Hall of Gorst a dreary, boring place. He'd been here a month this time and was anxious to return to Newcastle. He did not altogether trust the men he'd left in charge of Castletop, but then Esol trusted few men, and his Father least of all now.

Father cares nothing for my difficulties when he summons me here on short notice. He expects me to drop whatever I am doing and come running whenever he calls. But I have my own duties and responsibilities in Newcastle. Sometimes I think I am no more to him than another of his propitiating servants.

It took Esol two weeks of hard riding from get from to Gazlag from Newcastle, and he had just returned home when he was summoned back. He knew he could say whatever he wished about his Father in his own mind, but he dared not utter a word of it aloud. It was when his Father seemed to like you most that you had to watch your back. One could find himself Baele's best friend one minute and dead the next. His Father changed moods faster than a *drubot* changed direction in a storm, but Esol had to admit that what little affection his Father possessed was offered to his only son.

Growing up in this dreary place was much like a weed trying to push up through stony ground — much effort, little reward.

Esol had actually admired his Father once and craved his approval, something Baele seldom offered. The Lord of Gorst instead demanded obedience and loyalty, not affection. Esol had witnessed more than once the price a man might pay for saying the wrong thing, or if his Father suspected betrayal — torture, or death. It seemed to matter little to his majesty whether the man later proved innocent. And, as his Father grew older, Esol saw that he did not always differentiate between a man's guilt or innocence. Everyone was guilty of something, it seemed. He knew his Father liked deciding the fate of others.

Esol doubted his Father would kill his only son, but he did not want to test it. His Father's cruel and capricious nature both frightened and exhilarated him, for he shared some of the same traits.

The door creaked open, a servant beckoned Esol inside and he walked down the main aisle of the dark hall toward the dais, where his Father sat waiting.

"You are back, Esol, good, I have an errand for you."

Esol knew now that he would not be returning to Castletop anytime soon. He sighed.

"What errand, Father? Why have you not told me of this errand before now? I have been here for a month."

"The errand had been long in planning," replied Baele.

"And why keep me waiting outside the hall? You treat me like a guest in my own home, one I grew up in. I should not need an escort to enter my own hall."

Baele motioned his hand to dismiss his son's remark. "There is no use getting upset about it. You have your own home now at Castletop. If the servants detained you, I will have a word with them about it. Such was not my doing." But it was, of course.

"No need, Father." He did not want his Father's two closest servants to get into trouble on his account, for they had always been kind to him and he might need them later. He had plans of his own.

"Had you told me of this errand sooner, I would have had more time to prepare."

"Well, there is no use informing you of something that was

not altogether put together, is there?" Baele chortled, then, without warning flew into a rage. "Why do you always question my judgement? Am I not Lord here?"

Esol shrank back a little at the outburst. "Yes, Father, you are Lord of Gorst. But if I am to follow in your footsteps one day, you might keep me better informed."

A shadow crossed Baele's face, then passed. "You will be Lord here when I say so and not before!"

Esol took his Father's hand, a gesture that had always had a calming effect on him, for some reason. "Father ..." but Baele interrupted him before he could say anything further.

"Muji has disappeared, Esol. Those intruders have killed him! Only Fyri and Raji have returned from their errand."

"Perhaps Muji has lost his way, Father."

"No. I saw it in the Stone. He is dead!"

"I am sorry, Father."

"Well, you should be! You sent them!"

Baele looked at his son with malice and smiled. "You sent them!"

Esol replied, calmly, "You ordered me to send them, Father."

His words impinged.

"That is not the point," replied his Father. Baele smiled a crooked smile and his voice turned to syrup. "But you can make it up to me, son."

Esol recognized that look and voice and sighed in resignation. "What would you have me do this time, Father?"

Baele motioned Esol to his knees then stroked his head. Esol shrank back a little from his touch, but remained respectful.

"Get up!"

Esol stood. "What is it you want me to do?"

"Go north, to meet with our old allies. North lies our salvation. North lies our best hope for a victory over the West. North lies the little trick in my bag to get that old *hagid* Aneron, to draw him out, get the dragon out of his lair, so to speak." He smiled and chortled down in his throat.

A knot formed in Esol's stomach. "How far north Father?"

"As far north as you can possibly go."

Then Baele told him his plan.

Chapter 21: Parting Company

At their camp, just off the Southern Crossroads, the companions rose at dawn under a soft yellow sky and ate brefas, as the men of the company broke camp. Between bites, Stefen told them what they could expect on the next leg of their journey and drew a map in the dirt to illustrate.

"The north road — here — will take you to Malta, through these hills, which make a gradual climb north to the Eathen Mountains. From there it will take you about three days to reach the Southern Arch, which marks the entrance to the Golden City. It lies at the front edge of this plateau. Once you have completed your errand in the city, just follow the main road north, out of the city and exit beneath the Northern Arch. From there, the land begins a steep climb up to Mt. Athel. A narrow trail leads up to Egin Pass here, the place where your ancestors first crossed the mountains to Malta, in the First Age."

Eathelon and Darian looked at each other.

"That was just a side note. You should reach the Northern Crossroads — here — after two days more and, if you follow this trail east from there, you will reach Northwest Wood in another three and a half or four days."

"Is Egin Pass near Toldor's Keep?" asked Palo.

"No," replied Stefen, "I pointed it out to show Eathelon where his ancestors crossed after landing at *Eredian.* The pass is the only passage through the mountains to the western shores of Hamlan, which is why the Eldarin crossed there. I thought Eathelon might like to know."

"I thank you," said Eathelon. "It is the history my Mother taught me also."

"Egin Pass is usually open only in the summer months," added Darian.

"So, you take the company on this west road, then," Eathelon said to Stefen, pointing it out.

"Yes, the road turns north ahead and follows the Teb-Arnor River up almost to the Northern Crossroads. From there, we will take a narrow trail up into the Highland Gap, and on up to Toldor's Keep."

Eathelon smiled. "It looks as if we will all pass by the Northern Crossroads, but by different roads, at different times."

"That is likely," Stefen responded.

"Where does this road lead?" asked Palo, pointing to a large east-west line on the dirt map.

"That runs along the bottom of the hills of Malta, then turns north and follows the Harmen up to the southern tip of Northwest Wood. From there, it runs eastward, across the *Plains of Baerlan* to the Fyr Mountains. *Rampaatha*, it is called, East Road. It is the only road that links Northern Hamlet to Eastern Narda."

"It crosses the Great Dune Desert then," from Eathelon.

"Yes," replied Stefen. "From the Northern Crossroads, take this high trail eastward along the bottom of the Sylvan Mountains to the edge of the cliff that overlooks the valley of Elvenvale. The trail switchbacks down from there, into the valley. Cross the valley and enter Northwest Wood from here — where it bends in. It is the shortest route to Lingolia, city of the Elvenkin."

"We now have an idea where we are headed and about how long it should take us to reach our destination. We thank you, Stefen," said Eathelon.

"Wintereve is not far off, but your chances of making it to Lingolia before the snows arrive are good, I think," said Stefen.

"Can you tell us anything about the Elvenkin?" asked Palo.

"Not much," replied Stefen. "They keep to themselves and are wary of strangers, it is said. I suggest you keep to the valley until you reach this bend in the wood."

"I visited Lingolia once, with my Mother," Darian noted. "I do not fear the Elvenkin."

"Nor I," added Stefen. "I only meant to say the Elvenkin are wary of strangers because Eathelon and Palo are strangers here. I do not know if the Elvenkin will welcome you, but when you reach the wood, ask for Mengalan. He is Lord of the Elvenkin, who were once allied to Andolan. I advise you to keep your errand close, Eathelon. Discuss it first with Mengalan. His view of Andolan and my Father are unknown to me."

"You have no cause to worry," said Darian. "The Elvenkin are a fair and honest people."

"I only pass on the advice I feel I must offer. The Elvenkin have long been sundered from Andolan. I suggest you go with caution."

"We thank you for your advice, Stefen," added Eathelon.

"I dispatched a messenger to Andolan this morning, with news of our progress thus far, as the King requested," said Stefen. "I mentioned the incident in Brega."

"That is well," said Darian. "It is good that Aneron is forewarned, so he can turn his attention back to his duties and make the necessary preparations."

"Take care with your words, Darian," Stefen warned, though not unkindly.

Darian shrugged an apology. "I meant only to say that the King should have any news of what we already know is likely to come."

"Aneron is no fool, Darian," Stefen pointed out. "He knows."

They finished up the meal, helped clean up, then said goodbye to each other. Stefen and Arestor mounted their horses and signaled for the company to move out.

"Safe journey," said Stefen.

"Safe journey," replied the companions.

"I will show you the Keep when you return, Palo," Arestor stated, and he turned to ride off.

"We shall all meet again in Andolan," Stefen declared.

Meet in Andolan, yes, such is my hope, Eathelon confirmed to himself.

The three companions packed and mounted their horses then started off on the northeast trail toward Malta. The trail soon narrowed, forcing them to ride single file. Darian took the lead and Palo the rear. With conversation all but impossible now, they rode in silence and Eathelon turned his thoughts to his errand. Would he be able to find the Book of Stones in the Golden City? Or, perhaps one of the Stones? He doubted the latter.

After about an hour, the trail widened back out again and they rode abreast. They resumed casual conversation as they took in the sights and sounds of the surrounding lands. The high green hills soon swallowed them and after a time, colorful dots appeared on them — yellow, purple, pink and blue wildflowers. Eathelon recognized some of the trees that dotted the landscape, oak, cedar and pine, but he did not recognize some of the others.

Late in the day, clouds gathered overhead and the air turned chill. The temperature dropped quickly and they pulled on woolen cloaks against the cold. They camped at dusk in a small copse of pine and built a fire in a little hollow. Hungry after the long day's ride, they ate leftovers Stefen had provided, and talked. The clouded sky hid the moon and stars and they made a shelter against the possibility of rain. The night remained dry, but a gust of wind blew the shelter apart, exposing them to the cold. It blew the clouds away too, however, and they rose to a cold dawn and pale blue sky dotted with puffy white clouds, and the ghost of a crescent moon sitting above the horizon.

Eathelon, who had risen before his companions, walked to the top of a nearby hill, stood and looked north to the tall, rugged peaks of the Eathen Mountains. His thoughts strayed back to Melatui, to his Mother. For she ruled now over the Maagi, a dangerous position for her after the death of his Father. He decided to send her a thought-message, though he was not certain whether she would receive it, for Melatui was far away. Still, he would try.

He closed his eyes and formed the thought, then pictured her and sent it off: *I am here, in Malta Mother. We ride to the Golden City!*

His thoughts next strayed to Scirra, the young princess who had both intrigued and confused him. He wondered if he would see her again, though it seemed odd to him that he would even think of her. He'd met her only briefly and he knew she had been promised to another. It was but a fleeting thought and he turned instead to thoughts of his errand ahead, whose burden lay heavy on him. He stared at the tall, majestic Eathens, standing steadfast where they had stood all of the long ages of Narda.

Long before the Eldarin crossed Egin Pass to Malta have these mountains stood, and long after I am gone, and my children and their children, will they stand. And what will the cold north wind whisper to them of the Prince of the Mallorites? He paused. *Only that there came a man who wished to right a wrong, and not because he had to, but because it was the right thing to do.*

These words he offered to the north wind and watched as it carried his message up onto the high, white peaks of the Eathens. And there it would remain, he thought, until the peaks crumbled to the ground, in some far-off future age.

Having done this, he felt resolved, as he had on the cliff in Numar, and he strode back to camp with a renewed confidence and determination, for what he must do.

"Where did you go?" asked Palo, who was up, preparing brefas now, while Darian tended the horses.

"I walked to the top of that hill, to gaze at the Eathen Mountains. They are magnificent."

"They look rugged, not at all inviting," Palo observed. "The mountains of Melatui are lush and green. I prefer them."

"True, but the Eathens are magnificent," Eathelon responded, in a way that ended any further comment.

They ate a quick meal, packed up, mounted the horses and started off. After half a day's ride, great fields of golden flowers appeared, and soon the hills all around them were covered in a thick blanket of gold. Eathelon stopped them, in a place where the flowers grew close to the road, dismounted and walked over to inspect one. He had never seen a flower like it. He examined it closely, a fragile-looking bloom, shaped like a tiny cup atop a long green stem, its narrow leaves encircling the stem like a coiled snake.

"What is it?" he asked Darian.

"A maltinia," Darian replied. "They grow only in Malta."

Eathelon found and examined another small white, star-shaped bloom, that sat among the golden ones. Poised atop a thin pale stem, its face was turned upward, to the sky.

"What is this one?" he asked.

"A silmaria," replied Darian, dismounting and coming over to stand beside Eathelon. "The Eldarin brought maltinia seeds and planted these hills, around the Golden City. 'Malta' means 'gold', in Eolengwas, but you know that, of course. I believe it is, in part, how the Golden City got its name. 'Silmaria,' or 'silma,' means star, and is the name the Eldarin gave the white bloom, for its shape, but those blooms are native to Narda."

"Both blooms are rather unique," Eathelon stated.

"Yes. Wait until we look back on the hills of Malta from north of the city. You will find it a wondrous sight," Darian commented. "Maltinias bloom in all seasons, except winter, when they sleep. They return again with the Earlyspring thaw, and the return of the golden flowers has long been considered a sign that the Eldarin will also one day return."

"The hills of Malta are fair indeed," added Palo, who'd dismounted and stood nearby, staring at the golden hills.

"I am beginning to better understand why the Eldarin wish to return," Eathelon remarked. "My own heart could easily embrace this place, though I have not been here before. It almost seems like home to me."

Palo turned and looked at him.

Eathelon saw that Palo did not understand, but he just shrugged and gave him an encouraging smile.

They mounted and started off again toward the city and spent the night in the hills. It had turned bitter cold now, for Dèrnon — Latefall — was due any day. They set a tent, grateful for it and the blankets provided them, and for the leftovers Stefen had the cooks pack for them to take on this next part of their journey. They ate dried chikka meat, dark bread and soft cheese, and washed it down with a sweet light Holling Vale wine, *Riverdale*. Palo kept a fire going against the cold, and the three of them talked until well after dark.

"Malta seems deserted enough," said Eathelon, "as I would expect."

"Yes, though there are some who live here," said Darian.

"What do you mean?" asked Palo. "I thought the Golden City was deserted."

"It is. The Eldarin are gone, but Mengas live in Malta."

"Mengas?" asked Eathelon. "I have never heard of Mengas. That is not in our history."

"No, they did not exist before the Great War. They would not be written in Eldarin history," said Darian. "Mengas are a people dedicated to a life of service in Malta for as long as the Eldarin remain in exile. They choose to remain hidden. It is their way."

"What good are servants if there is no one to serve?" asked Palo.

Darian laughed. "You always seem to make a thoughtful point, Palo. Let me explain. During the war, Northmen killed many Eldarin in the Golden City and drove the rest out of Malta, as you know. They sacked the city and left it in ruin. Before King Feorn passed the throne to Aneron, he called for volunteers to rebuild the Golden City — 'for our Eldarin friends,' he said, 'and for their return. This we do to honor them for all they have done for the West.' That the Eldarin would return, Feorn never doubted, nor Aneron after him, though they both no doubt expected it to be before now. Aneron was a young man, vigorous and energetic when the Eldarin were driven from Narda. He is old now, and he had lost hope for their return, until you came along Eathelon, and renewed that hope."

"Then we have accomplished one small part of our errand," Eathelon claimed.

"Well Mengas are the volunteers. They have evolved into a dedicated group and they have restored much of the Golden City. The name 'Menga,' means servant, or service, in Eolengwas. Mengas made a pact to restore and care for the Golden City until the Eldarin return, however long that takes. Such service passes from one generation to the next. Mengas live in small, simply constructed homes built into the hills, or so it is said. They do not occupy any part of the Golden City, for it belongs to the Eldarin. Menga homes are meant to be temporary, easily dismantled, when their duty is done, it is said. They have gone far beyond what Feorn asked of them. Aneron said they have restored every building in Malta, including Eldarin homes, and they keep the city safe until such time as its owners can return to claim it. We will find Eldarin homes along this road, as we near the city, and others in the city itself."

A people dedicated to the restoration and preservation of the Golden City, who await the return of the Eldarin, and the Eldarin have no knowledge of it!

"Mengas are skilled at remaining hidden," continued Darian, "and skilled in many crafts, as must be evident. One cannot help but admire them."

"Narda holds a surprise around every turn," said Palo.

"Indeed," added Eathelon.

"Some good, some ill," Palo pointed out, rubbing his arm.

"There is likely much to see here," Darian offered. "Let us hope it is all good."

"But let us be prepared, if not," said Palo, ever the Warrior.

On the morning of the third day out from the Southern Crossroads, the companions rounded a bend in the road and the first Eldarin homes came into view. Here, a paved road began, of smooth, gray stone, similar to the main road of Andolan. They marveled at the homes, as they continued to the Golden City. Each had unique characteristics, but all shared a common architecture. They had various sizes and shapes of windows, but all were shuttered. Their front doors differed in color, but each had lothingel carvings around its perimeter. Almost every home had fruit or nut trees, and an herb garden, that included lothingel.

I dare not pick any, thought Eathelon. He wanted to, but it would not be right. *I not a thief.*

Some homes had fences of stone, some of wood, and some had arbors of ornate metal. Some yards had stone or wood bridges spanning a stream that wound from house to house, and most homes had a porch, or a balcony. Straight paths led to some front doors, winding paths to others, and some homes on the hill had stone steps leading to theirs. Eathelon half-expected people to come out to greet them, so well-kept and inviting were the homes. But the quiet was punctuated only by the gurgling of the brook, the murmuring of the trees, and the birds chirping happily away in them.

As they came closer to the city, Eathelon felt a thickness on the air, a sorrow that saddened him and contrasted with the beauty of the surrounding hills and pristine homes that sat empty. He felt joy and sorrow at the same time, a sort of beautiful sadness, but the feeling passed as they rode on.

The Eathen Mountains rose tall before them in the distance now, and the jagged peaks stood cold against a blue-gray sky. The landscape here was beautiful, but lifeless.

"We are spectators here Darian," said Eathelon, "all of us, including Mengas. We watch and wait, while the Golden City sleeps." *Will we be the ones to awaken it?*

On the last day before they expected to reach the Southern Arch, as night fell, Eathelon became conflicted. They needed to find a place to sleep and he had become increasingly guilty about camping in the golden hills. He did not wish to despoil the flowers. This road was lined with Eldarin homes, but if Mengas would not occupy them, neither could they. He mentioned it to Darian.

"I had planned to surprise you two, but since you brought it up, I will tell you. There is an inn ahead, not far now." Darian grinned.

"An inn," laughed Eathelon, "of course there would be an inn, and you would know of it!"

"An inn?" asked Palo, rubbing his backside.

"Yes, Palo, an inn — with a bed."

Palo grinned.

"That is a welcome surprise," Eathelon exclaimed.

"It has long been deserted, but with any luck, Mengas have restored it. too."

"That is well, Darian. Warrioring back home did not require sitting a horse all day. How do you do it?"

Darian laughed. "I am not the best one to ask, Palo. I have spent most of my life on a horse. I was practically born on one!"

"And I, on a boat," said Palo, showing his white teeth.

"Tell us about the inn," said Eathelon.

"I have not been to the Golden Hawk for many years, but if it is even partially restored, it will serve. It was built to house Nardan students who came into the city to study Eldarin history, customs and language. There are a few other inns in Malta, but the Golden Hawk is a favorite."

Eathelon laughed. "Where in Narda is there an inn that is not your favorite, Darian?"

"When you sit a horse all day, any inn is a favorite," grinned

Darian.

"Agreed," smiled Palo.

"Even in its deserted condition, Malta is hospitable to its guests," Eathelon noted.

"Yes, and the Golden Hawk's location suits our needs nicely," said Darian. He paused. "Aneron is an honorable King, Eathelon. I am fortunate to have had three such men in my life — my Eldarin Father, my Nardan Father, and my surrogate Father, the King."

"You are fortunate, indeed," agreed Eathelon. He thought about his own Father, King Maalo, and his Eldarin mentor, Celorn, who had also been like a father to him.

"Are we going to talk about this inn, or are we going to go find it?" asked Palo.

"Let us be off to the Golden Hawk then!" Darian paused. "And if any Mengas object, they can take it up with you!"

Palo made a "Warrior" face and both Darian and Eathelon laughed.

"Mengas hide, you said. They must dislike confrontation," said Eathelon.

"Most likely. I do not expect to see Mengas," responded Darian. "Palo's girth and stature alone would probably scare them half to death anyway."

They came to the top of the next hill and Darian pointed down to a wood and stone building ahead, on the right. "There it is," he pointed out, "the Golden Hawk."

They raced each other down the short distance and dismounted, laughing.

The inn looked like a large house with a wide porch. A low stone fence separated it from the road. They tied the horses to posts left for the purpose and entered through a small black wrought-iron gate in the fence. A sculpture of a large golden hawk, shining in the fading sun, sat on the roof, and a sign that hung down from the porch read: Inn of the Golden Hawk. The inn appeared to be restored.

"Well, like the Black Caat, there is no mistaking the name," grinned Palo.

They stabled the horses behind the inn, groomed, fed and settled them there for the night. Then they tried to open the inn's front door, but it was locked.

"Wait here," said Darian, and he disappeared around the side of the building.

A few minutes later, Eathelon and Palo heard a click and the front door swung open. Darian stood in the doorway, grinning.

"How did you get in?" asked Palo, "did you find a key? I could have kicked the door in, you know."

"No doubt," said Darian, "but then the door would be broken and our beds open to Mengas, or anything else that might wander in during the night. I found a back way in."

"Of course," grinned Eathelon.

They stepped through the door into a small foyer then into a long hallway. The door to a small dining hall stood open on the left. As they continued down the hall, they peeked through the doors to several sleeping rooms then selected one with four beds about halfway down and dropped off their belongings. They searched for and found a closet that held clean blankets and pillows, helped themselves to them and placed these on the beds in their room, then walked back to the dining room.

Palo saw a large fireplace, found some wood stacked on its hearth, and started to make a fire, but Darian stopped him.

"I may be better that we not announce our presence here."

Palo shrugged. "Mengas no doubt already know we are here, and I am cold."

"They know of our presence in Malta perhaps," said Darian, "but we did break into the Golden Hawk, after all."

Palo shrugged and put the wood back on the stack.

They went back and retrieved some food from their packs, selected a table at the back of the dining room, away from the single window, sat down and ate dried chikka meat, bread, cheese and drank what remained of the Riverdale wine. They talked together awhile then, exhausted from the long day of riding, retired to their beds.

Sometime in the middle of the night, Eathelon awoke to a loud *crash!* and a *thud!* He sat up. "What was that?"

"I will go investigate," said Darian, getting up, a frown on his face.

"Mengas?" whispered Palo.

"No," replied Darian.

"I will come, too," said Palo.

"No — stay with Eathelon. If I do not return in a few minutes, leave by the back door — down the hall to the end, then right. The door on the left is to the kitchen at the back of the inn. You can exit there and I will catch up."

Darian left, but quickly returned. "Come and see."

Eathelon and Palo followed him to the dining room. Darian picked up a single lamp with a dim light and shined it on the broken window, then led them over to a pile of broken glass on the floor.

"The crash we heard," Eathelon suggested.

"Yes," replied Darian, "and look at the cause."

"He shined it on the pile of broken glass and atop it, where a dead fyrcaat lay, its belly ripped open. The unmistakable wound had clearly been made by a sinter hawk."

"The hawks protect their namesake, it seems," said Palo.

"Darian, there is something I must tell you about these fyrcaats."

Palo gave him a look that said, "It's about time."

"We found another of these creatures at the Battle of Two Rivers monument," Eathelon stated.

"Go on," urged Darian.

"Fyrcaats have followed us since we set foot in Narda, though I do not know why."

"Fyrcaats have long been a nuisance in Narda, Eathelon, though they are not usually found this far west. I guessed the creatures set fire to the plains, and I saw one earlier on the ridge. I have long suspected Baele and his minions keep fyrcaats for pets, or to make mischief."

"Another thing, Darian. A sinter hawk intervened at the monument, or the fyrcaat would have injured me. I do not know why the hawk intervened."

Eathelon described the incident at the monument and how the fyrcaat had been killed in the same manner as the one here.

Palo bent to inspect the creature. "Like the one at the monument, this one has a collar," he pointed out.

"The collar does seem to imply the creature is someone's

pet," Darian remarked.

"We can guess whose," said Palo.

Silence.

"Fyrcaats are aggressive and dangerous," Darian offered, breaking the silence, "but you two are not the first to suffer such an attack."

"Perhaps so, but three consecutive ones?" Eathelon queried.

"That does seem more than a coincidence," replied Darian. "But this one did not attack — it flew into the window."

"Why would a fyrcaat attempt entry at all?" asked Eathelon.

"Perhaps it thought the window an opening," said Darian.

"Or hunger?" asked Palo. His remark struck Darian as funny, for some reason, and he laughed aloud.

"Make jest of me, if you will. I see no error in my comment," said Palo.

"There is nothing wrong with the comment, Palo," Darian claimed. "I meant no insult."

Palo looked unconvinced.

"I am not convinced the fyrcaat came here after you, Eathelon," Darian commented.

"I am convinced enough for us both," Eathelon replied.

"It is nearly dawn now, and we will not get any more sleep tonight., so we may as well pack up and head out." said Darian.

"What about the window and dead fyrcaat?" asked Palo. "Should we not clean it up?"

"No," Darian responded. "Leave it. We can slip out quietly and the Mengas will only find that a fyrcaat flew into the window in the dark and perished, its belly ripped open by a shard of glass. It is how the evidence reads. Perhaps they will place no more significance on it than that."

"Let us hope so," replied Eathelon.

They returned to their room, packed their belongings, put away the blankets and pillows and left the inn by the back door.

Baele's possession of the Stone may prove more dangerous than I thought, Eathelon mumbled to himself, as they rode off toward the inner city.

Chapter 22:
The Golden City

A pale yellow light painted the sky behind the hills of Malta, as the companions slipped unseen out of the Golden Hawk and made their way toward the center of the city.

Eathelon watched the remnants of a transparent moon fade away, as the sun rose above the gray-shadowed hills, turning them to gold. They rode all morning and reached the Southern Arch when the sun was straight up in the sky.

They gazed in awe at the magnificent stone arch, the southern entrance to the Golden City, for it stood as high as the walls of Andolan, and wide enough for 12 to ride through it abreast. It narrowed as it curved to the top and Eathelon saw that an intricate pattern of lothingel vines adorned it. He read aloud the words carved into it:

*a somï faévë: Eäldor * Aldárian * Faêtir*
*Málta sitaë * Nardåndo*

and translated:

*to our Fathers: Eäldor * Aldárian * Faêtir*
*The Golden City * Gateway to Narda*

As he said the words, something long asleep awakened in Eathelon. He'd come at last to his Mother's birthplace, the home of his Eldarin ancestors. He'd never expected to see this place of legend, the one place to which his Mother and her people longed to return. A chill went up his spine, and in that moment, a change was wrought in him. He felt sorrow, at first, then anger, anger for the Eldarin's betrayal by one of their own, anger for their loss of friends, family, homes and dignity, such an undeserved fate for a people who had brought many good things to Narda. And he knew in that moment that he was no longer just a Mallorite Prince who had come to Narda on an errand, but an Eldarin chosen by his people to bring them home.

I do not know how I will accomplish this task, but accomplish it, I must. And then I must also find a way to ensure that what happened to the Eldarin never again happens to anyone in Narda. The Stones hold a key, but what? He knew only that he needed to find the Book of Stones and recover the missing Stones. He hoped the book would tell him what he needed to know about how to use the five Stones. The book without the Stones would be useless, and the Stones without the book would be of little value. He hoped his Maagi Warrior blood would fuel the fire in him that he would need to accomplish his tasks, and that his Eldarin blood would guide his choices.

Darian rode up beside him, believing Eathelon absorbed in some dark thought, and attempted to pull him from it, "The Southern Arch is magnificent, is it not?"

Eathelon collected himself. "It is beyond words, Darian."

"Another feat of Eldarin architecture," Palo said, pulling alongside. He sensed the change in Eathelon and asked, "Are you alright?"

Eathelon smiled, "I am." He gave his horse a light kick and rode forward through the arch and Darian and Palo followed him into the realm of the Golden City.

They entered the flatter plateau and followed the main road toward the center of the city, passing homes similar to the ones they'd seen on the way to the Golden Hawk. These homes were narrow, two-story structures attached to one another. The yards were small and the paths to the front doors short. Some had stone wells or arbors with climbing vines, and all had gardens, thick with maltinia, silmaria, petiperl, blubel, dilli and lindili, which had begun to prepare for a winter sleep. Herbs grew in some window boxes — garlic, lothingel and ratintha among them.

The Golden City, once alive with activity, was now a ghost city. No one walked its streets, tended its gardens, stoked its fires, sold its wares. Eathelon imagined the streets filled with children walking home from school, and playing in yards, their parents setting lamps burning in windows, fires burning in hearths, the smoke curling up from their tall stone chimneys. But the companions were the only sign of life now. They passed home after home, building after building — a school, a library, shops. No Menga did they see, nor any sign Mengas had been here, except for the restored condition of the city, now a beautiful, empty shell, waiting for its occupants to return, waiting to be golden again.

"I do not understand how Mengas can come and go and keep the city in such good order, yet never be seen," observed Palo.

"They may be seen when they wish to be," said Darian. "It does not mean they have not seen us."

"Are these Mengas friendly?" Palo asked.

"They are neither friendly nor unfriendly," replied Darian. "They have lived up here for decades and few men venture here now, so it is no surprise that they keep to themselves. The Elvenkin are their only neighbors and, as was said, Elvenkin keep to themselves too, in their wood."

"Are the mercenaries of Rabellan still a threat to the Golden City?" asked Eathelon.

They pose little threat here now and I believe they dare not enter the Golden City. They sacked it and murdered the Eldarin." He raised his eyebrows. "They no doubt fear the ghosts of the dead."

"Ghosts of the dead?" Palo inquired.

"Said to be only legend, Palo," replied Darian, "though some believe them real enough."

"The Mengas do not fear these ghosts of the dead?" Palo continued.

"They have no reason to fear them, for they have rebuilt their city."

"Are you saying these ghosts are Eldarin?" asked Eathelon.

"I cannot say if they even exist," said Darian.

"How do Mengas know we are not allied to the East?" Palo questioned.

"A Menga can tell the difference between an Eldarin and a

mercenary. Do not worry. We will come to no harm from Mengas."

"I hope you are right," said Palo. "I am always ready for a fight should it come to that." He paused. "By the way, you mentioned that there are other inns in the city. Are we planning to stay in one? Our night at the Golden Hawk was cut short."

Darian laughed. "Yes, Palo. The King's Inn lies ahead, near the Great Hall of the Council, our destination. It once housed guests invited to audience there. Aneron and Landrin have both stayed there, and their Fathers before them."

"An inn built for royalty then," said Eathelon.

"Perhaps, but in that regard, you certainly qualify." Darian grinned.

"It is likely restored then," said Palo.

"No doubt," grinned Darian, "but do you care its condition as long as it has a soft bed?"

Palo smiled broadly — no reply needed.

They rode on and came to the heart of the city, the central plaza, the King's Inn straight ahead. Three other large buildings adjoined the plaza, all constructed with the same gray and white stone as the walls and structures of Andolan. The north building stood almost twice the size of the other two, and all faced inward toward the plaza. They stopped before a magnificent, sculptured fountain of marbled stone near the inn, and dismounted. Three men sat atop pizos on a stone platform in its center, an homage to the founding Fathers of the Eldarin races in Narda: Ealdor, a Syndar, faced north, Aldarian, a Nydar, west and Faetir, a Tynar east. Eathelon thought it an irony that Faetir, Father of the race that begat the enemy traitors and usurpers of the Eastern throne, faced east.

What an odd foreshadowing of events, he thought. But he knew Faetir could not have foreseen what he begat.

They walked around the fountain, admiring its beauty and workmanship, as water spilled in rivulets below the three Fathers onto the men, women and children, who worked and played in the fountain, water spilling from their jars, bowls, flower baskets and hands.

Eathelon had never seen such a unique, beautifully carved fountain, and it moved him. The stone figures seemed almost alive, in what must have been a happy life in the Golden City. He recognized each race by the characteristics he'd seen on the Eldarin survivors who reached Melatui — long narrow noses and chiseled features of the Syndar; oval faces, soft eyes and full mouths of the Nydar; round faces, almond-shaped eyes and narrow lips of the Tynar.

Stone benches placed around the fountain enabled one to sit and view it from any angle, under a shade tree, or in sunlight. A wide stone path wound around it and connected to larger paths that led to the surrounding buildings. Lush green grass grew in the open lawn around the plaza and a few hearty flowers still bloomed in its gardens, though most had already prepared for a winter sleep. Eathelon knew the Mengas would soon turn the fountain off, to keep it from damage in the coming winter freeze and he wondered if they had purposely left it on for their guests.

They tied the horses and left them to graze on the tender grass, then walked across the plaza to the north building. The stone columns, with their beautifully carved cornices, stood tall atop a shallow porch that wrapped around the building.

"The Great Hall of the Council," Darian proclaimed.

"Impressive," Palo stated.

"Indeed, our own Council building on Melatui is much smaller, though it is beautiful in its own right," said Eathelon.

The sun had fallen down the sky now and it cast fading rays onto the color-glass windows of the Great Hall, bouncing off a rainbow of light.

"Is that some sort of magic coming from the building?" asked Palo.

"The best kind," Darian replied. "That building was designed for the sun's rays to fall on the color-glass windows, as it rises and sets. The windows hold scenes of Nardan life, events, flora, fauna and they keep the activities inside the hall private, while entertaining those who wait outside. The spectacle has become known as The Dance of Light."

"You seem to know a lot about the Golden City," noted Eathelon. "Have you been here before?"

"I was here, long ago, but my Eldarin parents taught me most everything I know about the Golden City. Their families lived here ... for a time."

Eathelon had always thought of Numar as Darian's home and realized only now the significance of his friend's words.

They watched the Dance of Light until the sun fell far enough down for the colors to fade into shadow.

"Another of Narda's unique sights, for certain," said Palo.

Eathelon, mindful of his true purpose in coming, asked, "Darian, have you any idea where to find an entrance to the catacombs?"

"Why?"

"I need to go there to look for something."

"Eathelon, I doubt the catacombs have been opened since the Great War." Darian paused. "I did find an entrance once, long ago and by accident."

"Do you think you would be able to find it again?"

"I do not know. If my memory serves, there is an entrance somewhere inside of one of those buildings over there. Perhaps we can look tomorrow. Let us explore the Hall of the Great Council, now that we are here."

"You are certain the entrance is not in this hall?" asked Eathelon.

"Yes," replied Darian.

They walked up the steps onto the porch and stood before two high front doors of the Great Hall. Darian read aloud the words carved above them:

"Hheás émnin Máltåsémní"
Great Hall of the Council of Malta

"Shall we go in?" asked Eathelon.

"Wait," said Darian. He turned to the building on the west side of the plaza. The fading light and distance made it almost impossible to read the words carved into it, but he recalled them now:

"Hheás émnin Parmhisir"
"Great Hall of History"

"That one," he said, pointing to it, "the Great Hall of History. It once held all of the writings of Eldarin history and literature back to the First Age. The writings disappeared sometime before or during the Great War, Aneron said."

"What do you mean disappeared?" Eathelon inquired. "The Eldarin did not bring them to Melatui. If they are no longer here, they must lie at the bottom of the Southern Sea."

"If they are here, they have not yet been discovered." Darian paused and put his hand to his head.

"What is it?" asked Eathelon.

"The Hall of History," grinned Darian. "That is where we will find the entrance to the catacombs."

"Are you certain of this?" Eathelon asked.

"Certain, no, but that is where my intuition leads." He grinned. "Let us first drop our belongings off at the King's Inn and stable the horses. The building is not far. We can walk over to it."

"What is that other building?" queried Palo, pointing to the other one.

"The Great Hall of Justice," replied Darian. "It once held records of all of the justice proceedings handed down by the High Court. Tebor had those records burned in retaliation for the judgment passed on him, or so it is said. They are lost forever now. I know little else about it, but we will no doubt find it empty."

"For an Eldarin, Tebor was much flawed," said Palo.

That is a true enough statement, thought Eathelon.

"Indeed, he was Palo," replied Darian. "In fact, Tebor was so unlike an Eldarin that one might think him another race altogether."

"It seems that Baele inherited Tebor's flaws in abundance," noted Palo.

"Yes, so it seems," replied Darian. "And it is our misfortune that Baele's son Esol is cut from the same cloth, so to speak."

Eathelon found it difficult to understand how one man so flawed, and not even that powerful, at first, could heap such reckless ruin on the race that begat him. Such evil he found difficult to confront.

Darian said aloud, not so much from sight, but from

knowledge, the words carved into the stone face of the Hall of Justice:

"Hheás émnin Máltåzhəsémni"
Great Hall of Justice

"These three buildings once housed the government of Malta," said Darian, "which also stood as the central government of Narda, before the fall of the Eldarin. Their influence on the Nardan Kings was great. They organized and helped run the most effective government Narda has ever known." He paused. "It is my great honor to be counted among them."

"And mine," Eathelon added. "Now, let us make ourselves worthy of that honor. I have much to accomplish here and I will need the help of my two friends."

"And you have it," insisted Palo.

"Indeed," replied Darian.

He walked up to one of the huge doors of the Great Hall of the Council, pulled on its gold ring and it opened.

"I thought it would be locked," said Palo.

"Many Nardans came here in ages past and waited to audience in this Hall, but who is here now, to keep us out?"

"Mengas?" asked Palo.

"They would not bar our entry. Nothing of any real value remains here."

"Well," Eathelon suggested, "then let us go in."

They stepped through the huge doors into a wide foyer with a smooth gray marble floor and walls. Its vaulted ceiling held the image of a deep blue Nardan sky, with moon and stars. One star stood out from the rest and Eathelon immediately recognized it.

"*Forsil*," he pointed out, "star of the north. It has always beckoned me north, though I do not know why." Eathelon had gazed long upon it as a boy, and it had evoked feelings in him that he still did not fully understand.

The northernmost star burned brighter in the sky than any other star and had always been used in Eldarin navigation.

They crossed the foyer and stood before another set of high

ornate, carved wooden doors, also with gold rings in the center.

"These lead to the inner chamber," said Darian.

He opened one and they stepped through into a large rectangular room, with an amphitheater comprised of six levels of semi-circular stone platforms. Beautifully carved wooden benches sat along both side walls, beneath the color-glass windows. A high marble podium stood at the north end of the amphitheatre.

Eathelon walked over to it and discovered stone steps behind it leading to a high seat at the top. He climbed up and sat down.

"I can see everything in the amphitheater, on the benches and up in that balcony," he said, pointing.

"That is the seat for the Head of the Eldarin Council," said Darian. "The members sit in the amphitheater, the invited guests on those benches, and spectators sit up in the balcony."

The balcony wrapped around three sides of the large room, including over the entry doors, and Eathelon estimated it held more than 300 people.

Palo, meanwhile, had walked over to the north wall, behind the podium. "Eathelon, Darian, come and look."

They walked over to join Palo at a fireplace in the center of the north wall, stood and stared at the many name plates on the wall, above and beside the fireplace.

"These are the names of all of the Eldarin council members, by race, I think," Darian said. "Based on the date set for each, the names have been here since the inception of this Hall."

"Yet, there is room for more," noted Eathelon.

Palo gave them a puzzled look.

"Eldarin are a long-lived race, Palo, and Council seats are appointed for life," Darian clarified.

"So, I guessed," said Palo, "for I believe that to be true also for the Council members in Melatui."

"That is correct," agreed Eathelon. He mused that the wall, like the columns in the King's hall in Andolan, would one day fill up. When he looked more closely, he discovered that the center wall held Syndar names, the left wall Nydar names and the right wall the names of Tynar members. *There it is again, North, West and East, and this hall is built on the north end of the plaza.* He puzzled over it. "Look," he pointed out. "Under Tebor's nameplate is written the Eldarin word for 'traitor'. Few Tynar names appear after that date."

"Yes, the Eldarin banned the Tynar from the Council for many years after Tebor's treachery," added Darian, "though they eventually returned."

Eathelon began to better understand the significance of Tebor's loss and how it may have contributed to his desire for vengeance upon the Eldarin, though it was not until later that that was fully carried out ... by his heir, Baele.

"Tebor's treachery was no more the fault of innocent Tynar than the Nydar or Syndar," said Eathelon.

"I agree, but the High Court did not see it that way. They ruled against the Tynar, saying that they had not taken sufficient steps to restrain one of their own. It was the price they paid for Tebor's treachery."

"The Eldarin paid a far greater price," claimed Eathelon, but he was distracted, as he said it. He had just noticed some markings in the floor and made a guess what they were for. He made a mental note, but said nothing. Darian and Palo had evidently not noticed.

They turned and walked along the marble columns, spaced at intervals on either side of the hall, between the benches. A late arriving ray of waning sun filtered in through one of the color-glass windows and lingered, only for a fleeting moment, casting a faint rainbow of color around the room.

They continued their exploration, but saw little else, for the hall had been empty for some 60 years.

They exited the way they'd entered, walked back to the center of the plaza and walked the horses the short distance over to the King's Inn, for it was growing dark.

"I want to look for the entrance to the catacombs," remarked Eathelon.

"Tonight?" asked Darian.

"Yes," replied Eathelon. "It matters little if the sun is gone, if we walk underground."

"Well, light may better help me find the entrance," stated Darian.

"Then we will bring some," grinned Eathelon.

They approached the King's Inn and its sign announced it:

Lämindôl - King's Inn

From the outside, the inn looked much like the other buildings surrounding the plaza, with its tall columns and shallow porch. They located the stables behind it and found a lamp had already been set and food for the horses.

"Clearly, we are expected," said Eathelon.

"Indeed," replied Darian.

"Food for our horses, a lighted lamp. Perhaps Mengas are friendlier than I thought," said Palo.

They groomed and fed the horses, returned to the inn and entered through the unlocked front doors. Lamps burned, and a fire had been set in one of the fire pits in the lobby.

"As was said, we may not see them, but they have clearly seen us. This is their way of letting us know," said Darian.

They dropped their belongings and looked around. The marble floor and columns that held up the roof were even more elegant than those in the Great Hall, and the lobby held furnishings befitting royalty: colorful couches, chairs and inlaid tables with wrought-iron lamps, arranged in intimate settings, each with its own fire pit. They lit a few more lamps and continued the tour. They approached a long counter of smooth, polished wood and found, behind it, many small boxes that held keys.

Darian walked around behind the counter and removed a key from one of the boxes, then beckoned Eathelon and Palo to follow him. He led them to the far end of the foyer, up a winding staircase, to a balcony that overlooked it. He opened the door to Room 21, one of two large rooms on this level.

They stepped into a large sitting room with doors to sleeping rooms on either side. Eathelon opened the door to one of the sleeping rooms and found colorful rugs on the floor and a large four-poster bed, piled high with quilts and pillows. A small desk and chair sat against one wall, an armoire against another, and a small table by the bed held a water pitcher, towels and several small amenities. An unopened bottle of Holling Vale wine and 3 glasses had been placed on the desk.

"Your majesty," said Darian, bowing and grinning, "one of the royal suites!"

Eathelon waved him up with a chuckle, "Thank you, worthy guide."

"The sleeping room on the other side is no doubt as nice, and there is another royal suite on this level, room enough for us all," said Darian.

"How did you know about this room?" asked Eathelon.

"Easy," grinned Darian. "The boxes behind the counter had labels."

"This is cruel," Palo declared. "We will not want to leave!"

"For a fierce Warrior, you are certainly soft about your sleeping arrangements," asserted Darian.

"I never claimed to be fierce," replied Palo. "Stefen gave me that title. But even a Warrior is entitled to a few comforts, now and then."

"Well said Palo!" Darian slapped him on the back. "And I have no doubt you will be earning every one of them!"

Palo grunted.

After selecting their beds and placing their belongings in their chosen rooms, the three companions sat by the fire in the lobby and ate a small meal of leftovers. They took torches from the walls and lit them in the fire, then exited the inn.

Their torches penetrated the dark night and flickered in the cold wind, as they crossed the plaza to the Great Hall of History, where they again entered through unlocked doors.

They walked around the lobby, and Darian examined the space. "The entrance to the catacombs is somewhere in this building, but I will have to find something to bring back my memory. I have no idea where to start."

"How long since you were last here?" asked Palo.

"I was a boy. I visited this hall once, with my Mother."

"I thought you had been to the Golden City several times," said Palo.

"I have been to Malta several times, but I visited the Golden City, and this Hall only once before. Still, I am certain I can find the entrance to the catacombs."

Eathelon sighed. "Yes, but how long will it take?"

The floor of the Hall of History, like the other buildings, was made of marble. Three halls branched out from the foyer, and a large curving staircase on either side of the entrance led up to a mezzanine. The companions each took a hallway to explore.

Eathelon examined each of the rooms along the hall he'd chosen and found all similarly furnished, with stuffed chairs and couches, hand-crafted tables, wrought iron lamps and wall sconces, artwork, woven carpets and tapestries, and row upon row of empty bookshelves from floor to ceiling.

The companions completed their initial explorations and met back at the foyer to discuss what they'd found. None had seen any sign of an entrance to the catacombs. They sat down to discussed it.

"Have you any memory of its location?" Eathelon asked Darian.

"Only an impression, but my intuition tells me I will know it when I see it. None of the rooms I looked into jogged my memory. I have not looked in the right place."

"But you are certain the entrance to the catacombs lies in the Hall of History?" asked Eathelon.

"Yes, I am certain of this."

"Well, it is a start," said Palo, yawning. "What if we resume our search in the morning, Eathelon? It grows late and we have had a long day."

"I cannot say why Palo, but it is important to me that I find the entrance to the catacombs tonight."

"If you must," Palo yawned again.

"Does this foyer look familiar to you, Darian? Or one of the halls?"

"I was a boy when I found the entrance and even then, only by accident. Things look much different to me now. I must find something to bring back my memory."

"We have not looked upstairs," said Palo. "Perhaps it holds a key."

Darian looked at the staircase leading up to the mezzanine and shook his head. "I have no recollection at all of these stairs. Besides, the entrance to the catacombs would lead down, not up."

"Perhaps a look from a different vantage point will jog your memory," offered Palo.

"I do not think it will help, but I will go," Darian responded.

They all went up and looked down on the foyer below.

"Your suggestion has worked, Palo, I have an idea. Let us each take a different hall this time and make another search."

Palo shrugged.

They each took a different hall, and after quarter of an hour, Darian ran out of one of the rooms Eathelon had explored earlier, and yelled, "I have found it!"

"Where?" called Eathelon.

"End of the hall!" yelled Darian.

Eathelon and Palo followed his voice down the hall but didn't see him.

"Darian!" Eathelon called out.

"Last room ... in here!" came the muffled reply.

They entered the last room on the right. Eathelon did not see Darian, but he noticed the crumpled tapestry on the floor across the room and a door ajar in the wall behind it, "Darian?"

Darian peeked his head out and grinned. "This door was covered by the tapestry."

"But how did you know to look behind it?" asked Eathelon. "I saw it, but tapestries hang in all of the rooms."

"I did not, at first, then something about the scene brought back a memory," said Darian. "I stared at it awhile then remembered I had hidden behind it from my Mother. I pulled it down, revealing this door. I gave the door a push and it opened!"

"Does this lead to the catacombs then?" asked Palo.

"Come and see," grinned Darian.

They all stepped through the door into a small room, which like the outer room had many empty bookshelves. Eathelon decided it must have been used to store some of the books. Darian pointed to a shelf that stood out from the rest. He led them around behind it, to a large gaping black hole.

"I found it by accident ...again," Darian added.

"The entrance to the catacombs?" asked Eathelon.

"One entrance, at least, no doubt kept secret. Had I not discovered it earlier, I doubt we would ever have found it."

"How *did* you find it, did you remember?" asked Eathelon.

"No, I searched for a book."

"Darian, these shelves are empty," said Palo. "What do you mean you searched for a book?"

"The shelves are empty now, yes, but they were not empty when I first discovered this place. I simply tried to recall where I found the book earlier."

"You remembered then," said Palo.

"No," replied Darian. "I remembered climbing a shelf to reach a book that had caught my attention. I could not recall the exact shelf."

"Evidently you did," noted Eathelon.

"No," laughed Darian. "I climbed them all until one triggered the secret door. I had tripped the lever accidentally the first time and did so again when I climbed this shelf."

Darian gestured at the gaping hole. "Behold — the entrance to the catacombs!"

Eathelon stared into the black hole. "This cannot possibly be the only entrance to the catacombs."

"No, there is no doubt another, most likely in the hills. But this is the only entrance I know. It will have to do."

"It will do fine," insisted Eathelon.

"I used my torch to explore it only a short distance. The stairs leading down are steep and the way dark. I am not certain how far down it goes, or if the stairs are safe to walk."

"The stairs go to the bottom, however far that is," Palo said.

Darian laughed. Palo had a way of stating the obvious.

"Let us hope they are intact to the bottom," from Eathelon.

"These torches have burned long now," Palo stated. "We need new ones."

"We can take torches from the walls in the outer room," offered Darian. "They should burn long enough for us to reach bottom and return."

Palo retrieved three torches and lit them. They put out the others and left them for their return. Then Eathelon took the lead, Palo the rear, and the three of them stepped into the dark hole and began their descent into the catacombs.

Chapter 23:
The Catacombs of Malta

Eathelon navigated the steep stairs down the short, dark tunnel, holding his torch out before him to avert any missteps. The air in the tunnel smelled dank and stale.

"How far down do you think these stairs go?" asked Palo.

"The catacombs lie deep beneath the city," said Darian. "It is the resting place for the Eldarin since the First Age — and this is the Fifth. It is likely a long way down."

"These catacombs may be expansive, given the ages since they were made," said Eathelon. "I hope I can find what I search for, though Celorn did give me some idea of where to look."

They came to the end of the short tunnel and stepped out onto a stone platform.

"The air smells a little fresher here," Palo remarked.

"Agreed," said Darian. "There must be a fresh air source somewhere."

"That is good," Palo responded. "I care little enough for being underground. I have no desire to breathe foul air."

"Nor do we," confirmed Eathelon. He thrust his torch out beyond the platform, but saw little but black space.

Darian found a small alcove in the cave wall, and a lamp in it that still held oil. He lit the lamp.

"I am surprised to see oil still in the lamp," stated Eathelon.

"The oil does not diminish with time, only use," Darian said.

"That lamp has to have sat unused for 60 years," Eathelon pointed out.

"Mengas do not come down here?" asked Palo.

"I doubt they know about this place," replied Darian, "but

even if they did, what reason would they have to come here?"

The light from the alcove lamp did not reach far, but it illuminated the platform and the first few steps down.

"The cavern must be large," said Eathelon. "We cannot see how far down these stairs go in this blackness."

"That would explain the fresh air," Darian remarked.

"Over here," Palo called out. He had checked out the stairs leading down. "The stairs continue down here, but they look steep and worn. Parts of them may be broken. We will need to go with care."

"These steps are carved from stone," Eathelon said. "I cannot imagine how long it took to make them."

"Another feat of Eldarin architecture?" asked Palo.

Palo's remark broke the tension they felt, and Darian laughed. Eathelon joined in, and Palo laughed too, and the laughter bounced and echoed off of the cavern walls in a great cacophony of sound, almost as if a great host laughed with them.

"I should not be surprised if the Eldarin enlisted the help of the Lit'ls in making these stone stairs," Darian surmised. "That race is used to living in caves, it is said. They are miners and used to delving in stone."

Eathelon strained to look ahead in the dark, as the laughter faded away. "There is no way to know how far down these steps go, and I have no desire to join my ancestors early, nor have my companions do so. Let us go with care."

"We will have to trust the Eldarin architects, or whomever made these stair steps," said Darian. "Their skill in making them has likely kept them fit to walk, if it matches the skill of the other structures left us."

They started down the steps, Eathelon leading, his torch out in front of him. Darian and Palo followed him, single file. The stairs were narrow and had nothing to hold onto.

"Eldarin custom is to bring the dead here to rest," said Darian. "We burn the bodies of the dead, to release the spirit. The catacombs contain their ashes, not rotting flesh."

"We Maagi bury our dead," Palo commented, "but I see no error in it."

"Every race has its customs," Eathelon added. "It is not for anyone to judge one over the other."

Down, down they went, until they reached another platform. It, too, had an alcove, with a lamp, so Palo lit the lamp, and though Eathelon could not determine the condition of the next set of stairs, he knew he had no choice but to continue down.

"Wait," said Palo and he came forward to test the stairs. Satisfied they were sound enough, he let Eathelon continue to lead.

A little further down they came to a break in the stair and Eathelon almost fell through, but caught himself. "Hold! he said. The stair ahead is broken. Step over it."

They avoided the broken stair and continued down. The rest of the stairs proved sound enough and, as they descended, they reached platform after platform, each with an alcove and a lamp. Palo lit them as they descended, so that looking back up the way they had come, they saw a trail of lights to guide them back.

"This place would seem almost magical, were it not for the fact that it houses the dead," said Eathelon. "Look at these walls. They glow, and there are intricate carvings in them. I wish we had better light to see."

Eathelon could no longer be certain of the time, or how long it was taking them to descend, but they reached the bottom at last, and held their torches out to survey the cavern. When Eathelon looked up to see the dim trail of lights flickering above, he could not see all the way to the top, so knew they had come a long way down. He would need to find what he looked for before the lamps lighting the way back went out altogether.

My senses are distorted.

The cavern walls glowed and when he shone his light on the floor, it appeared to be made of marble, but upon closer inspection, he saw that it was only hard-packed dirt with some sort of iridescent particle in it that made it appear to be marble. They stood and took in the scene around them.

Eathelon heard quiet murmurings and a light breeze moved across his face.

"Do you feel the breeze?" he inquired.

"Breeze?" asked Darian. "We are far underground, Eathelon.

There is no breeze."

"I thought I felt something," Palo added, "but I am not certain. Still, the air is fresher here, so there must be a source. And I thought I saw something."

"What?" asked Darian.

"I do not know," Palo replied. "The image was not clear."

"We are imagining things," said Eathelon. "This place plays tricks with our minds. My senses feel distorted here."

"Mine, too," agreed Darian.

"We are underground, after all," stated Palo. "Without sun, moon or stars to orient us, it is no surprise our senses are distorted."

Satisfied with that explanation, they explored further and came upon three adjacent tunnels, each with two tall stone columns flanking it, and each leading off in a different direction. They lit the torches on the sides of the tunnels and it started a chain reaction of light that flooded the entire cavern.

"Well, that was unexpected!" exclaimed Eathelon.

"Indeed," Darian concurred.

They surveyed the huge cavern, and Eathelon read aloud the words carved in Eolengwas above each tunnel, as they moved from one to the other.

The words above the center tunnel read:

Ándo íeldra bána thóla faévë Syndar
(Gateway to the spirits of our Syndar Fathers)

And above the left tunnel:

Ándo íeldra bána thóla faévë Nydar
(Gateway to the spirits of our Nydar Fathers)

And the right:

Ándo íeldra bána thóla faévë Tynar
(Gateway to the spirits of our Tynar Fathers)

Even though he stood far underground, Eathelon knew the

direction each tunnel must lead: north for the Syndar, west for the Nydar, east for the Tynar, and his curiosity grew the more over its significance. He made a guess from his teachings that it had something to do with the direction each race took in their exploration of Narda. This probably also had influenced Tebor to set up his House in the East, for the Tynar must have explored there first. Whether or not this explanation would later prove correct, it satisfied him for the moment.

He started to enter the Syndar tunnel but Darian caught his arm and pulled him back. "We must stay together, Eathelon."

"But why not each take a tunnel?" Eathelon asked. "There are three tunnels and three of us."

"We cannot know what is down there," Darian stated bluntly. "I think it unwise for us to separate."

"You are not afraid of those ghosts of the dead, are you?" queried Eathelon.

"No, but this place has long been deserted. There may be fouler things down there than ghosts of the dead?"

"This I doubt," Eathelon countered. Then something touched his head. He brushed it away.

"Darian has a point," said Palo. "We should stay together."

"Agreed," Eathelon conceded.

"We can explore the Syndar tunnel first, if you like," Darian offered.

"No," replied Eathelon. "Let us first go to the tombs of your Fathers. It is fitting."

Darian nodded. They entered the Nydar tunnel and quickly covered the short distance to a smaller cavern. At its center sat a large stone tomb, with the carved figure of a sleeping man atop it. Eathelon knew it was Aldarian, first leader of the Nydar in Narda, for he had seen the same image in the fountain, facing west.

Darian walked up to the tomb, touched the hand of the sleeping man and smiled.

"I am his namesake, you know. He called his own son by my name."

They stood with him, in silence a moment.

"Does it not fill you with awe to see the resting place of our

Fathers Eathelon? Here lies the Father of my race in Narda, and the tombs of his sons and daughters, grandsons and granddaughters, down to my own Grandfather."

"Indeed," Eathelon agreed, "all of Malta and the Golden City fill me with awe, and no less this place."

"The Tombs of our Kings lie in the caves under Mt. Kinli, on Melatui," Palo interjected. "Eathelon's Father is among them." He said it almost as if to make a point for the Maagi blood in his Mallorite companion, but he may as well have been talking to air, for neither Darian nor Eathelon responded to his comment.

After a few minutes, Darian walked over to one of the walls and moved along it, slowly reading the names engraved on rows of silver plates. Eathelon walked behind him and, as Darian read the names, thought of the ancient ashes that lay behind each nameplate. He wondered if his ashes would lie here one day and he thought of the Eldarin lost at sea, including his friends Tomas and Marchal, for they would not now come to rest here. His eyes moistened at this thought and a shadow crossed his face, but he stayed the surge of grief that followed.

Darian stopped suddenly and Eathelon, lost in thought, nearly ran into the back of him. Darian stared at the nameplates of Aldarian's sons and daughters, and all in his line down to *Meoldor*.

"Eathelon thought of the story he'd been told of the Eldarin maiden in Northwest Wood, and of his desire to find her.

"Are you alright?" asked Darian.

"This place stirs feelings in me is all."

"And in me," said Darian.

Palo had not followed them, and Eathelon saw that he stood guard at the entrance to the cavern, ever his protector.

Darian continued his search and found his own ancestors, down to his Grandfather *Mengen*, his Father's Father. And seeing the name, Darian bowed his head and said aloud, "I would have liked to know you, Grandfather, for Mother said you were a good and honorable man."

Eathelon put a hand on Darian's shoulder — no words needed.

Palo watched from a distance.

"You found your Father's name?" asked Eathelon.

"No, he is not here. His ashes lie in the Tombs of the Kings in Andolan, placed there out of respect for his service to Aneron." Darian fell silent a moment. "I would like to bring him here one day, to lie with his own Fathers."

"When that day comes, Darian, I will help you bear him hence."

Darian smiled and nodded.

But these solemn moments quickly passed. Palo joined them and they continued to explore the tunnels running outward from the cavern, like the spokes of an incomplete wheel. As they explored, they noticed intricate patterns and markings on the walls and words written in Eolengwas, the ancient language of the Eldarin.

"Do you know what these markings say?" asked Palo.

"I do not," Darian replied.

"I recognize some of them," Eathelon stated, "but I cannot yet read all of the ancient Eolengwas."

The companions did not know what kind of iridescent material was present in the cave walls and floor that caused them to glow when the light shone on them, but the effect turned the catacombs into a magical underground realm, one worthy of the final resting place for the Eldarin. They quickly learned, however, that the tunnels led to more caverns and the caverns to more tunnels so, lest they become lost in the maze, they retraced their steps back to the main cavern.

"Some of these tunnels appear to be man-made," Darian noted, "though the caverns are clearly natural. It must have taken all of the past ages to make these catacombs."

"And perhaps even now, they are incomplete," offered Eathelon. "This cave system looks vast. There must be another entrance."

"No doubt," replied Darian, "but the way we came is the only way we know. I have no desire to become lost down here and join our ancestors in sleep."

"We must make the long climb back up those stairs, then," Palo stated.

"Yes," replied Darian. "But you said earlier you need to get into shape for warrioring." He slapped Palo on the back, then turned to Eathelon. "Let us go to the tombs of Lelar's Fathers now, where you will no doubt find your own lineage."

Eathelon nodded and smiled.

They followed the Syndar tunnel to its inner chamber knowing as they did, they would find Ealdor's tomb, as they had Aldarian's. And Ealdor's carven image lay atop his tomb also, but unlike Aldarian's, his eyes lay open, a brief smile upon his face. It made Eathelon smile. He knew the Nardans had deemed Ealdor a "god" of sorts — god of all things good in Narda. Ealdor had led the Eldarin in their explorations of Narda and had formed and led the Eldarin Council, which had helped stop the wars. He'd formed the central government and directed the building of the Golden City. A renaissance of culture had followed and spread throughout Narda, and the phrase "by the grace of Ealdor" had come into much use, both here and on Melatui. No Eldarin had had more influence on Narda than Ealdor — none, save one. The evil influence of the House of Tebor had been nearly as great as Ealdor's influence for good.

Eathelon walked around the tomb, then stood over its image, staring into his ancestor's eyes. And in that moment, he began to realize more fully what it meant to be the direct descendant of a Syndar Eldarin, of the god-Father of Narda. And what would this god-Father expect of him? Nothing less than he expected of himself, he decided.

"Are you ready to continue?" asked Darian.

"You two go ahead," replied Eathelon. "I would like a few more minutes more here."

"We will stay," declared Palo.

"Let us know when you are ready to go on," said Darian.

Eathelon walked along the cavern wall, reading the engraved silver nameplates, as Darian had done. He'd no idea what he expected to find, but his Eldarin instinct told him he would know it when he found it.

He heard faint, unintelligible whisperings again, and looked over to see Darian and Palo talking, though they took no notice of him. The back of Eathelon's neck began to prickle and his senses sharpened. He looked around, but saw nothing. He listened, but heard nothing more, so he took the short tunnel to a connected, smaller cavern, as they had done before in the Nydar tunnel. Darian and Palo followed, at a distance.

Eathelon searched the nameplates along the wall and stopped at one that read 'Talinia.' *Is that the name?* He'd written his instructions down in his journal, but it lay at the bottom of the Southern Sea. He would have to rely on his memory now.

He looked over at Darian and Palo. They were engaged in conversation, as they waited for him to find whatever he searched for. They acknowledged him with a nod and went back to their conversation.

Eathelon heard whisperings again and this time, he pulled his amulet from beneath his tunic and it began to glow, dimly at first, then with more intensity, until it bathed the cavern in a pale, green light. He could barely make out vague images of something, but he could not tell what. The light from the amulet attempted to reveal them, but they vanished. Eathelon felt curiosity, more than fear.

"What are you, or who?" he whispered. "Show yourselves. No harm will come to you." But he need not have whispered at all, for when he looked over at Darian and Palo, to see if they had heard, he found them frozen like statues, in mid-conversation. He examined his hands to be certain he could move them, and when he was certain he was not frozen, he laughed. *The amulet!*

He recalled the time Celorn had used it with his young apprentice, in the Great Hall on Melatui and all within had been frozen like Darian and Palo, all except himself and Celorn. That time it had lasted only a few minutes, as a simple demonstration of the power of the amulet. Several minutes had passed here — or had they? He could not be certain, for until now, he had used the power of the amulet only twice — once to light his way in the dark as he'd descended the cliff in Numar, and again at the Battle of Two Rivers monument. And he'd only remembered to use it because Celorn's image on the cliff had reminded him. "The amulet itself will show you," Celorn had said. Indeed. He recalled now that he had earlier thought about wanting more time to explore the catacombs, unhindered. He'd planned to return once Darian and Palo had gone to bed. Had the amulet sensed this? He did not know how it worked, but he knew he must take advantage of its power now to do what he needed to do.

He began a search for the name Celorn had given him, doing his best to recall it. He glanced over at Darian and Palo again to be certain they had not moved. They had not.

The name Talinia had tickled his memory, but he knew it was not correct. He continued his search and came upon a similar name, Talia. This time, the name registered and he examined it further. A symbol was carved just below the nameplate and an ancient Eldarin word *ándoparmindól* below it. He knew the word had something to do with a gate, or gateway. A novice at the ancient language, it was all he could work out. Whether by instinct, or out of curiosity, he touched his finger to the symbol and said this word over and over again, under his breath, trying to recall its full meaning: *ándoparmindól, ándoparmindól*. The dust began to fall away from the wall, the outline of a door appeared on the cavern wall and, when it had fully formed, he pushed on it and it opened. He stood before the gaping hole, one just large enough for a single man to enter.

More curious than frightened, Eathelon gave one last look at his friends, shrugged and, holding his torch out before him, stepped into the dark hole. He held his breath for a moment, then breathed a sigh of relief when the door did not close.

As his eyes adjusted to the light of a single torch, he saw that he had entered a very large room with a high ceiling. How large and how high, he could not tell for certain in the dark. He searched and found torches on the adjacent walls and lit them. The added light revealed row upon row of shelves that appeared to hold thousands and thousands of books. *These must be the books from the Hall of History,* he decided.

He walked over and plucked a book from the shelf and examined it briefly. He put it back and took another, then another.

These are the books of lineages of the Eldarin in Narda. Perhaps they foresaw war coming after all, and preserved their history here. Perhaps they also foresaw that one day they would return.

Whether by instinct or by some magic of the amulet, he had

found the place in the catacombs Celorn wanted him to find. He began a search for the Book of Stones.

It must be here, among these volumes, or else why would Celorn direct me to this place? He sighed. What did his mentor expect? He could not in 14 lifetimes search every volume on every shelf! There had to be an order to these volumes.

He searched further and found a cabinet with many little drawers. He opened one and found many small, metal plates He pulled one out and examined it, then did the same with another, and another. It was some kind of catalog system, he decided. He looked through the other drawers, by the light from his torch, and it became clear to him that the metal plates referred to the books on the shelves. They had evidently been placed in order by race, family name and date. He searched and found the plate with the volume number for his Mother's lineage, his lineage. He located the shelf, took the volume down and paged through it. The pages were thin, yet strong.

These volumes look as new as if they had just been made. What kind of material is this? Another Eldarin knowledge and skill lost, he decided.

He found his Mother's name — Lelar, daughter of Lothi and Lela. And next to his Mother's name, those of her brothers — Finli, the eldest and Tindar, the youngest. He found Celorn's name too. He knew Celorn, a Syndar and Head of the Eldarin Council must be in Ealdor's lineage. He continued and stopped on the name Mereador, a Syndar. It meant nothing to him. He read down the list of names and, only after doing so, realized how few Syndar had made it to Melatui and how many had left family behind. Finli, like Lelar had married a Maagi and they'd had a daughter, Earen, one only a little older than Eathelon, and his only cousin. Lelar's younger brother Tindar had perished at sea, a grievous loss, for he'd left no heir. Celorn's wife and child had also perished at sea and his mentor had never remarried.

Eathelon suddenly realized the full impact of Tebor's treachery and tried in vain to comprehend the mind of one who would betray his people and set up his own ruling House to later wipe them out. But he could not dwell on it. He must have been down here for hours! He began to feel an urgency to move on, but he had not found what he came for. He put the book back on the shelf and made another search, but he doubted the Book of Stones would be on these shelves with the lineages. He'd found nothing in the catalog drawers that mentioned the Book of Stones.

He heard whisperings in the dark again.

"Who is there?" he asked softly.

No reply.

How would he ever find the Book of Stones! He began to get angry, the disappointment set in as he walked back toward the entrance, extinguishing the torches on the walls, as he did. He vowed to return tomorrow, as he reached the door and hesitated. He turned back for one last look, stretching his torch out into the dark room.

He heard whisperings again and strained to understand the words. "Show yourself," he said. "No harm will come to you."

Silence.

He swung his torch from side to side, searching for the source and, when he did, the light reflected off of something in the corner, to his left. Curious, he walked over to see what it was, and there discovered something else he knew Celorn would want him to find — the stand for the missing Power Stone!

He examined the beautiful, ornate stand in the torchlight, and considered what to do with it. He could never carry it by himself, so decided it should remain hidden, until he could work out how to retrieve it. Had the voices been trying to guide him?

He was about to turn and leave, when he noticed the edge of something sticking out from behind the stand. He reached his arm around and tugged at it, until it came loose. He pulled it out and his heart skipped a beat. He had just found the Book of Stones! He set his torch down and tried to open it, but it was locked. Perhaps he could pry it open, but no, he did not want to damage it. *There must be a key.*

He searched the stand again, this time pulling it out to see all the way around it. His torch had nearly died now and he stared at the stand in frustration, barely able to see.

He took one of the torches off the wall and lit it with his dying one, then went back to the stand and made another search.

He let out a laugh. The key had been sitting there all the time, in plain view within the ornate decorations on the stand.

If you want to hide something, hide it in plain sight, Father said. Most people will not see it.

He took the key, opened the book and began to read it. His eyes went wide and a smile crept over his face. He closed and locked it, placed the key on the chain with his amulet, and tucked the book under his tunic. Exhilarated at the unexpected find, his task accomplished, he exited through the door in the cave wall and it groaned shut behind him. He turned back to look at it, as the outline of the door faded.

The amulet faded too, as he placed it, along with the key to the book, back under his tunic and went to look for Darian and Palo.

He found them in conversation, completely unaware of what had taken place.

"My errand here is finished," Eathelon announced. "We can leave, unless you two have other business here."

"I do not," Darian responded.

"I have nothing to look for," added Palo, "and my stomach is telling me it is time for a meal. How long have we been down here, do you know? I have felt my time sense distorted since we reached bottom, but the night must surely have passed by now."

Feeling somewhat guilty, Eathelon just replied, "I know what you mean, mine too. I have no idea of the time."

They walked back to the main cavern.

"Do either of you wish to visit the Tynar tunnel?" asked Eathelon.

"Not I," from Darian. "That history is known to us well enough."

"No, I wish to head back to the Kings Inn for a meal and some rest," yawned Palo. "I hope nothing is amiss up there."

"We should get back," Darian noted, "though I doubt anything is amiss."

They began the long, steep climb up the stairs, most of it in silence. Palo took up the rear and extinguished the lamps as they climbed. They reached the stone tunnel and navigated its steps to the anteroom, passed through the door and pushed the shelf back into place, hiding the secret passage. They exited through the door in the wall and replaced the tapestry to hide it, then walked back to the foyer and out of the Great Hall of History.

"Shards!" exclaimed Palo, "it is past dawn! We were down there all night! No wonder my stomach is saying it is time to eat."

"Imagine that," Eathelon remarked flatly, as they set off for the King's Inn. "Now that my errand here is finished, I want to set out for Northwest Wood as soon as possible."

"Let us take a meal at the King's Inn and a few hours rest first, as Palo suggested," said Darian.

"You found what you sought, then?" asked Palo.

"Yes," replied Eathelon. "And it may comfort you to know, Darian, that I also found the books missing from the Hall of History. They lie safe in a room, deep in the catacombs. I found them by accident."

"Then why did you not call us over?"

"I sought the Book of Stones, not the missing books of history, and did not wish to be delayed."

The answer satisfied Darian. "It is enough to know they are safe, I suppose."

"Let us go eat, rest and leave then," said Palo. "We need not stay here longer than is necessary and risk an encounter with those ghosts of the dead."

"Have we not just spent an entire night in the catacombs without incident Palo?"

"Yes, but I thought I saw something down there," Palo replied. "And did you not say you heard whisperings, Eathelon?"

"We probably only imagined it, Palo," said Eathelon.

But Palo looked unconvinced.

"When I first discovered the entrance to the catacombs, I heard whisperings," said Darian. "Perhaps it is not all imagination."

"Who are these ghosts of the dead supposed to be, anyway?" asked Palo.

"Some believe they are the spirits of the Eldarin who perished here," Darian replied.

"Or perhaps the spirits of those who died committing that foul deed," countered Eathelon. "The innocent have no need to remain."

"There is no need to fear them," Eathelon continued. "Even if they do exist, they would only be shadows. They cannot do us any harm."

"I do not fear them," said Palo.

"Enough talk of the ghosts of the dead," Darian insisted. "Let us go eat and rest."

Chapter 24:
The Ghosts of the Dead

The bitter cold air bit them, in the early morning, as they walked back to the King's Inn. They built two more fires in the fire pits of the lobby. The Mengas had already shown them they knew of the companion's arrival, so there was no reason to sit in a cold inn. They talked together, as they warmed their bodies and ate cold leftovers.

The leaves of the deciduous trees, both in Malta, and in far-off Northwest Wood had fully turned and the rising sun bathed them in hues of red, yellow and orange. Darian said the snows would soon arrive, for the tops of the Eathen Mountains already glistened white against the bright blue sky, far in the distance.

"We take the north road out of the city and pass beneath the Northern Arch, as Stefen suggested," said Eathelon, chewing a piece of dried chikka meat.

"How far is it from here to the Northern Crossroads, Darian?" asked Palo, as he washed down a piece of dark bread with water from his waterskin.

"About five days, if all goes well," Darian responded, taking a bite of cheese.

"What do you mean by that?" Palo inquired.

"I mean providing we have no interference from Mengas, ghosts of the dead, or any other such distractions." He grinned.

"I do not expect interference from Mengas," said Eathelon.

"Nor do I," replied Darian.

"How far is it from the Northern Crossroads to Northwest Wood?" asked Eathelon.

"Four days more, I should think," replied Darian. "Elvenvale lies empty now, 'tis said. The Elvenkin stay in their wood. We should not encounter Elvenkin until we enter their wood and, if we enter at the place Stefen suggested, it should take only a day or two more for us to reach Lingolia."

"10 days in all," said Eathelon. "We will likely reach the Northern Crossroads just behind Stefen and the company."

"Yes. Did you expect to meet them there?" asked Darian. "It takes six days or more for them to reach Toldor's Keep from the Southern Crossroads and Stefen seemed eager to arrive to the Keep and depart again before Wintereve."

"No, I did not expect to meet them," replied Eathelon.

"Let us rest now, before we ride out," said Palo, yawning.

They left the fires to burn down and retired to their rooms.

"I can take first watch," offered Darian, "and wake you in three hours."

"We need no watch, Darian," Eathelon remarked, "but do as you wish."

Palo nodded, yawned and went to sleep. He slept and woke with the same ease wherever he lay down, it seemed.

Eathelon had too much on his mind to fall asleep. He lay there, staring at the ceiling. On impulse, he felt under his tunic for the Book of Stones. Dare he draw it out? No, he dare not risk it, but his heart quickened a beat at the thought of what he may find when he could make a study of it. When he did fall asleep, another dream came to him.

* * *

He walked upon a paved road through a vast, empty desert, up and down between the sand dunes until, in the distance, the outline of dark, jagged, mountain peaks appeared, thrusting upward into the sky like sharpened daggers. He continued on and came to a village, a place of odd mud huts, like those of the Siipa tribe on one of the isles in Melatui's archipelago — flat roofs, narrow windows, cloth doors. Dim, narrow alleyways ran between the buildings, shaded by dark mud walls and it made the village uninviting. Few people walked its streets in the heat of the day — only those bent on some urgent errand, it seemed. But after dark, the village came alive. Lights appeared in the windows and fires blazed in hearths. People scurried this way and that, and it re-

minded Eathelon of the huge ants in the Melatui forests that scurried about in the cool of the evening, foraging for food and stockpiling it in their gigantic nests. The people of the village paid little attention to the cold desert, it seemed, as they shopped, gambled and drank in makeshift alehouses, filled with loud raucous music that split the night.

Eathelon walked unnoticed through the shabby village, and when he came to the other side of the desert, he followed a road north, over a rocky terrain. He saw, in the distance, a tower rising into the sky, and thought he heard a lady inside, weeping. A sinter hawk flew back and forth frantically at her window, then suddenly an arrow pierced it and it fell, twisting and turning to the ground below and its scream echoed in Eathelon's ears, and grew louder, and louder ...

* * *

"Eathelon! Wake up! Listen!" Palo whispered, with some urgency.

Eathelon sat up and tried to clear his head of the odd dream he'd just had.

"Do you hear it? Darian has gone to investigate," said Palo.

Darian returned a few minutes later, his face drawn and serious. "It is as I feared."

"What is it, Darian?" queried Palo.

"The ghosts of the dead ... they are here!"

"What? Where?" Eathelon questioned.

They followed Darian to the front of the inn and out onto the porch. The sky had turned black.

Have we slept all day? But Eathelon saw that black clouds had moved in, obscuring the sun. He peered out into the growing gloom and heard the unmistakable cry of a sinter hawk, but he could not see it.

The horses neighed and stamped in the stable behind the inn.

Eathelon strained to make out the shadowy outlines of the buildings across the plaza, when something whizzed past his head. He turned to see what it was, but it had moved by too quickly and disappeared.

He heard unintelligible mumblings, whisperings in the dark, like the ones he'd heard in the catacombs. "Show yourself!" he said, as he stepped off the porch.

Two sinter hawks streaked by and he glimpsed enough of them to see what they were.

"Do you feel them, Eathelon, and hear them?" Darian asked.

"The ghosts of the dead?" Palo seeking clarification.

"I think so," whispered Darian.

"Yes, I feel them and hear them, but I do not see them," Eathelon responded quietly.

"I doubt they want to be seen," said Darian.

Eathelon felt a hot breath on his face as another creature streaked by. *That was no sinter hawk!* "Palo — hand me a torch!"

Palo did.

Eathelon thrust it out into the dark, as another creature streaked by. This time he saw it. "Everyone inside!" he ordered, and he ran back up onto the porch.

They ran back into the inn and slammed the door shut as a scream pierced the night and something thudded into the door behind them.

"These are not ghosts of the dead," Eathelon declared, leaning against the door. "They are fyrcaats!"

"What?" exclaimed Darian. "So far north?"

"Indeed," replied Eathelon.

"Those creatures are still after us?" asked Palo, rubbing his arm where the fyrcaat barb had pierced him on the ridge.

"So, it seems Palo. Yet the sinter hawks are here, too. I believe they have come to our aid once again."

"These are your ghosts of the dead then, Darian," Palo said.

"No," replied Darian. "I know the difference between a fyrcaat and a ghost. And I heard the whisperings too."

"I heard them in the catacombs," Eathelon admitted.

"You did not tell us that down there," Palo pointed out.

"I thought at first I had imagined it."

"What does this all mean?" asked Palo.

"It means fyrcaats, sinter hawks and the ghosts of the dead

are probably all here," replied Darian. "Have I not been trying to tell you about these ghosts of the dead?"

"Yes, and I intend to put an end to this fyrcaat business too!" Palo started for the front door; his knife drawn.

Eathelon blocked his way. "You survived a poisoned fyrcaat barb once, by my skill and lothingel, Palo. We have no lothingel and I am not willing to lose another companion!" He paused. "I would like to know who sent the sinter hawks, though."

"Mengas?" asked Palo. "They clearly know of our presence here."

"I doubt anyone sends them," Darian responded. "These hawks protect their territory. The fyrcaats are intruders. The two are natural enemies."

"We have no time to look for answers," Eathelon declared. "We must leave and make for Northwest Wood, as planned. But first, we must wait out this battle." They went back to the fire pit, stoked the fire and waited.

The battle between the fyrcaats and sinter hawks lasted only a short time, however, and after all had gone quiet again the three of them stepped outside to find a mist now covered the city and a low-lying fog crept eerily over the grounds. No sign of any battle remained, not even the creature that had thudded into the front door, only the mark it left.

The companions went back and grabbed their belongings and exited the King's Inn. When they went to retrieve the horses, they saw, floating about in the mist, ghostly images of people, incomplete shadows, thin traces of men, women and children, some of their faces twisted in panic, fear or grief.

"See, did I not tell you? The ghosts of the dead!" whispered Darian.

"Indeed, you did," replied Eathelon.

Their whisperings and murmurings came from every direction and they just stood there, witnessing the scene before them, barely believing what they saw.

"Perhaps it is they who called the sinter hawks," Palo commented softly.

"Perhaps," said Darian. Then he added, "Perhaps Eathelon is right and they meant to protect us."

"Why do you think the ghosts of the dead have not appeared before now?" Eathelon asked in a whisper. "I wonder if Mengas have seen them."

"I doubt they appear to the Mengas, Eathelon. Perhaps they waited for an Eldarin to appear. Perhaps only now is the right time for them to show themselves. I once feared them, but no longer do."

"There is no need for us to fear our own kin, Darian."

Palo watched, but said only, "I do not fear them."

"You fear little, my Warrior friend," Eathelon noted, thankfully. "A fact for which I have always been grateful."

Eathelon stepped forward, into the mist and walked among the ghostly images. He felt a great compassion for these troubled spirits, who must feel compelled to remain. Words suddenly came to him and tumbled out of his mouth of their own accord: *a somë grási bána thóla; passarë pèsi,* "we thank you, spirits of the dead. You may go now, and be at peace, for you shall be avenged!"

There came a long, loud sigh, after which the voices diminished and the images began to dissolve and fade away into the mist. Then the mist itself dissolved and the dark clouds overhead diminished. A pale blue and yellow sky shone ahead in the crisp cold morning.

The companions retrieved the horses and secured their belongings, then mounted and set off across the plaza, past the huge fountain, which sat silent now, as the sun crawled slowly up the sky. They came to the main road and followed it north, around the Great Hall of the Council, and out of the city.

They passed through another region of Eldarin homes, as the road began a slow climb toward the Eathen Mountains, which loomed large ahead, and when they came to the Northern Arch, Eathelon stopped to read aloud the words carved into it:

May the grace of our Fathers keep you safe
on your journey north.

Indeed, thought Eathelon.

They passed under the arch and followed the road through

the vast northern hills of Malta, still golden with maltinias, and rode all day through the fields of gold, admiring the tenacity of the tiny golden teacups that danced on their long stems in the cold breeze, refusing to sleep, until Wintereve arrived as an enforcer requiring obedience.

They kept to a leisurely pace the rest of the day and, when the sun had fallen far down the sky, arrived to a place in the hills where Darian stopped them.

"Follow me," he said. "I have something to show you."

They followed him up onto a shelf of land that overlooked the road, and when they reached the top, they dismounted and followed Darian to its edge.

"Here now is the view I promised," said Darian.

As the sun sank between the peaks of the Eathen Mountains, it cast its dying rays over the fields of gold maltinias and bounced its rays off of the walls of the Great Hall of the Council in the city, turning everything to gold.

"The Golden City," smiled Eathelon.

"We would have missed it, had you not brought us up here, Darian," Palo noted. "It is a wondrous sight, for certain."

"I could not let that happen," Darian said. "I have seen it only once before myself, but I shall never tire of the sight."

Darian had somehow timed it exactly right, for the scene lasted only minutes before the hills and city fell into shadow. They made their way back down to the road and continued their northward trek.

Shortly after, they entered a region of dense trees that afforded them better protection and selected a place to camp. They feed and settled the horses, built a fire, ate and talked together into the night, then Palo took first watch. Eathelon relieved him after three hours and Darian took the final watch for three hours more.

They rose before dawn, mounted and continued to ride through the forested area, camping and risking fires for the next four nights. The sun warmed the days little and the nights grew colder, as they traveled north toward the mountains. Palo hunted rabet and dere, a nice change from the cold dried chikka meat, hard bread and sour cheese. The wine had long since disappeared, but they still had plenty of clean fresh water. The trees diminished again, as they rode farther north and, on the afternoon of the fifth day out of the Golden City, they arrived at the Northern Crossroads.

"Here the north road joins the east-west road," said Darian. "From here, that trail north rises steeply into the Highland Gap and connects to another, narrow trail that leads up to Toldor's Keep. That is the road taken by the company."

Palo examined the ground. "Indeed, they passed by here a few days ago, if I read these hoofprints correctly."

"We will stay the night here and take the east trail in the morning," said Darian.

"Four more days to the wood," remarked Eathelon, with growing excitement.

"Providing there are no more incidents," added Palo.

"That depends on the weather now," Darian claimed. "It is unpredictable this far north at this time of year. I doubt we will encounter any travelers on this trail."

They made a fire and Palo went off to hunt. He returned with three rabets, which he set roasting. The companions talked and ate together, grateful for fresh, warm roasted meat, which warmed their bellies, as the fire warmed their bodies.

"Have you thought at all about Farli and the Rangers, Darian?" Eathelon asked, as he plucked a piece of rabet off of its roasting stick and popped it into his mouth.

Darian blew on his rabet to cool it and said, "Farli is capable enough to act in my stead, which is why I left him in command. But I suppose I should try to get word to him, lest my men think me dead, or some other such folly." He laughed.

"Your men know you well enough, I am certain," said Palo, tearing a piece of meat off of his stick and overloading his mouth. "I doubt they will believe you have come to any harm."

"Well, they know, as I do, that conflict is unlikely this time of year." Darian wiped his mouth on his sleeve "Any conflict with the East is more likely to come after *Cármal - Winterend*. We should have the winter, at least, to tend to our errand and gather what information we can about any plans Baele may be making ... and make plans of our own."

"How certain are you that Baele is planning something?"

asked Eathelon, finishing up his rabet.

"We cannot be completely certain of his plans, but he has stewed in the juices of his earlier defeat overlong, and based on what the Rangers have discovered, the House of Toldor are recruiting Northmen again. It is why Aneron ordered the men to restore and fortify Toldor's Keep. But it will take time for Baele to bring to fruition any plan he makes, since he clearly has not already done so. The Northmen may again try to enter Hamlan through the Highland Gap, but the Gap is not easily traveled in winter. These things are somewhat predictable." He paused. "Besides, should Northmen attempt enter the Gap again, Andolan's soldiers will be ready for them this time."

"Why does Baele not simply invade through Numar?" asked Palo. "The climate there is more favorable and the overland route to Andolan less risky. Winter would not be a factor."

"You make a valid point, my Warrior friend. That is possible, I suppose, but consider this. A march from Numar is long and the southern plains well-guarded by Rangers. The grass, as you know, causes lethargy. In some ways, Baele's army is more vulnerable there. I believe he will want to put his strength in place before he attempts any invasion of Hamlan. It would increase his chance for success. No, Numar would not be his first choice. It is far too exposed."

"If he does recruit the Northmen and mercenaries of Rabellan into his army, Baele can hit Hamlan from more than one direction," said Eathelon, "his army from the south and the Northmen from the north. The mercenaries could approach from either side of the desert, yes?"

"Yes," Darian replied, "I thought of that. But if he invaded Numar, he would tip his hand before he could reach Andolan. Personally, I doubt his ability to coordinate an invasion from multiple directions anyway. He may be clever, but he is also mad and impulsive, qualities which do not make for good leadership."

"What about his son, Esol?" asked Palo.

"Yes, Esol is the greater concern," said Darian, thoughtfully.

"Baele's intentions seemed clear enough to me," Palo stated, rubbing his arm. "He did not send his fyrcaats after us as a diplomatic gesture."

"This is all speculation anyway," Darian said, "though not without some foundation. Besides, we do not know for certain that Baele was the one who sent those creatures after you."

"Who else could have sent them?" asked Eathelon.

"I do not know," replied Darian.

"We must make plans with whatever information we now have," Eathelon stated, "whether it has been validated or not." He paused. "I am grateful to have you here with us, Darian."

Darian nodded. "Hamlan is my home and the Eldarin my people. I will do anything I can to protect the West. And I believe you know me well enough by now to know I am a man of adventure." He grinned.

Eathelon grinned back.

"Three adventurers," boasted Palo. "I hope our end turns out better than our friends."

They fell silent at his reminder.

"Adventure always brings risk," Darian stated, "but we are trained for it, are we not?"

"Indeed, we are," Palo agreed.

Darian changed the subject. "What do you expect to find in Lingolia, Eathelon?"

"Anything I can learn about the Eldarin maiden for one, but mostly I hope to somehow rekindle the friendship between the Elvenkin and Andolan. I am told they were once allies. I believe the West will need them in the end. I do not know what sundered their alliance, and their friendship."

"War can create such breeches," Darian noted.

They continued the conversation awhile longer then, their bellies full and their bodies tired from the long day's ride, they settled in for the night. Palo gathered more wood, to keep the fire going through the night and Eathelon took first watch.

He sat by the fire, lost in thought and struggled to brush off an odd feeling of disappointment at missing Stefen and Arestor at the Northern Crossroads, though he'd not expected to meet them there. He thought about his journey thus far in Narda and concluded that, after the tragic shipwreck and loss of his friends more good than bad had followed. He could not foresee the future, so he would have to rely on his instincts and any information he could glean to plan ahead. He would need to raise all of his courage to overcome the dangers he knew must lay ahead, but thus far resources had somehow always appeared when he most needed them.

Seeing his companions were fast asleep, he decided to open the Book of Stones and he reached under his tunic and pulled it out. He unlocked it and began to read the pages by the firelight.

But Palo, as always, slept with one eye open.

Chapter 25: Elvenvale

Darian stood the final watch and stoked the fire, as Eathelon and Palo rose to a cold Midfall dawn. After a short brefas, they broke camp and set out eastward across the plateau to the long, shallow valley of Elvenvale. The white peaks of the Eathens rose high in the west behind them, and the dense trees of Northwest Wood filled the slopes of the Sylvan Mountains, to the north.

"It is a long day's ride to the eastern edge of the plateau," said Darian, "and the descent to Elvenvale from there is steep."

"Duly noted," Eathelon responded.

"Do Elvenkin live in the valley?" queried Palo.

"No longer, if they once did," replied Darian. "They are an ancient folk, who have lived in Northwest Wood many ages, long before the Eldarin arrived. They are the eldest race in Narda, though some creatures here are more ancient even than they."

"Like fyrcaats?" Palo asked.

"Most likely, yes, and sinter hawks and baerwolffs — and a few others. The Great White Birds are the eldest of all, it is said. I have never seen one myself."

"I have," Eathelon confirmed.

"Then you are fortunate," replied Darian.

"But I was groggy from being hit on the head so was not certain if what I saw was real, or imagined."

"They are real enough," Darian stated, "though sightings are rare. The Great White Birds do not appear to us often."

"What are they?" asked Palo.

"Guardians of Narda, it is said," replied Darian. "I know little of them. 'It is said they appear when they are most needed.'"

"Can they be summoned?" asked Eathelon.

"No," replied Darian. "I have heard they appear of their own free will."

"Well, I have no idea why one appeared to me then, but it is good to know it was not just my imagination."

"So, Elvenkin do not live in Elvenvale then," Palo restated, getting back to his question.

"No, they are a forest people. Woods and forests are the domain of Elvenkin. I doubt that they ever lived in Elvenvale, though the valley is under their protection."

"What about baerwolffs?" asked Palo. "You said their domain is in Elvenvale."

"That is true," Darian acknowledged. "I suppose an encounter with them is possible."

"Let us hope not," Eathelon chimed in.

They spoke thus, as they rode along. About mid-day, Eathelon noticed the sky beginning to darken. "We may be in for bad weather, from the look of that sky."

The days had grown short and the nights long up here, for they were far north now. They rode all day and thankfully, though the clouds gathered overhead, the weather held. They neared the edge of the eastern cliff, as the sun fell into the cradle of the Eathen mountains behind them.

"We will camp up here tonight," said Darian, "and begin our descent in the morning. It is not safe to attempt it in the dark."

They dismounted and walked to the edge of the plateau, and gazed out over the valley of Elvenvale, as the fading sun fell onto the tops of the deciduous trees of Northwest Wood and painted them in the colors of *Tolári – Midfall.*

"Behold the realm of the Elvenkin," said Darian.

"It is a fair sight," exclaimed Palo.

"Indeed, most of Hamlan thus far has been fair," replied Eathelon, "from Andolan to Harwyn and Forwyn Crossings, to Malta's golden hills and city, to the majestic Eathen Mountains and now this long green valley and dark forest — all sights I shall not forget."

"Nor I," agreed Palo.

"Numar was also fair to look upon once," Darian asserted, "though its landscape is much gentler. This is the first time I have seen Elvenvale from up here."

"I thought you said you had been here before," said Palo.

"I have been to Northwest Wood, but I did not enter it from here. I entered at its southern tip, on the other side of this valley."

Eathelon realized then that parts of their journey together would prove new to Darian.

Elvenvale fell into shadow, as the sun set, and Palo took off to hunt something up for supper. Eathelon and Darian groomed and fed the horses, set a camp and built a fire. Palo returned after a time with a small dere wrapped around his shoulders, much to Eathelon's delight. A full grown Nardan dere is only about two and a half feet tall, lean and tasty. This one would provide meat enough for them for several days.

Palo cleaned and set it roasting, then rummaged around in his pack and found a handful of small tubers, an onion, a clove of garlic and some herbs from Stefen's cooks. Eathelon and Darian smiled as the Warrior laid out a feast before them.

"You certainly make camping more pleasurable with your culinary skills, Palo," said Darian. "I believe you have outdone yourself this time."

Palo grinned, as they helped themselves to the food.

They sat long at the fire eating their fill and talking, as night deepened.

"Tell us more about Numar, Darian," said Eathelon. "What was it like growing up there?"

Darian paused to blow on a hot piece of meat and to take a bite, then he began. "The people of Numar were friendly, industrious, loyal and protective, for the most part. The few who knew of my ancestry, kept it quiet, for they knew well the penalty for revealing my secret. The East plundered Numar over time and most of the people fled to the cities. Only those of us who patrol the southern plains remained behind, primarily out of duty."

"Baele did that?" asked Palo.

"Baele and those in his employ," Darian responded.

"Did the people of Numar not fight back?" Palo queried.

"They did, with a militia of farmers and ranchers, and other angry men and women, but they stood no real chance against Baele's trained soldiers, let alone the mercenaries of Rabellan."

"Nor did the Eldarin," Eathelon said.

"No," replied Darian. "The Eldarin are intelligent and capable, but like the people of Numar, they found themselves ill equipped to protect themselves. And I can understand why. They had stopped war in Narda. How could they possibly foresee the evil that the House of Tebor begat? That House set the Northmen against the Golden City and the Eldarin had little warning or opportunity to defend themselves against the huge brutes. And Andolan's soldiers were too far away to help them." He paused. "The Eldarin are sorely missed here. They did much to make Narda safe and prosperous."

"They failed to predict their demise," Palo stated.

"Yes, though one can find evil in any group of people," claimed Darian, "it is the way of things, I suppose. But the House of Tebor changed Narda, undid many years of prosperity, for their own gain. All were blind to such evil, my Father said. People only see what they wish to see." He took a bite. "The West must restore Landrin to his throne. It is time."

"Well," Eathelon interjected, "That has everything to do with our errand. We must find a way to chase the House of Tebor out of Narda, for good."

Palo stood and swung an invisible sword through the air. "I am ready." Then he offered to take first watch. They finished up the meal and took Palo up on his offer.

Darian and Eathelon laid down for some much-needed rest and Darian relieved Palo after three hours. Eathelon took the final watch, during which he kept the fire stoked against the cold night and smoked what remained of the deremeat for the rest of their journey to Lingolia.

Darian and Palo rose in the cold morning and the companions ate brefas, as the sun spread its fiery fingers over Elvenvale, bringing it to life. But the sun could not wholly penetrate Northwest Wood, so dense was it with tall evergreens.

The meal done, they broke camp and began the long steep descent to the valley floor. The trail fell gradually at first, then became steep and it took them all day to pick their way carefully down, single file. Conversation was all but impossible, so they rode in silence much of the day, leaving each to his own thoughts. Eathelon took in the magnificent view as they descended, his payment for the trail's difficult challenge.

The plateau of Malta rose up behind them and the valley floor shrank before them, as they neared Elvenvale. The trees of Northwest Wood grew larger and larger, until the companions saw their true size and girth. At dusk, they came to a shelf above the valley floor and stopped. The sky had grown increasingly dark and had darkened fully now, as swollen black clouds loomed over the trees of wood and vale.

"We had better camp here tonight," Eathelon suggested. "This shelf of land offers a good vantage point and some protection, at least. It looks like we may be in for bad weather."

"Indeed," Darian agreed. "Wintereve is near now."

Palo tended the horses, while Darian set camp and Eathelon built a fire under a shallow overhang. The black night, devoid of moon or stars, quickly engulfed them and they wrapped themselves up in their heavy woolen cloaks against the bitter cold, for the fire alone was not sufficient to warm them.

They sat and ate the smoked deremeat, grateful for Palo's hunting and cooking prowess, and talked together. Just as they were finishing up the meal, they heard a long, high-pitched howl split the night, then another and another.

The horses whinnied and stamped their feet and would have bolted had they not been secured together.

"What was *that*?" asked Palo, walking over to help Darian and Eathelon calm the horses.

"It must have been a baerwolff cry," said Darian. "Those are the only creatures I know of that could make such a sound."

"The stuffed beast we saw at the inn," said Eathelon.

"Yes, though I have heard that they fear men more than men fear them," replied Darian.

"Let us hope so," Palo remarked.

"I have never encountered one," Darian offered, "but others

have said they only attack when provoked. They do run in packs, however, which makes them dangerous to one man. But we are three."

"How do you know if what you heard is even true?" asked Palo.

"I do not, for my part."

"Palo, you must not hunt alone," said Eathelon.

Palo scoffed. "I have slain a full grown baer, Eathelon — and that in my youth," he protested.

"I mean no disrespect for your ability, Palo," said Darian, "but one man alone, even a strong Warrior like you might still fall prey to a pack of hungry baerwolffs. Did you notice the size of that beast in Brega?"

"I did," replied Palo. "And I have slain beasts larger."

Eathelon looked at Palo, with a smile that melted Palo's resistance. "I have no desire to lose another companion, Palo, and most certainly not to a pack of baerwolffs."

Palo sighed. "I have long since learned to defer to your wisdom, Eathelon, despite my Warrior pride. I will not hunt alone."

"It is a useless argument anyway," said Darian. "You have already given us meat enough to reach Lingolia."

That ended their discussion about baerwolffs. They each picked a spot to lay down and settle in for the night.

Eathelon heard someone giggle.

"Did one of you just laugh at something?" he asked.

"Laugh? At what?" replied Darian. "There is nothing here to laugh about." He yawned and pulled a blanket over his head.

"I thought I heard someone laugh."

"I did not hear anything," yawned Palo.

Eathelon decided he must have imagined it.

"What do you know about the Elvenkin, Darian?" Eathelon inquired, with a yawn.

"Only what I learned of them on my one short visit to Lingolia, as a boy, and what I have heard from others." Darian yawned again. "My memory is not complete, but I shall never forget Lingolia."

"Why is that?" asked Palo.

"It seemed magical to me, unique, a place like no other."

"More magical than the Golden City?" Eathelon queried.

"The Golden City and its surrounds are unique in their own way, but Lingolia is more ancient and the Elvenkin ... very spiritual. They love all forms of art, but most especially music. They are diligent in their protection and care of the wood and its creatures, and highly skilled with bow and knife. Long have they protected their wood and this valley and kept them from intruders."

"Is that why they keep to themselves?" asked Palo.

"I do not know. They were once allied to Hamlan and they helped to defend Malta during the Great War. Many Elvenkin fell to give the Eldarin the opportunity to escape to their ships and they were sorely grieved to learn that the Eldarin they helped to save later perished at sea. Word of the debris that washed up on the shores of Numar went far and wide in Narda. Perhaps the loss was too great for them to bear and that is why they withdrew their allegiance to Andolan."

"Celorn holds the Elvenkin in high regard, as does my Mother," Eathelon stated.

"Stefen said the Elvenkin no longer care for Andolan, or for the West, though they are residents in it," noted Palo.

"No," Darian corrected, "He said the Elvenkin are wary of strangers, which is likely true enough. But Aneron and Stefen still hold the Elvenkin in high regard, even though they are sundered."

"We are strangers here," Palo pointed out. "Perhaps the Elvenkin will not be eager to welcome us, as Stefen implied."

"The Elvenkin have long memories, Palo, and I have visited them once before. I believe they will welcome us and be willing to hear your message. I believe that, in their hearts they too, desire the return of the Eldarin."

"Such is my hope," said Eathelon. "Do they know you are an Eldarin, Darian?"

"That is likely, for my Mother, a Nydar, made no attempt to hide the fact when we visited. But enough talk of the Elvenkin. We will meet them soon enough. Let us get some sleep." He yawned. "We have another long day of riding ahead of us tomorrow."

"I will take first watch," asserted Eathelon.

Darian and Palo agreed and were soon fast asleep.

Eathelon poked at the fire and stared out into the dark abyss beyond the shelf. He sat with his back against the cliff face, listening to the fire crackle and watching its embers rise into the air. Happily, they heard no more baerwolff cries. The time passed slowly, as it does when one wishes it to pass quickly, and just before his watch ended, Eathelon heard the giggle again.

"Who is there?" he whispered, looking around for the source.

A giggle.

"Show yourself," he insisted, softly. "I promise no harm will come to you."

Suddenly, a multitude of tiny lights flickered on and began to circle him, lighting up the camp. He thought they were embers from the fire he'd been watching, and a trick played on his mind. But the giggles said otherwise. He watched the tiny creatures with curiosity, did not fear them.

Darian woke up. "What is it, Eathelon?"

The lights flicked out in an instant.

"Nothing, Darian. Go back to sleep."

"Please come back," Eathelon whispered into the night.

But Darian, awake now got up and walked over to where Eathelon sat. "It is my turn at the watch anyway," he yawned. "Go get some sleep."

Disappointed the incident had been cut short, Eathelon grabbed a blanket and moved off to lay down. He found it difficult to get comfortable on the rocky shelf and he could not take his mind off of the tiny curious creatures flickering their lights and giggling softly. What were they? Darian had not mentioned them. But his curiosity would have to wait, for whatever they were, they did not return that night and, in the end, his eyes grew too heavy to remain open and he fell asleep.

When he awoke, Darian was getting up and Palo, who had stood the last watch, was stoking the fire. The sun was only a shadow behind the dark gray clouds that had continued to gather in the night, and the cold air penetrated them to the bone. Eathelon warmed himself by the fire and watched, concerned as the clouds covered the sky, shutting out any light or warmth from the sun. They decided to skip brefas and simply gathered more wood to take with them, for they did not want to search for it after they reached the valley floor, should the weather turn foul. Dry wood may be hard to find if the land became soaked.

They started on the trail, which wound down gradually from the shelf, twisting and turning as they rode single file, in silence again. The giant trees of Northwest Wood loomed closer with each step and, by the middle of the second day from the start of their descent, they came to the valley floor. As they did, the swollen clouds burst and dropped a torrent of freezing rain down on them. The rain turned almost at once to a freezing snow and blanketed them, the valley and the trees of the wood in pristine white, creating an almost magical, though unwelcome winter scene that hindered their progress. Not long after, they found themselves in the middle of a full-blown blizzard.

They searched for shelter as best they could in the blinding snowstorm and Eathelon lost his sense of direction, something rare for him. They stumbled onto a large grouping of boulders and pulled the horses into the space between them, one adequate enough for all of them to huddle together. A little farther in, the boulders touched at the top, creating a shelter of sorts, so they left the horses there and followed the maze through the giant rocks to a place large enough for the three of them to sit and make a fire. There they waited out the storm.

The blizzard raged through most of the night, the wind howling with ferocity across the open fields of Elvenvale. But with the fire and woolen cloaks to keep them warm, under the protection of the boulders, they were little affected, though none of them could sleep. Instead, they sat and talked all night, no need to set a watch.

The storm ended before dawn and they followed the maze back out and retrieved the horses. When they emerged from the boulders, they found a deep blanket of snow covered everything, including the trail. They discussed what to do.

"If we keep the wood to our left, we can ride eastward easily enough," said Darian.

"Yes, but without a visible trail, the horses may stumble into a hole and go lame," said Eathelon. "We cannot know what lies under the snow and we can ill afford to lose a horse. We dare not risk it."

"What would you have us do, then?" asked Palo. "Remain here?"

"We must consider all options," Eathelon replied.

"We could remain here until the snow melts off enough to pick up the trail again," Darian offered.

"Yes, but how long will that take?" questioned Palo.

"Too long," Eathelon responded. "We have already been much delayed in our errand. That is not our best option."

"It is colder here than the topmost peak of Mt. Malucan in the dead of winter," said Palo, stamping his feet and pulling his cloak more tightly around his huge frame.

"A snowfall this early in the season is not unusual, but neither is it common," Darian stated. "It does not look too deep. Perhaps the sun will melt it off in a few days. Waiting here may not be such a bad idea, Eathelon."

"It adds time to our errand we can ill afford," said Eathelon.

"I have another idea," declared Palo.

"What?" asked Darian.

"Look," he said. The weather had cleared enough to see the wood in the distance and Palo pointed to it. "Northwest Wood appears no more than half a day's ride from here. Why not make straight for the wood? You said yourself that once we enter, the Elvenkin will find us. We do not have to enter at the place Stefen suggested."

"What you say is true, Palo, but the distance to the wood may be deceptive, and look closer than it actually is," Darian remarked. "I believe it to be at least a day's ride. Lingolia is closer if we enter at the point Stefen suggested."

"Well, whatever choice we make, we are going to have the same problem of not knowing what lies beneath the snow," Eathelon declared. "You said yourself, Darian, you have never come this way before."

"I do not see why we should remain here when we can reach Lingolia sooner rather than later," challenged Palo. "You said yourself that you do not wish to further delay our errand, Eathelon. I say we make straight for the wood from here."

"We must consider his point," Eathelon stated.

Darian thought for a minute. "Alright, if we all agree, then we will make for the wood."

Eathelon and Palo nodded, so they mounted and started off across the white valley, but soon found themselves in deep snow that slowed their progress. By nightfall, they had covered only half the distance to the wood.

"The snow is deeper than it looked," said Palo.

Darian wore a look with an unspoken, "I told you so."

They searched for a place to make camp but found nothing promising on the open expanse of the valley and Eathelon grew uneasy about their decision. In the end, they camped on a small rise of land which at least gave them a view of the valley all around them.

They cleared away a patch of snow, made a fire to warm themselves and ate the smoked deremeat. Palo took first watch.

Eathelon lay back on his blanket, his head on his pack, and gazed up at the clear, darkening sky, now dotted with stars. He never tired of looking at the stars, nor lost his feeling of awe as he gazed at the pulsating multitude in the crowded sky. He recognized Forsil, as before, but few others. He had selected a spot a short distance away from his companions, for some privacy, in the hope that the tiny creatures that had appeared before would do so again. He was not disappointed, for as his eyelids grew heavy, he heard the giggles again. He sat up and peered into the dark. The tiny flickering lights came on — far away from the campfire, then blinked off. He looked over at Palo, but the Warrior was looking off in another direction — no doubt watching and listening for baerwolffs. Darian appeared to be asleep on the other side of the campfire.

"Show yourself," Eathelon whispered into the dark. "I promise no harm will come to you."

More giggles, then something made a soft landing on the end of his nose and began to pulsate with light. He looked cross-eyed at the tiny creature, not much bigger than a large insect. Several more flew around his head and his Eldarin intuition told him they tried to tell him something, but he did not understand their message. After a few minutes, as suddenly as they had appeared, the lights flickered out and the creatures disappeared into the night.

A moment later, a long piercing cry split the night, then another, and another. The hair stood up on the back of Eathelon's neck. Darian woke up and jumped to his feet. Palo drew his knife and peered into the dark.

"Baerwolffs!" exclaimed Darian. "And they sound nearby!"

"Too near," Eathelon declared, walking over to join him.

"I thought you told us the creatures are not much interested in men, Darian," said Palo.

"I said that is what I heard," Darian defended, as he peered into the dark night. "I also said I have never encountered one."

Palo scowled in the dark. "It looks like we are about to," he observed.

The horses stamped and whinnied and Eathelon tried to calm his horse, as he saddled it and loaded his pack. Palo and Darian did the same.

"Put out the fire!" Eathelon yelled.

Darian threw dirt on it and only after it had gone out, did they see the circle of yellow eyes staring at them from all around.

"Shards! We are surrounded!" Palo proclaimed.

"And unprotected," added Darian.

"We have only the slight advantage of the hill," Eathelon noted. "What should we do, Darian? Stand and fight, or make a run for the wood?"

"We are trapped here," replied Darian. "There is little else we can do but make a stand."

They took swords from their scabbards on the horses, ones Stefen had provided them, and prepared to make a stand, as the baerwolffs howled and the yellow eyes advanced.

They stood back to back facing out in different directions, ready to fight.

"I will be most unhappy if this ends badly," Eathelon confessed, as he prepared for what was coming.

"Do not underestimate us," Darian countered. "We can take the creatures."

"That depends entirely on how many there are," replied Eathelon.

Suddenly, there came a long sigh and a funnel of light spiraled up from the ground. It widened into a circle over their heads, and the circle grew wider and wider, moving out toward the yellow eyes, until it lay between the companions and the baerwolffs. The light intensified as it circled, and the yellow eyes blinked repeatedly, temporarily blinded by the bright light. The baerwolffs stopped their advance, for the moment.

The companions watched as a piece of the circle broke off and formed a long arrow pointing northward, to the wood, lighting a path in that direction.

"Make for the wood!" yelled Eathelon, deciphering the message.

They replaced the swords, jumped on the horses and took off at a full gallop, following the trail of light. The baerwolffs, recovered from their temporary blindness, took off at a hard run after them, howling wildly.

As the beasts gained on the riders, some of the lights overhead broke off and rallied behind them to slow the baerwolffs. The companions pushed their horses hard and the wood loomed closer and closer. Eathelon looked behind to see the baerwolffs beginning to tire. The beasts could run fast, but evidently could sustain their pace only over a short distance.

They reached the wood and tried to slow the horses, for they ran wildly into the wood, dodging trees and nearly throwing the riders to the ground. But when they realized the baerwolffs had not followed, the beasts eventually came under control.

The companions dismounted and spoke to the horses, calming them. Eathelon looked back through the thick stand of trees at the wood's edge and saw the yellow eyes staring back, but the baerwolffs did not enter. They remained safely outside the perimeter of the wood.

"It is fortunate for us that the creatures did not follow us into the wood," remarked Palo.

"And even more fortunate for them that they did not," said a voice.

They turned to see an Elvenkin step out from behind the trees.

"Northwest Wood belongs to the Elvenkin," he stated. "Why

have you entered here?"

Then a group of Elvenkin emerged behind him with bows, and pointed arrows at the companions.

"We seek Lord Mengalan," replied Darian, "to bring him a message of great importance."

"Tell me your message," the Elvenkin stated, so I may determine its importance. I am his ... emissary."

"The message is for Lord Mengalan's ears alone," said Eathelon, "and he alone may determine its importance. But know that we come in peace. We are friends, not enemies."

"Whether you are friends or enemies is not yet determined," the Elvenkin noted. He paused. "But I perceive no evil among you." He signaled the rest to put away their weapons.

He stepped forward and extended a hand to Darian. "You are an Eldarin, a Nydar."

"Yes." My companion here is also Eldarin, a Syndar. He tipped his head toward Eathelon. "I am Darian."

"I am *Tholin*. I did not expect to find an Eldarin. Your companion does resemble a Syndar, yet his color differs from that of any Syndar I have met. And your other companion is of a race I do not recognize."

"Correct," Eathelon confirmed. "My companion and I are not from Narda."

"I am Eathelon, a Mallorite from the isle of Melatui."

"And I am called Palo, a Maagi Warrior of that same isle," added Palo.

"I see there is a story here," surmised Tholin. "These names are new to me, yet I have lived long in Narda."

"And our tale is long," Darian claimed, adding, "but you are welcome to it."

"I wish to hear your tale, and if it pleases me, I will escort you to Lingolia myself. Then we will see whether or not Mengalan finds your message important, as you say."

"We thank you for your wisdom, Tholin," offered Eathelon.

Tholin nodded and beckoned them to follow him to their nearby camp. The rest of the Elvenkin followed behind, looking a little uncertain about Tholin's decision to let the strangers remain in the wood.

When they reached the camp, Tholin offered the companions food and drink and bid Eathelon tell his story. He told of their fateful voyage to Narda, of the shipwreck and loss of friends, but he did not tell all about their journey in Narda thus far. Tholin perceived that Eathelon held something back, but he nevertheless listened politely and asked few questions.

When the night had worn away, Tholin bid them all lay down and rest while the Elvenkin stood watch on the wood ... and on the companions for, as was said, Elvenkin are wary of strangers.

Chapter 26:
Northwest Wood

The sun filtered down through the tress of Northwest Wood at dawn, and glistened off of the snow-covered ground, revealing a picturesque landscape, though one of bitter cold. Tholin accepted the tale offered by the companions and agreed to escort them to the Elvenkin city to meet Lord Mengalan. So, after a brief meal, they all set out for Lingolia.

Eathelon tried not to stare at the unique features of the Elvenkin, whom he had never before seen. They had tall, lithe, slender bodies, and their ears were ever so slightly pointed at the top, which intrigued him. Tholin's long yellow hair fell well over his shoulders and his bright blue eyes sparkled when he spoke. His words tumbled out in a lyrical, almost poetic way and Eathelon had instantly liked him. Though he spoke little with the other Elvenkin, Eathelon observed the similarities among them.

"How far is it to Lingolia?" he asked Tholin.

"Two days, by this trail," Tholin replied.

The Elvenkin company rode in silence much of the time, with Eathelon and Tholin riding abreast, Palo and Darian behind them, all of them sandwiched between the other Elvenkin in the company, who scouted ahead, and covered the rear.

When Eathelon could hold his tongue no longer, he said, "I understand that the Elvenkin and Andolan were once allied."

"That is true," Tholin replied.

"And now?"

"Few words have passed between Lingolia and Andolan since the Great War. The Elvenkin no longer involve ourselves in Andolan's affairs."

"Do the affairs of Hamlan no longer concern the Elvenkin?"

"They did, and we paid a great price for that."

"So, too, did your allies, Tholin."

Tholin made no comment and a long pause ensued, so Eathelon decided to change the subject.

"I have heard tale of an Eldarin couple, and their child raised by Elvenkin in this wood. Is this true?"

Tholin smiled. "I have heard this also."

"You know of them, then?"

"What is your interest in this family?"

"They may have knowledge that would benefit my errand."

"Since I know nothing of your errand, I cannot say whether they would have knowledge to benefit it, or not."

"Can you tell me anything about them?"

"You ask much of me, for a stranger, Eathelon."

"I assure you my intentions are completely honorable. I only seek information that might prove useful to my errand."

Tholin paused. "I do not know why, but I believe you, Eathelon. I will tell you what I know. It is true the family made our wood their home, for a time. The child has grown, and she does abide in our wood, but she does not often come to Lingolia."

"That is unfortunate. And what of her parents?"

"That is another story."

"What can you tell me of the maiden then?"

"She is an ... unusual woman." Tholin's eyes sparkled as he spoke. "Her skin is as fair as a summer day, her hair dark as raaven feathers, her eyes like violets in Earlyspring and her voice like a songbird. She is as agile as a dere, yet hard-minded and steadfast as a *rulæn* tree. The Elvenkin are fond of her. We protect her, and I no less than the others." He looked directly at Eathelon and pinned him in his gaze. "We would protect her even to our own death."

His statement took Eathelon aback. "She is your wife, or betrothed?"

Tholin smiled. "No, Eathelon, she is my sister. Tholin and Meolin," he said in his lilting voice.

"Sister?" Eathelon felt a sense of relief, for no particular reason.

"She is my adopted sister, obviously," Tholin clarified. "My Father took her in when she was a child, and without her parents. She grew up here, in our wood, as you heard."

"What happened to her parents?"

"That is a long tale, though I will tell it if you wish to hear."

"I do."

"Then I will tell it over the mid-day meal, for your companions will no doubt wish to hear it also."

"Fair enough."

They rode on until one of Tholin's scouts, who'd gone to look for a place to camp, returned and took them to it. The Elvenkin prepared a meal, as the companions sat down at the fire with Tholin and he began his tale:

"Elvenkin are an ancient, long-lived race. I have lived nearly 80 turnings myself."

Eathelon commented, with some surprise, "I would have taken you for no more than Palo's age, 35 turnings."

"In Elvenkin years, I am yet young." Tholin paused to take a bite. "My Father has lived 130 turnings, yet there is life in him still."

"The Elvenkin are a remarkable race," said Palo.

Tholin smiled. "Before I tell you anything more about Meolin, I will tell you the tale of her parents, Mereador and *Melannor*." He paused to take a bite. "Mereador's Father, a Syndar Eldarin, was a senior member of the Eldarin Great Council in Malta. Melannor's Father was a Nydar member of the same Council. The couple fell in love but kept it a secret, knowing as they did that Eldarin custom forbade them to marry outside of their own races."

"I am familiar with that custom," Eathelon remarked. "It has changed."

"So, you said, though the union of Mereador and Melannor was a union between Eldarin races, not one outside of the Eldarin race, as was your Mother's union with your Father. But love recognizes neither race, nor custom."

"Especially when such custom is outdated," added Eathelon.

"No Maagi would have married outside of the Maagi race before the Eldarin arrived in Melatui," confirmed Palo. "Of course, no other race existed in Melatui before then, though there was another on one of the isles in the archipelago." He laughed, revealing a full mouth of white teeth. He took a bite of bread.

"Life sometimes brings unforeseen challenges and events which in turn force a change," mused Tholin.

"I know the truth of that," Eathelon responded.

"So, it was with Mereador and Melannor. Forbidden in love by their Fathers, yet unable to control their hearts, they remained conflicted. They did not wish to disobey, but they could not deny their love for one another, so they set out to Lingolia to counsel with Mengalan, for he is well known to have wisdom in matters of the heart. They left in secret, but Mengalan said their Fathers would have approved, for they would expect him to uphold the Eldarin custom."

"How old were they when they left to Northwest Wood?" asked Darian.

"Only 15 and 16, and few Eldarin had ever married that young," replied Tholin.

"Did Mengalan uphold the Eldarin custom and advise against the marriage?" from Palo.

"He had no opportunity to do so, for soon after the couple arrived in our wood, the Great War broke out. Mengalan sent as many Elvenkin as could be spared to the aid of the Golden City, which our scouts said was under heavy assault by mercenaries and Northmen. It proved most fortunate for the young couple that they reached the safety of the wood before the assault on the Golden City, for here, they remained protected. I was in my 20th turning and I joined the other Elvenkin and rode to the aid of the Eldarin. Mengalan and Mereador were with us also. Many Elvenkin fell defending the Golden City, for the battle was fierce and we were far outnumbered. Melannor remained in the wood with the women and children and the Elvenkin men appointed to protect them.

"We fought the eastern army, mercenaries and Northmen in Malta for many days and somehow survived, Mengalan, Mereador and I. But we returned to our wood, in defeat."

They finished the meal and Tholin suspended his tale until supper. They mounted and set off again.

The trail wound around and through an abundance of cedar,

pine, and hemlock trees, and large fern groves, including the tall blue rinna fern. Eathelon saw a blu-tailed sarow guarding its nest, and heard the tat, tat, tat of a woodpekir echoing through the forest, as it hunted a meal or drilled to store food for the winter. Latefall had left its mark here, for a thick carpet of fading leaves still covered the ground in many places and the trees that shed them stood almost bare now, preparing for the coming winter snows.

Eathelon noticed a tree he did not recognize, that became more prevalent in the forest, as they rode east. Taller and larger in girth than any other tree, it stood as a sentinel over the rest. Fascinated by its impressive height, girth and deep red, smooth bark, Eathelon had to satisfy his curiosity and asked, "Tholin, what is that tree? I have never before seen one."

"That is a rulæn, the eldest and strongest of all trees in the wood. Many Elvenkin build homes in them because they are as long-lived and steadfast as we are." He smiled.

"They are magnificent," said Eathelon.

Despite the bitter cold, Eathelon felt a warmth in this wood, and he felt lighter, as if the burdens he carried had been temporarily lifted from him. He could understand why the Elvenkin had little desire to leave it.

They set another camp at dusk, made a fire and sat down to supper. Tholin resumed his story:

"When he returned to Northwest Wood, Mereador had the sad task of telling Melannor that their parents had all perished in the raid on the Golden City. After a period of mourning, Eldarin custom no longer holding them back, the young couple asked Mengalan's permission to wed. They could not return to the Golden City, or even safely leave the wood, for Baele had put a price on the head of every Eldarin. But Mengalan counseled them to wait, saying if they were to remain in the wood, they must learn to care for it as the Elvenkin do. So, out of respect and gratitude, the couple agreed, and they spent the next five years learning the ways of the Elvenkin.

"During this time, we built a cottage for them in secret, a beautiful stone and wood cottage with a thatched roof of rulæn bark and shuttered windows. We built it near a stream and devised a way to bring water to the cottage and planted a garden there, and placed wildflowers in the window boxes.

"When Mengalan at last gave his consent for the couple to marry, the Elvenkin, who had come to love them, arranged the celebration in Midsummer, when the wildflowers are in high bloom and the songbirds' music abundant. The ceremony included both Eldarin and Elvenkin customs. Melannor looked beautiful in her long pale blue gown, and wore a crown of blubels, petiperls and silmaria, and Mereador looked regal in his traditional Syndar tunic, a crown of maltinia upon his head. After the ceremony, an Elvenkin procession led them to their cottage — a wedding gift. It was a joyous time for all."

Darian said thoughtfully, "Meolin is older than we thought then."

"No, she is not, for now comes the sad part of my tale. Mereador and Melannor longed for a child but after 10 years without result, resolved themselves to remain childless. The Elvenkin healers used all of their known remedies, to no avail. The years passed and the couple remained happy in the wood, but childless. Then, in her 50th year, Melannor found herself with child. The happy couple and all of Lingolia rejoiced with them."

"Melannor was not too old to bear a child?" asked Palo.

"No, for Eldarin, like Elvenkin, are long lived. There was little reason for concern."

"There must have been some risk," remarked Eathelon, as he thought about Aneron's wife and child, who'd recently died in childbirth.

"Elvenkin are skilled in such matters," continued Tholin. "The birth was without complication and Meolin entered the world a happy, healthy baby."

"I thought you said it was a sad tale," said Palo. "It seems happy enough."

"And it was ... for a time. For five years the family dwelt in the stone cottage by the stream, visiting Lingolia often. But 40 years had passed since the end of the war, and Mereador and Melannor longed to return home to the Golden City. Mengalan advised against it, for the Eldarin were under threat of death, if caught, but he was unable to dissuade them. He instead convinced them to leave Meolin behind in his care. The couple agreed and set off with a small company of Elvenkin along for protection. Mengalan knew it would take them more than a week to reach the Golden City by the west trail, so he did not expect them back for two and a half or three weeks. However, on the fifteenth day, Mereador and two Elvenkin returned, all of them gravely wounded. The rest of the Elvenkin lay dead in Elvenvale, they said, and Melannor was captured by mercenaries."

"After 40 years?" Eathelon asked. "And so near your wood?"

"Sadly yes, and we were sorely grieved that we let this happen, for the mercenaries did sometimes enter Elvenvale. They are lawless men, who care little for treaties, or sides, unless it benefits them directly. Baele had set a price on any Eldarin caught dead or alive and this had no expiration date, though I, for one, believe the mercenaries simply stumbled onto the Elvenkin company, saw a beautiful, vulnerable woman and seized the opportunity to take her captive, knowing she would bring a good price in Gazlag. Despite the trade agreement, the Eldarin are not safe in Narda even today."

"We know," said Darian, under his breath.

"Mereador and the two surviving Elvenkin spent several weeks recovering from their wounds, during which time one of them recalled a conversation he had overheard as he lay on the ground pretending to be dead. The mercenaries said they were taking Melannor to the Lord of Gorst. Sick with worry and regret, for having left the safety of the wood against Mengalan's advice, Mereador decided he would go to Gazlag to try to win her ransom, or otherwise rescue her. Some of us offered to accompany him, but he refused. I managed to convince him to let us escort him across the Great Dune Desert and up to the *Moors of Gorst*, for Gazlag was not far from there. He agreed, and when we reached the Moors, he insisted we all return home. He would watch and wait, he said, for the right time to attempt a rescue, but he must first discover exactly where and how she was being held. We could not dissuade him, so we left."

"He was either very brave, or very foolish," said Darian.

"Some of both," Tholin stated. "The Elvenkin in our company

returned to Northwest Wood, but I rode to East Wood, to counsel with my brother *Nathin*, who lives there. Together, we persuaded the Elvenkin of East Wood to watch over Mereador and keep him safe, which they do to this day."

"Mereador has never returned to see his daughter?" asked Eathelon.

"Yes, he visits now and then," said Tholin. "I believe he meant to return and I am certain he thought his task would be accomplished long before now. He lives on the Moors still, and it has been 20 years. He went half-crazy with grief and regret, and clothed himself in the robes of an old *Druid*, so the people of Gazlag would fear him and leave him alone. The *Druid on the Moors*, he is called now, and most people do fear him and leave him alone, so the purpose of his disguise has been achieved. But he is no Druid. He is, as was said, a Syndar Eldarin."

"And what of Meolin?" queried Eathelon. "He left his only child here, alone?"

"Meolin has never been alone and he sees her every few years. They have a bond of sorts, but he always returns to the Moors and he will not leave until Melannor is free, or death claims him. He knows she is imprisoned in the Tower of Gorst and has said on a clear night, when the wind blows from the east down over the Moors, he can hear her weep. I believe it is only the sound of the wind he hears, but it cuts his heart like a knife. His heart is broken and he holds himself to blame."

"It is a sad tale indeed," admitted Palo.

"What does Meolin think of this?" asked Eathelon.

"She grew up happy in our wood, away from all such sorrows and recalls little of her Mother and Father."

"She sounds more Elvenkin than Eldarin," Eathelon stated.

"She is gifted and has the benefit of both Elvenkin and Eldarin teachings. She is unique in that respect. All Elvenkin have a connection to the wood and its creatures, but Meolin commands them like no one else. Her love for the wood and its creatures is great."

"Your tale is sad Tholin, but its ending is not yet written," noted Eathelon. "Perhaps it may yet have a happy outcome."

"Such is our hope," said Tholin. He paused. "Come, my tale

has ended. Let us all get some rest. Tomorrow we reach Lingolia and I will take you to Lord Mengalan."

Eathelon laid down but found sleep difficult, as his mind swirled with thoughts of Lingolia, Meolin, the imprisoned Melannor, the Druid on the Moors, finding the missing Stones and figuring it all out somehow.

Chapter 27:
Lord of the Elvenkin

Eathelon fell asleep eventually, but something woke him up in the middle of the night. He stood and watched, as shadows of tree branches danced in the breeze that fanned them, by the light of a fire that still blazed in camp. Someone sat on the other side of it and, wide awake now, he walked over to join whoever it was. He found Tholin sitting with legs crossed and arms outstretched, encircled by the familiar flickering lights of the tiny creatures who'd led the companions out of harm's way in Elvenvale. Eathelon smiled and sat down beside him, and the creatures encircled him too, flicking their lights on and off, their giggles music to his ears. Then, without warning, the giggles stopped, the lights blinked off and they were gone.

"We awakened you," said Tholin.

"No, I could not sleep, a curse of late. Those were the creatures that brought us to you. I have frightened them off."

"The Firlis, yes. They are our friends. But you did not frighten them. They come and go of their own accord. They brought a message."

"What are they exactly?"

"Tiny, sentient beings who telepath with us. They have brought disturbing news."

"What news, if you do not mind my asking?" asked Eathelon.

"I do not. Do you recall that when you entered our wood the baerwolffs did not follow you?"

"Yes, you said it was fortunate for them that they did not."

"Yes, it is because I perceived a change in them that both surprised and frightened me. And having seen it, we would have killed them, had they entered, though not without regret. I believe they sensed this and withdrew."

"Baerwolffs are sentient too?" By now, Palo and Darian had awakened and walked over to join them.

"What is it? What has happened?" asked Darian.

Eathelon briefly explained.

Tholin continued, "No, Baerwolffs are not sentient like Firlis, who are intelligent as well as telepathic. But baerwolffs can sense danger. They have lived in peace with us in Elvenvale for a long time, but the ones that chased you are fey. I sensed they intended you harm."

"They most certainly did," claimed Palo. "They would have ripped us apart had they caught us, yet we did nothing to provoke them."

"Yes, the Firlis confirmed this. It is why they intervened and guided you to the wood. Someone has tampered with the baerwolffs."

"What do you mean, tampered with them?" Eathelon inquired. "Who?"

"As to who, I can make an educated guess," Darian responded. "But as to how ..."

"Again, the Firlis have provided the answer," said Tholin. "The mercenaries of Rabellan have tampered with the creatures' minds, though where they got the idea to do this or the wherewithal to do it, I cannot say. The Firlis have long kept watch on Elvenvale. They usually let us know when mercenaries are afoot there. Some of the mercenaries have even attempted to enter our wood, on occasion. We cannot keep them out of Elvenvale, but they enter our wood at their peril. None have ever left alive, so few, if any, attempt entry anymore."

Eathelon was gaining a new appreciation for having Elvenkin for allies.

"What do these mercenaries want with baerwolffs?" asked Palo. "And how can they make them sick in the head anyway? And how would the Firlis even know this?"

"As I said, they keep watch. The mercenaries use some sort of potion on the beasts. Such potions do exist. As to why they would tamper with the baerwolffs I assume it is to control, turn the beasts against us. It is no secret that the mercenaries are allied to the East. How do I know they are fey? I need no Firlis to tell me. The baerwolffs are usually docile with us, but I saw their hostility."

"A potion to alter a mind?" asked Eathelon. He knew something about potions, but had never heard of one that could alter a mind.

"Yes. Did you not hear the Firlis' speak?"

"I did, but I not understand anything they said. It sounded like ... laughter," Eathelon admitted.

Tholin chuckled. "That is because they eat giglrut, a tuber that grows in Elvenvale. It has become a staple of their diet. The Elvenkin have learned to understand them and we can read their thoughts. To others their speech sounds like laughter. They are ancient creatures, and we have both learned over the ages to mind-speak with each other."

"Their message was clear enough when they led us to your wood," exclaimed Darian.

"You are fortunate, in that regard," replied Tholin. "The Firlis perceived that you were friends, or they would not have helped you. Had they not helped, the baerwolffs may have killed you, though not without great cost to them, I am certain."

"We would have defended ourselves and possibly could have taken them," boasted Palo.

"I doubt the three of us, brave though we are, could have held off that huge pack for long," Darian countered.

"What about this potion?" Eathelon pressed.

"Some plants in Narda produce such effects, just as lothingel counteracts poison."

"I know of lothingel," Eathelon remarked, "and was fortunate enough to find some growing in Numar, which I used to counteract the poison from a fyrcaat barb Palo took in the arm."

"Fyrcaat barbs have been known to injure, or sometimes kill a man," said Tholin, "though such deaths are rare."

Palo rubbed his arm. "The pain was most unpleasant."

"Some potions can also kill, but these are few, and rare. There is evidently one that alters a mind and makes a creature do things it would not normally do. I do not know this potion, but clearly the mercenaries do, or they have been taught this by some apothecary. Only men of evil would do this thing to man or beast."

"From what we know, the mercenaries and men of the East would qualify in that regard," said Palo. "And it would explain the behavior of the fyrcaats, too."

"Fyrcaats are naturally aggressive, Palo, and can be controlled with conditioning," Tholin clarified. "I doubt there would be a need to use potions on them. The Fyrls tame them and some keep them for pets, but they would not harm one. Some men of the East turn the creature to evil. Baerwolffs are not normally aggressive, unless provoked or threatened. There has never been a baerwolff attack on an Elvenkin. Those beasts have definitely been tampered with."

"If mercenaries are afoot in Elvenvale, does it mean Baele is threatening the wood and the Elvenkin?"

"Yes, and no," replied Tholin. "Mercenaries have sometimes foraged for food in Elvenvale. Food is somewhat limited in the desert. But I believe they also keep watch on us for the East. They do not hunt here, but report what they see. We know Baele and his ilk." He paused. "Mengalan will not be pleased to hear this news."

They concluded the discussion, as the sun rose and spread its soft yellow rays over the wood, bringing the shadowed trees into focus. They took a meal then the Elvenkin broke camp and they started off on the last part of their journey to Lingolia.

As they came closer to the city, Eathelon noticed that the rulæn trees grew more dense and the blue rinna fern grew high and thick. The smooth, red-barked rulæns reached far into the sky, their branches fanning out widely, well above the ground. Homes came into view in some of the giant trees, with beautiful, intricately carved staircases winding up and around the trunks. Some had platforms with carved railings and some kind of pulley system to take the owners up and down the tree.

"Do you live in a tree?" Palo asked Tholin.

"No," he smiled, "though many Elvenkin do. My own house is built on a hill, at the edge of a canyon."

"Is Meolin's cottage near?" from Eathelon.

"No, it lies deep in the wood."

"How far are we from Lingolia?" Darian inquired.

"We are in Lingolia, for it is not a city, like Andolan or Brega, but a place of Elvenkin homes. This part of Northwest Wood is Lingolia."

Music began to play all around them, a low chant with a high light melody weaving over and under it, accompanied by a stringed instrument of some sort, and a soft, low beating drum.

"What is that?" asked Eathelon.

"The Elvenkin welcome us — it is our way."

"The music is … soothing," Darian commented.

"We find it so," agreed Tholin.

Eathelon felt the ground rise beneath his horse and his spirits rose with it.

"Lord Mengalan's home is not far now," Tholin remarked.

Eathelon's heart beat faster in his chest.

They rode on a little farther and came to a large multi-level structure, with a high roof, held up by beautifully carved pillars and cornices, and carved railings on its porches and balconies. A pair of beautifully carved high, wide doors sat at its entrance.

Tholin dismounted and the others followed. One of the Elvenkin took the horses and the rest left to their own homes. Tholin led the companions into a wide foyer and asked them to wait while he went to find Mengalan. The two soon returned, arm in arm, Mengalan only slightly shorter than Tholin. The Lord of the Elvenkin wore a long, grey tunic of finely embroidered cloth over smooth grey leggings and his long white hair fell below his shoulders, a silver circlet of silmaria on his brow. His expression was neither friendly, nor unfriendly, but his bright blue eyes sparkled and danced with interest.

Tholin turned to Eathelon and said, with a smile, "Welcome to our home, my friends. Lord Mengalan is my Father."

Eathelon smiled broadly at the announcement, but was not wholly surprised.

"Well met, My Lord," Eathelon responded. "We thank you for welcoming us into your home."

"Well met," replied Lord Mengalan.

"The Firlis deserve the credit for bringing them here, Father," Tholin noted. "This is Eathelon, Prince of the Mallorites,

Palo, a Maagi Warrior and Darian, a Nydar Eldarin, leader of the Rangers of Numar."

Mengalan smiled as each man was introduced, then said, "A Mallorite Prince, a Maagi Warrior and an Eldarin Ranger." He paused. "There is a story here. Few Eldarin are left in Narda and fewer still will admit to their ancestry." He looked at Darian. "You have been here before, I think."

"Indeed, My Lord, I came as a boy, with my Mother." Darian smiled, impressed that Mengalan would remember him.

"I rarely forget an Eldarin face, though yours has changed much. How is your Mother?"

"She has long since passed, My Lord."

"I am sorry. She was lovely." He paused. "But come! My table is set and you are no doubt tired and hungry from your long ride to my house. We will dine together and you can tell me where you are from and how you came to be here. Guests at my house are rare these days."

They followed him to the dining hall, where a table was set — not the long elegant table of Aneron's house, one more intimate, yet beautiful. Before they sat down, Tholin took his Father aside and spoke with him, briefly, then Mengalan called one of his staff over, said something to him, and the Elvenkin left the room on some errand.

Mengalan beckoned each guest to a chair — Darian and Palo to his right, Eathelon to his left. Tholin took the empty chair opposite his Father, and when all had been seated, the staff began to serve the food and drink. They brought baked fish, fresh from the Harmen River, fresh baked bread, winterberries, apples and some kind of baked tuber — purple, sweet and tasty.

They poured Holling Vale wine, *Riverdale*, a light red, and a sweet white wine, *Silverlight*. The meal had just begun when a door opened behind Tholin and a tall woman entered. Mengalan and Tholin rose to greet her, so the companions did too.

"My Father, you sent for me," said a soft voice.

Eathelon's heart skipped a beat when he saw her.

"Yes, My Daughter. Come and meet our guests and take supper with us."

Eathelon shot Tholin a glance and Tholin smiled then turned to his sister, as she walked toward them.

"Hello, My Sister," replied Tholin.

"Hello, My Brother," she spoke, casually.

This Elvenkin greeting intrigued Eathelon.

Meolin's eyes met Eathelon's briefly, and in that fleeting moment something unsaid passed between them. Eathelon knew it and knew that Meolin knew it, though neither acknowledged it. A warmth spread through his body, as he felt inexplicably drawn to this woman.

Meolin moved her tall frame with the grace and beauty of both Syndar and Elvenkin. The collar of her long, dark blue dress reached up her neck and a leather belt lay across her hips, the ornate hilt of a silver dagger showing above its scabbard. Her long black, wavy hair framed her face and covered her breasts, and curiosity danced in her blue-violet eyes. A silver circlet of lothingel with a single dark blue sapphire sat on her brow.

She took Eathelon's breath away.

"Honored guests, may I introduce my daughter, Meolin."

Eathelon stared in disbelief, then quickly regained his composure.

Mengalan introduced each companion by name and beckoned Meolin take the empty seat beside Eathelon. Tholin gave Eathelon a half-smile, as they all sat back down to supper.

They made small, cordial talk as they ate, for Mengalan had made it clear that Elvenkin custom forbade discussion of business matters during meals.

Meolin said to Darian, "You are Eldarin — Nydar, if I am not mistaken."

"You care correct, My Lady." He smiled at her and continued to eat.

She turned to Palo. "You are of a race I do not recognize."

"Indeed, My Lady, I am a Maagi Warrior, the native race of my isle, Melatui."

Eathelon smiled at Palo's good manners.

"You are fair tongued for a Warrior," Meolin pointed out.

"Thank you, My Lady."

"Where is this Melatui?" she asked.

"Far out in the Westmost Sea, My Lady," replied Palo.

"Interesting. I have not heard of the Maagi, nor of Melatui."

"The Eldarin settled there after they fled Narda, during the Great War," Eathelon stated.

Meolin turned to Mengalan. "Why have I not heard this tale before Father?"

"No one in Narda has heard this tale before now, My Daughter," Mengalan replied.

"It is why we have come, My Lady," Eathelon continued, "to bring this news to the people of Narda — that the Eldarin survived their voyage into exile and wish to return."

"You have journeyed far, Eathelon," Meolin said, politely.

"Indeed, My Lady, we have," replied Eathelon. He took a sip of wine, his heart pounding in his chest.

"You have Eldarin features — more Syndar, I believe, but your coloring is ... different."

"You are correct again, My Lady," Eathelon confirmed. He smiled at her.

Tholin watched with interest.

Before Eathelon could continue, Palo chimed in, "Eathelon is half-Eldarin and half-Maagi, My Lady." He chewed a piece of fish, reverting somewhat to his Warrior ways, now that his ancestry was out.

"Really? Which half is which?" Meolin asked with a smile, directed at Eathelon.

Eathelon blushed. Darian and Tholin suppressed a laugh and Palo nearly choked on his fish.

Mengalan smiled a half-smile. "Meolin," he said, "please mind your manners." He turned to Eathelon, "I apologize for my daughter's remark. Her mouth sometimes moves ahead of her good sense."

"I am not offended, My Lord," replied Eathelon. He smiled at Meolin and her smile back left no doubt that she'd meant what she'd said. Her comment did not upset him, it only amused and intrigued him, though he chided himself for blushing.

The conversation turned to a cordial hum throughout the rest of the meal, until Eathelon reached for the fruit platter and the amulet tumbled out of his tunic and began to glow. He quickly put it back.

Mengalan saw it and smiled.

"A gift from my Eldarin teacher," Eathelon stated, apologetically.

"Celorn, yes. Surely he told you I gave it to him."

"He did, My Lord and I planned to reveal it at a more … appropriate time."

"It gladdens my heart to know Celorn made it safely to Melatui and that he gifted you the amulet," said Mengalan. "You may keep it, Eathelon. I believe you will have more need of it later than I."

"I thank you, My Lord."

They finished up the meal and Mengalan announced, "Supper is concluded. We have business to discuss now. Please follow me."

Mengalan led them down a long hall to a large room with 12 ornate chairs arranged in a circle, half already occupied.

"This is the Elvenkin Circle of Chairs," Mengalan said, as they entered the room. "Here we discuss matters of great importance to the Elvenkin."

Lighted sconces on three walls cast an abundance of light onto the beautiful furnishings, and Eathelon saw, through the tall windows in the fourth wall, the dim twinkling of emerging starts in the night sky.

Meolin and Tholin walked over to two of the empty chairs and sat down. Mengalan introduced the companions to the rest of the Elvenkin, then directed them to take three of the four remaining chairs. Mengalan took the last one, at the head of the circle, and called the Circle of Chairs to order.

Chapter 28:
Visitors in Lingolia

Mengalan had Eathelon tell his story to all of those seated at the Circle of Chairs, so Eathelon began by telling how the Eldarin had come to Melatui after being forced out of Narda and intermarried with the Maagi, creating a new race, the Mallorites. He told how Celorn had survived the journey and, as head of the Eldarin Council, arranged the marriage of Eathelon's Syndar Eldarin Mother to Maalo, his Maagi Warrior Father, the King, in order to bring peace to the isle. He told how his Father had died under mysterious circumstances, on the eve of their departure and how his Eldarin Mother now ruled the isle in his stead.

"So, you are heir to the throne then," said an Elvenkin.

"Yes, sire," replied Eathelon.

He continued, with great passion, "The Eldarin wish to return to the Golden City. It is why Palo and I, and two friends, made the journey here, one in which our ship and both friends were lost."

"Many Eldarin perished when they fled Narda," another Elvenkin pointed out. "You barely survived the journey yourself. How then, do the Eldarin expect to survive the journey back?"

"My companions and I sailed the Westmost Sea. We completed most of the voyage without difficulty. It was not until a storm blew us off course into the Southern Sea that we shipwrecked. The Eldarin who sailed the Westmost Sea arrived safely to our isle."

"Continue, Eathelon," said Mengalan.

Eathelon told the Council about the five Seeing Stones, how the History Stone is with Celorn on Melatui, and how they saved the Earth Stone from the bottom of the sea and returned it safely to Aneron, in Andolan

"Celorn bid us find the remaining Stones," he remarked. "He believes they are here in Narda, somewhere, but we fear Baele may have one of them. Palo has come to aid me in my search and Darian has joined us. We have journeyed far to ask the Elvenkin for aid in accomplishing our errand."

A murmur ran through the Circle of Chairs.

Eathelon went on to describe the encounters with fyrcaats, the incidents at Harwyn and Brega, and the encounter with baerwolffs.

"Someone has tampered with the baerwolffs." declared Tholin. "This I have seen with my own eyes, and the Firlis have confirmed it."

Another murmur went through the Circle.

"This is ill news," exclaimed an Elvenkin.

"Ill news indeed," Tholin agreed.

"Continue," Mengalan said to Eathelon.

He mentioned the recent passing of Aneron's wife and baby son.

"We heard this grievous news about the Queen and her child," Mengalan remarked, "and were sorely grieved."

"I find it difficult to understand," added an Elvenkin. "Andolan's healers are no less skilled than our own."

"Many feel as you do," Darian claimed, "but that puzzle is one for the Captain of the Guard, or the King's son to unravel."

Eathelon told of his failed search for the Power Stone in the Golden City, but he made no mention of finding the Book of Stones.

"The Power Stone is said to hold a key to unlocking the full power of the Stones," Eathelon declared. "Without it, should the House of Tebor move against the West, the Stones will be of little aid to us in the conflict."

"What do these Stones do?" asked an Elvenkin.

"That is something we must discover," replied Eathelon.

"Then I see little value in your searching for them," responded an Elvenkin, "if we cannot know what help they would be once found."

"Let us not be hasty to discourage Eathelon from his errand," countered Mengalan.

"The House if Tebor must not take the West," said Darian, "or we risk them taking over all of Narda. Do not forget that Baele had the Eldarin murdered, exiled and placed under death sentence here."

"We know well that tale," Mengalan reassured them, and he shifted uneasily in his chair.

Eathelon thought he saw a suppressed smile on Mengalan's face, like a caat who has eaten a blu-tailed sarow and attempted at once to conceal it.

The discussion at the Circle of Chairs continued for two hours more and, when nothing of value had been decided, Mengalan stood and stated, "The hour grows late. Let us adjourn this Council until tomorrow morning."

The Elvenkin all stood and began to file out of the room.

Eathelon had seen Meolin stare at him now and then, as he spoke and guessed her interest had been in his tales. When she rose to leave, however, she smiled warmly at him, a change in her demeanor from their earlier supper. He felt drawn to her and could not take his eyes off of her. She exuded strength and confidence, yet was in every way a beautiful woman, and her insouciance and odd sense of humor at supper had intrigued him.

Tholin led their guests to sleeping quarters in the guest area of his Father's house. They slept well in the soft beds, fires warming the rooms, grateful to be spared another night on the hard ground, in the cold, and having to stand watch.

They woke at dawn, dressed and walked to the dining hall for brefas. Tholin awaited them there, but neither Mengalan nor Meolin joined them for the meal. They made idle talk at the table, then finished up and walked to the meeting at the Circle of Chairs. The Elvenkin who'd attended the previous night, and who Tholin said held positions of importance in Lingolia, greeted each of them by name.

When everyone had been seated, Mengalan called the Circle to order and said, "Tell us, Eathelon, how is our old friend, Celorn?"

"He is as well, My Lord, though impatient to return. He grows older with each turning and wants to return to the Golden City before he passes, so his ashes may be laid to rest in the

Catacombs of Malta, with his ancestors."

An Elvenkin spoke up and exclaimed, "I find it odd that Celorn, as leader of the Eldarin, permitted the intermarriage of your Syndar Mother and Maagi Father, against Eldarin custom."

"He not only permitted it, but arranged it, as was said," Eathelon replied. "The Eldarin realized, after the Great War, that they no longer possessed the necessary skills to defeat their enemies, even with help from their allies."

"It is true that the Eldarin were ill prepared for war," noted another Elvenkin.

"And failed to predict it, putting us all at risk," said another.

"They ended our senseless wars, with diplomacy," said Mengalan, "and turned our skills to more productive endeavors. They relied on Andolan's soldiers, and on the Elvenkin's prowess with bow and arrow to protect them. That we failed in this, is no fault of theirs."

"The Eldarin hold you blameless," Eathelon remarked. "The Elvenkin came to their aid and perished. They hold themselves to blame for their defeat, and exile has changed their point of view. They have had to rethink their old ways and customs. They intermarried with the Maagi to prevent another defeat at the hands of the House of Tebor. Should they find a way to return, the Eldarin want to be able to defend their own home."

"Then why not simply have the Maagi fight for them?" asked an Elvenkin.

"Celorn thought at first to do this," replied Eathelon.

But before Eathelon could continue, Palo stood up and said, "I shall answer your question. We Maagi can be impulsive, short-tempered and are often poorly organized. It is no doubt why we went fought amongst ourselves. I say this though I hold my race in high regard, for I know well our weaknesses. The Eldarin are an intelligent, organized and wise race, but lack the physical prowess to defend themselves as well as they should, as proven in the Great War. Eathelon is a Mallorite. He possesses both the skill to fight and the wisdom to know when to use it. Such was Celorn's foresight in creating the Mallorite race."

"I can see the wisdom in Celorn's decision," said Mengalan. "I see also that there is wisdom in both a Mallorite, and a Maagi

Warrior."

Palo smiled and nodded. "The Eldarin race is dominant in Eathelon, though he is as much a Maagi Warrior as I." He sat down.

A heated discussion ensued among the members of the Circle.

One Elvenkin stood up and proclaimed, "We helped the Eldarin during the Great War and lost many family and friends." He sat back down.

"And the Eldarin still perished," pointed out another.

"Dare we risk it?" asked another. "Eathelon's errand will invite war."

"War will find us, whether he invites it, or not," said another.

"Eldan, an Elvenkin of some repute, stood up. "The Eldarin did much for Narda. Should we desert them because we suffered loss when their own loss was far greater than our own?"

More discussion ensued and went on, until Mengalan brought the meeting back to order.

"The Eldarin's lack of skill in war and inability to predict their demise almost wiped them out," Eathelon asserted. "The Elvenkin have both foresight and skill in defense. The Eldarin were once your allies, and your friends, and friends to the many races in Narda. For this reason, if no other, you must consider offering your help to bring them home. This is the primary reason we have risked our lives to come here, though we did not expect to walk into a conflict that has evidently been brewing for some time. Still, we are here now and we will not desert our errand."

"We will take all of this under consideration," Mengalan assured him.

"Our skill in trees, with creatures of the forest and our prowess with bow and arrow are unequaled in Narda," claimed an Elvenkin.

"It is true," said another. "We must not fear to defend what is right."

Eathelon stood, "Good members of the Circle, I ask that you decide here whether or not the Elvenkin will aid us in bringing the Eldarin back to Narda. The time to accomplish our errand grows short. I must find the missing Stones before Baele finds them, if we are to stand fast against the House of Tebor. I do not know how I will accomplish this, but my companions and I will complete my errand alone, if we must. I need your decision." He sat back down.

Darian stood. "Members of this Circle, the people of Numar were ravaged by the East during the Great War because they were disorganized and poorly armed. They did not lack courage, but the skill to adequately defend themselves. It was for this reason my Father formed the Rangers of Numar. Andolan did not fall because it is a stronghold, manned by trained soldiers. Many regions of Hamlan lie unprotected to this day. Toldor's Keep is being restored and will offer protection from a Northmen invasion, which protects your wood. Andolan has not forgotten its northern allies, even if you have chosen to sunder that alliance. I ask that you consider these points in making your decision." He sat back down.

Mengalan rubbed his chin, thoughtfully. "We have remained sequestered in our wood for too long. We will consider your words." He paused. "What news do you bring of Aneron? I have not seen or spoken to my old friend in too long, not even in his time of sorrow."

"He grieves, My Lord," said Darian, "but Eathelon has restored his hope, with the return of the Earth Stone, with news that the Eldarin live and wish to return. Aneron has agreed to give Eathelon whatever aid he can to help bring his friends home, for they were not only friends, but trusted advisors."

"Aneron's help is of no small value," noted Eldan.

The other Elvenkin murmured in agreement.

"And have you any news of Landrin?" Mengalan asked.

"He remains in exile on Suvrii, My Lord," replied Darian, "but the two Kings remain connected and exchange messages as often as possible. Their sons are Narda's future Kings and Aneron's negotiations with Baele spared Landrin's life."

"We are familiar with the agreement," said an Elvenkin, "but doubt the sincerity of the House of Tebor to keep it."

"He has kept it these many years," added another.

"His patience is running out, it would seem," said another.

Mengalan stood. "Thank you, good members of the Circle.

Let us end this debate. The Elvenkin have remained sequestered and sundered from Andolan long enough. We once ruled Narda together — Celorn, Aneron, Landrin and I. It is time for us to mend this breach. There was great strength in that alliance."

Eathelon breathed a sigh of relief.

There followed some minor disagreement, expressed by a few of the members.

"We paid a heavy price for that alliance, as was said," an Elvenkin pointed out.

"And the Eldarin paid a heavier price, as was said," replied Eldan.

"What aid has Andolan offered us of late?" queried an Elvenkin.

"I was not aware that we asked him for aid," replied another.

"Andolan has long protected Hamlan well, and are we not residents of Hamlan?" asked an Elvenkin.

"We are residents of our wood!" remarked the Elvenkin who had first spoken.

Mengalan permitted the argument to continue for about half an hour, then one by one, the members began to state their willingness to mend the breach with Andolan.

"Good members of the Circle, your friendship and your aid are most welcome," said Eathelon.

The door to the chamber suddenly opened and Meolin entered. Eathelon did a double take, for she wore a dark green tunic over brown leggings, her silver-handled knife secure in its leather scabbard across her body — an image much different from the dress he'd seen her wear at supper the previous night. No circlet sat on her forehead, and her black wavy hair had been braided back on the sides with thin pieces of leather. Her blue-violet eyes sparkled as she entered and she looked more Elvenkin Warrior than Eldarin maiden. He could not take his eyes off of her.

She made no apology for entering late, but simply sat down and announced, with a smile, "I had other business to attend to." Then she turned to Mengalan and said, "What have I missed, My Father?"

As if her behavior were both expected and excused, Mengalan replied, "We were discussing old friends." He turned to Eathelon. "Now that Meolin has joined us, I will make something known to all of you that I have long kept secret from everyone here."

Meolin and Tholin looked at their Father with curiosity, as a loud murmur went through the Circle, for he did not usually keep secrets from them. Mengalan waited patiently for them to settle down, and when they quieted, he continued.

He addressed Eathelon directly. "One of the Stones you seek is here, in Lingolia."

Another audible gasp went through the Circle, as Eathelon stared at Mengalan, almost in disbelief. His heart skipped a beat and he leaned forward in his chair and asked, "Which Stone, My Lord?"

"The one you sought in the Golden City — though I realized its importance only now, during this discussion."

"The Power Stone?" The words tumbled out of Eathelon's mouth as he barely contained his excitement. "What turn of good fortune is this?"

Mengalan smiled. "So, I guessed. I did not realize the Stone's significance at the time of its discovery, though I knew it had some importance to the Eldarin. But they were no longer here, and though I did not know if any had survived their exile, I knew it prudent for me to keep the Stone here, in the wood, lest it fall into the hands of the House of Tebor."

"You are wise in that regard, My Lord. Please tell me how you came to discover the Stone," Eathelon inquired. "I would like to hear the tale."

"As would I," added Darian.

"So, would we," echoed the rest of the Circle.

"The tale is not long," Mengalan said. "When the Great War broke out, the Eldarin called for aid, so I sent a large company of Elvenkin to help fortify defense of the Golden City. I left just enough Elvenkin behind to defend our southern border from the mercenaries we guessed might attempt to enter from Elvenvale. Tholin and I organized and led a second company behind the first, but we arrived to find the Golden City already taken, for it had been overrun by Northmen. Many wounded, dying and dead Eldarin and Elvenkin lay scattered about, and seeing we were too late, we retreated into the hills. Meolin's Father had been with the first company and had survived, along with some of the other Elvenkin, so they joined us."

Eathelon glanced at Meolin. Her expression remained unchanged.

"As we retreated into the hills, we stumbled upon many wounded and dead Eldarin, laying among the flowers. We did what we could for them, but most were beyond our skill. When I scouted ahead for a safe way back to Northwest Wood, a glimmer of fading sunlight shone off of something in the grass and caught my eye. I stopped to investigate and found an Eldarin near death. There was nothing I could do for him, his wounds were too severe. With his last strength, he grabbed my tunic and pulled me down, my ear to his mouth, and whispered, 'Take it and keep it safe.' Then he died. I did not know what he meant, so I made a search and found the Stone beneath his body. I did not know what it was then, but knew if it had been important enough for this Eldarin to give his life protecting it, I must carry out his wish. I was alone, so hid it beneath my tunic. When we returned to Lingolia, I locked it away in my private quarters, where it has since remained, untouched."

"You did not attempt to examine it, or use it?" asked Eathelon.

"No, for it does not belong to me, nor to any Elvenkin. The Eldarin alone would know and understand its use and I knew they would want it back. Your presence here has confirmed this."

"You have foresight, My Lord," said Eathelon. "We are grateful that the one who found the Stone had wisdom and honor enough to keep it safe."

Mengalan nodded.

Eathelon stood and addressed the Circle. "A piece of our puzzle concerning the fate of the Stones has been solved here. Five Stones there are, and three are safe. Celorn keeps one in Melatui, Aneron one in Andolan, and this one is here, in Lingolia. Baele likely has another, and should that prove true, it will be necessary for us to take it from him. But that is not the problem of the Elvenkin, or this Circle. One missing Stone remains — the Wind Stone, which Celorn said Landrin kept at Castletop. The exiled King may have taken it with him to the Flax Isles. If so, it will need to be retrieved and returned to its rightful place at Castletop, which is in enemy hands. These Stones are of no value outside of their designated places, and only the five Stones together offer power enough to be of use to the West."

"How can we help?" asked Mengalan.

"I ask now for the wisdom and counsel of each member of this Circle. There is much to decided here. I must go east to look for the missing Stones. If I take time now to return the Power Stone to the Golden City, my errand might fail. I must locate the missing Stones before Baele does or take them from him. The usurper will want to scratch his itch to take over Narda before this is done, if what you all say is true. The baerwolffs of Elvenvale are fey and the mercenaries on the move, it is said. The Northmen are likely being recruited by the East, as we speak. The time to recover the Stones is likely shorter than we think. I ask your guidance and your aid in my quest to find the missing Stones."

There ensued a long silence.

"We will counsel you, Eathelon," promised Mengalan.

"Why should we?" queried an Elvenkin. "We will pay a great price again, if we join any conflict with the House of Tebor."

"The House of Tebor will strike Hamlan whether or not we offer aid to our allies," Eldan responded. "Should we deny them because we fear our own losses? We will lose our wood anyway, should Hamlan fall. There is no choice here."

"The Eldarin are our friends," noted an Elvenkin. "We must help Eathelon."

"Yes, Andolan would come to our aid if asked" added another Elvenkin. "Can we do less?"

They all began to talk at once, and Eathelon did not understand all that was discussed. He quickly realized that not every Elvenkin present was convinced of Mengalan's offer of aid.

Meolin did not speak and Eathelon perceived that she held something back.

Mengalan finally brought the Circle of Chairs back to order.

"Good members, it has been decided. We will give our advice and aid to Eathelon and his companions." That ended further discussion.

Mengalan was about to adjourn the meeting when there came an urgent knock on the chamber door and an Elvenkin burst in and walked over to speak with Mengalan.

"My apology for the interruption, My Lord, but a Lit'l messenger has just arrived with an urgent message for this Council."

"Alright, send him in."

The Elvenkin left and returned with the Lit'l.

The small man bowed before Mengalan, then addressed the Circle. "My Lords," he said, then turning to Meolin, added, "My Lady."

His eyes scanned the others seated there and he cleared his throat.

"Pray, what is your message?" asked Mengalan, not unkindly.

"One I fear you will not wish to hear, My Lord. Lord Rini calls for aid, but my message also concerns your wood."

"Go on."

"Aynor is under attack by Northmen. We have all taken refuge in our mountain caves. The Northmen are more than thrice our size and we cannot easily defend ourselves against them. We call for aid from our southern neighbors. If Northmen are afoot in Aynor, your wood is at risk, also."

"Northmen — in Aynor?" asked Tholin.

"Yes, My Lord. They have not yet reached your wood, but it is only a matter of time before they do. They are looting our city now and I fear the Lit'ls may not survive unless aid comes soon. If Aynor falls, Lingolia will be at risk. Long have the Lit'ls kept watch on your northern borders."

"Northmen attacked Aynor without warning, or provocation?" asked an Elvenkin.

"Yes, My Lord. I raised the alarm myself, which is why we had time to flee to the caves."

"Tell us what happened," said Mengalan.

"I am Oni, My Lord, a Lit'l hunter. Last week, my friend and hunting partner, Hagi and I hiked west in the Sylvan Mountains, to hunt. We go every year though we had a later start than usual, this time. We accumulated many pelts for market and started for home, when Hagi, walking ahead, stumbled onto a group of Northmen and was captured. He yelled a warning, so I escaped. I wanted to go back for him," he choked up a little, then composed himself, "but had I done so, it would have meant certain death for us both. I barely escaped myself and knew I had to get back to Aynor to sound the alarm. No Lit'l in our history has ever survived a Northman attack. I assumed Hagi dead and ran back to warn the city as fast as I could. Lord Rini opened the caves and the city was evacuating even as he sent me here to warn you and ask for aid. I left Aynor four days ago."

"Four days!" exclaimed an Elvenkin. "Have you wings to fly?"

Oni smiled. "No, My Lord, I traveled by boat down the Harmen, though the current is swift and dangerous and, when I could no longer manage it, I ran the rest of the way."

"You are very brave, Oni," said Mengalan. "We thank you for bringing this warning, and thank Lord Rini for sending you. Go and take food and rest now, while we discuss your request."

"Thank you, My Lord, but please do not delay your answer. The Lit'ls are in dire need of aid. We cannot stand against the Northmen alone, though I believe they may already regret that they tried to loot our city." He smiled. "We set traps and ... well, the Northmen are not a very intelligent folk." Oni smiled.

"I see," Mengalan responded, smiling, "that the stature of a Lit'l is not always measured in inches alone."

Oni turned to leave, but stopped when he heard Eathelon speak.

"I will help you," Eathelon proclaimed, standing up.

"What?" asked Mengalan.

"And I," boasted Palo, standing.

Darian stood, too.

"My companions and I will help you defend Aynor against the Northmen."

"We must not invite war," commented an Elvenkin.

"War is upon you, whether you would invite it or not," Darian pointed out.

"Eathelon is right," said Mengalan. "The Elvenkin will send

aid."

Eathelon heard a murmur go through the Circle.

"I thank you, My Lord," said Oni, bowing low, "on behalf of my people."

Meolin stood and announced, "Before you leave here, Oni, there is something I want to show you."

Mengalan nodded his consent. Meolin led Oni toward the door, saying, "Anyone else who wishes to come, may do so."

The Elvenkin remained seated, but Eathelon, curious, headed for the door and Palo and Darian followed too, as Meolin led Oni out of the room. They walked down a long hallway, into another hall, up some stairs and out onto a covered balcony, on the third level of the house. An elaborate carved railing overlooked a wide, green lawn with a garden on its perimeter and large pines around it on three sides. The lawn held a fountain, and in it the figure of an Eldarin woman, a sinter hawk on her shoulder and animals at her feet, and drinking at the fountain's edge. Eathelon made a mental note to ask Tholin about it.

They followed Meolin to a door at the far end of the balcony. A sign above it read: *passarë mella weluné a béda, thinta, thóla.*, Eathelon immediately recognized it: *Enter, friend, be healed in body, mind and spirit.*

A House of Healing.

They followed Meolin through the door and down a short corridor, with doors on either side. She stopped at one and opened the door, signaling for the rest to be quiet as they entered. A dim light inside cast its rays onto a small bed in the center of the room.

"You have visitors," Meolin said, softly.

Eathelon saw the figure of a child in the middle of the bed, a thin blanket atop his body, his splinted legs sticking out.

Making a guess, Oni hurried over to the bed and looked closely at the patient.

The patient opened his eyes and blinked, then stared at the visitor, until recognition came to his glazed eyes.

"Oni?" he whispered.

"Hagi?" replied Oni, tears filling his eyes. "You're alive!"

Hagi smiled weakly.

"But ... how? I thought you ... I wanted to come back for you, but …"

Hagi lifted a finger to his friend's lips. "I'd have done the same. You are here now. That is all that matters to me."

Oni clasped his friend's hand, while the others looked on.

"But, how? Are you alright?"

"I am … mending," Hagi whispered. "As to how — ask the Lady. If not for her, I would lie dead among the fern, in the Sylvan Forest."

"Your stay must be brief," said Meolin, kindly. "Hagi is still mending, but you may return tomorrow."

Oni promised to return in the morning, and they all started back to the Circle of Chairs, then Oni stopped them part of the way back. "Please, My Lady, tell me how you found Hagi … if the tale is not long."

Meolin smiled. "Alright. The tale is not long, so I will tell it."

They gathered around her, as she told the story:

"I left on an errand to the northeastern part of the wood, near the place where the Harmen enters. The whisperings of the trees drew me there and I did not know why, so I decided to go investigate. Three Elvenkin accompanied me and we scouted the wood as we rode, watching for any danger, uncertain of what we looked for. Late, on the second day, shortly after we made camp, a blu-tailed sarow came to me and fluttered about wildly with an urgent message. It begged me follow, so we did, and it led us to a thicket of high rinna fern and once there, it dove in and out, repeating its message. Night was near and after a brief search, one of my companions called out, 'Asíminé lámatha — over here!' He had found Hagi, cold to the touch, half dead and out of his mind with pain. The blue-tailed sarow, having delivered its message left. My companions made a fire and placed blankets over Hagi's body to warm him, while I looked for herbs to make a potion. I forced this between Hagi's lips to help ease his pain and my companions made a carry-bed, from tree limbs and blankets. We lifted Hagi carefully onto it, placed it between two of our horses and set off for Lingolia. We carried him as gently as possible, so the trip took longer than we knew wise, but we did not wish to further injure him. I was afraid he would die before we reached the healers, but he proved stronger than I thought. I sent one of my companions ahead, to have them prepare to receive Hagi, and I gave Hagi the herb potion I made every hour or so. By the time we arrived in Lingolia, he looked better and felt warmer, but still drifted in and out of consciousness. Our healers are skilled and Hagi is mending, but there is some doubt about whether he will ever walk again. We do not tell him this, of course."

"Hagi is the first Lit'l in our history to survive a Northman attack," Oni proclaimed. "He is a hero!"

Meolin smiled down at the Lit'l. "I believe the true hero stands before us."

Oni smiled back, tears filling his eyes.

Eathelon looked at Meolin with admiration, and she acknowledged him with a nod. Her eyes softened as they met his.

"Come," said Eathelon, "Let us get back to the Circle. We have much planning to do, if we are to aid the Lit'ls."

"And take the Stone back to the Golden City," added Darian.

"And discover why mercenaries have tampered with the baerwolffs," from Palo.

"Yes," said Meolin, "the baerwolffs may not always be in our favor, but they are creatures of our realm and, as such, entitled to our protection."

They walked back to the Circle of Chairs, where the Elvenkin waited.

"We have discussed the situation in your absence," said Mengalan, "and are all in agreement now that our purpose aligns with yours, Eathelon. We too, wish for the return of the Eldarin. The alliance with Andolan is now restored. It is an alliance of hope."

"That is well, My Father," spoke Meolin. "Hope has long eluded the Elvenkin and I, for one, welcome it here."

Mengalan nodded and smiled.

Eathelon's eyes met Meolin's. Was it the anticipation of battle he felt, or something else that fueled his emotions? He hoped his errand would succeed, but was that all he hoped?

There ensued a great discussion about the invasion of Aynor by Northmen, and the waxing intentions of the House of Tebor toward the West. It turned into a council of war, one in which the fate of Narda might well depend on the decisions made now, at the Circle of Chairs.

* * *

Find out what happens next in Book Two, *Paths of Fyr* in the continuing *Tales of Narda* adventure series.

Glossary of Terms

Aldo (*All-doe*) the Fire Stone, a Tynar Seontir, of opaque deep red set in a bronze base decorated with flames.

Aldona (Al *do* na) Earlyfall.

Alisia (Uh-*lee*-see-uh) the eldest daughter of the Elvenkin Nathin and *Tiana*.

Aneron (*An*-er-on) King of Hamlan, King of the West.

Antebba (An-*teh*-buh) a seaport on the west end of Tebe Inlet, a major trading port for western Narda, *Flax* and the Flax Isles.

Andolan (An-*do*-lun) the fortress city built into the Brunhyl, which houses the King of the West, his government and most of the citizens of Hamlan.

Aresten (A-*res*-tun) Captain of the Guard of Hamlan, Arestor's Father.

Arestor (A-*res*-tor) son and heir of the Captain of the Guard of Hamlan.

Aynor (*A*-nor) city of the Lit'ls, in the Sylvan Mountains near the source of the Harmen River.

Baele (Bay-*elle*) self-proclaimed Lord of the East, of the House of Tebor, usurper of the Eastern throne; his line are descendants of the Tynar Eldarin.

Baat a small bat in the caves of Narda.

Baer a small black bear of the forests of Narda.

Baerwolff large animal with a baer body and wolff head that lives only in Elvenvale.

Bali (*Bah*-lee) a large seaport in *Balortin*, on the western coast of Narda.

Balor Bay (*Bah*-lor Bay) a large bay in Balortin, the major fishing region for western Narda.

Balortin (*Bal*-ortin) city on the western coast known for shipbuilding and fishing.

Banth a seaport on the northeast coast of Grenelan near the Bay of Gorst.

Battle of Two Rivers site of an early battle that destroyed Toldor's Keep, one in which Teold, the only son of King Toldor fell; it lies above Forwyn Crossing near Harna Falls.

Bay of Fauber (Bay of *Faw*-bur) a long, narrow bay between Flax and the Lowlands, fed by the Islin River.

Bay of Gorst a bay between Gorst and Grenelan, fed by the *Ramas River*.

Bay of Hond a large bay between south Newelan and the Hond peninsula, fed by the River Dansen.

Began (*Bay*-gin) sire of the House of Began, lineage of the Kings of the East.

Benold (*Bay*-nold) capital city of northern Grenelen.

Bezlar (Bez-*lar*) a major city of southern Gorst.

Birra (*beer*-uh) large black spy bird of the East.

Blu-tailed sarow (*sorrow*) a small blue-tailed bird of the forests of Narda.

Blubel a small, delicate, blue bell-shaped wildflower of Narda.

Brefas first meal of the day.

Brega (*Bray*-guh) a small city in the Grenhyl north of Harwyn Crossing.

Brenin (Brennan) servant of *Lord Valdir's* deceased father.

Brik leader of a small band of Northmen.

Brunhyl (*Broon*-hill) or Brown Hills that separate Southern Hamlet from Holling Vale; so-called because they are brown most of the year.

Caleopsi grass (Kay-lee-*op*-see) a tall grass of the plains of Numar that causes drowsiness and irritation until one becomes immune to its effects.

Carmindol (*Car*-min-dol) Lamplighter Inn, a small inn in Andolan.

Castellan Valley (Cas-*tel*-lan Valley) the vast, dry desert region between the Sylvan Mountains and Fyr Mountains.

Castletop home of the House of Began in Newcastle.

Catacombs of Malta subterranean Eldarin burial grounds beneath the Golden City.

Celorn (*K*-lorn) Syndar head of the Eldarin Council in Melatui.

Ché caat (Shay cat) a domesticated caat that can shrink to the size of a mouse or grow to the size of a large dog, then return to normal at will.

Chikka a small, tasty wildfowl, sometimes domesticated by farmers and raised for food; akin to a grouse.

Ciara (See-*are*-uh) youngest daughter of Nathin and Tiana.

Conteberi (*con*-tuh-berry) a small pig-like animal of the flatlands and lower slopes of the mountains of Melatui.

Corbellan (Kor-*bell*-un) an old fortress in the northern part of the Castellan Valley, captured and occupied by the armies of the House of Tebor.

Cornth a major seaport at the southern tip of Newelan, a port-of-call for the trade ships between Eastern and Western Narda, the Flax Isles and Hond.

Danil (*Dan*-ul) grandson of *Nami*, owner of *The Old Bookshop* in Heath.

Dansen River primary river of Eastern Narda that flows from the Fyr Mountains above East Wood, down to the Bay of Hond, used to transport goods and people between Grenelan, Newelan and Hond.

Dar Bartil Proprietor of *Dar Bartil's Bed and Supper*, the major inn of Heath.

Darian leader of the Rangers of Numar and one of Eathelon's companions.

Debat (de-*baht*) a village in Deblan at the northwestern foot of the Eathen Mountains.

Denton a port city near the mouth of the Teb-Arnor River on the peninsula that forms the southern side of Balor Bay.

Dilli a purple wildflower of Narda.

Druid an ancient religious order thought to practice mysticism; no Druids actually exist in Narda, they are only a myth.

Druid on the Moors Meolin's father, Mereador, who assumed the guise of a Druid to hide his identity.

Drubot (*drew*-baht) a small, light dugout canoe with a single sail.

Eastmost Sea the sea on the east coast of Narda.

East Wood a dense wood on the eastern slopes of the Fyr Mountains near the source of the River Dansen, populated by Elvenkin.

Eathelon (Atalon) Prince of the Mallorites, son of Maalo, King of Melatui and Lelar, his Syndar Eldarin mother living in exile. His name means *wise warrior.*

Eathen Mountains (*Eee*-tun Mountains) highest of the mountain ranges of Narda; it runs north and south along Narda's western side.

Egin Pass (*Eee*-gun Pass) a high mountain pass in the Eathen Mountains beneath Mt. Athel, the only direct route inland to Malta from the west coast of Narda.

Eldan (El-*dan*) an Elvenkin of Northwest Wood.

Eldarin (El-*dare*-in) the colonizers of Narda in the First Age, trusted advisors to the Kings of Narda; the three Eldarin races are Syndar, Nydar and Tynar.

Elvenkin an ancient race of elf-like beings living in Northwest Wood and East Wood, once allies of the Eldarin and the

Kings of Narda.

Eolengwas (Ay-oh-*len*-gwas) the ancient language of the Eldarin, it later devolved into the common speech of Narda.

Eredian (Air-*rid*-e-un) the landing place of the Eldarin in Narda on the northwest coast in the First Age.

Erl an old Fyrl geologist living in the caves under the Fyr Mountains.

Esol (*Ee*-sul) evil son of Lord Baele of the House of Tebor.

Faramon (*Fare*-a-mon) an Elvenkin who befriends Eathelon and his companions.

Fargo primary seaport of Flax, at the entrance to the Bay of Fauber.

Farli (*Far*-lee) Darian's lieutenant who leads the Rangers of Numar in Darian's absence.

Fellin a city in northern Flax near the top of the Bay of Fauber.

Firlis (*fur*-lees) tiny telepathic creatures of Elvenvale, whose bodies can glow at will and whose speech sounds like giggles from eating *giglrut.*

Flax a region in eastern Narda, south of the River *Niwe*, flanked by the Bay of Fauber, separated from Newelan by the *Nahyl*.

Flaxling a horse bred in Flax used primarily by the Rangers of Numar; akin to a halflinger.

Flax Isles islands in the Southern Sea comprised of two large and several small isles, the largest of which is Suvrii, a key trading port and home to the exiled King of the East and his family.

Flik Lord Rini's son-in-law.

Forth a seaport far north on the west coast of Narda.

Forsil (*For*-sul) the northernmost visible star in the Nardan sky, a key navigation point for sailors.

Forwyn Crossing northern crossing of the Teb-Arnor River that lies between Southern and Northern Hamlets.

Fyr Crossing (*Fire* Crossing) a pass thru the Fyr Mountains between the Castellan Valley and Gorst.

Fyrls (*Fī*-ruhls) once called Fyr-Lit'ls, cousins to the Lit'ls of Aynor, they live in the caves beneath the Fyr Mountains.

Fyrcaat (*fire*-cat) ancient caat-dragon of Narda, with a long sleek hairless body, skin like leather, long slender legs, and wings and varied in color from common mottled green-brown to red-brown, yellow-brown and (rare) brown-blue; fierce and menacing in temperament, it has pointed ears, yellow eyes, a short-reaching fiery breath and a long tail with poisonous barbs.

Fyr Mountains (*Fire* Mountains) longest and widest, ancient volcanic mountain range of Narda, it extends from northern Gorst down into Newelan.

Gazlag (*Gaz*-lag) capital city of Gorst.

Giglrut (*giggle*-root) an edible tuber that offers a refreshed, uplifting sensation; it grows in Elvenvale and is a staple in the diet of the Firlis, making their speech sound like giggles, which is how giglrut got its name.

Giinabird (*gin*-uh-bird) a large, tasty, flightless bird of the plains, akin to a pheasant.

Gorst the northernmost region of eastern Narda, seat of the House of Tebor.

Gorthag northernmost city on the east coast of Gorst.

Grenelan (Gren-*ellen*) the region in eastern Narda between Gorst and Newelan, divided by the Rym Mountains.

Grenhyl (*Gren*-hill), Green coastal hills of Southern Hamlet; Brega, Holling Vale and Hollin all lie in the Grenhyl.

Haga (*Ha*-guh) primary seaport of northern Grenelen, on the Bay of Gorst.

Hagi (*Hah*-gee <hard g>) a Lit'l hunter of Aynor, Oni's hunting partner.

Hagid (*Ha*-gid) a Nardan slang term used to denote an evil, malicious person.

Hamin (*Hay*-min) Administrator of the House of Healing in Andolan.

Hamlan (*Ham*-lin) the region of western Narda ruled by the King of the West.

Hamstead (*Ham*-sted) a village in Hamlan between Heath and Harwyn Crossing.

Harmen River a major river of Narda, sourced in the Sylvan Mountains near Aynor, that flows south through Northwest Wood and joins the Teb-Arnor at Harna Falls then branches tributaries into the Lowlands as it flows south to Tebe Inlet,

Harwyn Crossing (*Har*-win) southern crossing of the Teb-Arnor River, south of Brega.

Hawir (*How*-ur) an Elvenkin of Northwest Wood.

Heath (Heeth) a major city between Antebba and Andolan.

Heidl (*Hi*-dul) a healer in Newcastle who is also a spy for the West.

Highland Gap a narrow mountain pass on the east side of the Eathen Mountains, the only direct passage from the Northern Reaches into Hamlan.

Hinthu (*Hin*-too) the only trading port of Hond, it lies at the tip of the peninsula.

Hod a Ranger of Numar under Darian's command, posted in Heath.

Hollin the primary city of Holling Vale.

Holling Vale the wine-growing region of western Narda that lies between the Grenhyl and coastal hills north of Balortin; it produces 90 percent of the wines of western Narda.

Hond the peninsula at the southern tip of Grenelan, a farming delta and fishing region for eastern Narda.

Hoona Monkey a small monkey of Melatui with a bottom like a baboon.

Islin River (*Eyes*-lin) a river in western Narda that forks off of the River Harmen at the southern tip of Northwest Wood and flows south to the Bay of Fauber, branching tributaries into the eastern side of the Lowlands.

Jan a Ranger of Numar under Darian's command, posted in Heath.

Landon the prince son of King Landrin, heir to the Eastern throne.

Landrin deposed King of the East living in exile in the Flax Isles, a friend and ally to Aneron, King of the West.

Laurin (*Low*-rin) an Elvenkin of Northwest Wood.

Leaf a Nardan variety of tobacco.

Lelar (*Lay*-lar) Syndar Eldarin mother of Eathelon, Queen of Melatui.

Lesil (*Le*-zul) a spy for the West who travels on trade ships between the Flax Isles, Antebba and Cornth to gather information for the West.

Lian (*Lee*-un) eldest son of the Elvenkin Nathin and Tiana.

Liana (Lee-*ah*-na) princess daughter of King Landrin.

Linea (Li-*nay*-uh) Elvenkin wife of Lord Valdir.

Lindili a yellow wildflower of Narda.

Lit'l a race of Nardans, perfectly proportioned little people who stand about three feet tall on average as adults.

Lothan (*Lo*- thin) an Elvenkin of East Wood.

Lord Valdir (Lord Val-*deer*) Elvenkin Lord of East Wood, a distant cousin to Lord Mengalan, of Northwest Wood.

Lothingel (*low*-thingul) a healing herb of the Eldarin which can counteract poisons.

Lowlands an uninhabitable region that divides western from eastern Narda, characterized by uncharted waterways, bogs, marshes, poisonous flora and fauna and various other creatures of unknown origin; the *Trelks*, though now extinct, are thought to have originated there.

*Maagi (maj-*eye*)* native warrior race of Melatui.

*Maalo (Mah-*lo*)* Eathelon's father, the Maagi warrior king of Melatui.

*Malea (*Muh-*lee*-uh*)* a young girl rescued from eastern soldiers by Eathelon, *M.C.* and the Druid.

Mallorite Eathelon's race, the new race created by the intermarriage of Eldarin and Maagi.

*Malta (mahl-*tuh*)* the region in northern Hamlan that houses the Eldarin's Golden City.

Maltinia (mal-tin-ee-uh) a golden flower of the Eldarin that covers the hills of Malta.

*Marchal (Mar-*shul*)* Eathelon's friend and member of his crew.

The Marshes the uninhabited area at the northern end of the Lowlands which contains tall grasses, reeds, bogs, pools and several poisonous species of flora and fauna.

Mayurna (May-*yur*-nuh) the Eldarin name for Melatui, named after the ship that brought their ancestors to Narda; the name translates to *Morningstar.*

M.C. nickname of the *moorcaat, Moreopolinopholes* because his name is too long and too difficult for most to pronounce.

Melannor (*Mel*-uh-nor) Mereador's Nydar Eldarin wife, Meolin's mother.

Mellærna (May-*yur*-nuh) the ancient Eldarin spelling for Mayurna, pronounced the same.

Melatui (Mel-a-*too*-ee) the Maagi isle on which the Eldarin settled after they fled Narda during the Great War, home of Eathelon and Palo.

Mengalan (Men-*gay*-lin) Lord of the Elvenkin of Northwest Wood.

Meolin (May-oh-lin) daughter of Melannor and Mereador, an Eldarin raised by Elvenkin in Northwest Wood.

Mereador (Mary-*a*-door) a Syndar Eldarin, Meolin's father, also known as the "Druid on the Moors."

Merlon (*Mur*-lon) a seaport on the southern coast of *Newelan*.

Midnight the ché caat mascot of the Black Caat Inn.

Moors of Gorst a hilly area of northern Gorst at the foot of the Fyr Mountains, often covered in mist and fog.

Moorcaat a large ancient intelligent caat of Narda with an ability to telepath and change his coat to blend in with his environment.

Moreopolinopholes (Mor-ee-oh-pole-in-*off*-oh-lees) the moorcaat M.C., thought to be the only living moorcaat in Narda; he is very old, has a sense of humor and lives on the Moors of Gorst with the Druid.

Mt. Athel (*A*-thul) the highest peak in the Eathen Mountains at 14,950 feet, it has a year-round glacier at the top and is the source of the Teb-Arnor River.

Mt. Fava (Fa-vuh) a high peak on Suvrii, where the exiled King of the East has built his home.

Mt. Kinli (*Kin*-lee) a mountain on Melatui under which the Tombs of the Kings lie, where Eathelon's father is buried.

Mt. Malucan (*Mal*-oo-cahn) a mountain peak on Melatui.

Mt. Melani (Meh-*lahn*-ee) Melatui's highest peak.

Nahyl (*Nay*-hill) or *Naked Hills,* an extension of the Fyr Mountains that lie between Flax and Newelan and are so-called because they are barren except for hearty scrub plants; the yellow stone of the Nahyl was used to build the city of Newcastle and Castletop.

Nami (*Nah*-mee) Darian's friend and owner of *The Old Bookshop* in Heath.

Narda (*Nar*-duh) the planet colonized by the Eldarin in the First Age, subject of the Tales of Narda, a fantasy adventure.

Naoli (Nay-*oh*-lee) a deserted coastal city of Numar.

Nathin (*Nay*-thin) the Elvenkin brother of Tholin who lives in East Wood.

Newcastle capital city of Newelan, seat of government for eastern Narda, home of The House of Began until overthrown by Baele, Lord of Gorst and occupied by Eastern soldiers led by Esol, Baele's son.

Newelan (New-*ellen*) southern region of eastern Narda bordered by the River Dansen, East Wood, the Nahyl and the Southern Sea.

Niwe River (*Nee*-wuh River) a river flowing west out of the Fyr Mountains, south of Fyr Crossing, down into the eastern side of the Lowlands where it joins the Islin above the Bay of Fauber.

Nolin (*No*-lin) youngest son of the Elvenkin Nathin and Tiana.

Northwest Wood home of the Elvenkin, it lies between the Sylvan and Eathen Mountains.

Numar (*New*-mar) the southernmost region of Hamlan and Darian's homeland.

Nydar Eldarin (*Ni*-dar El-*dare*-in) one of three Eldarin races who colonized Narda in the First Age; they are primarily engineers and architects of the major structures of Narda.

Oni (*Oh*-nee) a Lit'l hunter of Aynor, Hagi's friend and hunting partner.

Orte (*Or*-tay) the Eorth Stone, a Nydar Eldarin Seontir of opaque dark green set in a silver base decorated with lothingel.

Paalam a tropical tree of the Flax Isles.

Parma the History Stone, a Syndar Eldarin Seontir of opaque white with multi-colored veins, the Eldarin teaching stone, it sits atop a short gold stand in the shape of an open book with a pair of hands atop it which holds the Stone.

Petiperl (*petty*-purl) a delicate, soft pink flower growing in the wooded areas of Narda, akin to a tiny peony.

Pizo (peezo) the breed of horse used by the King's Guard of Andolan, akin to an all-black gypsy vanner.

Plains of Baerlan (Plains of *Bare*-lin) the barren desert region that sits between Northwest Wood and the Fyr Mountains.

Pynth (Pinth) primary city of southern Grenelan which lies south of the Rym Mountains and north of the River Dansen.

Pyru (*Pie*-roo) a port on the eastern coast of Grenelan used to import goods from western Narda and Gorst.

Queen's Rose a deep red rose named for Aneron's former wife, Siri, mother of Stefen and Scirra.

Rabellan (Rah-*bell*-in) city in the desert at the southern end of the Plains of Baerlan inhabited by mercenaries, who are outcasts and criminals.

Rabet (*ra*-bit) a large brown rabbit with long ears, found on the plains and in the woods of Narda.

Raesta (Ray-*es*-ta) a port city on the southeastern coast of Hamlan, whose primary export is brew.

Ramas River (*Rah*-mus) a river in eastern Narda that flows from the Fyr Mountains into the Bay of Gorst, creating a natural divide between Gorst and Grenelan.

Razlan (*Raz*-lin) a southern port of Gorst located across the Bay of Gorst from Haga, used for trade between Razlan and Haga.

Rena (Rena) Earlyspring.

Rini (*Ri*-nee) Lord of the Lit'ls.

Rinna Fern a high blue fern of Nardan forests that can grow to six feet or higher and often grows in large thickets.

Rulæn (*roo*-lun) tallest and most majestic tree of Northwest Wood and East Wood, it has a smooth red-bark, can reach 200 feet or higher, lives hundreds of years and houses some of the Elvenkin families.

Rym Mountains (Rim) a mountain range that extends almost to the coast of the Eastmost Sea and divides Grenelan in two, north and south.

Saluna Meadows (Suh-*luna*) a wide meadow in Melatui near the Tocuni River.

Sark warden of the prison under Castletop in Newelan.

Scirra (*Shear*-uh) princess daughter of King Aneron.

Shandlir (*Shand*-lur) a Nardan loyal to King Landrin and the House of Began, given sanctuary in East Wood after refusing to live in Newelan under Esol's rule following the Great War.

Silmaria (Sil-*mare*-ee-uh) a white, star-shaped bloom native to Narda.

Sinda companion to Liana, former companion to Aliana, King Landrin's deceased wife.

Sinter Hawk a large, ancient telepathic hawk of Narda, used as a messenger bird by the Eldarin and Elvenkin.

Siri (*Seer*-ee) King Aneron's first (deceased) wife, mother of Scirra and Stefen.

Seontir (*Say*-un-teer) ancient "Seeing Stones" of the Eldarin, five in all: Aldo, the Fire Stone, Orte, the Eorth Stone, Ule, the Wind Stone, Parma, the History Stone, and Yala, the Power Stone.

Snivl (*sni*-vul) a large, worm-like creature of the Great Dune Desert.

Soba (*So*-buh) Lord of the Fyrls.

Somi (*So*-mee) an old jeweler on Tìvia, second largest island in the Flax Isles.

Southern Sea the sea at the southern coast of Narda, prone to sudden violent storms.

Spyglas (*spy*-glass) a small telescope used to see things far away.

Stagar (*Stag*-are) a seaport in Gorst on the northeastern edge of the Bay of Gorst.

Stefen (*Ste*-fin) prince son of King Aneron.

Suvrii (*Soo*-vree) largest of the Flax Isles and the island on which King Landrin and his family live.

Sylmar (*Sil*-mar) an Eldarin resort on the southern banks of the River Dansen below East Wood, used by Nardans as a spiritual retreat, but now largely abandoned.

Sylvan Mountains (*Sil*-vin Mountains) northern mountain range of Narda that divides Hamlan from the Northern Reaches.

Syndar Eldarin (*Sin*-dahr El-*dare*-in) eldest and wisest of the Eldarin races, rulers of the Great Council, teachers and healers of Narda.

Tanbark Sails are sails made from the bark of the *hymil* tree, a conifer of the forests of Narda and Melatui; the Eldarin created hymil farms on the slopes of the *Grenhyl* to meet demand and to ensure the trees did not become extinct from over harvesting; tanbark sails are used in sailing because they are more durable than cloth sails.

Teb-Arnor River (Teb-*Ar*-nur) the major river of western Narda whose origin lies on the eastern slope of Mt. Athel, it joins with the Harmen River at Harna Falls then flows south to the Westmost Sea; wild and swift in the north, it runs through deep chasms and is not navigable until it passes below Harwyn Crossing.

Tebe Inlet (Teb-bee *In*-let) a small bay on the east coast of Hamlan at the southern tip of the Lowlands.

Tebor (Te-*bor*) sire of the House of Tebor, a rogue Tynar Eldarin, traitor and creator of the lineage of Baele and Esol, enemies of the West.

Tiana (Tee-*ah*-nuh) Elvenkin wife of Nathin.

Tinith (*Tin*-ith) an Elvenkin of Northwest Wood.

Tivia (*Ti*-vee-uh) second largest isle of the Flax Isles.

Tocuni River (Toe-*coo*-nee) a large river in Melatui, sourced in Mt. Malucan.

Toldor (*Tol*-dur) sire of the House of Toldor, lineage of Aneron and Kings of the West, and lineage also of the Captains of the Guard.

Toldor's Keep Hamlan's northern fortress on the eastern slope of Mt. Athel in the Highland Gap, built during King Toldor's reign in the First Age.

Tomas (*Toe*-mas) Eathelon's friend and member of his crew.

Trelk a creature of the Lowlands, akin to a small troll, now extinct. They earlier migrated to the Moors of Gorst, where the Moorcaats killed them all.

Tualo (Too-*ah*-low) Palo's deceased father, a Maagi Warrior Chief and close friend of King Maalo.

Tull a large beast used by the Northmen in battle.

Tynar Eldarin (*Ty*-nar El-*dare*-in) youngest of the Eldarin races, the Tynar are primarily craftsmen, farmers, smithies and ranchers.

Ule (*Oo*-lay) the Wind Stone, a Nydar Seontir of opaque dark blue, set in a silver base decorated with sun, moon and clouds.

Ulu (*Oo*-loo) Palo's mother.

Vinte (*Vin*-tay) the topmost peak in the Brunhyl at the 10th level of Andolan, the level which houses the King's family and the Watchtower.

Westmost Sea the western sea in which Eathelon began his journey to Narda.

Yala (*Yah*-la) the Power Stone, a Syndar Eldarin Seontir of clear crystal, set in a gold base decorated with celestial bodies.

Donna Casselman

A native of Southern California, Donna has enjoyed careers as a writer, illustrator, composer, singer, producer, computer industry pioneer, business consultant and mother. Fantasy writing is her current passion.

Her published works include poetry, articles in the natural health sciences and technical theatrical scripts, some of which she also directed.

She is a founding member of The Hollywood Writer's Society, a group that helped to inspire and instruct writers and showcase their works. No stranger to the stage, Donna has sung in jazz and chamber groups, in choirs and has performed and worked with many celebrities. She combined her business acumen and performing arts ability to produce musical theater.

It was during the years when Donna traveled extensively abroad that she discovered the magical works of Tolkien and the seeds for *Tales of Narda* were planted. Her fascination with languages, cultures, travel and unforgettable characters permeate her novel.

Prolific in all endeavors, Donna's first fantasy adventure story takes four books to tell and depicts an original and rich world with its own languages, history, art, genealogy, creatures and geography. After *Tales of Narda* is launched, Donna plans to continue the adventure story and create other worlds in book and film that will intrigue, inspire, excite and entertain readers and viewers.

Made in the USA
Columbia, SC
14 July 2022